22

STRIKE THE BLOOD

DAWN TRIUMPHANT

Gakuto Mikumo

Illustration by Manyako

Kojou Akatsuki

The Fourth Primogenitor

The world's mightiest—and
laziest—vampire

Yukina Himeragi
Sword Shaman
The Lion King Agency's
beautiful observer

Avrora Florestina
Kaleid Blood
The Twelfth Sleeping Princess

Nagisa Akatsuki

Sister of the Fourth Primogenitor

Naive, innocent, loud,
and wise little sister

Shizuri Kasugaya
Castiella

Paladin

Pure and noble knight of
the fiery blade

Sayaka Kirasaka
Shamanic War Dancer
Elegant dancer and shooter of
the magic bullet

Contents

Design / Hirokazu Watanabe (2725, Inc.)

STRIKE THE BLOOD

Dawn Triumphant

22

GAKUTO MIKUMO

ILLUSTRATION BY
MANYAKO

YEN
ON

NEW YORK

STRIKE THE BLOOD, Volume 22
GAKUTO MIKUMO

Translation by Jeremiah Bourque
Cover art by Manyako

This book is a work of fiction. Names, characters, places, and incidents are
the product of the author's imagination or are used fictitiously. Any resemblance to
actual events, locales, or persons, living or dead, is coincidental.

STRIKE THE BLOOD Vol.22
©Gakuto Mikumo 2020
Edited by Dengeki Bunko
First published in Japan in 2020 by KADOKAWA CORPORATION, Tokyo.
English translation rights arranged with KADOKAWA CORPORATION, Tokyo,
through Tuttle-Mori Agency, Inc., Tokyo.

English translation © 2022 by Yen Press, LLC

Yen On
150 West 30th Street, 19th Floor
New York, NY 10001

Visit us at yenpress.com
facebook.com/yenpress
twitter.com/yenpress
yenpress.tumblr.com
instagram.com/yenpress

First Yen On Edition: November 2022
Edited by Yen On Editorial: Leilah Labossiere, Payton Campbell
Designed by Yen Press Design: Wendy Chan

Yen On is an imprint of Yen Press, LLC.
The Yen On name and logo are trademarks of Yen Press, LLC.

The publisher is not responsible for websites (or their content) that are not owned by the publisher.

Library of Congress Cataloging-in-Publication Data
Names: Mikumo, Gakuto, author.| Manyako, illustrator. | Bourque, Jeremiah, translator.
Title: Strike the blood / Gakuto Mikumo, Manyako ; translation by Jeremiah Bourque.
Other titles: Sutoraiku za buraddo. English
Description: New York, NY : Yen On, 2016–
Identifiers: LCCN 2015041522 | ISBN 9780316345477 (v. 1 : pbk.) |
ISBN 9780316345491 (v. 2 : pbk.) | ISBN 9780316345514 (v. 3 : pbk.) |
ISBN 9780316345538 (v. 4 : pbk.) | ISBN 9780316345569 (v. 5 : pbk.) |
ISBN 9780316345583 (v. 6 : pbk.) | ISBN 9780316562652 (v. 7 : pbk.) |
ISBN 9780316442084 (v. 8 : pbk.) | ISBN 9780316442107 (v. 9 : pbk.) |
ISBN 9780316442121 (v. 10 : pbk.) | ISBN 9780316442145 (v. 11 : pbk.) |
ISBN 9780316442183 (v. 12 : pbk.) |ISBN 9781975384838 (v. 13 : pbk.) |
ISBN 9781975332587 (v. 14 : pbk.) |ISBN 9781975332600 (v. 15 : pbk.) |
ISBN 9781975332624 (v. 16 : pbk.) |ISBN 9781975332648 (v. 17 : pbk.) |
ISBN 9781975332662 (v. 18 : pbk.) |ISBN 9781975332686 (v. 19 : pbk.) |
ISBN 9781975338541 (v. 20 : pbk.) |ISBN 9781975338565 (v. 21 : pbk.) |
ISBN 9781975341510 (v. 22 : pbk.)
Subjects: CYAC: Vampires—Fiction. | BISAC: FICTION / Science Fiction / Adventure.
Classification: LCC PZ7.1.M555 Su 2016 | DDC [Fic]—dc23
LC record available at http://lccn.loc.gov/2015041522

ISBNs: 978-1-9753-4151-0 (paperback)
978-1-9753-4152-7 (ebook)

10 9 8 7 6 5 4 3 2 1

LSC-C

Printed in the United States of America

INTRO

The girl did not know the island's name.

The monorail darted through the steel-colored city, looking down at the transparent blue sky.

It was a world where ground and sky were reversed.

Overhead, everything was covered by the aquamarine surface of the sea. The artificial isle floated upon its glimmering waves. From the steel-colored island resembling a decrepit ruin, countless buildings towered toward the sky below.

The girl gazed without a word upon this scenery scrolling past her car window.

Following the spiraling path of the track, the monorail car continued its gentle turn. Through the glass, the sun's rays flickered at every angle, illuminating the shine of the girl's golden hair like a rainbow.

The train finally decelerated and slid into the station.

This was the end of the line—the last station on her commute to school.

The door made a slight sound as it opened. Passengers spewed out all at once.

These were girls wearing identical uniforms. Mingling amid the throng, she, too, headed to school.

She did not know the name of the school.

It was a campus covered in a clear glass dome like a big goldfish bowl.

The girls spent day after day in peaceful classrooms. The familiar scenery was always the same. This was the everyday life they had enjoyed many times over.

At some point, though, a tiny change occurred in the supposedly stagnant background.

The clamor of the girls' voices echoed through the formerly tranquil school halls.

Delight. Sadness. Anger. Lamentations. The unresponsive, doll-like girls had begun to display emotions—unique, varied emotions. They were like princesses from a fairy tale awakening from a long slumber.

Stopped time had resumed its flow, and the world began to undergo a visible change.

She knew the reason why.

She knew that her existence was the cause behind the changes occurring in the world around her—

"Morning, Avrora. There's a dead end ahead."

When she separated from the ranks of the girls heading to class and went down a dark stairway, she heard someone call her name.

A classmate with mature-looking eyes was waiting for Avrora's arrival at the entrance to the underground warehouse.

She had slender curves and an affable, smiling face. Her steel-colored hair swayed as the classmate gave Avrora a friendly wave.

"…So it is thee, Glenda…Guardian of the Corridor."

Avrora's expression did not change as she halted, gazing at the girl at the bottom of the staircase as she spoke.

Surprised and delighted by Avrora's unexpected reaction, the girl with silver hair blinked several times.

"Why are you talking like that, Ava? You sound like some sort of princess."

"…A princess I am not. I am a doll, a handcrafted vessel to contain Beast Vassals."

Avrora quietly shook her head at Glenda's teasing smile.

Glenda fell into silence for but a moment. Her tiny smile felt a little bleak.

"So you remembered."

"The time for games is at an end. 'Twas a pleasant dream nonetheless."

Avrora commented quietly as she glanced down at the top of her uniform.

Glenda's eyes softened with relief.

"That so? I'm glad you had fun with it. That's what Cain wanted, after all. I wonder if the other girls are pleased, too."

The chime announcing the start of classes rang in the distance. Avrora turned away from Glenda without a word.

She could see girls in school uniforms sitting down in the glass-covered classroom. It was a false tranquility. Their daily lives were a sham.

Avrora knew, though. She knew just what price the man once known as the Sinful God had paid to grant this to them.

"Did you find the classroom? The classroom where the secrets of the world are locked away?"

Glenda's smile vanished as she asked Avrora this with a serious expression.

"Though I have yet to unravel that mystery, the mist hath cleared from my memories."

Avrora laughed a bit at her own expense.

Poking out from her lips were pointed, pure white fangs. Her blue eyes blazed like flames as she glared at what lay behind Glenda—a spiraling stairway, partially emerging from a thick, steel-colored wall.

"Accordingly, I know this world's true form—come forth, Minelauva Iris—!"

Fresh, slick blood gushed from Avrora's outstretched right arm.

This became a crimson mist imbued with demonic energy, finally changing into the form of a huge humanoid beast. It transformed into a beautiful Beast Vassal enveloped by rainbow flames—a Valkyrie gripping a sword of light.

This was Beast Vassal Number Six of the Fourth Primogenitor, the World's Mightiest Vampire. Minelauva Iris's ability was that of Severing.

The rainbow-colored sword of light wielded by the Valkyrie tore through the corridor wall with the greatest of ease. No, what Avrora's Beast Vassal had sliced apart was an intricate illusion—part of the powerful barrier surrounding the school.

The false image vanished from the corridor, causing the rest of the supposedly cut-off stairway to come into view.

Beyond that was not the interior of a school. Spreading around the spiraling stairway was the sky, endless azure without a single obstruction. One misstep going down the glass stairway and she would doubtlessly keep on falling until she reached the ends of the sky.

Yet Avrora did not falter, calmly beginning to descend the stairs.

"You go, Avrora! ...See...ya!"

She heard Glenda's voice in her ear, but when Avrora looked back, Glenda had already vanished from sight. All that remained were the sounds of wings flapping and the silhouette of an enormous dragon receding in the distance.

The spiral stairway continued.

One step at a time, Avrora continued descending the stairs toward a destination she knew had to be at the end. It was the same as climbing toward the highest reaches of the sky.

The lower she went into the sky, the more her sense of up and down blurred. She gradually became unable to tell whether she was going down stairs or rising into the sky, or whether there even was a difference.

Just as she had reached a point where she was completely unable to feel her body's weight, Avrora arrived at the end of the spiral stairway.

At the foot of the stairs was a room floating right in the middle of the sky like a moon under the noonday sun.

It was a tiny, cylindrical space seeming like the very center of the world. This was the secret room Glenda had told her about.

Avrora did not know the tiny room's name. She did know who was in it, however.

The one seated in the place in which the secrets of the world were locked away was he who ruled those worldly secrets—in other words, the King of Nod.

Breathing deeply several times, Avrora went down the final rung.

The cramped room had steel-colored walls.

It was a dark place reminiscent of a pipeline buried deep under a city. The walls were lined with countless monitors embedded in them like mosaic tiles. They displayed scenes of worlds that were not Nod, worlds far away.

Illuminated by the glow from these monitors was a peculiar creature sitting in a tattered chair.

The tiny figure looked like a toy that had been thrown away—

"Yo. So you came, Lil' Twelfth. Been waiting for ya."

The badly sewn teddy bear modeled after a lovable animal looked up at Avrora.

"Keh-keh."

"Our ancestors came down from the sky."

Ladli Ren still had a crimson lollipop in her mouth as she mused to herself.

She wore long boots, a checkered skirt and a necktie, a sleeveless white shirt, and a top hat with a red ribbon attached. The girl's outfit was surreal, something that seemed to hail straight from a theatrical stage.

Based on her looks, she seemed to be around seventeen or eighteen years old. Her soft, long hair was an ashen color, nearly black. She had pure white skin that lacked even a hint of the flush of life, and her red, cherry-like eyes were highly distinctive. Sharp canine teeth poked out from the gap of her mouth as she kept the lollipop stuck in her mouth.

"Hence, they named themselves the Devas, so as never to forget they were visitors from the sky and not of the peoples on the surface. No one remembers that anymore, though."

Ladli's sweet voice continued to boast.

She was in the master control room on the topmost floor of Arnica Quad—the corporate headquarters for Magna Ataraxia Research floating in the Pacific Ocean's Celebes Sea.

Incorporating a small island from the Talauds to form a single giant facility, Arnica Quad was more akin to a military fortress than an office building. Connected to branch companies and factories in every corner of the world via its electronic network, it had complete control of its own communications net, allowing it to issue detailed instructions in mere milliseconds. This capability was so crucial that it had amply earned its status as the "brain" of the multinational corporate conglomerate known as MAR.

Accordingly, security for Arnica Quad was heavy. It possessed independent defensive combat capabilities ranging from patrol boats to fighter aircraft, and each of the forty-six operators working in the command room had a strict military air about them. In that context, Ladli's presence with her theatrical outfit looked extremely out of place.

Not a single person would dare reproach her for this.

After all, she was the one and only principal executive of the corporation and the little sister of Shahryar Ren, president of MAR.

"—The Holy Grounds Treaty Organization aircraft carrier strike fleet has commenced field operations."

The report from a young defense operator interrupted Ladli's soliloquy.

Invisible tension ran through the command room. The employees' reactions held an air of resignation rather than surprise. They'd known from the beginning that the HGTO would become MAR's foe.

MAR had assisted the Order of the End, a sorcerous criminal organization. MAR had interfered with a Demon Sanctuary's neutrality, instigating the civil conflict known as the Electoral War. During this dispute, they had made use of the captured Fourth Primogenitor, opening the gate to Nod—all were crystal-clear breaches of the Holy Grounds Treaty, so MAR could not avoid an outpouring of international scorn.

If that had been the end of it, there would still have been room for negotiations. MAR could apologize and pay out a fortune in compensation. At the very least, a full-on armed clash could surely have been avoided.

The fact that MAR special forces under Shahryar Ren's command were attempting to monopolize the legacy that the Sinful God had left behind in Nod had decisively turned the HGTO against them.

The Legacy of the Sinful God was a strategic weapon of mass destruction. Shahryar Ren's desire for this made clear that his objective was to rule the world.

Even without that, MAR had accumulated so much power in its expansion into a giant international conglomerate that it was viewed as an eyesore across the globe. Various national governments had quietly banded together to begin attacking MAR through legal or even extralegal means: the freezing of assets, the sealing of factories and offices, arrests of executives and employees, and even direct attacks by force of arms—

For all the economic power it could boast, MAR was a civilian corporation in the end—a leaf in the wind against the force of a tornado. MAR strongholds were being taken over across the globe. In two short days, the corporation had lost virtually all of its capabilities.

The last stronghold remaining was its headquarters, Arnica Quad.

"The main force is the Magallanica Pacific Fleet. Aircraft Carrier *Yurlungur* and six missile destroyers confirmed. The island is already within range of Long-Range Land Attack Projectiles."

The operator read off the information gleaned from unmanned reconnaissance craft. The calm and businesslike tone could not conceal the turmoil within.

"A grand showing against a mere civilian corporation, isn't it? Did they really think sending a fleet would make us roll out the red carpet?"

Ladli sighed with a look of exasperation. A strange atmosphere fell over the command room.

The Holy Grounds Treaty Organization had dispatched an amount of firepower able to wipe a small nation off the map in a single night. One could only call it complete overkill for subjugating a single corporate headquarters. There was no doubt they were wary of MAR, but that could not have been the only reason.

"Well, not that I don't understand what they're thinking. They're just crushing us along the way. Their real target is Itogami Island, surely."

Ladli laughed scornfully, then happily turned around.

At present, the gate to Nod existed only in the sky above Itogami Island. If one conquered Itogami Island, you could pour in as much military power as you pleased, enabling that party to wipe out Shahryar Ren and his MAR forces in Nod. It was a simple but effective means of dealing with the problem. Taking over Arnica Quad was a preliminary step, live-fire training doubling as a morale-boosting exercise.

"This is dangerous. Lady Ladli, you must escape."

The security department chief, whom everyone called Colonel for short, urged Ladli in a sober tone of voice. Arnica Quad was already within the HGTO battle fleet's firing range. It was probably only a matter of time before they began attacking in earnest.

Given the situation, the only company employees left at MAR were either pure Devas or clans with Deva blood flowing through them—in other words, coconspirators of Shahryar Ren. The HGTO side was no doubt aware of this. They would surely seek to mercilessly exterminate Ladli and the others for the sake of eliminating future concerns, yet—

"Run? Me?"

Ladli's eyes went round as if taken a little by surprise. Then the corners of her lips rose with amusement.

"Of course not. Right now it's far more dangerous outside of Quad."

"But, Lady Ladli…"

"More importantly, warn all hands that someone's trying to lay a finger on us. We have incoming."

"Eh?"

The security chief frowned, perplexed.

The very next moment, Arnica Quad was slammed by an unanticipated blow.

Blast winds blew and raged like a tornado, violently shaking the entire island.

The stout exterior wall of the command room was on par with a nuclear shelter, yet it creaked as if crying out. It was not the ground, but space itself that was shaking. An object of immense mass suddenly emerged from another world.

"Situation report!"

The security chief angrily shouted at the nearby operators. His voice was overridden by the sounds of countless alarms echoing across the room. Even Arnica Quad's information management capacity was unable to ascertain the true nature of the anomaly that had appeared out of the blue.

"A Necropolis. The final fiefdoms left to the seventeen Deva clans, and the symbols of their martial might."

In contrast to her skittish subordinates, Ladli's expression was bright and cheerful.

Operating a console without even having to touch it with her hands, she switched to real-time imagery sent from an unmanned reconnaissance craft. The bizarre sight displayed on the giant monitor made everyone in the control room draw in their breath.

It was an enormous sphere similar to a snow dome.

The sphere was a little under a kilometer in diameter. Its surface was composed of stone and steel. From its appearance, one might think it was the result of taking a castle city from the Middle Ages and forcing it into a round shape.

Ignoring the power of gravity, the sphere floated in the sky above the Pacific Ocean.

The spherical castle floating in midair was an ominous structure that seemed to have come straight out of a surrealist work of art. The fortress of the Devas emerging from another world was one of the cities known as Necropolis.

"You mean…the Necropolises are real?"

The security chef's murmur trickled out from his lips.

This Necropolis had emerged at a point ten kilometers south of the Talaud Island chain. It was perfectly positioned to shield Arnica Quad from the HGTO fleet's approach.

"The Necropolis came to support us? But that means…"

"It will be bathed in concentrated gunfire from the enemy fleet, yes."

Ladli spoke in a sober tone as if it wasn't any concern to her.

The Necropolis was a powerful weapon built with Deva technology, but seven thousand years had already passed since it had vanished from the surface. Humanity's technology had risen by leaps and bounds during that time, certainly rivaling the Devas of old in military might at the very least. A straight-up gunfight with a cutting-edge fleet would be a hard fight even for the Necropolis.

"Flying objects from enemy fleet confirmed. Total numbers sixt…no, thirty-two. Roughly eighty percent reaching the Necropolis."

The operator shouted with a tense tenor. The missile destroyers had fired ground attack cruise missiles. They were most likely armed with ritual warheads for demolishing facilities.

The Necropolis, also known as the Otherworldly Castle, existed simultaneously in that world and another, giving it powerful resistance to all physical attacks. This magical bulwark had caused humanity much grief in wars of old, but there was no guarantee it could withstand the latest ritual warheads.

"Should we counterattack?"

The security chief checked with Ladli. She, however, waved a hand with a relaxed smile.

"It's fine, it's fine. Just leave them be."

"But at this rate—"

"Sure, the Necropolises come off as moldy antiques compared to mankind's weapons nowadays. On top of that, the Devas have no demon soldiers or human peoples on their side anymore. We can't fight a proper war like his."

Ladli spoke these words with an indifferent air.

The missiles launched by the HGTO fleet would probably arrive at the Necropolis in less than thirty seconds. If they eliminated the Necropolis, Arnica Quad would be their next attack target.

Though she knew this full well, Ladli's smile was undiminished.

"Yet these are but trifling concerns. The greatest power of the Devas is not dependent on sorcerous technology or the number of soldiers at our command."

Ladli's words had not even finished when something was shot out from the Necropolis.

It was not an interceptor missile or a high-output laser or anything of the sort. It was a simple metal round fired out of a large, primitive cannon barrel.

After tracing a parabolic arc as it flew through the sky, the shell burst apart midair in a stretch of open sky. Flying out from the scattering fragments was a glimmering sphere resembling a jewel.

"...What the?! A doll...no, a woman?!"

The security chief scowled when he noticed the strange silhouette encased inside the sphere.

It was a naked girl with her knees tucked under her chin as she slept. The young girl slept inside the gemstone like a mosquito encased in amber.

"Everyone has forgotten how the betrayal of Cain the Sinful God sealed away the Devas' greatest power, leading to humanity's victory in The Great Cleansing of days gone by."

Ladli broke out into giggles.

Pulled down by the force of gravity, the gemstone would cross paths with the cruise missiles in midflight—the second the employees watching thought this, the sleeping girl suddenly opened her eyes, glimmering blue eyes glowing like flames.

"Demonic energy response increasing! It's a vampire's Beast Vassal! It's materializing!"

The pale-faced operator's report sent the command room into an uproar.

A vampire was summoning a Beast Vassal. In itself, this elicited no special surprise. Being able to detect that Beast Vassal's demonic energy from a place ten kilometers removed was a different matter entirely.

Few existing vampires were able to summon Beast Vassals of such power. Really, it would be rather bad if more existed.

"This is crazy… This demonic energy capacity is on par with the Beast Vassals of the three primogenitors?! If it's released without any restraint, this part of the sea will be unapproachable due to magical contamination…!"

The security chief's voice was full of terror.

The violence and destructiveness of a Beast Vassal was not the truly frightening part. Those who had inherited the knowledge of the Devas knew this well.

Beast Vassals were beings akin to flames. Weaker ones could be completely controlled through the actions of the summoner and could be dismissed once the need for them had passed.

Overly powerful Beast Vassals, however, were very difficult to dismiss. Just like it was arduous to snuff out a massive conflagration, powerful Beast Vassals were beings beyond the control of advanced peoples.

These beings sought to destroy everything and consume magical energy without limit in accordance with their cravings. Once summoned, these Beast Vassals could never be dismissed so long as magical energy was present. They vanished only when all magical energy in the surrounding area ran dry—in other words, only when any and all information, including the memories of living creatures, was erased.

The Beast Vassal summoned by the girl inside the jewel was a huge eyeball blazing like the sun. Perhaps it was better to call this a mass of white flesh with a blazing centipede wrapped around it. In human terms, the shape of the monster was simply repulsive.

Flying cruise missiles were blown apart one after another as the Beast Vassal's flames engulfed them. The Beast Vassal roared with delight as it consumed the magical energy scattered in the process. Then, with incredible speed belying its great size, the Beast Vassal assailed the HGTO fleet.

The destroyers' main guns spewed flames. Fighter jets launched from the aircraft carrier boldly challenged the Beast Vassal as well.

The Beast Vassal did not stop, however. Its demonic energy flames explosively swelled, enveloping the entirety of the fleet. Within those flames, the fleet was embroiled in a single moment.

The fighter jets were vaporized without a trace. The destroyers sank instantly one after another. The enormous aircraft carrier dissolved and melted away, steam gushing from the sea as the vessel sank.

The destruction was overwhelmingly one-sided. Arnica Quad's control room fell so silent that one could have heard a pin drop.

"So they are finally in your hands, Brother."

Amid that silence, Ladli abruptly mused aloud.

Biting apart the crimson candy giving off a scent of fresh blood, she narrowed her eyes and formed a tiny smile.

"The Deadly Sin of the Devas, sealed in Nod by Cain the Sinful God—the Beast Vassal Warheads."

CHAPTER ONE
THE ITOGAMI ISLAND
PURCHASE

1

Kojou Akatsuki had a dream.

He dreamed of going down a transparent, spiral stairway.

There was nothing around the stairs. There was only the vastness of unobstructed blue sky.

Overhead, he could make out the hazy sight of a calm, mirrorlike, deep blue sea.

It was a strange world where sea and sky were inverted. Alone in this upside-down world, Kojou continued descending the long staircase. He was clutching a bouquet of thorny roses, the red petals glossy like drops of red blood.

This is a pretty vivid dream, thought Kojou.

He felt like he was reliving a scene out of someone else's past.

He heard the faint ringing of a bell mixed with the sounds of the strong sea breeze blowing.

At the end of the transparent spiraling stairway was a tiny peninsula enveloped by mist.

The ground was bare rock with moss growing on it. He saw an old building at the tip of the cape. It was a decrepit, stonework bell tower.

Someone was standing in front of the bell tower. It was a small figure wearing a pure white wedding dress. Kojou's heart leaped in his chest the instant the sun's rays illuminated the girl's back.

The nostalgic longing welling up in him was almost enough to drive him mad.

He instinctively understood that he'd come to this place to meet her.

Her face was hidden by a multilayered veil.

Kojou stepped down onto the bit of land floating in the sky, and he approached the decrepit bell tower.

The bell continued to ring. Her dress fluttered in the strong breeze.

When the girl in the wedding dress turned toward him, Kojou sensed she was softly smiling at him.

She came running and leaped into Kojou's arms, and she slowly pulled the veil back.

Startled, Kojou drew in a sharp breath.

Appearing from under the pure white veil was a badly sewn teddy bear patterned after some adorable animal.

Looking up at him, so close that their lips might touch, it laughed sardonically.

"Keh-keh…"

"U…uaaaaaaaaaaaaaaaaaaaaa!!"

Kojou screamed as he woke up.

He was nauseated from terror. His entire body was rigid, his back sticky and drenched with sweat.

Kojou fiercely shook his head and deeply exhaled in an attempt to drive the haunting image of Mogwai in a wedding dress out of his mind. He told himself it was only a dream and inwardly calmed his shaky nerves.

Yes, Kojou had been dreaming—a nonsensical dream that was the worst and most ominous nightmare imaginable. Putting a hand over his heart, which still beat quite fiercely, Kojou slowly shifted his gaze.

He was in a spacious, unfamiliar room. It had a thick carpet, an extravagant bed, and a number of large, multiperson sofas and guest tables against the wall. He was in a suite at a five-star hotel in Keystone Gate.

Exhausted from the berserk episode the night before, Kojou and the others had stayed overnight at a hotel under Gigafloat Management Corporation control. It wasn't out of consideration for Kojou, victor in the Electoral War—more accurately, they were isolating him. They must have figured it was better to put a vampire who might go berserk at any moment somewhere they could watch him rather than leave him to his own devices.

The hands of the clock at his bedside told him it was a little before noon. He'd arrived at the hotel just before daybreak, so he must have slept almost seven hours.

Maybe owing to the awfulness of the dream, however, his entire body felt heavy. His chest hurt, and his stiff limbs limited his movement.

Feels almost like someone's lying on top of my blanket, thought Kojou. The very next moment, a human figure filled his vision. It was a black-haired girl whose presence he could not sense—

"Sen...pai..."

"Uwaaaaaaaaaaaaaaaa!!"

Kojou screamed when the soft voice whispering in his ear reminded him of Mogwai from the dream. For some reason, the shoulders of the figure lying on top of Kojou trembled out of nervousness.

"P-please be quiet, senpai! It is me! Himeragi!"

The figure earnestly called out to Kojou while pushing him down as he tried to thrash away. Her familiar voice finally made Kojou stop screaming.

"H-Himeragi...?"

"Yes. Who in the world did you think I was...?"

Looking down at the weakly moaning Kojou, Yukina exhaled with a perplexed air.

She probably never expected the boy once called the World's Mightiest Vampire to be that afraid of anything. Her pouty expression made her seem slighted somehow.

Yukina was wearing a nightgown provided by the hotel rather than her usual clothes. That was why he didn't immediately recognize her.

"Wait a sec... Himeragi, why are you in my room? Wasn't it locked?"

Kojou inquired in a tone that still sounded a little sleepy. Being a suite room in a high-class hotel, last he'd checked, the bedrooms had imposing electronic locks.

Yukina spoke her next words like they were a matter of course.

"I opened it with a *shikigami*."

"Why...?!"

"So that others would not notice. Everyone else should still be asleep."

Yukina explained with a peculiar degree of calm. A great many of his friends were beat-up and exhausted from bringing Kojou back to sanity when he had been possessed by Beast Vassals and on a rampage. Those girls were likely still sleeping soundly at that very moment. Yukina had apparently seized the opportunity to sneak into Kojou's bedroom.

"Is this something you don't want anyone else to see?"

Kojou lowered his own voice as he followed up. He didn't think a forthright girl like Yukina would resort to breaking and entering without a good reason. It was only natural for him to think some unavoidable circumstance had left her with no other option.

"Well, kind of."

Yet for some reason, Yukina averted her eyes, seemingly uncomfortable with Kojou's unwavering gaze.

Kneeling formally on top of the bed, she squirmed around a little as if she was hesitating to say something.

"Himeragi?"

"Er, um…senpai, you've regained your vampiric powers, I take it?"

"Seems like it. Guess you could say the end result is that Ki Juran-barada saved my ass."

Kojou twisted his lips as he raised his right hand to his eye level and clenched it. Yukina nodded in apparent agreement.

"So you intend to enter Nod and bring Miss Avrora back hereafter."

"Yeah. That was the deal."

Kojou made a pained smile and shrugged his shoulders. Ki Juran-barada, the First Primogenitor, promised to provide Kojou with power on par with the Fourth Primogenitor. Kojou was to repay him by stopping Shahryar Ren's actions in Nod—that was the agreement made between the two of them.

His methods were really out there, but Ki had fulfilled his promise to Kojou. It was Kojou's turn to keep his end of the bargain.

"That is why, beforehand…I would like to do…that, with you."

Yukina's cheeks reddened as she murmured haltingly, unable to meet Kojou's eyes.

"That?"

Kojou grimaced suspiciously. He didn't know what Yukina was trying to say.

"I mean *that*. You know…using a vampire primogenitor's demonic energy for the purpose of establishing, via a contagion ritual, a magical system to offset the excessive spiritual energy created by the Divine Oscillation Effect activation."

"…Huh?"

Is this some kind of new spell? pondered the bewildered Kojou.

For some reason, Kojou's vague reaction made Yukina's voice flustered and angry.

"Goodness! I am telling you to please drink my blood!"

"R-right…well, you should've said that to start with… Er, why all of a sudden?"

Kojou was still a little confused as he sat up.

Yukina had been dispatched by the Lion King Agency to serve as his watcher. If anything, she was someone who should be scolding Kojou for vampiric acts without a very good reason. Even if you could justify it in an emergency where many lives hung in the balance, it wasn't like her to seek out vampiric acts of Kojou in a situation lacking immediate danger.

He'd heard offhand that the one bitten felt pleasure during vampiric acts and that this became addictive over time. *Don't tell me a girl like her got addicted to having me drink her blood*, Kojou began to worry, but Yukina spoke with her usual serious tone.

"If I do not reestablish a spiritual pathway with senpai, I will not be able to use Snowdrift Wolf. That would be very inconvenient when we go to Nod, would it not?"

"Ahhh…"

So that's what it is, thought Kojou as he sighed in relief. The backlash from using the powerful divine armament called Snowdrift Wolf had the dangerous side effect known as angelification.

Powerful spiritual energy coursing back from the purging spear transformed the flesh, shifting one's very existence into a higher dimension—in other words, one ran the risk of vanishing from the mortal realm entirely.

It wasn't a hindrance to daily life, but any use of powerful spiritual energy would push her farther down the path to angelification. In other words, she couldn't endure employing Snowdrift Wolf in combat.

To avert this issue, Yukina and Kojou had formed a provisional Blood Servant pact.

This allowed his vampire primogenitor's inexhaustible demonic energy to offset the excess spiritual energy coursing through her body. Thanks to Kojou relinquishing the power of the Fourth Primogenitor, that pact had already been rescinded.

That was why Yukina had snuck into Kojou's bedroom. Her objective was to reestablish the provisional pact so that she could use Snowdrift Wolf once more.

To become a vampire's Blood Servant, you needed a mutual sharing of physical parts to serve as catalysts for the spiritual pathway. These catalysts could be pieces of Kojou's flesh and bone sealed into a pact ring, or Yukina's own bodily fluids—in other words, blood.

In short, Yukina needed to have Kojou drink her blood so she could fulfill her objective. So she'd slipped into his room under cover of darkness. He got that. He got that, but…

"Himeragi, you plan on going to Nod, too…?"

Kojou seemed genuinely surprised.

"Hah?!"

Yukina's eyes flew wide open in astonishment.

"Is that not obvious?! I am your watcher, senpai! Or is it somehow inconvenient for me to see you with Miss Avrora?!"

"This's got nothin' to do with Avrora…! I'm worried about you, Himeragi!"

Kojou sullenly argued back in the face of the incredible force of Yukina's statements.

Yukina pouted as she stared at Kojou.

"About…me?"

"Now, I know how strong you are. I recognize that. But when push comes to shove, that's against demons, right? Against a guy like Shahryar Ren with his own private army, you can't do anything, Snowdrift Wolf or not. Am I wrong?"

"Are you saying I will be a hindrance to you, senpai?"

Yukina retorted, an aggravated expression still on her face, but Kojou wouldn't back down. She'd shed a great deal of blood in the past half day for the sake of dragging Kojou back from his berserk state. Properly speaking, she was in a state that required rest in a hospital. He couldn't take her to a dangerous battlefield.

"Himeragi, I'm grateful you stopped my rampage, but because of that, you're nowhere near top form. That's why you should rest this time around. I'll bring back Avrora before you know it."

Kojou spoke with a painstakingly formal tone.

Listening to his words, Yukina sighed deeply, as if yielding to Kojou's persuasion.

"I understand."

"Th-that so?"

Kojou patted his chest, relieved that he'd come to an understanding with Yukina much more smoothly than he'd expected. That was when Kojou's vision swayed.

Without a word, Yukina had firmly shoved Kojou down onto the bed. Looking down at Kojou with emotionless eyes, she undid the buttons of her nightgown one by one.

"—Er, Himeragi?! What do you think you're doing?! Hold on a…?!"

"If you say you will not drink my blood, I will make you want to."

Yukina spoke in a flat tone of voice. Kojou panicked as he looked up at the completely glassy expression in her eyes.

"No, wait, why?! Hold on, Himeragi! Calm down!"

"What is the matter, senpai? How does it feel to be shoved down and rendered immobile by the underclassman you called a hindrance? Senpai, I endured my feelings of embarrassment to come and meet you like this, and then you went and decided on your own not to drink my blood…!"

Yukina looked down at Kojou as she spoke provocatively. Apparently calling her useless in combat had really gotten to her.

"Isn't that shifting the goalposts?! Also, using physical enchantment ain't fair!"

"Be a good boy and drink my blood. I'm very familiar with what arouses you, senpai—"

Yukina grabbed hold of the back of her hair and bundled it together to make it seem short. Normally it was very hard to tell, but she had apparently taken great note of Nagisa's hairstyle.

"Hold on a sec! Why do you think I'm aroused when I look at Nagisa?! That's a pretty fundamental misunderstanding!"

Kojou shouted in indignation. The trigger for vampiric acts was not hunger or thirst but sexual arousal—in other words, lust. Yukina apparently thought that girls like his little sister Nagisa were his type. Kojou was used to people telling him he had a sister complex, but even he couldn't let a misunderstanding like this slide.

"Then what kind of girl's blood *would* you drink?! Even though you… told me before that I was cute…"

"Y-yeah. I get it. You're cute. You're cute, Himeragi. So calm down a bit, and let's talk this over…!"

Figuring he'd better do something about Yukina's blatantly sour, bent-out-of-shape mood, Kojou tried to compliment her to his utmost. Kojou's flattering words didn't come off as sincere, making Yukina puff her cheeks in annoyance, but the next moment…

"…Kojou?"

Kojou and Yukina gasped when they heard a quiet voice from the bedroom entrance.

Wearing a plain T-shirt, Nagisa Akatsuki gazed, mystified, at the sight of Kojou and Yukina tangled on top of the bed. Since they were siblings, Nagisa had been sleeping in the other bedroom in Kojou's suite.

"N-Nagisa?!"

"Nagisa?!"

"…Yukina? What are you doing on the bed with Kojou?"

When Nagisa inquired without any change in expression, Yukina timidly shook her head.

"Y-you are mistaken, Nagisa… This was out of profound, unavoidable circumstances…"

"Yukina, were you thinking of having Kojou drink your blood?"

In an extremely calm voice, Nagisa sought to confirm her deduction. Yukina nodded awkwardly.

"Y-yeah…I require a spiritual pathway with senpai to block Snowdrift Wolf's side effects, so I need senpai to drink my blood to serve as a catalyst for this, so, ah…"

"…Hmm, I see. So you really need him to, huh?"

"N-Nagisa?"

Nagisa's completely unexpected response left Kojou and Yukina glancing at each other.

It would have been natural for her to be far more surprised, worked up, or even bursting out in anger. They were grateful Nagisa was taking it well, but she was so coolheaded that it worried them.

"It's all right, Yukina. I'll help, too."

Nagisa smiled gently and headed out of Kojou's bedroom. With no clue as to what was happening, Kojou and Yukina remained close against one another as they fell silent.

Humming all the way, Nagisa returned about ninety seconds later. Her right hand was gripping a large kitchen knife with a blade some seven inches long.

"Eh?"

"Uh, umm, Nagisa? What's with the kitchen knife?"

Yukina paled. Kojou's voice went shrill. Nagisa went *Mmm*, tilting her head with a mystified expression.

"Oh, this? It's a steel chef's knife. These high-end hotel suites are really something else. I mean, they even have real kitchens in them."

"No, I mean why are you holding a kitchen knife?"

"Well, the sharper the blade, the less you'll have to suffer, Kojou."

Nagisa grinned as she ran a finger along the kitchen knife down to the tip of the blade.

"N-Nagisa?"

Yukina's voice was trembling as she tried to stop Nagisa's approach. Nagisa, however, nodded to her with an expression filled with a tragic sense of duty.

"Yukina, don't worry. I get it."

"Er…what do you get?"

"Sorry, Kojou."

Nagisa bit her lip hard as she reversed her grip on the kitchen knife. Then, without any hesitation whatsoever, she swung it down toward Kojou's heart.

"U-uaaaaa!!"

Kojou yelped and rolled across the top of the bed. Nagisa's kitchen knife sliced the pillow apart, causing the goose down packed within to fly into the air.

"Why are you running, Kojou?"

Nagisa spoke with an irritated tone. She was genuinely peeved at Kojou for dodging her.

"Wait, Nagisa, senpai has done nothing wrong! I am the one who tried to coerce him into…!"

"Anyway, calm down! We can talk this out…!"

"I am calm, Kojou. Yukina wants you to drink her blood, right? Then I have no choice but to stab you."

"Why?!"

Bloodlust rose from Nagisa as she raised the kitchen knife high. Kojou and Yukina double-teamed her to try to hold her back. Nagisa, unconvinced, vigorously resisted.

The three were fiercely jostling around like this when Kojou sensed yet another person at the bedroom door.

Standing there, with her suite room smart key in hand, was Asagi Aiba. Clad in a tight-fitting suit for some reason, she gazed at the sight of Kojou and the others thrashing around with a kitchen knife, murmuring with weariness from the very bottom of her soul.

"What in the world are you doing?"

2

"Ow ow ow ow…hurts like I got beat up all over…"

Kojou dragged along his tattered body as he gazed up at the late-night sky.

Dregs of demonic energy scattered by the berserk Beast Vassals still lingered thickly over the container base in Island East.

It was around half a day before Kojou woke up at the high-class hotel in Keystone Gate, right after the Beast Vassal's rampage had been quelled and Kojou had been brought back to sanity.

"But of course…you were in a berserk stage brimming with demonic energy to the point you could not maintain human form, and on top of that, you employed all twelve Beast Vassals in that berserk state."

Shizuri Kasugaya raised her voice in exasperation as she stood behind the tottering Kojou.

Though dressed in a bunny suit for no clear reason, she wore the expression of someone who'd just run a full marathon. He could hardly blame her, given that she'd been fighting primogenitor-class Beast Vassals head-on. It felt like her gleaming, pristine white hair had been cruelly sullied in the process.

Kojou was just as exhausted as she was. Thanks to having been exposed to enough demonic energy to transform his flesh and blood, his entire body's cells were under incredible strain. It would take time to recover even with a vampire's immortal flesh.

Kojou and Shizuri were the only two remaining in the ridiculously spacious container yard.

Yuuma Tokoyogi had gone on ahead to take Yukina, who'd collapsed from major blood loss, to a medical facility. Lydianne was driving her tank around the harbor outskirts with Asagi aboard, no doubt to assess the damage from the rampaging Beast Vassals.

Left behind, the tottering Kojou was making his way toward urban areas on foot. All he could do was endure the pain coursing through his body, but he was really, really hungry. His school uniform was in tatters as an aftereffect of his rampage. He would have loved a cold shower right then, because he felt icky all over from sweat, grime, and coagulated blood.

"You truly are a high-maintenance vampire."

Approaching Kojou, Shizuri put her shoulder right against his. She gazed at Kojou and the questioning look on his face as she pulled Kojou's arm to her as if she were about to judo-flip him on his back.

"Cas? What are you doing?"

"I am lending you my shoulder. Even if it was an emergency measure to bring the Electoral War to an end, I am your Blood Servant nonetheless."

"Er, that's too much. You're all beat-up yourself, right?"

Kojou calmly pointed this out to her. Her bunny suit had distracted him from noticing sooner, but when he looked more closely, Shizuri's entire body was covered in bandages. Her legs were shaking, too. She'd been heavily wounded in the fighting at Keystone Gate the day before to begin with. Normally it should've been hard for her to even stand.

Even if Shizuri's cooperation had been indispensable to stop the Beast Vassals' rampage, Kojou was more aghast than impressed that she'd gone onto the battlefield with her body in such a state.

Yet Shizuri forced herself to support Kojou's shoulders, largely out of sheer stubbornness.

"This is nothing to a Paladin of Gisella!"

"You realize you have tears in your eyes, right…?"

"Ghhh…"

Shizuri's cheeks were twitching from pain, yet she made no move to distance herself from Kojou. Giving up on persuading her, Kojou headed to the entrance of the container yard with them pressed against one another, each mutually supporting the other's weight.

He could make out tents illuminated by floodlights on the other side of ground scarred from the Beast Vassals' attacks.

The tents seemed to have been put up to treat the wounded and cook food for them. Lured by the scent of soup, Kojou and Shizuri quickened their pace.

"Kojou!"

Kojou suddenly heard someone calling his name.

From the other side of white steam rising from asphalt torn up in aftershocks of the Beast Vassals' attacks, a small girl wearing a Saikai Academy uniform ran over with a nervous expression.

"Nagisa? What are you doing out here…?"

Kojou posed that question as he gazed dumbfounded at the unexpected appearance of his little sister.

He'd heard a lot of people had lent a hand to stop his rampage, but for Nagisa to have been among them was news to him. Kojou couldn't hide how the thought of his little sister seeing him violent and having lost all reason shook him deeply.

"Never mind that, come quick! Kano's in trouble!"

Paying her older brother's gloom no mind, Nagisa anxiously spoke at hyper speed.

"Kanase is…? Don't tell me she's here, too?!"

Kojou was bewildered as his expression hardened.

Kanon Kanase, bearing the blood of the Aldegian royal family, was a spirit medium with power on par with Yukina and her peers, but she hadn't taken Attack Mage combat training. Kanon participating in combat against those black Beast Vassals was reckless beyond all doubt.

"Please! Hurry!"

Nagisa ran off, leading Kojou and Shizuri. Kojou forgot about the pain in his body as he followed.

The white mist got thicker as they pressed on. Instead of steam gushing out of molten asphalt, the air was frigid, tingling his skin. The low temperature was normally impossible for Itogami Island's tropical climate. However, snow was falling.

"*Cosa?* What is with that mass of ice…?!"

Shizuri, running alongside Kojou, halted in abject shock.

A nook outside the container yard was covered by an ice sculpture. It was a giant mass of ice, as if a raging tornado had been frozen solid.

"Don't tell me this is…angelification?"

Kojou uttered those words because he had seen such a spectacle before.

"Angelification?"

Shizuri glared at Kojou as she echoed his words. *Yeah*, said Kojou, clenching his jaw as he nodded.

"Something exactly like this happened when Kanase was turning into a Faux-Angel once before, freezing everything it touched in the area. It's not as complete as it was back then, though…"

"Faux-Angel? Where the practitioner shifts into a higher-dimensional being as an effect of high-density spiritual energy?"

A crease formed on Shizuri's brow. The existence of Faux-Angels was an Aldegian national secret, but Shizuri already knew about Yukina as a precedent. She had to understand that using vast spiritual energy beyond human limitations ran the risk of someone vanishing from the mortal realm.

"—Affirmative. I believe it is the effect of her using a divine armament from the Kingdom of Aldegia to face The Blood's Beast Vassals."

The one who responded to Shizuri's comment was a blue-haired girl waiting for them within the mist—a homunculus wearing a maid outfit.

"Astarte…!"

Kojou ran over to the girl in maid clothes.

He was worried about Kanon proceeding down the path of angelification, but Astarte's life was exposed to just as much peril. She was an experimental, artificial Beast Vassal symbiote. A Beast Vassal forcibly implanted into her exhausted the homunculus's life span at an incredible rate.

Until recently, Kojou had shouldered the burden of the demonic energy required to use her Beast Vassal, but that supply of demonic energy had been cut. Kojou's spiritual pathway with her had been severed when he'd relinquished the power of the Fourth Primogenitor.

"Are you all right? No, ain't no way you are if you used your Beast Vassal without the Fourth Primogenitor's demonic energy—"

"I am not suffering any hindrance to operational activity at the present time. I recommend securing Kanon Kanase as the higher priority. I anticipate Nina Adelard has been frozen in Kanon Kanase's vicinity."

Astarte spoke in a flat tone that betrayed no emotion.

The Beast Vassal dwelling within her was whittling down her life span that very moment, yet she was telling him he should rescue Kanon first regardless, no doubt because Kanon was in just that life-threatening a situation. It seemed that Nina had been caught up in the freezing, but the nonsensical alchemist was in no immediate danger, so he decided he would save her later.

"Though…what should I do, bust the Aldegian divine arm thingy?"

Kojou inquired as he glared at the sight of Kanon deep inside the transparent block of ice. The uniform-wearing Kanon had a bracelet with a dull golden glow on her left wrist. That was probably the divine armament in question.

Kanon's divine armament, responding to the vast spiritual energy in her angelicizing body, was continuing to emit incredible cold.

Destroying only the divine armament and leaving Kanon unscathed was a tall order for Kojou's powers. Kojou's Beast Vassals were excessively strong, making them unsuited to precise, pinpoint attacks. The same went for Astarte's Beast Vassal and Shizuri's Hauras.

"…She possesses a ring."

Beside Kojou, Shizuri sank into thought, belatedly speaking as if she'd remembered something.

"Ring?"

"A ring identical to mine and Yukina Himeragi's, sealing a portion of your flesh as a catalyst."

When a questioning look came over Kojou, Shizuri thrust her left hand toward him. The silver-colored ring on her ring finger greatly resembled Yukina's.

"I see now... That's from the knife that Zana chick stabbed me with...!"

Kojou murmured as he recalled a vague memory from just before his rampage. Zana had given Yukina metal with Kojou's vampiric flesh sealed inside, which they were supposed to use to assemble Blood Servants for Kojou.

Yukina had it changed into rings and had given one to Shizuri. That was why Kojou drinking Shizuri's blood was all it took to make her his Blood Servant.

If Shizuri's words were to be believed, Kanon had the same kind of ring as she did.

"...So, if I drink Kanon's blood, it might stop her from angelicizing."

Kojou glared at the mass of ice before him, quietly regulating his breath as he hardened his resolve.

With the thick ice in the way, he couldn't tell if Kanon actually had on the ring. He could only pray she was still wearing it.

"Based on similar circumstances, I judge the possibility to be high. Accordingly, I recommend you attempt a vampiric act."

When Astarte said that, she summoned her own Beast Vassal without giving Kojou the slightest chance to stop her. Giant, rainbow-glimmering arms spread forth like wings, clawing away at the mass of ice impeding their path.

"Kojou can save Kano if he drinks her blood?"

Nagisa questioned and worriedly gazed up at Kojou. He gave her a slight nod.

"Well...probably."

"I'm so glad...then, please! Drink Kano's blood quick!"

"Er...you say quick, but..."

Kojou's lips twisted nervously as a cold sweat formed at his temples.

This was something generally misunderstood, but the trigger for vampiric urges was lust, not hunger. If you had to categorize it, vampiric acts were more similar to sexual acts. Even Kojou couldn't just drink anyone's blood at the drop of a hat, particularly with his little sister watching.

"Um…Nagisa Akatsuki, I would be grateful if you could move a short distance away from this place…"

Shizuri acted considerate for once and tried to get Nagisa to give them some space.

Nagisa blinked hard and looked back at Shizuri.

"Eh…? Why?"

"If you must know, this is, er…you will find out when you are older!"

"…Huh?"

Shizuri's roundabout explanation made Nagisa suspicious. Well, her reaction was only natural. Of course she wouldn't easily accept being ordered to go somewhere else when her older brother was trying to save her close friend.

Kojou looked skyward and sighed. Exhibiting lust for Kanon under Nagisa's watchful eye was a pretty tall order, but that didn't mean they had time to persuade her, either. The clock was ticking as Kanon's angelification advanced and Astarte's life was whittling away.

"Astarte. Can you search for Nina and get her out while I'm in contact with Kanon?"

"*—Accept.*"

The homunculus girl curtly assented to Kojou's instructions. Kojou turned toward Shizuri and continued.

"Cas, your sword… It's not dirty or unsanitary or anything?"

"Unsanitary? You are referring to Hauras? How rude! I keep it properly maintained!"

"…They say sexual desires increase when a creature's life is in danger, right?"

"Huh? Kojou, what in the world are you thinking? You don't mean…"

Kojou's sudden question made Shizuri's expression harden. According to theory, life-threatening crises stimulated a creature's reproductive instincts for the perpetuation of the species.

On top of that, Shizuri's Hauras was a demonic blade that stole the demonic energy of those it cut in order to increase its strength. It was entirely likely that a vampire's normal instinct would be to drink someone else's blood in order to replenish the stolen demonic energy.

"Sorry, but I don't have time to worry about it. Please, watcher. Hit me with everything you got."

A taunting smile came over Kojou as he looked at Shizuri.

"This man…!"

Shizuri's lips twisted in disgust. Kojou was telling her to slash him in order to provoke vampiric urges toward Kanon. On top of being reckless, it was such an uncertain method that she really didn't want to go along with it.

If it was the only way to save Kanon, though, she could understand his logic.

Since Yukina wasn't there, the duty of cutting Kojou fell to Shizuri.

After all, Shizuri was the watcher of Kojou Akatsuki just as much as Yukina was.

"…Shizuri?"

A bewildered expression came over Nagisa as she watched Shizuri smoothly draw her long sword. No surprise she hadn't realized what Shizuri's objective was.

Astarte's Beast Vassal broke through the mass of ice and exposed Kanon's body.

Kojou and Shizuri approached Kanon, leaving the worried Nagisa watching on from behind. When he spotted Nina midway, frozen and fallen to the ground, he picked her up and tossed her toward Astarte before picking up the unconscious Kanon.

"Cas!"

"…*Scusa*…do not hold this against me!"

Shizuri grimaced and poised her sword. When Kojou turned toward her, she thrust her long sword's blade into Kojou's flank.

The malevolent, undulating, flame-like blade penetrated Kojou's flesh with barely any resistance. Fresh blood gushed of the wound with great force. She'd delivered exactly what Kojou had ordered: a grievous wound making him feel as if his life was at risk.

"Kojou?!"

Nagisa was dumbfounded as she gasped, but Kojou had no time to consider her feelings.

"Shit, that really hurts…!"

With the long sword still stabbing him, Kojou pressed a hand to his side as he peered down at Kanon's face.

Enveloped by the light of spiritual essence, Kanon's beauty was positively divine. Her silver hair glowed. You could practically see through her skin. She looked like a serene work of art. Under normal circumstances, maybe that would have kept her from being a target of his vampiric impulses.

Kojou, however, had drunk Kanon's blood several days before. The memory of the warmth and softness he'd felt at the time was still crystal clear.

On top of that, thanks to the great amount of demonic energy stolen by Hauras, Kojou was incredibly hungry that moment, hungry enough to summon his vampiric urges.

"Aka...tsuki...I am so glad...you are safe."

Having vaguely regained consciousness, Kanon smiled weakly and looked up at Kojou.

Kojou strongly embraced her body without a word. Even on the verge of vanishing altogether, Kanon was still more worried about Kojou's safety than her own.

"Sorry, Kanase. I still need you here in our world."

Kojou ferociously bared his fangs. Kanon looked up at him and nodded.

"Yes...so you do."

She offered her slender neck. Kojou's fangs sank in. Nagisa and Shizuri watched in silence. The ring on Kanon's finger gave off a faint, silvery glow.

Tiny fragments of shattered ice fell around Kojou and Kanon's bodies as if they were glimmering snow.

"——So that's all she wrote, all during the time we were mopping up after your rampage, too."

Asagi sighed wearily as she gazed at the security camera footage playing on her smartphone screen.

This was taking place inside an elevator continuing to the central block of Itogami Island's Keystone Gate, the Gigafloat Management Corporation's headquarters.

"Whaddaya mean, all she wrote?! And why are you treatin' that being on camera like it's normal?!"

Sulking and glaring at Asagi's exasperated face, Kojou raised his voice in outright objection. Sure, he'd drunk Kanon's blood outdoors, but no one had said a word about it being caught on video from start to finish.

"Why so surprised? Of course there were security cameras there. The whole Island Guard mobilized to stop your rampage."

"U...ghhh..."

Asagi's casual and eminently correct version of events left Kojou at a loss for words.

Kojou drank Kanon's blood inside the operational theater under Island Guard surveillance. Since he was the operation's target, it wasn't all that hard to imagine they'd kept tabs on Kojou's movements with spy satellites or surveillance drones and the like. That data would technically be secret, but Asagi was the sort of person who could access such data with ease.

He hadn't intended to feel guilt for it, but the fact remained that vampiric acts were underpinned by sexual desire. When he thought about it calmly, being recorded drinking Kanon's blood really was embarrassing.

On top of that, right after he'd finished drinking from Kanon, Kojou drank Astarte's blood, too. When he thought about that on surveillance, his face felt red enough to catch fire at any moment.

"In other words, that is how Nagisa misunderstood that senpai must suffer grave wounds and lose a great deal of blood in order to engage in vampiric actions."

Yukina spoke in a calm tone. Now Kojou understood the reason behind Nagisa suddenly fetching a kitchen knife when she learned Yukina was trying to have Kojou drink her blood. Nagisa had it in her head that he needed to be wounded before he could drink anyone's blood.

"Pretty much. Guess Nagisa can switch mental gears on a dime, just like her big brother, who acts all cool and doesn't mind if he gets hurt if it's to save a friend?"

Asagi looked up at Kojou with a strained, sarcastic smile.

"I'm so happy for you. She doesn't actually think of you as the living embodiment of lust, carried away by his passions and drinking from every girl he can put his hands on."

"What do you mean, every girl I can put my hands on…?"

Kojou sighed in exasperation. Still, he couldn't deny that Asagi's assertion had a valid point. Such a violent misunderstanding weighed on his mind a little, but he'd much rather be respected by his little sister than scorned.

"Setting aside how Nagisa got the wool pulled over her eyes as a result, the fact remains that you assaulted Kojou in his sleep to have him drink your blood, right, Himeragi?"

Asagi checked to confirm this with Yukina while they switched to an Employees Only elevator. Since he was taken completely by surprise, Yukina's voice was shrill from a fair touch of nerves.

"Y-you are mistaken. No, you are not mistaken that I tried to have him drink my blood, but if I do not have a pact with Akatsuki-senpai, I cannot use Snowdrift Wolf so…you are mistaken!"

"Hey, I'm not going to stop you. It just annoys me to have you sneaking around like that. It's not like anyone turned you down in advance."

Asagi leaned against the interior wall of the elevator and let out a deep, irritable sigh. Kojou covered his eyes and shook his head at her statement, which seemed a bit off the mark.

"Er, this isn't an issue of consent…"

"If you have nowhere dark and out of the way, just do it in front of everyone. If I wanted to do it with Kojou, that's what I'd do."

"It's not that I *want* to do stuff like that with Himeragi, either."

"…It is not that you want to do that with me, either…stuff like that, you say…is that so…"

Hearing Kojou's words of instant rebuttal, Yukina lowered her voice. For some reason, Asagi shifted her gaze toward the obviously peeved look on Yukina's face with apparent sympathy.

"So what then? It's not like Nagisa's here. You gonna do it now?"

"Eh?! N-no, that would be…"

Yukina's cheeks reddened as she emphatically shook her head.

Asagi shrugged her shoulders a little, smiling with a hint of relief.

"That so. I'm glad. I don't want to keep our guest waiting forever."

"...Guest?"

Kojou squinted suspiciously at the mature suit Asagi was wearing. The kitchen knife incident with Nagisa had taken up so much of his attention that he couldn't remember having actually found out the reason Asagi had requested his and Yukina's presence.

Asagi looked back at the bewildered Kojou and Yukina with exasperation. Her smile faded as her face turned serious.

"A somewhat troublesome guest has come to see you."

The stopped elevator's doors opened. Kojou and Yukina were wary of the weighty atmosphere hovering in the corridor as they stepped into the inner sanctum of the Gigafloat Management Corporation.

3

The scenery from forty meters below sea level sprawled beyond huge, pressure-resistant windows.

There, sunlight illuminating the surface of the sea and the blue gradients of the deep produced a beautiful backdrop to gaze at from the huge round table placed in the room. It was a VIP conference room under Keystone Gate.

"How do you do, Fourth Primogenitor?"

Waiting for Kojou and company at the back of the conference room was a young woman wearing clothes so flashy, you'd think it was the stage outfit for an idol singer. Her outward age didn't seem much different from that of Kojou and the girls. She had fluttery, ashen hair and skin as white as snow. Her red eyes were as bright as cherry tomatoes. A seductive smile crossed her lips as she touched a hand to her top hat with a big ribbon on it.

"...No, that would be the Former Fourth Primogenitor, Mr. Kojou Akatsuki, ruler of Itogami City-State."

"Who are you?"

Kojou responded bluntly to the woman addressing him with a shrewd look on her face.

Even though Kojou obviously looked wary, the expression of the woman in the gaudy outfit changed little. She gave him an exaggerated, theatrical bow as she began introducing herself in fluent Japanese.

"I am most pleased to meet you. I am Ladli Ren, principal executive of Magna Ataraxia Research. I hope we become well acquainted."

"You're with MAR…?!"

"Ladli…*Ren?*"

Kojou and Yukina exclaimed simultaneously. The corners of the girl's lips rose with delight.

"Yes, Shahryar Ren, president of our corporation, is my older brother. I am truly apologetic about the disturbances my brother has caused all of you of late."

Ladli's lips formed a teasing smile as she shifted her gaze upward. Then she touched the tip of her hat as if she'd just realized something.

"Ahhh, please do not mind the outfit. As you must be well aware, we Devas are sensitive to sunlight. This hat is to prevent sunburn. *Giggle.*"

"…!"

When Ladli announced her true nature, Kojou watched her, subconsciously going on guard.

If she really was a Deva, there was a good chance she could use what Shahryar Ren had termed divine energy to launch strange attacks. He couldn't let his guard down, for the woman was a far more dangerous individual than she appeared.

"So what does an executive of MAR want with the Gigafloat Management Corporation? Don't tell me you've come to drag your brother home?"

Asagi questioned Ladli bluntly. Ladli sadly shook her head as she took out a tiny box she could fit in the palm of her hand. It was a 3D holographic projector, MAR's latest model.

"Unfortunately, I can do no such thing. First, see here? It's a sphere… just kidding."

"That's…?"

Frostily ignoring Ladli's playfulness, Kojou and the others paid attention to the 3D image floating in midair. On display inside the sphere some two meters in diameter was a fleet of warships traversing the sea. It looked like footage shot by a military unmanned recon vehicle.

"The North American Union's Pacific Long-Range Strike Fleet, huh?"

Asagi gave the fleet in the footage one glance before snorting with scorn.

Asagi had duked it out with a multinational armada from the Holy Grounds Treaty Organization during the War of the Primogenitors. The NAU's battle fleet had been included in that armada.

"Quite correct, Miss Priestess of Cain. Or perhaps I should call it a punitive fleet dispatched by the HGTO to conquer Itogami Island and invade Nod?"

Ladli nodded courteously. Kojou glared at Ladli in surprise.

"Conquer Itogami Island...?!"

"Yes, most likely. If they gain control of Itogami Island, the world's only open route to Nod, it doesn't matter what Shahryar might be planning, or so the thinking probably went."

"Worst case, they might just blow Itogami Island off the map."

Ladli and Asagi spoke in sequence. Kojou felt a mild sense of déjà vu as he shook his head. This would be the second time Itogami Island had become the HGTO's attack target.

Last time, Kojou had managed to cut the attack short using a primogenitor's veto power, but he couldn't play the same card twice. Currently, Kojou was not the Fourth Primogenitor, and the HGTO viewed Shahryar Ren in Nod as its enemy, not Itogami Island. Now that Ren had been deemed a terrorist, the HGTO had every justification in the world to attack him.

"So, what? You want to fight alongside Itogami Island? You're telling us to lend our strength to resist the HGTO together?"

Asagi sat in a nearby chair and rested her cheek against her palm, elbow on the conference table.

Kojou looked at Asagi in surprise. MAR had made an enemy out of the HGTO—or really, the entire world. Even if it was just being caught up in the mess, Itogami Island had become the HGTO's attack target just as much. Ladli's and Kojou's team joining hands had some merit to it.

"Fighting alongside—? No, no, perish the thought."

Unexpectedly, Ladli readily rejected Asagi's words. Circling her index finger around, she sped up the holographic feed.

"More importantly, watch this footage to the end. You'll see something very interesting."

Before Ladli's words had even finished, the sound of an explosion echoed through the room. One of the destroyers in the fleet in the 3D image sank in an instant.

"…Eh?!"

Asagi's eyes widened, and her jaw dropped. Apparently even she hadn't expected this development.

"What the—?! What in the world are they fighting?!"

Kojou squinted and peered into the flame-enveloped 3D imagery. Just before the destroyer sank, something enveloped by blinding light flew right over it. It didn't have a trail like a gun shell or a missile. The movements were animated, like those of a wild beast.

"That's…a Beast Vassal?! But whose…?"

Yukina spoke in a daze. Coldly lording over the area, standing on the bow of the sinking destroyer, was a giant cephalopod with its whole body enveloped by demonic energy lightning.

Judging from the size of the destroyer, the monster had to be over ten meters tall. Of course, this was no creature from the natural world. It was a summoned beast from another world with a body of dense demonic energy—a vampire's Beast Vassal.

Yet even vampiric Beast Vassals would not find sinking a destroyer equipped with magical defenses an easy task. Few vampires could use Beast Vassals on such a scale, nearly rivaling the primogenitors.

The Beast Vassal's host was nowhere to be seen in the image.

The Beast Vassal attacking the HGTO battle fleet with the power of a primogenitor had no host. It was simply destroying everything in sight according to its instincts.

"Beast Vassal Warheads, huh?"

Gazing at the raging Beast Vassal, Kojou wore a neutral expression as he let those words slip.

"…Senpai?"

Kojou's uncharacteristically calm reaction puzzled Yukina.

For her part, Ladli looked back at Kojou with a satisfied smile.

"I see, you've seen the memories of other primogenitors. So, you know the truth about the past, then."

"Yeah."

Kojou confirmed with a single word.

Beast Vassal Warheads—that was the name of the strategic weapons the Devas had employed in The Great Cleansing of Old. Their incredible might had inflicted grievous damage on the alliance of rebelling humans and demons, culminating in the destruction of Deva cities and civilization itself.

"Masses of demonic energy giving in to instinct and destroying everything in sight—such are summoned beasts from another world. This is the original version of Beast Vassals. A Beast Vassal Warhead is a weapon that seals them inside a warhead until they can be fired into an enemy formation."

Ladli continued explaining with a musical air.

"The principle is very simple, but the power is, as you can see for yourselves, overwhelming. After all, these are wild, untamed Beast Vassals. The downside is that they cannot be ordered to attack specific targets or limit their attack range, so their only use is for genocidal warfare."

"Sealing Beast Vassals...but how...?"

Yukina's voice quivered as she inquired.

A Beast Vassal was a mass of dense demonic energy summoned from another world. Even merely existing in that world required the exhaustion of a vast amount of "sacrifices"—demonic energy, spiritual energy, life force energy, and even people's memories. They maintained their physical manifestations by greedily devouring any and all information they could.

No sorcerous device existed that could seal such a monster, save a single exception—

"Are you not quite familiar with it?"

Ladli smiled elegantly, seemingly seeing right through Yukina's thoughts.

Yukina fell silent, unable to hide her inner turmoil. The only things that could seal a Beast Vassal consuming vast "sacrifices" were unaging, undying vampires with infinite negative life force energy.

"Don't tell me, this weapon uses...artificial vampires...?"

The look in Yukina's eyes sharpened as she glared at Ladli.

The MAR executive casually accepted that gaze as she strongly puffed out her chest.

"Please, rest at ease. The artificial vampires employed in Beast Vassal Warheads are factory-made and possess neither emotions nor wills of their own. It is quite all right. They are mere weapons of might…*giggle*."

"Why, you…!"

Ladli's scornful demeanor brought Kojou's anger to the surface. Ladli raised her fine eyebrows with a slightly disconcerted look.

"Don't get angry at me. They were constructed in antiquity, thousands of years ago—before The Great Cleansing, it is said."

"…I see…so Shahryar Ren went to Nod to bring Beast Vassal Warheads back with him, then."

Asagi casually asserted this with an unmoved voice.

Yes, nodded Ladli proudly in reply.

Flames spewed from a fourth destroyer displayed in the 3D imagery.

The remaining ships desperately continued to engage in combat, but normal weapons were virtually powerless against a huge, rampaging Beast Vassal. The destruction of the entire fleet was probably only a matter of time.

"This is the Legacy that Cain the Sinful God sealed away in Nod—six thousand four hundred and fifty-two Beast Vassal Warheads. Had Cain not sealed them, the Devas would never have lost to humanity in The Great Cleansing. After all, that number of warheads is enough to destroy the surface three times over."

Ladli casually revealed this frightening information. In other words, if Shahryar Ren had his hands on the rest of the Beast Vassal Warheads in Nod, he already had enough power to destroy the world and then some.

"So Shahryar Ren's goal is to get his hands on the Beast Vassal Warheads in Nod?"

"I would say not his objective so much as one part of his plans. The Beast Vassal Warheads are merely a means to an end."

Kojou shivered as he asked, and a suggestive smile came over Ladli's lips. She put her hands together in front of her breasts with a clap, straightening up as she turned straight toward Kojou and the others.

"So I have come with a business proposal."

"…Proposal?"

"Yes. Please sell Itogami Island to MAR. Everything, the island populace included."

"Huh…?"

For a moment, Ladli's sudden statement left Kojou reeling and unable to process what she had said. Yukina was just as surprised as he was. Asagi was the only one who merely covered her eyes a little and let out a languid sigh.

"In other words, you want us to hand rulership rights over Itogami City-State to you. You'll pay fair compensation and ensure the citizens' safety and guarantee their rights as subjects of the Devas—something along those lines? You probably have the fine details of the rights we'd request already laid out."

"…The gist being, quietly sit and obey while you guys occupy Itogami Island?"

Kojou looked like he was nursing a headache as he double-checked.

Very much so, said Ladli's narrowed eyes as she smiled.

"I believe the terms are extremely favorable. It seems Shahryar intends to bring the entire world under Deva rule, which would make war unavoidable. However, coming under our rule sooner rather than later would avoid exposure to the flames of war. It will be teatime, not wartime, for you."

"Favorable terms, my foot. Itogami Island getting destroyed is a big problem for you, isn't it?"

Asagi spoke with a sardonic smile.

"I do not refute this. I also understand how you resent being threatened with Beast Vassals and the like to force you to obey us."

Ladli accepted Asagi's words without any attempt at a rebuttal. Then she turned a sharp gaze toward Kojou, seemingly testing him.

"However, are you not the same, Kojou Akatsuki, ruling people through the violent power we call Beast Vassals? What is your basis for assuming you would be a better ruler of Itogami Island than we would?"

Ghhh, went Kojou's low groan. Ladli's question struck Kojou's doubts with pinpoint accuracy.

It wasn't as if he'd wanted to sit on Itogami Island's throne. He certainly didn't think he had the qualifications or right to rule Itogami Island. By rights, it was nonsensical for a student and minor like Kojou to sit at the negotiating table that would determine Itogami Island's destiny.

"At the very least, MAR employs a large number of skilled specialists and possesses the know-how to move as an organization. We possess the financial power to hire the right people and the technology to allow people to live prosperous lives. Is it not obvious to the residents of Itogami Island which would serve as the better statesman?"

Ladli's words were like rubbing salt into Kojou's self-conscious wounds. Kojou couldn't manage a response, leaving Yukina and Asagi to speak in his stead.

"I do not believe it is for you to decide what the residents of Itogami Island wish."

"Nope, and Kojou's the one who did the hard work bringing the Electoral War chaos to an end. The people who fanned the flames of the conflict that made the citizens suffer are in no position to complain."

"Oh myyy…it hurts when you put it like thaaat…"

How vexing, Ladli's strained smile seemed to say as she shook her head.

"However, what is it that you think, Kojou Akatsuki? Do you genuinely desire to rule Itogami Island? Would you not be satisfied with saving Dodekatos? If so, why not help us?"

It was easy to tell that Ladli's mention of an unexpected name threw Kojou off-balance. His whole reason for regaining vampire powers wasn't for the sake of being Itogami Island's ruler, let alone saving the world. He was motivated to save the girl named Avrora Florestina, and that was all.

"…Help, you say?"

"Yes. Now that the gate to Nod is open, we do not require her any longer. I shall attempt to persuade my brother to return her to you. Or is her return such a strange turn? Mm? …Just kidding."

Ladli spoke in a jovial tone. *Are you messing with me?* broadcast the twitch of Kojou's temple, but she apparently had no particular ill intent.

"I am providing you with two options. Hand over your right to rule Itogami Island to us and avoid unnecessary conflict or make enemies of MAR and the Devas and fight us to the last."

Peace, Ladli seemed to say as she grinned and held up two fingers in a peace sign.

"I will not insist that you make a decision immediately. There is still time, so please eat a good meal, take your time, and make a good judgment. Ah, also, this is my business card. Business is my business, so to speak."

Pulling a business card out from somewhere and unveiling it like prize merchandise, Ladli left it on the table and waved *bye-bye*. This signaled that the meeting was at an end.

4

"Ick...these sunrays are truly abominable."

When a Gigafloat Management Corporation employee saw Ladli Ren out to the lobby, she covered her eyes in irritation as she peered at the blue sky visible beyond the revolving doors.

To Ladli and other Devas, the light of the sun was a lethal menace. Mere reflected light inflamed their skin, and light shining through glass could burn their flesh off. If exposed to direct sunlight, she'd probably end up a pile of ash.

"What is Brother thinking, knowing this and sending his precious little sister to this tropical nation? Sunlight is some fright, I tell you."

Ladli muttered idle jokes to herself as she took out a sorcerous device resembling a brooch. This was a teleportation device using MAR's latest technology.

The downsides were that it depleted a vast amount of magical energy and could only jump to preregistered coordinates, but the convenience of a nonsorcerer being able to use teleportation so easily was overwhelming. The device was the reason why Ladli could visit the Gigafloat Management Corporation during daylight hours without any concern for the rays of the sun.

The MAR Inc. business jet that had brought Ladli to Itogami Island from the Talaud Islands was waiting at Itogami Island Central Airport. To avoid annoying customs procedures, Ladli pressed the switch of the teleportation device to port straight into the plane. However...

"Dear me…?"

A magic circle glowed as it hovered in the area around Ladli, but it shattered and dissipated. Ladli puffed out her cheeks when she realized someone had interfered with it from the outside.

"I am sorry, but I deployed a barrier to seal your spatial control magic. You cannot leave this building."

Ladli heard a man's voice from behind her. The low voice was not aggressive, but it was dignified and direct.

"My, my, the Duke of Severin, Your Excellency, Velesh Aradahl, is it?"

Approaching from the back of the lobby was a man with long hair, wearing an old-fashioned frock coat. This was Velesh Aradahl, chairman of the Imperial Parliament of the Warlord's Empire, said to be a vital retainer and confidant of the First Primogenitor.

Attending him from behind were four vampires dressed in black. If all of them were noble-rank vampires, they wielded heavy firepower rivaling an infantry battalion.

In addition, a lone woman waved a hand from a short distance away. She was a vividly beautiful woman with hair that was red bordering on blond.

When Ladli looked at that woman, her lips formed a sarcastic grin.

"Even Her Royal Highness, Queen Zana Lashka? I am exceedingly honored to have an audience with you, even if you are the seventy-second, the very bottom of the queen litter."

"How dare you…!"

Ladli's insolent statement brought Aradahl's anger to the surface, but Zana, the one supposedly being scorned, stopped Aradahl with a composed demeanor.

"It's fine, really. It's the truth, after all… It would be pitiful if I couldn't let the ramblings of someone seven millennia my elder slide."

"Hah?!"

Ladli's eyebrows rose high when she heard Zana's mocking words.

"Elder who?! Time flows differently inside the Necropolis so I'm every bit as young as I physically appear! And you don't age so you're in the same boat!"

"My age isn't even one tenth of yours!"

"... *Tch.*"

After roughly clicking her tongue, Ladli regulated her breathing and changed her tone to gloss that part over.

"So what is your business with me? If you have come to offer your surrender, I will at least consider it."

"Those are precisely my words to you, Ladli Ren."

Aradahl spoke with a deadly serious demeanor. The four vampires behind him stepped up as if moving to surround Ladli.

"The Holy Grounds Treaty Organization has issued international arrest warrants for all MAR personnel as large-scale terrorism suspects. Disarm yourself and surrender. If you do not, you will face the Imperial Knights of the Warlord's Empire."

"It's best if you let us capture you here. Fallgazer and Chaos Bride's people are far bloodier. They're prowling all over Itogami Island looking for you, you know?"

Zana warned her in a tone blatantly intended to fan her fears.

The publicly acknowledged vampire primogenitors numbered three. Their retainers, the soldiers of the three Dominions, were all affiliated with the HGTO, but that didn't mean they cooperated with one another. Each was probably moving independently to target Ladli, competing over the same prey.

They had more reason to target Ladli than the simple fact she was an MAR employee. Ladli was Shahryar Ren's little sister and played the role of Shahryar's Deva connection to the surface. Whether she was a hostage or a source of information, Ladli's value was priceless. Of course, the interrogation that would follow Ladli's apprehension would be... severe.

Zana's assertion was this—compared to the mysterious Fallen Dynasty and the Chaos Zone renowned for its cruelty, their Warlord's Empire was far more reasonable.

This, though, was premised on being able to actually capture Ladli in the first place.

"How unfortunate. This would have been so much faster if you'd surrendered."

Ladli took out a lollipop and twirled it around in her hand. What had begun as a single candy became a trio of them at some point.

"But you know, I suppose the retainers of the three primogenitors, the betrayers who took humanity's side during The Great Cleansing, wouldn't serve the Devas at this late stage."

Ladli smashed the lollipops in her hand against the floor. The candy sticks impaled the limestone floor, then bounced off with incredible force. This was different from Deva divine energy or vampiric demonic energy, but a malevolent power smelling of blood.

"—Velesh!"

Sensing something was wrong, Zana instructed Aradahl to attack.

Aradahl's subordinates summoned Beast Vassals all at once.

Zana's Divine Oscillation Effect was able to seal Ladli's teleport magic, but MAR technology derived from Deva relics was an unknown factor. They needed to completely neutralize Ladli before she could pull any funny business, even if it meant killing her, but—

"Of course, we Devas have no intention of forgiving you, either."

The attacks unleashed by those Beast Vassals bounced off before ever reaching Ladli. A white figure suddenly appeared in front of Ladli, receiving the Beast Vassals head-on and striking them down.

"What…?!"

Aradahl's cheeks contorted in surprise.

Standing all around Ladli were humanoid monsters, each covered in a white exoskeleton.

They were two meters tall, or perhaps more. Their legs were unusually long, and their torsos rather thin. They looked like a cross between fossilized dinosaurs pieced back together in a museum and ferocious carnivorous insects. Ladli had used the fragments of the candies she smashed on the floor as catalysts to summon them.

"What are these things…?! Sorcerous weapons?"

Aradahl exclaimed as he summoned his own Beast Vassal. He didn't think the monsters with exoskeletons could contain enough internal organs to qualify as demons or even proper living creatures, but…

"No…they are living creatures! They are deploying powerful bio-fields! Our Beast Vassals are bouncing off…u-uoooo!!"

Aradahl's vampire subordinate was wounded when he sustained a counterattack from the monsters. They had incredible agility and brute force belying their fossilized appearance. Even Imperial Knights, the elites of the Warlord's Empire, were being overwhelmed by only three of them.

"Living creatures, you say…?!"

"Don't tell me these are…Dragon Tooth Warriors…?! Ewww, not cute!"

Silver-colored metal knuckles over her hands, Zana shielded the wounded Imperial Knight and punched one white monster into the air. Yet even showering it in Zana's Divine Oscillation Effect, able to neutralize sorcerous weapons, did not stop the monsters in their tracks. The only result was a tiny crack running along its bony, skull-like face.

"Dragon Tooth Warriors…?! I see, these are Spartoi?!"

"Yes. They are sorcerous soldiers, grown from the fangs of my brother's ancient dragon friend. Now, my good Spartoi, put your fangs into it!"

Glancing at the surprised Aradahl, Ladli urged the monsters onward.

Aradahl, wearing his own Beast Vassal like a suit of armor, blocked the Spartoi attacks. Nonetheless, the monsters were fine after coming into contact with Aradahl's Beast Vassal, one that supposedly destroyed all that it touched.

Spartoi were legendary artificial demons created from dragon teeth. Just like the dragons from which they hailed, they possessed a powerful resistance to demonic energy. That was why even vampiric Beast Vassals could not destroy them with ease.

"Tch…gouge, Invidia!"

Becoming impatient, Aradahl summoned a fresh Beast Vassal, a long sword the color of utter darkness.

Swinging the Intelligent Weapon with his own hands, he sliced across a white monster's torso, shattering it. He'd used the vast amount of demonic energy within to break through the Spartoi's defensive barrier through sheer force.

"That is His Excellency, Velesh Aradahl for you… I thought it'd take five or six cutting-edge fighter jets to take down each one grown, but you sure blew that estimate out of the sky."

Ladli sadly shook her head as she gazed down at the shattered Spartoi fragments.

Aradahl ignored her laments and ordered the Beast Vassal Invidia to attack.

By rights, the pitch-black great sword was a Beast Vassal meant for destroying castle walls and other fortifications. Barring a monster like the Fourth Primogenitor, it was unthinkable to summon it for melee combat due to its excessive power. Any enemy would be blown away without leaving a trace.

"What…?"

Aradahl, feeling an unusual level of resistance through his Beast Vassal, let a perplexed utterance slip past his lips.

Ladli, a wisp of a girl, had blocked the blade of Invidia, over five times her own height. More precisely, Aradahl's Beast Vassal had been stopped cold by the steel-colored cane that had appeared in Ladli's hands.

"A sorcerous device of the Sinful God?!"

"More precisely, a sorcerous device of the Devas."

An impetuous smile spread across Ladli's face as she swung the cane like a practiced stage magician.

There were many mysteries concerning the sorcerous devices called Legacies of the Sinful God. The simple fact that Ladli possessed such a device meant it was likely her staff's abilities posed an enormous threat to Aradahl. Judging it was foolish to approach her without knowing what its effect might be, Aradahl put distance between them.

"Velesh, above!"

Realizing Ladli had lobbed an attack, Zana called out from behind Aradahl.

"Lady Zana…?!"

"Destroy the building's roof! Devas are weak to sunlight!"

"Oh my."

I'm in sooo much trouble, Ladli's touch of her hand against her cheek seemed to say. Itogami Island, the artificial isle of everlasting summer, no doubt had powerful sunlight pouring down upon the building's exterior at that very moment. Now that she couldn't teleport, Ladli had no way to escape the sun.

Aradahl did not hesitate. Ladli, who had lived for years exceeding Aradahl and the rest, was a monster underneath her adorable appearance. One couldn't beat her by being picky about the means. Aradahl understood that full well from their brief battle with her.

"Awaken, Acedia!"

Aradahl summoned a new Beast Vassal. This was a whiplike long sword with a notched blade reaching dozens of meters in length. The enormous shockwave it generated easily pulverized the lobby's ceiling, wiping out both it and the upper-floor structures without a trace.

Somehow, Ladli seemed amused as she looked up. Her eyes were unshaken. The light of the sun that should have poured down from overhead barely even brightened her flesh.

Aradahl had completely destroyed the structure's roof, yet the midday sky was nowhere to be seen. For the sun was obstructed by a gargantuan sphere around a whole kilometer in diameter, which floated in the sky above Keystone Gate.

"Hee-hee, guess the roof didn't go poof. Just kidding."

Ladli touched a hand to her hat with a cutesy smile.

"How could this…! A Necropolis…?!"

Aradahl somehow wrung out a cry.

A Necropolis, fortress of the Devas, had appeared from another world.

The fortress was carrying Beast Vassal Warheads transported from Nod. Its appearance in the sky over Itogami Island meant Ladli had effectively taken all of Itogami Island hostage.

"To be honest, it would be a little awkward if your liege the First Primogenitor came out, but he's not on this island anymore. The fact that he sent a young, bottom-feeder queen like you to face me is proof enough. Just knowing that is a plus."

Ladli spoke casually with a musical lilt to her voice as she surveyed Aradahl and company. Her sociable smile warped into a cruel sneer as her large eyes emitted a crimson glow.

"As thanks, I will be as gentle as possible when I break you. Did you think children who haven't lived even a thousand years could win against me, Ladli Ren?"

"…!!"

Ladli's question overlapped with Zana's cry. Fresh blood scattered as Zana's sensual body whirled in midair. Zana had been unable to block the divine energy Ladli had unleashed as an invisible blade.

"My lady!"

When Aradahl instantly tried to shield Zana, the severing of his left leg caused him to tumble. The divine energy Ladli emitted had rent even Aradahl's Beast Vassal armor.

Looking down at the prone Aradahl, Ladli turned her steel-colored cane toward him.

"Regret your actions, lesser creatures crawling over ground stained with your own blood."

The girl's eyes displayed no emotion as she murmured.

CHAPTER TWO
WHEREABOUTS OF
THE RINGS

1

It was the ruin of a steel-colored city—

Shahryar Ren toyed with the dagger-shaped sorcerous device in his pocket as he looked up at the starless night sky.

The urban site was Senra, an ancient artificial island floating upon the Great Sea of Nod. Dozens of transport helicopters had landed in an open area on the coast, turning it into a makeshift military base. The soldiers assembled there numbered roughly four hundred, elite special forces made up of personnel hand-picked from private military corporations under MAR's corporate banner.

Using the functions of Itogami Island's Keystone Gate, he had opened the gate to Nod and obtained the Legacy of Cain the Sinful God: the Beast Vassal Warheads. They'd repelled the HGTO battle fleet and called forth the Necropolis to seal Itogami Island's airspace. All of that had gone according to Ren's plans.

Yet Avrora Florestina, the Fourth Primogenitor who should have been in their custody, had escaped. They still didn't know her whereabouts. This fact faintly annoyed Ren.

"NAU battle fleet has withdrawn beyond the Beast Vassal Warheads' effective range. Number of ships remaining: four. Number of survivors: unknown."

A female soldier assigned to coms spoke in a worked-up tone. With nothing but a tarp drawn over their heads, the fifteen-odd soldiers gathered in the field command post continued analyzing messages and data from the surface.

A makeshift projection screen displayed footage of warships enveloped with flames as they sank. A single Beast Vassal summoned with Beast Vassal Warheads had virtually destroyed the world's mightiest aircraft carrier strike group, the pride of the NAU.

"Tell the Necropolis pursuit is unnecessary. We require survivors to spread fear of the Beast Vassal Warheads for us."

Ren moved under the tarp as he spoke with a cool, detached air.

Exterminating the NAU fleet was not MAR's objective. Driving home the power of the Beast Vassal Warheads into the minds of the world's people was far more important. The more that humanity understood how foolish it was to defy the Devas, the smoother Ren's rule would become.

"With this, the HGTO will likely abandon its attack on Itogami Island. How are the three primogenitors moving?"

"The Second Primogenitor Fallgazer has appeared in the Celebes Sea, and the Third Primogenitor Chaos Bride has appeared in the North Pacific Ocean. They have begun dealing with the respective Beast Vassal Warheads."

"Well, that is hardly a surprise."

Ren gave the female soldier a satisfied nod in reply. The only things that could stop a Beast Vassal summoned with a Beast Vassal Warhead were the even more powerful Beast Vassals controlled by the three vampire primogenitors. They would scatter across the globe, steeling themselves against the Necropolises to protect the Holy Grounds Treaty Organization signatory nations and their very own Dominions.

In other words, they had no choice but to distance themselves from Itogami Island. The primogenitors didn't have the luxury of impeding Ren's plan.

"—*The immediate threats seem to have receded, President Ren.*"

"*Next, we can only pray humanity is not foolish enough to defy us now that they have witnessed the might of the Beast Vassal Warheads.*"

Suddenly, a pair of husky male voices interjected, and the image on the screen switched over. The female soldier let out a little yelp as two fantastical male figures floated on the screen.

One was a white-haired elder wearing an over-the-top outfit like a priest from antiquity. The other was a black-haired man wearing a beautiful, ornate robe reminiscent of a noble from the Middle Ages. Both had skin as pale as that of the dead. Sharp canine teeth resembling fangs poked out from the gaps of their lips. It had been centuries since Ren had been acquainted with their faces.

"Duke Kul Zu. Lord Alda Ba. I am grateful that you both responded to my abrupt summons."

Ren bowed courteously. Both men of noble rank were pureblood descendants of the Devas, few in number in the present era. They were rulers of their own Necropolises allied with Ren.

The two rulers smiled as they watched Ren bow his head.

"*It is merely doing our part as Devas. We have beheld for ourselves the might of the Beast Vassal Warheads you provided us.*"

"*As promised, our own castles shall emerge. My own Ba Castle will appear over the South Pacific, and Duke Kul Zu's castle shall appear in the North Pacific. None shall approach Itogami Island.*"

"Very good. I will hasten the resupply of Beast Vassal Warheads."

Ren spoke to his two coconspirators. The night before, MAR had transported a total of seven Beast Vassal Warheads from Nod. Ren had divided four, over half of that number, to Kul Zu and Alda Ba as samples. Their end of the deal was to mobilize their Necropolises and drive HGTO military forces back.

"*However, I am surprised that of the seventeen Deva clans, we are the only ones participating in this conflict.*"

The white-haired elder—Kul Zu—spoke to Ren as if making light banter. A tiny smile appeared on Alda Ba's face as he concurred.

"*Just so. Perhaps the others have gone soft, or perhaps they are too afraid...*"

"It is likely they do not trust me as of yet."

Ren's expression did not change as he spoke quite calmly.

At present, the Necropolises numbered seventeen. In other words, a mere seventeen families were the only ruling class Devas to have survived The Great Cleansing of Old. When Shahryar Ren called upon all of them to ally with him, Kul Zu and Alda Ba were the only ones to respond. The remainder, the vast majority of the Devas, did not believe Ren's plan would succeed.

"However, this is not a concern. Once it becomes clear I have gained complete control over Nod, the other clans will no doubt be forced to adjust their thinking. If they do not, they will be destroyed by my hand, and that will be that."

"How dependable. We expect great things from you, O new leader."

"We shall be off, then."

The two allies smiled cheerfully and broke off the call. Though the gate was in an opened state, being able to converse with Ren while in Nod without any time lag was difficult even with MAR's technological prowess. That they had accomplished this with ease showed that the two were truly fit to call themselves descendants of the Devas.

Yet at the same time, the two had conveyed their internal discomfort with Ren.

Both of them feared Ren might try to be the ruler not only of mankind, but even of the Devas themselves. If Ren displayed the slightest opening, the two probably would likely rescind their alliance and turn on MAR in an instant.

"Such an unpalatable bunch, when you are the ones who have gone soft…"

Ren let a brief soliloquy slip from his lips.

A bell-like voice rolling with laughter coursed over the transmitter immediately after. The image switched without prompting, and a young woman wearing a gaudy outfit appeared on-screen.

"I suppose they are…so unpalatable, one would not eat them at a banquet… Just kidding."

"Ladli…you heard the transmission just now?"

Ren glared with a stern face and slightly cleared his throat as his little sister laughed with delight. Sensing that her older brother was irritated with her, Ladli shrugged her shoulders slightly.

"Well, it's fine, isn't it? They did move their Necropolises, as a matter of fact, and a hundred and forty Spartoi are considerable firepower."

"I know. It demonstrates that they, too, are quite serious about this."

Ren's disgruntled expression didn't change as he nodded.

The Spartoi generated from the fangs of Kreyd the Flame Dragon actually weren't constructed using MAR technology, but through sorcerous manipulation from the Zu family and biological manipulation in the Ba family's hands—the two had provided these technologies, outside MAR's own specialties without restraint, finally reaching the operational phase.

Had they not done so, mass-producing sorcerous troops in such a brief time would have been impossible. Whatever thoughts rested at the bottom of their psyches, their dedication had proven them to be allies for the time being.

"Now then, Brother. How goes the delivery of Beast Vassal Warheads?"

"The work is advancing, but removing the barriers seems to be taking time."

Ren's face grimaced unpleasantly. The over six thousand Beast Vassal Warheads sealed in the artificial isle of Senra were protected by special, powerful barriers that were a hard fight for even MAR's sorcerous engineers to lift. This was why they had transported only a scant seven Beast Vassal Warheads to the surface.

"Is that so? I ask that you please hurry as much as possible, though. If the supply of Beast Vassal Warheads falls behind, I'm the one who will receive an earful from those two."

Ladli wasted no time beating around the bush. *I know*, Ren nodded curtly in reply.

Ren was someone who prioritized efficiency and rationality. Normally he didn't appreciate Ladli's antics. To be blunt, he found them distinctly unpleasant. To the Devas, beings with near infinite life spans, the instinct to preserve the species ran thin. Naturally, this meant they had little love for close relations.

Ren had appointed Ladli to a crucial post in spite of all this because she possessed great talent. If not, he would never have handed full command rights of MAR forces on the surface to her, little sister or not.

This same Ladli brought her hands together in front of her breasts as if she'd only just remembered something.

"Ahhh, come to mention it, Kojou Akatsuki seems to have obtained the Beast Vassals of The Blood."

"The Blood's Beast Vassals, you say…? I see, this is the work of the First Primogenitor's Blood Servant…"

A single one of Ren's eyebrows twitched. He recalled that Zana Lashka had been present at the site of the decisive battle between Kojou

Akatsuki and The Blood. He was surprised to learn that Zana's objective was recovering The Blood's Beast Vassals, but it was far from an impossible feat. After all, The Blood's black Beast Vassals were *special* Beast Vassals with properties identical to those of the Fourth Primogenitor's.

"Kojou Akatsuki's objective is getting Dodekatos back, I'm sure. What will you do? He has the Star Beast Vassal prototypes, plus he has the Priestess of Cain on his side, so they'll be trouble if we leave them be. The Priestess of Cain is a real pain, don't you know."

Ladli smiled as she spoke, quite proud of herself. Ren glared at his little sister with emotionless eyes.

"Don't let Kojou Akatsuki into Nod."

"Huh? That's it?"

"That's what I gave you all that combat strength for."

Ladli seemed perplexed, but Ren ignored her. Ladli puffed up her cheeks and pouted.

"Why not just give Dodekatos to him? He's a boy in the springtime of youth, so if you give him the girl he likes, I think he'll just leave you alone. Probably."

"Unfortunately, I can do no such thing. Tie him down on the surface until I'm done here. That's an order."

"Wait a... Brother...!"

Ignoring Ladli's attempts to argue, Ren hung up from his end.

Kojou Akatsuki regaining his vampiric powers was outside of Ren's expectations but not enough to interfere with his plans. He was no threat to Ren so long as he remained on the surface. Even so, he felt a concern, an unpleasantness that he could not quite put into words, almost like something tickling the back of his throat.

Kojou Akatsuki was no more than a mere human, yet temporary or not, he had once called himself the Fourth Primogenitor, and now he had new black Beast Vassals in his hands. Ren was unable to hide his dismay over this unpleasant fact.

"...It would seem you are...having a hard time...Shahryar Ren."

Ren let out a strained laugh, slowly turning to face the low voice addressing him from a distance.

Standing at the entrance to the tarp structure was a large-statured man wearing a mask with a lizard skull motif. He was not a fellow Deva, nor did he seem to have any human sociability whatsoever, so it felt a bit odd having him show consideration to Ren.

"Ahh, Kreyd, my friend. How does it feel being back in Nod after so long?"

"It feels...nostalgic. But...do not forget. You have yet...to fulfill the pact between us."

The dragon-man spoke in a flat voice. It was raspy, leaving a portion of his words difficult to make out, because his vocal cords were made differently from those of a human being.

"I am well aware, Guardian of the Corridor. You must understand as well. Dodekatos...no, the Fourth Primogenitor holds the power to open gates to Nod, and gates *from Nod* as well."

Ren spoke with a calm tenor. Nod was not at the end of the world. It was the boundary that bordered other worlds. Through that realm, it was possible to reach far-off lands one normally had no way of reaching. The homeland of Kreyd's fellow dragons was one such far-off land.

"Nod is the single corridor leading to Else, the Eastern Lands. Opening the gate for that corridor requires Avrora Florestina, the Fourth Primogenitor. If you wish to return to your homeland, you should retrieve her first."

"Where is Avrora Florestina?"

The eyes of the ancient dragon Kreyd glowed behind his mask.

Ren slowly lifted his face upward.

"She is not in this ruined city. That is why searching for her has taken so much time."

"...The sky...I see! Glenda...I take it?"

Kreyd's entire body emitted bloodlust resembling a wave of heat as his flesh swelled, doubling in size. Ren looked back at the sturdy dragon-man.

"MAR special forces are heading to recover Avrora now. You could always lend them a hand, though."

"Understood..."

Kreyd violently stripped off the robe he wore. His flesh, entirely covered in copper scales, progressively changed into the form of an enormous dragon. Ren narrowed his eyes as he watched, dazzled by the sight of Kreyd flapping his magma-colored wings and sailing into the skies.

Daybreak in Nod always came suddenly. At some point, the sky had begun to brighten, and rays of light trickling in from the direction of the sea shone upon the sky.

"These abominable sunrays."

Ren practically fled the tarp, heading toward his personal resting space installed in one of the transport helicopters.

Nod's sun was dimmer and smaller than that of the surface world, but its glow was lethal to the Devas all the same. Ren would be forced to spend his time inside a structure shuttered against sunlight until night arrived once more. It was like spending time inside a darkened prison.

"Just a little longer…just a little longer, you filthy humans, and the world will be mine…"

Shahryar Ren's sleeping place came with a naked girl bound by chains.

She was a sacrifice offered to him by the populace of a Necropolis, one of the pathetic humans artificially grown to serve as a blood supply, food for the Devas. She was a living doll without free will.

Ren bit into the defenseless girl's neck, drinking her dull-tasting blood plasma, all the while dreaming of the instant when he subjugated the humans, weeping and wailing with fear, and moistened his throat with their warm, raw blood—

2

"We have finished our analysis of the ring."

Sami Arashima, a sorcerous engineer of the Bureau of Astrology, returned to the tent with a ring in a vinyl bag.

They were on the tip of Island East—Itogami Island's container base. A great many Attack Mages and guardsmen remained assembled that day at the place Kojou Akatsuki's Beast Vassals had raged the night before. They were observing the gate leading to Nod that had appeared in the sky above Itogami Island.

Priestesses of the Six Blades of the Bureau of Astrology and Attack Mages of the Lion King Agency could be seen among that group.

"The ring itself is made of high-purity Ashglow Silver but contains faint impurities, organic matter originating from vampire flesh. It is impossible to separate the two due to how strongly they are bonded with the metal, or more to the point, they have molecularly bonded together to form some kind of sorcerous device."

Sami explained this in a tone more befitting an elegant music teacher than a proficient sorcerous engineer.

Kiriha Kisaki glared at this partner of hers with a cold expression. Sami was a beautiful, cheerful, and sociable woman, but she had the shortcoming of being excessively roundabout and chatty when a subject had piqued her interest.

"Your conclusions?"

Sami pursed her lips, pouting slightly at the bluntness of Kiriha's question.

"This is a magical object spiritually linking Mr. Kojou Akatsuki with someone else. It has no use other than this, but put another way, the wielder of the ring connected to him in this manner would seem able to draw upon his supposedly inexhaustible demonic energy however she sees fit."

"So it provides status on par with the Blood Servants of the primogenitors, in other words."

Kiriha cut Sami short before she could give another long-winded explanation. *Yes*, said Sami's smile.

"…So what are you going to do, Kiriha?"

"Meaning?"

"Will you form a pact with him?"

"Me? Become Kojou Akatsuki's servant…?"

Kiriha openly grimaced.

Realizing that the Lion King Agency Attack Mages sitting at the next table over—Sayaka Kirasaka, Yuiri Haba, and Shio Hikawa—were desperately trying to eavesdrop, Kiriha exhaled with annoyance.

Properly speaking, the ring Kiriha had asked Sami to analyze was something she'd received from Yukina Himeragi of the Lion King Agency. Kiriha had been a candidate to be one of the twelve Blood Servants supposedly required to bring the rampaging Kojou Akatsuki to a halt.

Asagi Aiba, however, had proposed a change of plans at the eleventh hour, and in the end, Kiriha had not become Kojou Akatsuki's servant. Kojou Akatsuki had somehow regained control over the Beast Vassals, and all should have been well in the land. Even Kiriha couldn't hide her bewilderment at facing an issue she'd thought had already been settled.

"The Bureau of Astrology seems to desire as much, since strength on the level of a Blood Servant of a primogenitor-class vampire is very difficult to acquire. Kiriha, if you really don't want to, I don't mind doing it in your place."

"...Are you serious, Sami?"

"Yes. I don't mind having a younger spouse."

Sami grinned. Kiriha couldn't tell from her expression just how seriously she had said it. Kiriha sullenly twisted her lips and rested her cheek upon her palm—whereupon her eyes met those of Sayaka, observing with a sidelong glance. That instant, a cruel glint shone from deep in Kiriha's eyes.

"Hold on...you have a point... Being Kojou Akatsuki's Blood Servant wouldn't be so bad, actually."

Kiriha deliberately nodded in grandiose fashion as she accepted the ring from Sami.

Sure, when she thought about it calmly, the Bureau of Astrology's proposal wasn't a raw deal whatsoever. Becoming Kojou Akatsuki's servant meant your combat abilities would rise by leaps and bounds, and she would be unaging and undying on top of that. In that case, Kiriha making Kojou Akatsuki weak in the knees for her and giving the other girls heartburn was the far more amusing option.

"Hah?! Hold it right there, Kiriha Kisaki! Are you seriously saying that?!"

Inevitably, Sayaka Kirasaka easily fell for Kiriha's taunting, lobbing complaints while looking as if she were crushing something with her teeth. Kiriha put on a face as if she were noticing Sayaka's presence for the very first time.

"My, Sayaka Kirasaka? You were listening?"

"I can hear you whether I want to or not!"

Kicking away the metal pipe chair she was sitting in, Sayaka closed the distance with Kiriha. Kiriha calmly watched her do so with a limp wrist and a mystified look.

"What are you so nervous about? I'd meant to become Kojou Akatsuki's servant from the beginning, yes? Did I not say so just yesterday?"

"It was a different situation back then!! Kojou's not berserk anymore so there's no need for you to become his Blood Servant!"

"Whether that man is in his right mind or not isn't a big deal to me."

"It's a really big deal!!"

Sayaka's face was beet red as she rebutted. Kiriha was desperately holding back her laughter, letting only the tiniest sexy expression come over her face.

"I don't hate that man, though…*giggle*, as opposed to a man-hater like you."

"Wha…I—I don't particularly…mind Kojou Akatsuki…"

"Do you love him?"

Kiriha verbally backed Sayaka into a corner. Sayaka was startled, her entire body freezing unnaturally.

"O-of course I don't! Who'd love a man hanging around my Yukina like that…"

"Nah, if it's one or the other, it's Yukina Himeragi hanging around him, I think…"

"Well, in Yukii's case, that's her mission, so yeah."

Overhearing the exchange between Kiriha and Sayaka, Shio Hikawa and Yuiri Haba chimed in with oddly appropriate banter. Sayaka shut up the pair with a single glare.

"A-anyway, hand that ring back to the Lion King Agency, Kiriha Kisaki!"

"Huh? You don't even want to be Kojou Akatsuki's Blood Servant, so you have no right saying such a thing. If anything, shouldn't you be the one relinquishing your ring? That goes for the two of you as well."

Evading Sayaka when she tried to steal the ring by force, Kiriha addressed the two other Lion King Agency Attack Mages. Yuiri Haba was a bit flustered as she shook her head.

"Wait, wait, we never said we wouldn't become his servants. Right, Shio?"

"Eh?! Er…yesterday I kind of went along with the flow then and there, but when I calmly thought things over, I was, like, it might be too soon for that. Maybe we could start off by going shopping when I have time off and holding hands and…ah…er…it doesn't have to be just the two of us, you can come with us, Yuiri…"

For whatever reason, Shio Hikawa had turned timid and blushy as she murmured quietly to herself.

"S...Shio?"

"Her delusions are quite vivid, aren't they...?"

Yuiri and Kiriha couldn't hide how Shio's sudden revelation of her maidenly side left them at a loss.

"Whatever, just give the ring back! I'm confiscating it!"

Sayaka raged in an attempt to snatch back the ring, but the next moment, Sami, toying with her smartphone off by herself, went *Oh my* and furrowed her brow in surprise.

"I am sorry, Kiriha. Unfortunately, we must abandon that plan. Please forget all about it."

"...What is the meaning of this, I wonder?"

Kiriha looked back at Sami as a grave expression came over her, staring with vivid displeasure.

Not that she'd genuinely wanted to be Kojou Akatsuki's servant, but she fiercely resisted the idea of simply forgetting about it. That was just how Kiriha's personality worked.

"The situation seems to have changed... It would appear the government of Japan has agreed to a cease-fire with MAR."

Sami, well aware of how troublesome Kiriha could be when she wanted to, continued in a tone of voice broadcasting that this was not her idea.

Both the Lion King Agency and the Bureau of Astrology were special agencies operating under the Japanese government. If the government of Japan had a cease-fire with MAR, none of them could lay a hand upon it. Of course, that made cooperating with Kojou a difficult affair.

"Cease-fire negotiations...why all of a sudden like this?"

Sayaka commented in a daze. Kiriha let out a sigh with a weary expression.

"The Beast Vassal Warheads are the reason, I take it?"

"Yes. If the Beast Vassal Warheads brought back from Nod were fired at the Tokyo Metropolis on the Japanese mainland, it is estimated there would be a maximum of seven million two hundred thousand casualties. At present, only primogenitor-class vampires are able to face Beast Vassal Warheads, but they cannot protect every region of the globe."

Sami replied with a somewhat conflicted look.

Yuiri and Shio seemed perplexed as they traded glances.

"So, what? We should be MAR's lapdogs?"

"This is going just like Shahryar Ren wants…!"

"I really do not care for this."

Kiriha clicked her tongue with annoyance. Threats against the Japanese government had resulted in Kiriha and company being unable to raise a hand against terrorists—it was a result she found difficult to accept. Her irritation made her want to lash out against someone, but Kiriha touched a hand to her chin and sank into serious thought.

Then a second later.

"—!!"

The four Attack Mages present stood up at once as if they'd been slapped, each drawing her weapon. Sami responded only a moment later. They felt an incredibly strong "power" approaching, a strange power differing from the demonic and spiritual powers known to Kiriha and the rest. This power rivaled that of a vampire primogenitor—

"What is this pressure…?! Where is it coming from…?!"

Kiriha honed her consciousness and searched for the source of this power, but the power was too strong for her to pinpoint its source. Its overwhelming presence seemed to cover the entirety of the ground at their feet, something that left the Lion King Agency Attack Mages just as perplexed.

The ground at the center of the tent Kiriha and the others were in was being encroached upon by a steel-colored shadow resembling a mirror.

They were stricken by a powerful, unpleasant feeling, like a precursor to being caught up in a large-scale teleport. The shadow-encroached ground ferociously swayed, and an enormous demon beast floated up from it.

It was a beautiful dragon covered in scales with a mane the color of steel.

"Daaaaaaaaaaaaaaaaaaaaah—!!"

The steel-colored dragon emerging from within the shadow made a high-pitched roar. Caught up in the wind raging around its huge body, Kiriha and the others were blown straight out of the tent.

"—A dragon?!"

Kiriha froze in shock for but the briefest of moments. Twirling her lead-colored forked spear, Kiriha instantly adopted an attack posture. Priestesses of the Six Blades from the Bureau of Astrology were experts in anti–demon beast combat. She could think of any number of rituals effective against even a dragon over ten meters long.

Responding to the ritual energy Kiriha sent coursing into it, her forked spear emitted a dull glow. Activating her pseudo-spatial severing ritual, she girded herself for slashing at the dragon's throat, but someone suddenly stepped in the way before Kiriha could launch her attack.

"Wait, Miss Kisaki! Not her!"

Yuiri Haba of the Lion King Agency stood before Kiriha. The appearance of an unexpected interloper slightly slowed Kiriha's attack.

During that time, the steel-colored dragon changed shape, going from a huge dragon to a human girl—a little girl with steely hair.

"Glenda! Where have you been all this time?"

Lowering her raised recurve bow, Shio Hikawa raced over to the girl.

Sayaka and Kiriha stared at Shio and Yuiri's actions in confusion. They'd heard of the dragon being of unknown origin called Glenda, but they couldn't hide their surprise at seeing her in the flesh. Her being able to use teleportation was news to them, too.

"Yuiri! Shio! Come! Come save Ava!"

Now that she was in human form, Glenda pleaded with Yuiri and Shio in a voice every bit as young as she looked. *What does she mean?* wondered the perplexed Kiriha and Sayaka, but Yuiri immediately realized what she meant.

"Ava? You mean Avrora?"

"Dah!!"

"You're telling us to come, but how…?"

Shio looked overhead as she posed the question.

Avrora Florestina, the new Fourth Primogenitor, was probably in Nod that very moment. Reaching Nod meant going through the gate in the sky over Itogami Island, but that gate opened only at night.

Glenda, however, seemed impatient, wrapping her arms around the reluctant Yuiri and Shio as she changed into a huge dragon once more.

"Daaaah!!"

"Ehh?! Wait a…?!"

"G-Glenda?!"

Yuiri and Shio yelped as the steely dragon put them on her back and glared at the ground. That instant, a large, ripple-like sway occurred in the ground upon which Kiriha and Sayaka stood.

A silvery shadow like a watery surface spread farther. The tips of Sayaka's toes sank into the ground. The shadow covering the ground under Kiriha's feet was serving as a gate connecting to Nod.

"The encroachment of Nod...! Don't tell me this dragon can...?!"

Pulling the shaken Kiriha into the mix, the huge dragon flew right into the steely shadow. Yuiri's and Shio's faces were frozen stiff as they progressively sank into the shadow and vanished from sight.

Finally, the dragon's tail was engulfed, and the steely shadow vanished.

The only things left were the metal pipe chairs, worktables, and the remnants of a tent strewn all around, and Sayaka and Sami, standing stiff and dumbfounded.

"The hell...what in the world's going on?! Hikawa! Haba! Kiriha Kisaki!"

Sayaka fell into a fit of panic, dropping her silver long sword to the ground as she shouted, but there was no reply forthcoming. Realizing something had happened, Island Guard members were gathering around, but not a single soul really understood what had just taken place.

"This is...quite vexing."

Amid the uproar surrounding them caused by that abrupt strangeness, Sami Arashima's expression was unchanged as she began thinking up the report she'd send to HQ.

The tilting sun was beginning to paint the western sky with a golden glow.

3

Itogami City General Sorcerous Hospital was a medical agency specializing in demons directly overseen by the Gigafloat Management Corporation.

The medical wing was near the center of Itogami Island, giving it a great across-the-canal view of the Keystone Gate lobby Aradahl had destroyed with his Beast Vassal. The giant spherical fortress floating in the sky above was also highly visible.

"Hah…that bastard really put on a show."

Gazing at the sorry sight of Keystone Gate from his patient room window with a sardonic smile on his face was Schtola D, paroled sorcerous criminal. The youth had a crude look on his face reminiscent of a street gang member.

Thanks to being wounded all over his body, his foul look didn't seem very imposing at the moment. The night before, he'd challenged Shahryar Ren to combat, only to suffer critical, near-fatal wounds himself.

"That Necropolis is Castle Kalenaren of the Ren family. Damn it all…!"

Schtola D's cheeks twisted as he gazed at the fortress floating in mid-air. The blatant foulness of his tongue was just as rumored, but it didn't feel all that scary since he came off as a pouting child.

"Necropolis?"

Asagi parroted back the unfamiliar term. She'd come to visit Schtola D, a fellow Deva, to wring out information on Ladli Ren.

"…The castles where Deva royalty and nobles hold court. According to legend, they're phantom cities that wander the borders between the real world and another, I think? The Devas left on the surface during The Great Cleansing dream for eternity inside the Necropolises, biding their time until their eventual return…"

Motoki Yaze, tagging along with Asagi, explained in an overdramatic tone, but…

"Ain't nothin' as high an' mighty as that. They're just monster mansions of useless geezers who won't hurry up and die already…"

"*Keh*," spat out Schtola D as he spoke.

By rights, he was a fiendish criminal who should've been shut inside the Prison Barrier, but contrary to expectations, he'd been cooperative with Asagi and Yaze. He probably was desperate for any visitor he could talk to. He was bound to his bed, unable to move a muscle, and the other occupant of the room, Bruté Dumblegraff, was a man of exceedingly few words, apparently leaving Schtola D bored stiff.

"Geezers…aren't those your buddies?"

Asagi asked with a suspicious tone. Schtola D and the Ren siblings were both self-declared Devas. Asagi and Yaze didn't know how to distinguish between them.

For his part, Schtola D's face suddenly went red with indignation.

"Haah? Who's whose buddy, you stupid jerk! I'll kill ya, Priestess of Cain or not… damnit, that hurts! These wounds hurt!"

"Gravely wounded patients shouldn't get all excited, then…!"

Asagi turned a pitying look toward Schtola D as he trashed around on the bed.

"Oh, shaddap, shit-jerk. Look, after the piece-of-shit Great Cleansing, proud Devas, you know, like me, cut off all ties with the human world and created a highly developed spiritual civilization on an isolated plateau in South America, unlike you monkeys! And that was thousands of years ago!"

"Highly developed spiritual civilization…?"

"You got a problem with that, haaah?!"

The dubious expression coming over Asagi's face made Schtola D angrily shout with teary eyes.

"Well, fine. And?"

Asagi bluntly prodded him to continue. Schtola D's fists trembled from obvious irritation.

"The crappy folks left in the Necropolises are like livin' corpses that ain't taken a step forward in thousands of years. They think the whole unaging and undying bit is grand and stay locked up in their flyin' tombs, obsessed with their pathetic authority and tryin' to retake their past glory. So don't you dare lump me together with those shitheads beyond saving, you idiot!"

"Well, now I know the gist of it…"

"Ahhh, that so?"

Worn out by his own anger, Schtola D slumped back against his bed, closing his eyes and taking several moments to put his breathing in order.

"…So you wanna know the Necropolises' weaknesses?"

"Eh?"

"Didn't ya come all this way to talk to me to get me to tell ya? Hey, if you don't wanna hear it, that's fine with me."

"Wait, Schtola D, tell me about it. Ahhh, right, want to eat some jelly?"

Asagi picked up a cup of jelly sitting on top of the table, dangling it in front of the young Deva. For a moment, Schtola D looked back at Asagi in abject shock.

"No, I don't! An' that's my leftover hospital food, ain't it?!"

"You don't need it? I can have it, then?"

"What, you're gonna eat it?!"

"I like this brand of jelly. They served it a lot at the cafeteria in primary school way back…"

Asagi cheerfully explained as she began digging into the jelly. Schtola D gazed at her with an exasperated look for a time, finally sighing with an offhanded air.

"First, it goes like this. Physical attacks don't work against a Necropolis. It's like Spiky-Face said earlier, even if a Necropolis appears in the real world, half its existence is still in another one. No matter how showy the attacks you pound into it from this side, it ain't gonna do damage through the otherworld wall in the way."

"I see…so it's constructed like a vat made with a vacuum insulation spell…"

"I got no idea what the hell that is."

Whether appropriate or not, Asagi's example was so difficult to understand that it left Schtola D replying with annoyance.

"If attacks don't pass through from the outside, would attacks from within work?"

Yaze inquired in a sober tone.

Among the Beast Vassals serving Kojou Akatsuki was a twin-headed dragon, a Dimension Eater that could inflict damage regardless of dimensional walls. The effects on surrounding space would be too great to let it chew its way through an entire Necropolis, but it might be viable if they could open no more than a breach to invade the Necropolis's innards.

Schtola D went *hmmm* as he thought about it.

"Well, I suppose so. I ain't heard of anyone gettin' into a Necropolis and comin' back alive, though."

"Why not?"

"The shitty bastards livin' in those Necropolises have been holed up in those cramped castles for thousands o' years. Their retainers have some pretty damn tweaked-up defenses for those castles. It's a way for 'em to kill time."

Murmuring those words, Schtola D lowered his eyes as if enduring a memory haunting him all over again.

"They got most of the bunch from my village, too. That guy—that bastard Shahryar Ren—lured us into his castle on purpose so he could have fun with us! He was watchin' while my pals died!"

"That so…"

Yaze's expression grew graver as he sank into silence. He felt like he finally understood why Schtola D hated Ren despite both of them being Devas. Apparently, the whole reason he'd been captured as a sorcerous criminal was because ordinary civilians had been caught up in his repeated attacks on MAR for the purpose of defeating Ren. That collateral damage couldn't be undone, but Yaze could empathize with him to a fair extent.

"What happened to that dragon…?"

Bruté Dumblegraff, who'd kept silent up to that point, spoke from the adjacent bed through the thin curtain separating the two.

"Dragon? You mean the flame dragon called Kreyd?"

Yaze remembered the copper-colored dragon he'd encountered back at the warehouse district in Island East. They'd thought he was a member of the Order of the End, but the dragon was actually a coconspirator of Shahryar Ren.

"Pretty sure that dragon went to Nod along with Shahryar Ren."

Asagi calmly answered Dumblegraff's question.

Upon hearing this, the dragon slayer man fell silent on the other side of the curtain. He'd lost his battle with Kreyd and had been unable to stop the flame dragon from crossing over to Nod. He apparently felt responsible for the result.

"Hey, you, you're a dragon slayer…a Georgius, right? Why do you have that much of a hate-on for dragons?"

Asagi followed up, her interest piqued. She thought he might ignore her, but Dumblegraff was unexpectedly open about it.

"There is no reason. I am a Georgius built by the Church for that purpose."

"Even so, there have to be extenuating circumstances. What did the Western European Church make the Georgiuses for?"

"…Because dragons are invaders, or so I was told."

After a silent pause, Dumblegraff quietly spoke. Asagi narrowed her eyes with a dubious look.

"Invaders…?"

"The dragons on this planet are scouts; therefore, we kill them before they can carry information back to their kind."

"…Scouts…like recon troops? So they came as spies…but where from?"

Dumblegraff's explanation was so lacking in words that Yaze felt a strong sense of bewilderment. At present, it was impossible for Yaze to judge if he was speaking the truth or simply false dogma that had been fed to him long ago.

For some reason, Asagi readily nodded.

"I see. It makes sense."

"Eh…?! Asagi, you buy his story?"

Yaze pressed the point with his childhood friend in a tiny voice. Asagi looked apathetic as she spoke.

"I don't completely buy it, but to me, it doesn't look like he's lying."

"Well, I'm with you there, but…"

"Either way, we're putting dragon countermeasures on the back burner. We have to do something about these Necropolises first."

"I guess you have a point… Otherwise we won't be able to send Kojou off to Nod."

It didn't sit well with Yaze, though he had no choice but to accept that Asagi was right. Yaze's brow creased as he sighed deeply.

Either way, they'd gotten the information they needed. There seemed to be no reason to stay in that hospital room any longer. Yaze and Asagi nodded to one another, about to head out the door at virtually the same time.

That was when Schtola D opened his mouth once more.

"Wait, Priestess of Cain. You said the Fourth Primogenitor…Kojou Akatsuki, was it? Tell that jerk something for me."

"Tell Kojou what?"

Asagi stood still and looked back. Schtola D nodded with a sulky look on his face.

"Yeah. It's pathetic, but I'm stuck in this bed, so tell 'im to kill that shit bastard Shahryar Ren for me, would you…please."

Asagi raised her eyebrows, somewhat surprised as she saw Schtola D reverently lower his head. Then a powerful grin came over her.

"…Okay. Even if it's not killing him, it'll be half killing him for sure. I'll make Kojou take responsibility."

"Fine with me."

Schtola D murmured in satisfaction and closed his eyes. Turning their backs to him, Asagi and Yaze left the hospital room.

"…You sure you should be making a promise like that? Half killing Shahryar Ren… If he knew we were in negotiations to sell Itogami Island to MAR, wouldn't he totally flip his lid?"

Yaze asked Asagi this as they walked down a dreary hospital corridor.

Asagi nodded without any change in expression.

"I suppose so."

"Er…even you suppose so…"

"It's all right, though. That's not gonna happen."

Asagi showed off a toothy smile. Asagi's behavior perplexed Yaze.

"How can you be so sure?"

"MAR…or rather Ladli Ren has a huge misunderstanding about one thing."

"Misunderstanding?"

"Yeah. She thinks Kojou's someone who'll budge from weighing the pros and cons in purchase negotiations."

The instant she spoke Kojou's name, Asagi's smiling face was enveloped by a bright, vibrant glow.

Somehow, the tone of the words she spoke sounded loving and proud.

"It takes a complete idiot immune to that kind of logic to rule *this* island."

4

The place that had once been the lobby of Keystone Gate looked like the impact site of a huge meteorite. There was a large pile of rubble twenty meters or so in diameter and dust hovering in the air on top of that.

"Yuuma!"

Noticing the girl standing amid that dust, Kojou spoke her name.

The girl wearing a sports brand parka over her tall, slim physique— Yuuma Tokoyogi—waved a hand as she saw Kojou and Yukina approach, seeming amused for some reason.

"Heya, Kojou. Himeragi, too. You two came awful quick."

"The heck is all this? What a mess…"

"What in the world happened?"

Kojou and Yukina both spoke up as they surveyed the sorry state of the lobby once more.

Both of them had returned to their hotel after finishing their meeting with Ladli Ren about twenty minutes before. Immediately after, they felt incredible amounts of demonic energy being thrown around nearby, destroying the roof of the structure.

On top of that, a spherical castle of unknown origin had appeared in the sky above Keystone Gate. Thanks to that, Kojou and Yukina were left very confused, so they came to the lobby—now reduced to an impact site—to find out what the situation was.

"Ladli Ren."

Yuuma looked back at the stiffly standing pair with a small, strained smile. She was working as an assistant to Natsuki Minamiya in the Attack Mage Section, so she had to have more info than Kojou and Yukina at the very least.

"Imperial Knights from the Warlord's Empire tried to apprehend Ladli Ren. There are international arrest warrants for all MAR employees as terrorist suspects, see."

"So Warlord's Empire guys took Pun Girl for a ride? "

Kojou questioned back in surprise. If Ladli had been captured by the Warlord's Empire, Kojou and his side couldn't negotiate with her any way you sliced it.

Yuuma, though, blinked in minor bewilderment.

"Pun Girl? Ahhh…no, Ladli Ren went back home without harm, to her at least."

"…'To her at least'?"

What does that mean? they both wondered as they tilted their heads together. It was just then that they heard a familiar, high-pitched voice on the other side of that pile of rubble.

"There! Tanker, underneath! Get this pillar out of the way!"

"Indeed. Understood. Hangest on!"

With the boisterous whine of a motor, a crimson robot tank picked up a stupidly huge piece of concrete and violently cast it aside. It was the brand-new two-seater that Lydianne Didier had dubbed *Momiji*.

Guiding that tank was the World's Mightiest Succubus—Yume Eguchi, Lilith aka the Witch of the Night. The girls, staying at the same hotel Kojou was, had apparently raced straight to the site of the collapse to begin rescue operations for victims caught up in the incident.

Yume with her powerful mental abilities was well suited to searching for survivors buried under rubble, and Lydianne's tank, far more mobile than heavy machinery, truly shined at a disaster site like this. Kojou wasn't in a hurry to admit it, but the two primary schoolers were a lot more useful here than a top-class vampire like him. The Island Guard members finally gathering on the scene watched on, reassured by the girls' dependable work.

Kojou and Yukina both drew in their breaths when they realized just what Lydianne's tank was dragging out of the rubble. These were gleaming, vermillion statues with glossy surfaces. They numbered two. The beautifully shaped transparent statues resembling rubies looked awfully familiar.

"Aradahl…?!"

"Miss Zana…!"

Both exclaimed simultaneously. The vermillion statues emerging from inside the rubble were perfectly patterned after Aradahl and Zana. Their heights, figures, and even expressions were spitting images of the live versions.

"This is petrification…no, jewelification?"

Yukina murmured while touching the statues that had been dug up.

"Jewelification? Wait, transmutation…?!"

Kojou's face stiffened as he exclaimed. Transmutation was a master-level alchemical technique, one of the few ways of completely nullifying an immortal vampire. Rather than destroying the flesh, it was transformed into inorganic matter, sealing away a vampire's vital functions and preventing all regeneration. Kojou had gone through the same thing when he'd fought against the Wiseman's Blood.

All the same, transmuting a vampire with powerful resistance to magic was a difficult feat even for the very top alchemists. Short of a monster on the level of Wiseman's Blood, it should have been impossible.

"—This is Ladli Ren's doing."

Just as Kojou wondered who could have done this, Yuuma told him.

"She defeated Aradahl and Zana…? All by herself?"

Kojou looked at Yuuma in shock.

Even if she wasn't as young as she looked, Ladli Ren was a slender, lovely woman. Even if she could take on normal demons and Attack Mages, he hadn't thought she was capable of the same against the likes of Aradahl and Zana.

Yuuma, though, shook her head with a slightly conflicted look on her face.

"She didn't just put those two out of action. I simply took the four subordinates Chairman Aradahl brought with him to the hospital. All of them were Old Guard vampires, but it'll be three days before any of them can move again. Weaker vampires might have been completely annihilated."

"So Pun Girl did all of that…"

Kojou's expression grew graver still. Yukina was at a loss for words, too. Yukina had actually fought Zana, so she knew just how strong the woman was. Word of her defeat had to leave Yukina feeling incredulous, yet she and Aradahl were right there, turned to gemstones for all to see.

The fact that neither body had so much as a scratch after being buried in rubble had to mean they were as hard as real gemstones. Bringing about such a complete transmutation required frighteningly high-end magic, which made lifting the spell all the more difficult. At the very least, Kojou himself had no clue as to how they could be returned to their original states.

"—I see. They employed the same technology used to construct the Beast Vassal Warheads, I presume. If primogenitor-class Beast Vassals can be sealed, neutralizing noble-class vampires and a primogenitor's Blood Servant is no impossible feet."

Kojou was still lost before the sight of the jewelified Aradahl and Zana when an elegant, laughing voice suddenly greeted his ears. When he looked around in surprise, Kojou locked eyes with a beautiful, blue-eyed, silver-haired woman, the princess of the Northern European Kingdom of Aldegia, extolled as the second coming of Freya.

"La Folia…!"

"It seems you have regained your power, Kojou. I am quite relieved."

Narrowing her deep, lake-blue eyes, La Folia Rihavein smiled charmingly.

He knew that the princess, realizing the peril Kojou and others had fallen in, had come running all the way from Aldegia. Kojou more or less figured she'd come to meet him. All the same, the princess's sudden appearance left Kojou shaken and twitching his cheeks. He had something of a hard time dealing with the black-hearted, scheming princess, one of the world's leading strategists.

Still, the fact remained that, without her help, they'd never have been able to deal with the black Beast Vassals making Kojou run amok. Of course he felt grateful.

"Ahhh, er, I heard you and your people did a ton to help me. You were a big help."

Kojou regained his senses and conveyed his thanks to La Folia. The silver-haired princess shook her head in feigned, exaggerated surprise.

"My, you do not need to thank me. I owed you for the disturbance in Aldegia, and it is only natural for a wife to aid a husband in distress. Is that not so, Yukina?"

"Y-yes…so it is, although Akatsuki-senpai is not your husband so far as society is concerned."

In spite of being a little overwhelmed by the princess's force, Yukina still managed to make that contrary assertion. La Folia let Yukina's rebuttal glide past as if she'd never heard it.

"Besides, where saving Kanon is concerned, I believe it is I who should be thanking you, Kojou."

"Ahhh…well that was kinda my fault to begin with…"

Kojou was touching a hand to the back of his head as he spoke when he gasped, a guarded expression coming over him. La Folia had casually pointed out the fact Kojou had drunk Kanon's blood in order to prevent Kanon from angelicizing.

"Hold on a sec. Why does even La Folia know about me and Kanase?"

"This was a matter of life and death for a member of our royal family, after all."

La Folia calmly spoke these words as she produced a laminated photo taken surreptitiously. It showed the decisive moment when Kojou bit into Kanon's neck.

"Someone snuck a shot of us?! Wait, so Miss Justina not being at Kanase's side at the time was because...!"

"*Giggle*...well, I wonder?"

La Folia playfully stuck out her tongue as she beat around the bush.

Kojou sighed with a stern expression on his face. For some reason, he was getting the feeling the surreptitious photo handed to Yukina was making her mood sour further the more she looked at it. It was dangerous to let La Folia continue to set the pace. Judging this, Kojou forced a change in subject.

"More importantly, you all right, La Folia? If Kanase might angelicize from overusing spiritual energy, won't the same happen to you?"

"Oh my, if you are so concerned about my physical condition, perhaps you should do what you did to Kanon with me? Right here, right now?"

La Folia's eyes sparkled as she looked at Kojou.

Her unexpected proposal made Kojou's eyes bulge as he looked around the area.

"Right now?! Here?! That's a little..."

"*Giggle*...then with all haste."

"No, ah, that's too much haste...!"

"Come, Yukina. Please give me my ring."

"Eh?"

Yukina, thrown off from the sudden invocation of her name, raised a clueless voice.

La Folia smiled and stared at Yukina as if to test her.

"You still have rings left from those you received from Zana Lashka, yes?"

"Ah...er, well, yes..."

Yukina took a silver ring out from her uniform pocket. The pact ring sealed a portion of Kojou's body within, a catalyst for the sake of producing a mimic vampiric Blood Servant.

"I, too, expended spiritual energy beyond my limits to seal the rampaging black Beast Vassals. If it is a countermeasure against angelification, I believe that qualifies me to be Kojou's servant just as much as you and Kanon?"

"That...may be so..."

Yukina's words vaguely trailed off. Her expression told them she didn't really know if it was a good thing to hand that ring to La Folia.

"Aaa…"

That moment, La Folia let out a tiny moan, losing her balance as if she was dizzy.

"La Folia…?!"

Yukina instantly reached out with her hand to support the tottering princess. Slipping right past Yukina's flank, La Folia twirled around to face her again. The princess's fingers were grasping the silver-colored ring. She'd plucked it from inside Yukina's hand in the moment they passed each other.

"I see. So this is a catalyst ring."

"Wh-when did you…?!"

The suggestive way La Folia lifted up the ring made Yukina stare with a shocked expression.

The princess swiftly put the stolen ring on her ring finger.

"Zana Lashka provided eleven rings in total. Of these, the Attack Mages of the Lion King Agency and the Bureau of Astrology have taken four. The ogre of the Castiella family took one for the sake of bringing the Electoral War to a close. Kanon has used one to halt her angelification… Now that I have taken this one, this would leave four."

"No, that leaves three. I'm taking mine right now."

While Yukina was distracted, a tiny hand came in from a blind spot and snatched another ring from her hand. A smile of relief came over the small primary schooler wearing a beret now that she'd obtained her own ring.

"Eh?! Yume…?! But that's…"

"I understand. This is just a preview."

"P-preview?"

"Yes. You just watch. In another three years, I'll be able to be lovey-dovey with Mister Kojou as much as Miss Yukina and everyone else!"

"Wait…wait a moment. I am not lovey-dovey with Akatsuki-senpai…!"

Yukina was desperately trying to deny it, but Kojou was thinking, *That's not the problem here, sheesh.*

For her part, La Folia shot the primary schooler a gaze as if they were powerful enemies on equal footing.

"Yume Eguchi, also known as Lilith, the World's Mightiest Succubus, yes? As I shall be Kojou's lawful wife, I cannot have you frittering around him."

"Princess La Folia of Aldegia, I am surprised, you are just as pretty as the rumors say. However, I will someday snatch the throne of lawful wife from you!"

"Why is La Folia being his lawful wife being taken for granted...?!"

Yukina muttered in a quiet voice so that neither Yume nor La Folia could hear her. It was then that a tall, slender girl appeared right behind Yukina without the slightest warning.

"Hmmm...if you have a spare one, I guess I'll grab one for myself."

"M-Miss Yuuma, you too?! Wait a... Give that! Give that back!"

With a light *toss*, Yuuma whisked away a third ring. Realizing this, Yukina hurriedly tried to take it back, but the height difference between the two meant Yuuma could raise her hands too high for Yukina to reach.

"Return it...? I cannot comply with your request. Properly speaking, these are Kojou's to administer and not yours, are they not? Right, Kojou?"

La Folia critiqued Yukina's words with a calm tenor. The blackhearted princess was in her element when it came to negotiations like this.

"Ahhh...well, feels like it now that you mention it..."

Kojou hesitantly acknowledged what La Folia was saying. Yes, Zana Lashka had directly handed the rings to Yukina, but that was because Kojou had fallen unconscious from Zana having carved a hole in his chest. Under normal circumstances, Kojou should've held the rings because the pacts were being made with him.

"Uuu..."

Exposed not only to La Folia's objecting gaze but those of Yume and Yuuma as well, Yukina reluctantly handed the final ring over to Kojou.

Kojou sighed wearily before simply stuffing the thing into his pocket.

"So what of the acts of vampirism? Shall we do them here and now?"

Watching that course of events with visible satisfaction, La Folia looked up at Kojou and posed her inquiry. Kojou reactively distanced himself from the princess.

"In a situation like this? Like hell I can!"

"You do not need to be concerned for my sake…having others see… that might well be a turn-on, *giggle*."

"The fact that I can't tell how much you're joking is really scarin' me…!"

"Well, let us leave it at receiving the ring for the time being."

Pfft, went the tiny laughter escaping La Folia's lips as she gracefully shrugged her shoulders.

"You need not be concerned for my physical condition. Unlike Kanon, I did not employ my spell with my flesh alone. Large-scale spells employed by the Royal Family of Aldegia are fashioned with support from a spiritual reactor as a premise."

"So Kanase pushed herself too hard takin' a Beast Vassal on all by herself, huh?"

I get it, said Kojou, accepting La Folia's explanation. *Yes*, said the princess's smile.

"I suppose she did. It must indeed be the power of love?"

"Er, love…she's kind to everyone, right?"

"…I suppose we can leave it at that."

For once, La Folia murmured in a slightly exasperated tone of voice. She then shifted her gaze to the jewelified Aradahl and Zana once more.

"More importantly, the immediate issue is what to do about them."

"Himeragi, can't you use your spear to lift the jewelification?"

Kojou suddenly thought of something and asked Yukina. Yukina sank into thought with a serious look on her face.

"I believe it is possible. Snowdrift Wolf cannot reverse normal petrification, but their current state seems to be a type of sealing so—"

"Yeah, but you should probably pass on that anyway."

Yuuma interrupted Yukina midsentence. Kojou looked at Yuuma with a bit of surprise.

"Why's that?"

"Himeragi's spear might be able to neutralize the magical energy, but the shock from destroying the seal with brute force from the outside might wreck the cells of people on the inside. If you're gonna lift it, better to take your time and do it slow."

"…So it's like thawing frozen food, then."

Kojou aired a silly-sounding comparison, but even he could understand how the more powerful the magic, the bigger the backlash from lifting it.

"Besides, Snowdrift Wolf's attack would inflict damage on Chairman Aradahl to begin with so…"

"Ahhh…"

Yukina's apologetic-sounding explanation made Kojou back down for good. The Divine Oscillation Effect emitted by her spear neutralized demonic energy, allowing it to inflict lethal damage to vampires.

"It is no doubt safest to return them to the Warlord's Empire without any excessive intervention, though in that case, the standing of Chairman Aradahl might become somewhat frayed."

La Folia spoke in a thoughtful tone.

If word of Aradahl, feared as a vampire of martial prowess, being neutralized by a little Deva girl spread through his homeland, it would likely be a humiliating stain on his reputation. Losing only his status as chairman of the Imperial Parliament would be the light version. Failing that, he might have his lands and title stripped from him—Kojou couldn't even dismiss the worst possibility that he might be executed. If that happened, Kojou would have an awful time sleeping at night.

La Folia sank into thought with rare earnestness.

"If possible, I truly do not wish to pass on an opportunity to put him greatly in my debt…"

"Debt, sheesh…"

Kojou sighed wearily at the princess's very calculating words.

The very next moment, a reserved voice flowed from the robot tank's speakers.

"Ah…ladies and gentlemen…I pray you, pardon me. Concerning Sir Aradahl and Lady Zana…"

"Lydianne?"

Knowing how high-tension "Tanker" normally was, her meek demeanor made Kojou look back with deep suspicion.

A pile of rubble. Island Guard members hastily moving to and fro. Hovering dust particles illuminated by the rays of the setting sun through the broken ceiling. The scene was the same as before.

Nothing was happening to throw Lydianne into a state of confusion. Nothing, save one tiny change—

"The remains of both have vanished."

"…?!"

The sudden disappearance of the jewelified Aradahl and Zana made Yukina, Yuuma, and even La Folia gape.

None of them had felt someone taking Aradahl and Zana away. There was no trace of someone having used teleportation. The two jewel statues that had been there were simply gone.

It was a small anomaly with neither the objective nor the means being known to them. Amid Yukina and the others' unrest over this mystery—

Er, they aren't remains, damnit, Kojou thought to reassure himself.

5

"…So in the end, you never did find Aradahl or Zana Lashka?"

Wearing an elaborate dress, Natsuki Minamiya sat in an antique chair complete with armrests that seemed terribly out of place, and she inquired with a haughty demeanor.

The location was Itogami Island Sorcery Lab Number Six—the laboratory of Kensei Kanase. Despite this, the space that should have by rights been occupied by magical devices and books had already been almost halfway transformed into Natsuki's personal fiefdom. Examples included a triple cake stand and a tea set, or perhaps the teddy bears on the leather-covered sofa. Perhaps it was stress from Natsuki's audaciousness, acting like she owned the place, that made Kensei Kanase's expression, gloomy under normal circumstances, even darker.

Not that this was directly related to Kojou and company.

"Yes. I would not think someone could have used heavy magic at such a range without anyone noticing…not only myself, but Miss Yuuma and Princess La Folia were present as well."

"Lydianne said her tank's sensors didn't pick up anything, either."

After Yukina had explained in an overly serious tone, Kojou tossed in his own extra comment.

Inside the room were Natsuki; Kojou; Yukina; the owner of the room, Kensei Kanase; and one Shizuri Kasugaya Castiella, currently recuperating from her wounds. Yukina's superior, Yukari Endou, had been the one to summon them, but she'd apparently been called away on urgent business, delaying her arrival.

Kojou and Yukina were killing time at that point so they reported the Ladli incident to Natsuki.

"I can't really judge anything from your explanations at this point. There's simply too little information."

Listening to the pair's explanation to the end, Natsuki voiced her exceedingly sensible take on it. The incident had left Kojou and Yukina confused, so of course Natsuki couldn't get much from their report.

"Well, that figures. I thought Natsuki of all people might have some idea what happened but…"

"Don't address your teacher by her first name."

Natsuki languidly recrossed her legs, glaring at Kojou with a chilling look.

"The Tokoyogi girl stayed behind to examine the scene, right? You should leave it to her. Or are you that worried about the First Primogenitor's bride?"

"Nah, and sayin' it that way will give people the wrong idea…! Ain't like I was thinkin' about Miss Zana, 'cause she's another man's wife!"

Unable to pin down whether Natsuki's question was joking or serious, Kojou hastened to refute her. Natsuki gave him a brief snort.

"I suppose not. You've managed to get brides of your own."

"…Brides?"

Whaddaya mean? thought Kojou, tilting his head in earnest confusion when he abruptly turned his eyes toward Shizuri Kasugaya Castiella in a corner of the room. The ogre with white hair that gleamed like snow was covered in bandages as she rested on a bed.

"You're not talking about Cas, are you?"

"Hah?! What is with that blatant dissatisfaction upon your face…?! More importantly, who is this Cas?!"

Shizuri fiercely objected, glaring at Kojou with a distinct grimace.

"Just so you know, this is a provisional pact for the purpose of halting the rampage of your Beast Vassals, nothing more. Do not think that even my heart is yours to do with as you…plea…ugh!"

Shizuri, thrusting her left hand with the ring on it as she wailed, was reminded of the pain of her wounds, flopping right back onto the bed and moaning in anguish. She'd clearly gotten too worked up.

"Er, the pact stuff's no big deal, but more importantly, you all right...? You haven't gotten worse since this morning?"

"No big deal?! Er, these bandages are simply because this quack made such a big fuss!"

Baring her teeth at Kojou's insensitive words, Shizuri glared angrily at Kensei Kanase. Kensei shook his head a little as if he'd taken offense.

"That is because I am a sorcerous engineer, not a doctor. It is not so much that treating patients is not my specialty. I simply have no interest in it. I had hoped that because you were an ogre, a rare species, your skeletal structure might be a little more unique...alas."

"Would you please stop treating me like a rare variety of deep-sea fish?!"

Kensei's words betraying no emotions made Shizuri raise a high-pitched, incoherent growl. *They're both real pieces of work*, Kojou thought wearily.

"Anyway, guess no need to worry 'bout Cas."

"Yes. Compared to twenty-four hours ago, she has two more broken ribs and six more torn tendons or so, but that is of no great concern. She should be able to move by tonight."

Kensei's calm explanation made Kojou's eyes bulge in surprise.

"Ain't that way too fast for healing? Ogres are tough, but their healing ability's standard human level, right?"

"It is the blessing of a paladin."

"Provisional pact or not, she is a primogenitor-class vampiric Blood Servant nonetheless, a considerable boon. A true Blood Servant would gain regenerative ability on par with a vampire, so compared to that, the effect is somewhat lessened."

Hmph, huffed Shizuri, puffing her chest out with pride. Kensei completely ignored her as he gave that serious reply.

As Kojou's Blood Servant, Shizuri was currently able to receive replenishment from his inexhaustible supply of demonic energy. The demonic energy stimulated her cells, wringing more natural healing out of her flesh. That was Shizuri's special privilege as a demon.

"I see... In that case, pretty glad I made that pact with you."

A relieved smile came over Kojou as he spoke. Shizuri had more or less forced herself to become Kojou's Blood Servant to stop the black Beast Vassals' rampage, but if that ended up pulling her out of trouble, it was good news as far as Kojou was concerned. It also considerably eased his sense of guilt.

"Er, ahhh, well…it is not a bad thing."

Maybe Kojou being so glad surprised her, for Shizuri's cheeks reddened as if she was blushing. At the same time, Yukina, listening to Kojou and Shizuri's conversation from beside him, adopted a terribly blank expression. Kojou didn't know the reason why, but her mood seemed to have sharply worsened.

Feeling the need to escape from her glacial aura, Kojou took a sip of lukewarm tea and reached a hand toward the *onigiri* that was, for whatever reason, sitting on the cake stand. Supper was being prepared for employees working at the lab, but he'd been waiting for so long that he figured taking a single bite wouldn't be a big deal.

"Huh…this *onigiri*, did Kanase make this?"

Kojou murmured in surprise just as he took his first nibble of the *onigiri*. It tasted just like the *onigiri* made by Kanon Kanase he'd had just recently.

Natsuki gazed at Kojou with deep interest.

"Oh, you can tell? I suppose it's…you know…the food made by your own servant must taste special to you."

Kensei's eyebrows moved with a sullen twitch. Kanon Kanase, his adopted daughter, had become Kojou's Blood Servant just as Shizuri had. He seemed to have remembered as much at that very moment.

"…Is that so, senpai?"

Yukina remained expressionless as she inquired in a flat voice. *As if*, thought Kojou as he shook his head.

"It ain't that; they're just the same as the ones Kanase had me eat after I helped her bake them… Er, come to think of it, where is Kanase anyway?"

"Kanase has gone to Saikai Academy with Nina Adelard."

When Kojou desperately tried to dodge the topic, Yukina sighed and spoke, perhaps taking pity on him.

"…With Nina? To school?"

"That's because the alchemist girl will be useful repairing the wrecked campus. A little prodding and she'll probably do it on her own."

Natsuki explained to the perplexed Kojou. *So she'll be working for free*, thought Kojou, feeling rare sympathy for Nina.

A moment later, the door to the lab opened, and a tall, slender girl walked in.

It was Sayaka Kirasaka, whom he'd parted ways with last night at the container yard. She was hugging a golden-eyed black cat against her chest. This was the familiar of Yukari Endou, Yukina's mentor.

"—I am sorry to make you wait, Yukina, and former Fourth Primogenitor lad. Our superiors are in a bit of a tizzy."

The black cat addressed Kojou and company with a sarcastic tone.

Sayaka and the black cat were the only ones entering the room. There was no sign of Yuiri or Shio, who had previously worked with Sayaka, or Kiriha Kisaki, either.

"Were Miss Yuiri and Miss Shio not with you?"

Yukina shifted a questioning gaze toward Sayaka. For whatever reason, Sayaka's shoulders trembled with a heavy twitch.

"Eh?! A…ahhh, Yuiri Haba and Shio Hikawa…right, the gate! They're observing the gate to Nod! They're definitely not missing or anything like that!"

"R-right…"

Yukina vaguely nodded as she watched Sayaka's suspicious behavior. Sayaka could rarely be described as calm, but she was really off the rails that day.

"What do you mean, the Lion King Agency's high-ups are in a tizzy?"

Kojou, all done with munching on the rest of the *onigiri*, posed that question to Endou. The black cat shook its head.

"That should be obvious…the Necropolises of the Devas and the Beast Vassal Warheads. I heard you've met with Ladli Ren. You've seen the footage of that fleet, I take it?"

"Well, kinda… So that was the real deal?"

"The NAU has acknowledged it has withdrawn the fleet it had dispatched after sustaining a heavy strike. It's been on a loop on news channels around the world, too. Sayaka, show them the photo from earlier."

"Y-yes."

Nodding with a rigid expression, Sayaka took out her smartphone. It was displaying the nighttime landscape of Itogami Island. Floating in the sky above it were complex magic circles resembling geometric shapes—the gate connecting that world to Nod.

Small transport craft were visible right by the gate. Kojou recognized the model.

"MAR transport choppers...I take it?"

"They were most likely carrying Beast Vassal Warheads from Nod."

Affirming Kojou's comment, Yukari continued. Kojou was a little put off by how her reply sounded like it wasn't any problem of hers.

"No one noticed those choppers?"

"No one had time to. Someone's Beast Vassals were on a rampage on the surface, you see."

"Ugh..."

Having his own accountability pointed out to him in an unexpected fashion made Kojou's words stick in his throat.

Apparently, it was none other than Kojou's Beast Vassals that had ensured MAR could transport the Beast Vassal Warheads without anyone noticing, with the beasts acting as decoys. Not even Shahryar Ren was likely to have planned it that way. From Kojou's perspective, it was an unfortunate coincidence.

"Considering the helicopters' carrying capacity, we estimate they have brought a maximum of twelve Beast Vassal Warheads from Nod. It was likely less than that, but we can ill afford to be optimistic under the circumstances."

"...So they've already used two, leaving ten left at most."

Natsuki spoke, picking up where Yukari had left off.

"However, we have no idea where in the world the Deva cities serving as firing platforms might appear. Small wonder the HGTO signatory nations are frightened out of their wits."

"We kinda heard about that part from La Folia."

Kojou spoke with a voice tinged with anger lacking any outlet. La Folia had told Kojou and company about the Deva Necropolises, but her home nation of Aldegia was one such HGTO signatory. If La Folia and her knights took hostile action against MAR, there was no guarantee Aldegia's capital city wouldn't become a Beast Vassal Warheads target. Hence, La Folia told Kojou and the others she could not cooperate with them. All she could do was watch—for the moment, at least.

"It is not just the Kingdom of Aldegia. The government of Japan is also in negotiations with MAR."

Natsuki told Kojou this with a calm air. Kojou leaned forward in spontaneous surprise.

"The Japanese government's negotiating with them... What about Itogami Island?"

"Itogami Island City-State is treated as a self-governing territory within the country of Japan. Worst case, *they'll sell you out.*"

Natsuki spoke in a cold, dismissive voice.

Itogami Island's political situation since the War of the Primogenitors remained unstable and vague. Though it had the right to govern its own affairs and engage in foreign relations, national defense and law enforcement remained in the hands of the government of Japan. That was why Natsuki, a Japanese Federal Attack Mage, and the Lion King Agency were able to operate as they had previously.

So if MAR demanded the ceding of its territorial rights for Itogami Island, the government of Japan couldn't refuse. MAR had the Beast Vassal Warheads after all.

"Then why did Ladli Ren come to the Gigafloat Management Corporation? If she can persuade the government of Japan, additional negotiations with the Itogami Island side are meaningless..."

Yukina seemed perplexed as she murmured to herself.

"Even if they end up occupying it either way, the residents of Itogami Island will have a much easier time accepting it that way than if the Japanese government decides all on its own."

Natsuki voiced that realistic deduction.

"The problem is, it doesn't end with Itogami Island. If the Devas really do have their hands on over six thousand warheads, the whole world will come under their rule in the exact same way. Even if they understand that will be the result, deep down the politicians don't want to sacrifice their own people."

"That's all the more reason not to sit on our butts in a place like this. I've gotta drag Shahryar Ren out of Nod before the Devas get their hands on any more warheads…"

Kojou unwittingly slammed his fist down on a work bench as he raised his voice.

Natsuki quietly lowered her eyes. Then she shifted her gaze overhead.

"I suppose so, but if we know that, the Devas know it, too. That's why they brought that big thing floating in the sky."

"So we've gotta do something about the Necropolises before we can go to Nod…"

The gravity of the issue they faced really sank in again.

According to the measurements taken by Lydianne's tank, the Necropolis was floating in the sky some two thousand meters above the island. It was neatly positioned to seal the entrance to the gate.

"You can't use your Beast Vassals to blow it away while it's sitting over the island. We can't even estimate the damage that'd come from fragments falling into urban areas."

Natsuki warned Kojou as if seeing straight through his thoughts. It was not impossible for the black Beast Vassals obtained by Kojou to destroy the spherical castle a kilometer in diameter.

The Deva fortress was protected by a powerful magical barrier. There was no absolute guarantee Kojou's attacks would even be effective against it, and even if they were, a single fragment of the Necropolis falling onto the surface would be a catastrophe.

"Well, that doesn't mean we can just sit on our hands and watch. Or do you seriously plan on selling the island off to Ladli Ren?"

"The Attack Mage Section is working with the Lion King Agency on a countermeasure. Don't worry too much and behave yourself. If you go on a rampage by your lonesome, it'll be yesterday all over again."

"…Ain't like yesterday was 'cause I wanted it. Well, I've seen Cas already, so since you say so, I'll behave and go home."

With Natsuki firmly driving her point home, Kojou grudgingly rose to his feet.

If he could, he'd have liked to go grab Avrora and bring her back that second, but even Kojou understood that wasn't feasible. It grated on him, but the Deva Necropolis and the Beast Vassal Warheads weren't things Kojou could deal with by himself.

Watching with worry as Kojou's shoulders slumped and he headed for the exit, Yukina started following him out of habit. Yukari abruptly called her to a halt.

"Wait, Yukina. You stay here."

"…Master?"

"Yesterday you lost enough blood to collapse. Can you work if the situation demands it? I will arrange for healing spells. You will rest here with Koyomi until I give you permission to leave."

Yukari's black cat familiar spoke to the surprised Yukina in a firm tone of voice.

"With Lady Shizuka…? But my duty is to be Akatsuki-senpai's watcher…"

Yukina softly resisted her master's arbitrary command, but the black cat leered right back.

"You can leave that duty to Gisella."

"Gisella…to Miss Kasugaya?"

Yukina had a perplexed expression as she looked at Shizuri there on the bed. Shizuri stripped off the bandage wrapped around her arm, leaping to her feet as if waiting for that very moment.

"You may leave this to me! It is my duty as a Paladin of Gisella to guide Kojou Akatsuki so he commits no wickedness! You are injured, so you should take your time and rest!"

"Injured…but does that not also apply to Miss Kasugaya…"

Yukina glared at Yukari's black cat familiar with reproachful, half-lidded eyes. The black cat exhaled with an innocent look, gazing up at the face of the tall girl holding the cat against her chest.

"For peace of mind, let us assign one more. You do not mind, Sayaka?"

Twitch, went Sayaka, her body going rigid when she heard her name, almost like she was afraid of something.

"N-no."

When Sayaka nodded with a cornered expression, Kojou thought it just a little strange. He knew Sayaka was a man hater, but he didn't think just being Kojou's watcher was anything to make her tense at this late stage.

For her part, Sayaka bit her lip and hugged the instrument case sheathing her long sword against her chest.

Yukina stared at her blatantly unnatural reaction without a word.

6

Waiting for Kojou upon his return from Keystone Gate were Asagi and Yaze, and the primary schooler duo of Lydianne and Yume.

"So you ended up crawling back with dishonor?"

Looking at Kojou coming back with Shizuri and Sayaka, Asagi seemed weary to her very soul.

They were in a room at a luxury hotel in Keystone Gate. It was the living room of the suite Kojou had stayed in the night before. The room was broad and the ceiling was high, but thanks to Lydianne's robot tank being present, the interior felt oddly cramped. Kojou felt like a criminal summoned to a court-martial.

"Whaddaya mean, crawl back? Well, I guess I understand your reaction over forcin' an injured person back on duty."

Kojou rebutted with a look of dissatisfaction. *Wha—?*, thought Shizuri, taking offense and glaring at Kojou.

"By an injured person forced back on duty, are you possibly referring to me?!"

How rude, the childlike puffing of Shizuri's cheeks seemed to say. Kojou let out a sigh like it was a heap of trouble.

"Who else here fits the bill? And what, it's a bad thing comin' back here? It ain't like I can stay overnight at my place with Cas and Kirasaka, right…?"

Even if they were both acquaintances, he figured even Nagisa would blow her lid if her big brother came back home with a pair of girls in tow. It'd be better if they could use Yukina's apartment right beside the Akatsuki residence, but Sayaka had completely forgotten to borrow her key.

Normally, Sayaka would be overjoyed to take the key and have a legal, aboveboard way of entering Yukina's living space, so it was a slipup quite unlike her.

"Well, it's fine, I suppose. This hotel doesn't have any guests besides us, and there's some stuff I wanted to ask Kirasaka anyway."

"You want to ask Kirasaka stuff?"

Kojou found that a little surprising as he looked at Asagi, dressed in her own plain-looking clothes.

Asagi and the others nodded all at once in response. The charged atmosphere pricked at Kojou's skin, causing him and Shizuri to trade glances. Sayaka's expression hardened even further.

"Something smells fishy. Doesn't it, Miss Kirasaka?"

Asagi rested her cheek against her palm, smiling with only the corners of her lips. Sayaka nervously shook her head.

"E-excuse me?! I properly bathed today, I'll have you know?! Twice at that!"

"That's not what she means. What are you planning, Miss Sayaka?"

Yume looked straight up at Sayaka as she inquired.

Trying to escape from their sharp gazes, Sayaka subconsciously averted her eyes.

"I am not p-planning anything..."

"Come to think of it, the Island Guard's been sending up some odd complaints. They're having a hard time getting in touch with Kiriha Kisaki of the Bureau of Astrology. They're fussing over what to do about the divine armaments she used and left behind at the container yard..."

"I-is that so... The Bureau of Astrology really likes causing trouble...!"

Yaze's casual comment made Sayaka's voice go shrill. Sayaka was extremely capable as an Attack Mage, but she was surprisingly fragile on the mental front, especially in the face of unexpected circumstances. Now that her poker face had been stripped away, she barely had a leg to stand on.

"That's the face of someone who knows something, isn't it?"

Yume slowly posed that question like a cruel serpent cornering its prey. Sayaka looked very nervous as she fiercely shook her head.

"Y-you're wrong. It's not me; Glenda, she..."

"Glenda?"

The look in Kojou's eyes sharpened when an unexpected name was brought up.

With everyone present glaring at her, Sayaka nodded with a forlorn look of resignation.

"Yeah. That girl suddenly appeared and took Hikawa, Haba, and Kiriha Kisaki away somewhere."

"Whaddaya mean, somewhere?"

"I don't even know…!"

Kojou pressed the point, causing Sayaka to shout loudly, her nerves frayed.

Asagi touched a hand to her lips. *Hmm*, she thought, briefly exhaling. "Now I see…"

"Ring any bells, Asagi??"

Yaze grimaced in mild surprise, but Asagi bluntly shook her head.

"Only a little bit, but it's probably fine to let the girls be. Glenda's not our enemy."

"Ain't really worried about that."

Kojou made a pained smile as he breathed out. It was unthinkable for Glenda to do harm to Kojou and others with malice aforethought. At the very least, everyone who knew her thought so.

"The Lion King Agency knows that, too, so they're not nervous about that part. Well, probably not."

Asagi shrugged her shoulders as she agreed with him.

Yaze stared intently at Sayaka with a dubious look.

"So what Kirasaka-baby's people are up to is separate from this whole Glenda thing?"

"Y-yeah…"

Overwhelmed, Sayaka nodded reflexively. Then she gasped and came back to her senses.

"Y-you're wrong! I didn't mean that Master and the others are planning something right now… You're wrong!"

"Hmmm…"

Asagi gazed coolly at the flustered Sayaka, and then…

"Tanker."

"Understood."

Lydianne took out a cell phone marketed to children, operating it with a practiced hand. The robot tank seated at the center of the room suddenly went into motion, its telescopic manipulator firmly pinning Sayaka's arms to her body from behind.

"Ah, wait a—?! What the—?! What are you pulling?!"

Sayaka thrashed, trying to shake off the manipulator holding her in its grip, but however much her clothing became disheveled, the robot tank didn't even twitch.

Asagi's gaze became frostier still as she watched Sayaka defenselessly held aloft.

"Yume, please."

"Yes. I am sorry, Miss Sayaka."

Yume moved in front of Sayaka and closed her eyes. When she opened her eyelids once more, Yume's eyes emitted a dazzling glow like those of a cat seeing in the darkness. Black wings woven of demonic energy floated up from her back.

When Sayaka realized this, an air of undiluted terror came over her face.

"D-don't tell me you plan on using succubus powers to make me spill my secrets?! I-it's no use; even if you do that, I'll never tell a soul that I'm actually in love with Yukina!"

"………"

We know that already, said the odd expressions coming over pretty much everyone in the room. Shizuri was the only one bulging her eyes, speechless.

For her part, now that saying the first part had lit a fire under her, Sayaka began rambling on her own without anyone having bothered to ask.

"I love her, so what gives?! Yukina seems to have more fun when she's with Kojou Akatsuki than when she's with me…! The two are always flirty-flirt, lovey-dovey, uuu…hate, I hate Kojou Akatsuki! I want to lick my Yukina's neck, I want to breathe in the scent of my Yukina's hair…!"

"Wh-what the heck is this…?"

Stricken by dizziness, Kojou clutched his head. Yume Eguchi, the Witch of the Night reborn, had mind control abilities. It wasn't impossible for her overwhelming power of domination to control others by force, but its main use was to unveil the darkness in another's heart and make them act in accordance with their secret desires.

That said, even Yume was red-faced and a bit thrown off, having never thought Sayaka's true feelings would be embarrassing to this absurd extent.

"I feel like hiding under a rock just from hearing all this."

"Um, I am quite sorry. My ability only makes the target reveal her hidden feelings, so…"

Asagi put a hand on her forelocks with a constrained look. Yume hung her head, crestfallen. Yume's succubus ability apparently wasn't so convenient; you only got the answers to the specific questions you wanted.

Sayaka paid no heed to the dejected looks all around her, voice fraying as she became even more agitated.

"Uuu…and what's with Kojou Akatsuki, his face is plain, but once in a while, the side of his face looks really cool, he's sweaty but it smells kinda nice, hearing his voice calms me down, and he even carried me bridal style, I mean if he can make Yukina his servant, take me, too, damnit…!"

"…Huh?"

When Sayaka began to ramble on like she was completely drunk, her words threw Kojou for a loop.

Beside him, Shizuri stared at Kojou with a sullen gaze for some reason.

"How wonderful. You are so popular."

"Nah, if I seriously did that, it'd be a big mess…"

Kojou replied, just barely maintaining his mental calm. Sayaka was not in control of herself at the moment, so it'd be a disaster later if he acted based on thinking they were Sayaka's real feelings.

Unaware of Kojou's melancholy, Sayaka shook her head in anguish, off in her own little world.

"Ahhh…but it's not meant to be… If we destroy Itogami Island, I can't be with Kojou Akatsuki anymore…!"

"…Hah?!"

Asagi, barely listening to Sayaka's confession from lack of interest, paled as she stood up.

"Destroy Itogami Island? What's this all about, Kirasaka?!"

Kojou's face was tense, too, as he closed the distance with Sayaka. Sayaka shook her head like a child being scolded.

"I don't know, either…! The Three Saints and the Attack Mage Section decided it! They said if they break the keystone and Itogami Island sinks, the gate to Nod will close, too…!"

"Break the…keystone, you say…?"

Kojou was beside himself as he weakly murmured the words.

Two hundred and twenty meters under the surface of the sea, in an eternal prison beyond the reach of light, was Keystone Gate's lowest stratum. Kojou gritted his teeth when he recalled the stone pillar sealed within...

7

A powerful night breeze blew through the enormous cracks carved into the wall.

Bare girders, concrete fragments—Kojou climbed over the rubble piled up in the lobby of Keystone Gate's topmost floor and climbed onto its half-destroyed roof.

It was after ten PM. Beneath them, he could see the skyline of Itogami Island. The way the moonlight shone on the surface of the nighttime sea surrounding it gave off a luster like a sleek fabric.

When he looked at the night sky, it was covered with strange magic circles. Right at the center of these circles floated a sphere resembling a dark moon—the Necropolis. The Deva castle impeded all intrusion into Nod.

Kojou reached his right hand toward the Necropolis in the sky far above. It couldn't have been too far for the black Beast Vassals he'd inherited from The Blood to reach it, but Kojou lowered his right hand without summoning a Beast Vassal. At the moment, it was neither Shahryar Ren in Nod nor the Deva Necropolis that threatened the island.

"What an awful sight, huh? The Blood, he just came to someone else's island and did whatever the hell he liked."

He suddenly heard a voice below him. Appearing atop what was left of the emergency stairs was a high school girl with an extravagant hairstyle.

"Asagi..."

Perplexed, Kojou reached out with his hand and pulled up the wobbling girl. Deftly stepping on the twisted steel rungs, she managed to find a safe place to stop.

Asagi wore a white T-shirt and a pleated skirt like that of a school uniform. Compared to her usual attire, this look left a rather plain impression. Her makeup was simpler for once, making her seem younger, which made her also seem a little harder to approach. She was a girl with a pretty face to begin with.

"This is the last place you met Avrora, isn't it?"

In contrast to Kojou hesitating over that gap, Asagi asked Kojou that question in her normal speaking tone.

"Yeah."

Kojou gave a rather curt reply and nodded. This was the site of Kojou's final battle with The Blood and so, too, the place where he'd relinquished the Fourth Primogenitor's Beast Vassals to Avrora.

Right after, though, Shahryar Ren had used a sorcerous device to take over Avrora, using her as a sacrifice with which to open the gate and whisking her away to Nod.

"The Deva Necropolises and the Beast Vassal Warheads… If I hadn't let her out of my grasp back then, none of this annoying stuff would've happened, huh?"

Kojou smiled weakly at his own expense. He knew regrets were meaningless. The instant he'd lost his vampire powers, it was impossible for him to stop Shahryar Ren. Even so, the fact remained: That instant, Kojou let go of Avrora's hand.

"Maybe so."

Asagi spoke calmly, neither consoling Kojou nor blaming him.

"But she's still alive, and we are, too."

"Ah…"

Her words made Kojou gasp briefly.

She was right. Nothing was over yet. Shahryar Ren didn't rule the surface. Kojou controlled the black Beast Vassals and had regained his vampire powers. And Avrora was alive. The fact that the gate to Nod was still open served as proof.

Seeing that the spark had returned to Kojou's eyes, Asagi smiled in satisfaction.

"We got a report from the Island Guard captain who went to Kensei Kanase's lab. Natsuki and the Lion King Agency people left it a while ago. They upped the number of guardsmen at Keystone Gate, but if Natsuki's working with them, their odds are pretty bad, to be blunt."

Asagi took out her smartphone as she spoke. She must have come all the way up to Keystone Gate's roof just to convey this information to Kojou.

"Natsuki seriously plans to wreck Itogami Island?"

Kojou was asking himself this with an incredulous look on his face. Natsuki Minamiya, the Witch of the Void, was Kojou and Asagi's homeroom teacher as well as an Attack Mage assigned to Itogami Island. Before Kojou obtained the power of the Fourth Primogenitor, she'd apprehended numerous sorcerous criminals, saving Itogami Island from danger many times over.

Yet Natsuki was an Attack Mage assigned to the Attack Mage Section of the police, a Federal Attack Mage in the employ of the Japanese government. If the government of Japan ordered her to destroy Itogami Island, she had no choice but to obey. The same went for Yukina, an agent of the Lion King Agency.

"It adds up. If there's no Itogami Island, the gate to Nod can't be maintained. If the gate vanishes, Shahryar Ren won't be able to return to this world so no more Beast Vassal Warheads get through."

Asagi voiced a set of objective facts.

The number of Beast Vassal Warheads was ten at most, and probably fewer than that, in reality. If they closed their eyes to significant casualties, these weren't numbers the vampire primogenitors were unable to deal with. Even if several large cities were wiped out, at least some would surely find that preferable to the Devas ruling the world.

"At the very least, the Holy Grounds Treaty Organization has no reason to object to the operation. They meant to sink the island to begin with. Even if Natsuki and her girls fail, they don't lose a thing either way."

Asagi's detached commentary sent a shiver down Kojou's spine. The thought of Natsuki destroying the island seemed preposterous, but it was swiftly sounding more and more real.

"She's gonna sink the island…"

Kojou murmured softly as he looked down at the Itogami Island cityscape spread beneath them.

The lights of the city shone amid the darkness of night. Each and every one of those lights represented the living, breathing people dwelling on the island. These were the lives of residents of a Demon Sanctuary, where humanity and demonkind coexisted without conflict.

If the keystone was destroyed, Itogami Island wouldn't last more than a few hours. It would be like a suspension bridge losing its anchorages. Without any support for their mass, the four gigafloats—North, South,

East, and West—would capsize, collide, or maybe start to float adrift. Of course, the populace would lose their former lives, and the scenery they remembered, forever—

As Kojou pictured this worst possible future, emotions hovered in his eyes: despair, apprehension—and anger.

Asagi looked toward Kojou with a soft gaze. Then she spoke with a gentle smile.

"I love you, Kojou."

"Eh?"

Kojou blinked his eyes in a daze. He didn't immediately grasp what she'd just said to him, the reason being that Asagi's tone was just that unnatural, that unburdened.

"I've loved you since way back, and this island, too."

Asagi peered directly into Kojou's eyes. Kojou was breathless as her unwavering gaze shot right through him. Asagi softly narrowed her eyes. Then she continued with crisp, clear words.

"That's why I won't let anyone destroy this island. No way, no how."

"Asagi…what are you thinking?"

Gazing at the small but ferocious smile on Asagi's face, Kojou followed up uneasily. He'd seen that look of hers before. It was the same look on her face when she'd kicked off a war with the HGTO all by herself for the sake of protecting Itogami Island.

"Itogami Island is the one place the Devas can't lob a Beast Vassal Warhead at. The island is their one and only route into Nod. They can't sink us, like it or not."

"In other words…we're the only ones who can oppose them…?"

Kojou felt a shiver run up his spine.

The government of Japan couldn't defy Shahryar Ren, or the Kingdom of Aldegia, or the primogenitors' Dominions. Their homelands and the citizens thereof had been taken hostage by the Beast Vassal Warheads.

For Kojou and other Itogami Island residents, however, this was not so.

MAR couldn't use the warheads on Itogami Island. That's why they feared Kojou and company. Only the residents of Itogami Island could defy Deva rule, because they were able to make enemies of MAR. Ladli Ren had entered into negotiations to purchase Itogami Island for this very reason.

"Ring."

As Kojou stood still and defenseless, Asagi thrust her left hand toward him.

"Eh?"

Kojou blinked hard and looked at Asagi. She breathed raggedly.

"You still have rings from the ones Zana Lashka gave you, right? Gimme."

"But that's…"

Kojou took out a silver-colored ring. This was a pact ring magically sealing a piece of Kojou's body—a catalyst with which to create a vampiric Blood Servant.

Kojou fiercely hesitated before handing his friend Asagi such a ring. As he hesitated, Asagi grabbed him by the collar and drew her face close to his.

"Even if you can't forget about Avrora, hell, even if you love someone else, that's fine with me. If it takes a hundred years or a thousand, I'll make you love me the most—so give me the chance."

Asagi whispered into Kojou's ear.

Her long lashes, her eyes full of triumph, her glossy lips, her white skin, her sweet scent prickling at his nostrils—Kojou felt a great thirst, and his canine teeth were stricken with a terrible ache.

"You're…really fine with this, Asagi…?"

Doing as she insisted, he slid the ring onto her delicate finger.

As she gazed at the silvery glow of the ring, a satisfied smile came over Asagi, after which she used that left hand to push up her side bangs. Offering her slender, exposed neck, she lifted her chin, gently closing her eyes.

"You and me, Kojou. We're gonna save the world."

Hearing these words, a vow spoken like a magic spell, Kojou plunged his fangs into Asagi's neck.

Asagi let out a pained breath as sweet, crimson fluid coursed into Kojou's throat.

Along with the blood memories of the Priestess of Cain—

CHAPTER THREE
BETRAYAL

1

The sound of wind rushed in her ears. There was a faint scent of the sea breeze. Something grazed her cheek with the softness of a plush toy. It was a long mane that smelled sweet like a flower.

"Shio! Wake up, Shio!"

"Yui…ri?"

The fierce shake of her shoulder woke Shio Hikawa. The first thing she saw was the familiar face of her best friend. Yuiri Haba's eyes wavered with concern, and Shio saw huge wings slicing through the wind behind her friend. They were dragon wings that gleamed like steel.

"Glenda…huh? Oh yeah…Glenda jumped out in front of us and…"

Shio vigorously shook her head as bits of memories started coming back to her.

Glenda had suddenly appeared out of nowhere, generating encroachment of Nod to form a gate she'd dragged them through. Apparently, Shio and company were on Glenda's back that very moment, flying God knows where.

Judging from the state of her body, Shio figured she hadn't been unconscious for very long. They shouldn't have been that far from Itogami Island yet—when she had that thought, Shio began to look around, then Yuiri pointed overhead with a grave expression.

"Shio, look!"

"Eh?"

Bewildered, Shio looked up, and her eyes were greeted by the twinkling surface of the sea. Shio gaped at the bizarre sight. An aquamarine sea covered the space over her head. A cloud-covered sky stretched below her. Losing her sense of up and down, Shio desperately clung to the dragon's mane. She felt like she was having a nightmare.

"What is…this place…?"

Shio looked around in a daze at a world where earth and sky had traded places. With no landmarks to go by, she couldn't make a proper estimate of distance, but the sea above their heads was at an altitude of two or three thousand meters at minimum.

At the center of the vast sea were the silhouettes of countless islands swirling in a spiral pattern. She had a sense of déjà vu as she gazed at the ruin of a steel-colored city—an artificial isle.

"That island…that's not Itogami Island, right? Seems to be an…artificial isle, though…"

Yuiri spoke with a perplexed expression. Shio shook her head in silence, unable to answer her.

"They resemble the structures of New Itogami Island, yes."

An unhappy-looking Kiriha appeared from behind Shio and Yuiri atop Glenda's swaying mane. Apparently, she'd carefully climbed up Glenda's long tail.

"Kiriha Kisaki, so you were safe and sound, too…"

"Yes. You must find that quite unfortunate."

Kiriha gave the surprised Shio a sardonic reply. Yuiri looked between the artificial isle above them and Kiriha's face.

"It really does seem like New Itogami Island… Then this might be…"

"Nod—is that not the most likely, especially when you add her controlling the encroachment of Nod?"

Kiriha shrugged her shoulders as she spoke. Shio felt dizzy yet again. Sure, they'd been observing the gate from the surface, but visiting Nod herself without any kind of preparation—emotional or otherwise—was well outside her expectations.

"What in the world's going on, Glenda? Where are you taking us?"

Yuiri posed this question to Glenda in the tone of a scolding mother speaking to a young daughter, yet the steely dragon merely twitched her ears without looking back. She was looking not at the artificial isle above them, but at the sea of clouds spread before their eyes.

In a gap between the white, cotton candy–like clouds stood a single strip of land, resembling a cape with cliffs on both sides. Glenda was heading straight toward this cape in the sky.

"It would seem that structure is our destination."

Kiriha calmly pointed this out, glaring at the artificial structure on the tip of the cape. It was a tall structure resembling a bell tower.

"Is that a…church?"

"It looks like a dam control facility to me…"

Yuiri and Shio tilted their heads, murmuring respectively. The cape floating among the clouds had a pointed tower standing upon it, a beautiful yet bizarre sight.

"*Daa———h!!*"

Glenda roared loudly as if to announce her return.

Making one, big circle in the air above the tower, she began to plunge toward the cape. They were actually heading toward the sky, so perhaps it was more accurate to call it a precipitous rise. Shio's confused thoughts were mulling over this issue when Glenda's entire body was suddenly wrapped in a steely twinkle.

The dragon's huge body rapidly contracted, and her voluminous mane turned into long hair.

Glenda released her dragon form and returned to the body of a young girl. This, naturally, meant the girls riding on her back were hurled into the air.

"G-Glenda?! Waiiiit!"

"If you throw us off from here…die…we're gonna die…!"

"Tch…!"

As Yuiri and Shio shrieked fervently, Kiriha silently girded her body to break the fall, but however long she waited, the anticipated impact of their landing failed to arrive.

After all, they weren't falling. They were certainly moving downward, but the force of it was far softer than they had imagined.

Freed from the force of gravity, their bodies were light, almost like they were standing on the clouds—since, as a matter of fact, they were above the clouds, the feeling might well have been a natural one to have.

Like astronauts on a spacewalk, Shio and company awkwardly flailed their limbs as they landed on the cape amid the clouds. The light sensation conveyed through the soles of their feet felt like they'd landed on a papier-mâché bridge.

"It doesn't…hurt?"

"It's like walking on the moon."

The lightness of their bodies felt strange enough for Yuiri and Kiriha to let out perplexed comments.

"Are the laws of physics different from our world…?"

Shio touched the moss-covered soil as she speculated. It wasn't like anything she'd expected, but this was part of Nod. The inversion of sky and ground and the strength of gravity were probably things they just needed to accept as is.

On the other hand, having brought Shio and company this far, Glenda was back to her usual invigorated self.

"Daa—!! Yuiri! Shio!"

"Wait a… Glenda?!"

Unable to support the weight of the leaping dragon girl, Yuiri wobbled backward. The weak gravity made planting her feet ineffective.

"You little… I was so worried! Where have you been all this time?!"

"Dah…"

Scolded by Yuiri in a firm tone, Glenda wilted and hung her head. Exhaling with deep relief, Yuiri hugged Glenda to her chest.

"I'm so glad you're safe…"

"Dah…"

Eh-heh-heh, Glenda's happy, narrowed eyes seemed to say as she glomped Yuiri. Shio's expression was taut as she gazed at the pair's heartwarming reunion.

"So where is this, Glenda? Are we really in Nod?"

"Certainly you told us to come save Avrora Florestina?"

"Dah! Ava!"

Responding to Kiriha's question, Glenda gasped and lifted her head. The dragon girl shifted her eyes to the little, steel-colored tower standing at the very tip of the cape.

As if responding to her gaze, the door to the tower opened. Though scarred and a shadow of itself, it was a thick metallic door.

Poking her head out from inside was a little girl hugging a teddy bear. She had vivid, golden hair that seemed to change color like a rainbow and had blue vampiric eyes that glowed like flames.

"Avrora...?!"

Yuiri called out the girl's name. The small, golden-haired vampire's shoulders quivered like she was frightened.

"You're really Avrora?"

Shio was flustered by the lightness of her body as she approached the girl. Avrora hugged the teddy bear tighter against her chest, seemingly firming up her resolve as she opened her mouth.

"H-how hast thou...come to this place?"

"Er, we're not really sure ourselves..."

She seemed conflicted, grimacing as she looked at Glenda, but the one girl who seemed capable of explaining the situation simply smiled innocently as she hugged Yuiri.

"Avrora, are you all right? We heard Kojou handed the power of the Fourth Primogenitor to you..."

Yuiri inquired in Shio's place. Avrora's eyes settled upon the ring on Yuiri's left hand. In sequence, she then shifted her gaze to Shio and Kiriha's left hands, and the ring fingers of each.

"Rings of the pact..."

"Aaa...! Y-you're wrong. You're wrong, these are..."

"R-right! Kojou hasn't done anything to us at all... Not yet...!"

Avrora's halting comment made Shio and Yuiri vigorously shake their heads. "Dah?" said Glenda, tilting her head as she looked up at the immensely flustered pair.

"Whatever but...what is that badly sewn creature?"

Good grief, thought Kiriha with a sigh before asking this question. She was staring straight at the teddy bear Avrora was hugging against her chest. Kiriha was dubious that the bizarre mascot character of unknown provenance had been modeled after an actual living creature.

"Keh-keh...ain't you a rude one, Priestess of the Bureau of Astrology."

The teddy bear suddenly moved its googly eyes and looked at Kiriha.

"I-it talked?!"

"It's alive?!"

Shio and Yuiri exclaimed in surprise. Seeing the duo's shock made Avrora tense her body, too.

"What are you?"

Instantly leaping back, Kiriha drew her lead-colored spear from the case on her back, a forked spear with a tip like that of a tuning fork. This was the Bureau of Astrology's Ricercare, but even with the tip of this spear pointed at it, the badly sewn teddy bear smiled without showing the slightest hint of fear.

"Let's see. That's a long story, but for starters, on Itogami Island they call me Mogwai."

"...Mogwai?"

Kiriha glared sharply at the teddy bear's sarcastic tone.

"I've heard of it. That's the artificial intelligence Asagi Aiba designed, right? It's like the avatar of the five supercomputers managing Itogami Island or something..."

Shio commented as she vaguely recalled this information.

Hmph, thought Kiriha as she slightly lowered her guard.

"I see...so the partner of the Priestess of Cain, in other words?"

"What are you doing in Nod? And that body...it's real, right?"

Yuiri voiced her quite natural doubts, but the badly sewn teddy bear made a deliberate shrug of its shoulders and shifted its eyes overhead.

"Can we save that question for later? It's gonna be pretty dangerous if we don't deal with that first."

"...That?"

Shio shifted her gaze on cue.

Mixed in with the sound of the sea breeze was the sound of tilt rotor transport craft in flight.

Transport craft flying from the artificial isle floating on the sea overhead were coming down to land on the cape. Shio supposed that actually meant the other side was coming up, but at any rate, they were definitely closing with Shio and the others.

"Who's that?"

"MAR special forces. Looks like one platoon for now."

"Shahryar Ren's men...! You don't mean they're after Avrora?"

"Dah!!"

Glenda excitedly affirmed Shio's question. Come to think of it, she'd pleaded with Shio and the others to save Avrora in the first place.

Seeing Glenda so worked up that she was breathing heavily through her nose, Mogwai laughed with a sardonic *Keh-keh*.

"Well, I suppose that's half their objective."

"And the other half?"

Kiriha had a frosty expression as she pressed Mogwai for more details.

With a deft curl of one of his stubby arms, Mogwai pointed at the tower behind him.

"That. The facility itself."

"Facility…? What is this place anyway?"

Yuiri blinked hard and turned back to the steel-colored tower all over again.

The question made Mogwai raise the corners of his mouth in a leering grin as he paused for effect. Baring his jagged teeth, he puffed out his chest with what somehow seemed like pride.

"Just the management core of Artificial Isle Senra—the system for keepin' six thousand four hundred Beast Vassal Warheads sealed up…no biggie."

2

The elevator Yukina was in quietly descended. Inside the cramped cage were Yukina, Natsuki, and Yukari Endou's black cat familiar.

It couldn't have been just Yukina's imagination that the atmosphere felt weighty and oppressive. This was the underwater nineteenth stratum of Keystone Gate. The exterior water pressure had to already be near five atmospheres' worth.

The elevator reached the bottom and the door opened.

In front, she could see a bulwark resembling a vault door of unbelievable thickness. It had multiple, highly detailed barriers stretched across its surface. To an Attack Mage like Yukina, just gazing at it made her breathing feel labored.

Four heavily armed guardsmen stood before the barriers. They had brought a fair number of security pods to stand alongside them. Noticing Yukina and company's approach, they trained their guns all at once.

These were short military machine guns, probably loaded with anti-demon silver iridium alloy rounds.

"Halt! Halt right now! Who goes there?!"

The guardsman warned them in a voice filled with hostility. They were guarding the most vital section of Itogami Island. The group had unconditional permission to fire on anyone approaching without permission.

The guardsmen didn't pull the trigger because they saw Natsuki walking out of the elevator.

"...Attack Mage Minamiya? What are you doing here...?"

Bewildered expressions came over the guardsmen. Natsuki was a legendary Attack Mage, practically a celebrity, and also worked as the Island Guard's tactics instructor. Small wonder they were incapable of pegging her as a foe.

"Guard detail for the keystone's isolation bulwark, I take it."

Natsuki walked toward the bulwark as she posed that question.

When the perplexed guardsmen nodded, she shot them a cold smile.

"Good work. Good night."

Swinging her still-folded fan without warning, she caused the air around her to distort, creating a shockwave that struck the guardsmen. The guardsmen were unable to even cry out as she blew them away. The shaking went straight to their brains, so they probably didn't understand what was going on from start to finish.

Detecting an abnormality, the security pods instantly shifted to combat mode.

Pure white arrows of light mercilessly assailed them.

This was spirit archery, a high-level spell employed for sniping. Yukari's black cat familiar employed this to fire sixteen arrows simultaneously. The sixteen security pods were destroyed in a single instant, their functions completely coming to a halt.

They'd toyed with the Island Guard's finest as if they were children. Yukina looked completely beside herself as she watched the two masters utterly crushing their opposition.

"Now then, it is your turn, Sword Shaman of the Lion King Agency."

Natsuki turned toward Yukina and spoke with the calm tone of one reading off a death sentence.

"Are we really...destroying Itogami Island?"

Yukina asked back in a cracked voice.

What Natsuki and company were trying to do was to invade Keystone Gate's lowest stratum and destroy the keystone within. With the connector for Itogami Island's gigafloats destroyed, they would lose their balance and split off or collide, holding on for no more than half a day before sinking. The city known as Itogami Island would vanish without a trace.

"I believe we've been over that already?"

Natsuki sighed as she glared at the hesitant Yukina.

"Relax. The situation isn't like when that Lotharingian Armed Apostle went on a rampage here. New Itogami Island is in the surrounding sea. Even if this island sinks, the residents have plenty of time to evacuate."

"B...but...!"

"Hurry, Yukina Himeragi. If MAR brings Beast Vassal Warheads out of Nod, it will only increase the number of dead."

"Khh...!"

Yukina bit her lip and clenched her spear.

If Itogami Island was gone, the gate to Nod appearing in the sky above the island would be gone, too. Shahryar Ren would lose his way to return to that world, so the number of Beast Vassal Warheads brought from Nod would not increase. As a result, the number of people potentially sacrificed in conflict would likely diminish dramatically. All Yukina had to do was destroy Itogami Island—

"Snowdrift Wolf...!"

Yukina thrust her spear into the barriers covering the bulwark. Letting up a high-pitched sound like the echo of a girl's scream, the multilayered barriers were torn asunder without any resistance.

"Well done. I'll teleport us to the lowest level."

Natsuki nodded emotionlessly as she spoke.

Before Natsuki, master of spatial control magic, resilient metal bulwarks and corridors laid out in labyrinth-like manners were utterly meaningless. The instant the barrier vanished from the corridors, there was no longer any way to prevent her intrusion.

The scenery around them rippled, and they instantly arrived at Keystone Gate's lowest stratum, some two hundred and twenty meters below sea level.

This was a prison at the seafloor beyond the reach of light. Yukina's eardrums pleaded in pain from the severe difference in atmospheric pressure.

The stout exterior wall designed to resist water pressure was shaped like a cylinder.

The four wire cables stretching toward the exterior walls each fastened onto one of the main four Gigafloats to East, West, North, and South. Each cable was attached to the metal anchor inside an enormous winch.

The center of this anchor was pierced by a single stone pillar.

This was the keystone supporting several million tons of force to keep Itogami Island connected—this stone pillar, not even a meter in diameter, was Itogami Island's Achilles' heel.

"So this is the keystone's new barrier…"

Yukina was a little overwhelmed as she gazed up at the spiraling barrier enveloping the anchor.

Once upon a time, the center of the keystone employed the remains of a Saint, a holy relic of the Western European Church. The miracle wrought by the holy relic literally held up the Demon Sanctuary of Itogami Island.

The assault by Lotharingian Armed Apostle Rudolf Eustach had exposed this dark side of Itogami Island. Furthermore, advances in sorcerous technology in recent years had made it possible to produce a keystone of sufficient strength without relying upon the holy relic's miracle.

Half a year after that incident, the holy relic had been returned to the Western European Church, swapped with Itogami Island's new keystone. This was the rainbow-colored stone pillar before Yukina's eyes.

Compared to others Yukina had seen in her life, the barrier enveloping the stone pillar was built with overwhelming beauty and simplicity. It was actually a crystallized monolithic barrier.

Resembling a finely polished gemstone, this special barrier possessed high strength and endurance. This object was the pinnacle of sorcerous engineering, of which only a handful of successes existed in the entire world.

"Even the Order of the End was not able to lay a hand on Itogami Island's most fortified area. Even my Guardian cannot destroy this. It is supposedly designed so that it can resist attacks by the Fourth Primogenitor's Beast Vassals, at least in theory."

Natsuki calmly explained. The resilient barrier strengthened for the sake of turning it into a powerful keystone also served as an absolute bulwark protecting it from external attack.

Even if someone managed to get to Keystone Gate's lowest stratum, there was no physical method with which to destroy the keystone.

"But your spear is the one exception, Yukina Himeragi. The Schneewaltzer's Divine Oscillation Effect able to rend any barrier can destroy this bulwark."

Natsuki thrust this cruel fact onto Yukina. Only Yukina could destroy the keystone. In other words, Yukina herself had to decide whether or not Itogami Island sank.

"…I…must…"

Yukina's hands, gripping her spear, trembled.

Closing her eyes, she saw the scenery of Itogami Island in the back of her mind. The scent of the sea breeze, the sounds of the seagulls, the white waves, the dazzling rays of the sun—it was a city where demonkind and humanity lived side by side. Yukina's memories of Itogami Island always included a certain boy within them.

"Yukina Himeragi. That is enough. You have done well."

While Yukina was frozen in place, she heard a delicate, gentle voice from behind.

Turning in surprise, Yukina saw a young woman in a wheelchair.

Her hair was in an unadorned triple braid and she wore painfully plain glasses. Her face was average, to the point where Yukina would forget it the instant she averted her eyes, yet the spiritual essence enveloping the girl's entire body was vivid and ferocious.

"Lady…Koyomi Shizuka…"

In a daze, Yukina spoke the name of the head of the Three Saints of the Lion King Agency.

"If you cannot decide, no matter what, then please hand me the spear. Even if it is not as much as you, I, too, love Itogami Island—therefore, allow me to bear the sin of sinking this island."

Still in the wheelchair, Koyomi Shizuka approached Yukina and extended her right hand toward Yukina. She, possessor of an extreme level of spiritual energy, could wield Snowdrift Wolf just like Yukina. Once, she'd actually wielded Snowdrift Wolf to crush Kojou Akatsuki.

If Yukina handed Snowdrift Wolf to her, it probably would be easier. Maybe it would let her walk away without the guilt of destroying Itogami Island weighing on her conscience.

Yukina, however, shook her head, strongly gripping her spear anew.

"Thank you very much for your consideration. This is my duty, however."

Turning her back to Shizuka and the others once more, Yukina faced the keystone. The spiritual energy flowing into the silver-colored spear made it emit the pale glow of the Divine Oscillation Effect. All she had to do was rend the barrier before her eyes, and all would be over.

The battle with the Devas, her mission to be Kojou Akatsuki's watcher, everything—

"I am sorry, senpai… I am sorry, everyone…!"

Violently shaking her head as she wiped away her tears, Yukina regulated her breathing. Poising the light-imbued silvery spear, she thrust it toward the center of the barrier.

That very moment, she heard the powerful echo of the voice of a boy who shouldn't have been there.

"Do it, Astarte!"

"—Accept."

"…?!!"

Yukina exclaimed as a rose-colored radiance suddenly buried her field of vision.

The tip of the silver-colored spear Yukina had thrust forward was halted by a giant wing just short of touching the barrier. No, this was no wing—it was a giant arm, the right arm of a humanoid Beast Vassal enveloped in the same Divine Oscillation Effect that Snowdrift Wolf employed.

"Execute, Rhododactylos—"

The small homunculus girl appearing out of thin air stood before Yukina enveloped in her own summoned Beast Vassal. The sight severely shook Yukina.

Once upon a time, Yukina had witnessed the same sight in the same place, yet their positions had been reversed.

Back then, Yukina had protected the keystone when Astarte had tried to destroy it. Now Astarte, as an ally of Kojou Akatsuki, was trying to stop Yukina—

"Sorry, Natsuki. This time I'm getting in your way."

A ferocious smile came over Kojou as the Beast Vassal–enveloped Astarte stood behind him.

Yukina was frozen, unable to move. The very last person in the world she wanted to witness her trying to sink Itogami Island had appeared with no warning. Her mind had gone blank. She had no idea what to do. She felt like she was having a nightmare.

"Kojou Akatsuki…why are you here?"

Natsuki inquired in the silent Yukina's stead. Kojou seemed amused as he curled up the corners of his lips.

"Why? I'm the ruler of Itogami Island, y'know? It's only right that I protect this island, even if it makes me the enemy of the world."

"So Kirasaka let it slip?"

Koyomi Shizuka checked with a gentle tone. For some reason, her faintly anger-tinged voice made Kojou grimace with a conflicted look.

"Forgive her, 'kay? She got a big helping of Yume's mind control."

"…Yume Eguchi, Witch of the Night, you say?"

Koyomi Shizuka sighed sullenly. Yume Eguchi was the World's Mightiest Succubus, able to bring even Leviathan, Weapon of the Gods, under her control. Even if Sayaka was a Shamanic War Dancer of the Lion King Agency, she couldn't resist if Yume got serious, even less when Sayaka already had a guilty conscience.

"That girl is simply too kind. I had her keep watch over the lad because I thought her unsuited for this mission, but that seems to have backfired."

Yukari Endou borrowed her familiar's tongue to grumble offhandedly. To Yukina, Yukari's words sounded like she was blaming herself. Precisely because Sayaka wasn't suited for it, the duty fell to Yukari to fulfill in Sayaka's place.

"—But you coming here doesn't change the bottom line."

Natsuki Minamiya solemnly pushed the still-stunned Yukina aside and stood before Kojou. The ghastly aura emitted by her entire body made Kojou reflexively go on guard.

"We will destroy the keystone. Or do you really think your abilities are enough to stop us?"

Not waiting for the answer to her own question, Natsuki began her attacks. Her target was not Kojou but rested behind him—Astarte, enveloped by her humanoid Beast Vassal.

Silver-colored chains spewing from midair assailed Astarte from four directions, wrapping her tight. These chains were Natsuki's divine sorcerous devices known as *Drómi*. These stout chains, able to bind even the Beast Vassals of the Fourth Primogenitor, rendered Astarte immobile.

"Sword Shaman! Destroy the keystone while you have the chance!"

Natsuki shouted at Yukina. Astarte's humanoid Beast Vassal bearing the same ability was the only thing that could block Snowdrift Wolf's Divine Oscillation Effect. Now that her humanoid Beast Vassal was pinned in place, Yukina could destroy the keystone with ease.

"Himeragi, don't! …Whoa there?!"

When Yukina hoisted her spear, Kojou nervously leaped out before her, but countless arrows of light poured down straight at Kojou. It was Yukari Endou's Spirit Archery.

Yukina turned her eyes away from Kojou as he fled in panic and faced the keystone. Kojou's black Beast Vassals were too powerful for him to freely employ them in such a narrow space. Yukina, Kojou Akatsuki's watcher, knew this better than anyone. Borrowing the black cat's body, Yukari was able to exhibit only half of her real potential, but she was more than a match for Kojou under these conditions.

"Figures it's too tough to take all of you at once…!"

Kojou commented with an anguished expression, probably grasping that fact for himself. Responding to his complaint was a carefree voice with a laugh tossed in.

"Yeah, not with just Kojou and Astarte."

"—?!!"

Yukina's field of vision swayed like a ripple, a precursor of teleportation magic. She instantly moved back. A faceless knight construct clad in rusty blue armor appeared before her. This was the devil's familiar that protected Yuuma Tokoyogi.

"Miss Yuuma?!"

A tall, slender girl wearing a sports brand parka landed in front of the keystone. Her blue knight construct attended behind her.

"Thanks a bunch, Himeragi. With the bulwark's barrier destroyed, I could jump straight down here. Even I'd get tired running down forty flights of emergency stairs."

Yuuma Tokoyogi gave Yukina a friendly smile.

Yukina groaned *ghh*, her voice caught in her throat.

Keystone Gate's isolation section was blocked off by a powerful barrier that made intrusion via teleport impossible. Yukina was the invader who'd destroyed that barrier. Yuuma, bearing the same witch powers as Natsuki, was able to jump straight to Keystone Gate's lowest stratum herself as a result. Sending Kojou and Astarte into that chamber had been Yuuma's work.

"Le Bleu—!"

Yuuma ordered her own Guardian to attack. The blue knight construct turned its sword not toward Yukina, but to the chains binding Astarte's Beast Vassal.

A swaying in space itself transferred to the chains, faintly loosening the Beast Vassal's bindings. Astarte did not let her chance slip, shaking off Natsuki's chains with brute force.

"Go, Sword Shaman!"

Natsuki shot out fresh chains in an attempt to seal Astarte's movements once more, but Yuuma's Guardian beat all of them out of the air. None reached Astarte.

Natsuki's real goal wasn't to bind Astarte, though—it was to slow her down. The chains obstructed Astarte's field of vision, delaying her motion by a single instant. During this time, Yukina raced through the gap between the Beast Vassal's legs.

"—Snowdrift Wolf!"

"I will not allow it!"

When Yukina's spear thrust toward the keystone, it bounced back with a fierce shower of sparks. A high-pitched sound of two metallic objects clashing accompanied the numbness in Yukina's arms. Hiding in the shadow of the Beast Vassal, a white-haired ogre had halted Yukina's attack with her crimson long sword.

"Shizuri Kasugaya Castiella...!"

"I will not allow it, Yukina Himeragi. As a Paladin of Gisella...no, as a survivor of the lost Demon Sanctuary of Iroise, I will not permit you to sink Itogami Island!"

"Khhh...!"

Yukina was wobbling from losing her balance when Shizuri thrust her shoulder forward. Bracing for the ogre's angry charge, Yukina was blown into the air. She instantly back-flipped on one hand a few times to put distance between them, but this ended up putting her far from the keystone.

When Yukina entered a combat stance once more, Shizuri poised her long sword in turn. The undulating flame-like blade was thrusting forward, a stance specialized for attack—the basic stance of a paladin.

"Besides, I always did want to pay you back. Even if I was brainwashed and controlled at the time, I wish to return in kind the unsightly, humiliating way you defeated me. This is our rematch!"

As she glared provocatively at Yukina, a ferocious smile came over Shizuri. Overwhelmed by that resolute gaze, Yukina strongly clenched her jaw.

3

Brutal combat unfolded in various parts of the isolation chamber with cables stretching through it.

Kojou Akatsuki was running blindly from the arrows of light pouring down upon him like a meteor shower when the rose-colored Beast Vassal controlled by Astarte stretched a giant arm out to try and support him. Shizuri Kasugaya and Yukina Himeragi continued close-quarters combat, literally sending sparks flying from point-blank range.

Also, Yuuma Tokoyogi was taking on Natsuki Minamiya, the Witch of the Void, arrayed in a war of spells on equal terms.

"—Sorry, Teach. I can't act freely 'cause of my pact with my devil, but there's just one exception."

Yuuma unleashed invisible shockwaves wrought from spatial control that assailed Natsuki from four sides.

Tch, Natsuki sullenly clicked her tongue as she teleported, evading Yuuma's attack.

Undeterred, Yuuma continued attacking. Using her witch's magical calculation potential to its utmost limit, she slammed shockwaves into Natsuki's teleport destination. Natsuki engaged in dizzying teleports as she counterattacked as well. The two witches swapped locations at high speed as they unleashed surreal, inhuman levels of magical energy.

"I can attack you, and only you, anytime I want! You're the one who locked away my mother—Aya Tokoyogi!"

Yuuma's Guardian roared as it assaulted Natsuki with a blade of void.

In exchange for the powerful magical energy she obtained, a witch was bound by her pact with her devil. If she acted in defiance of that pact, the witch's Guardian would instantly take the witch's life.

The pact Yuuma made with a devil was for the sake of freeing Aya Tokoyogi, her biological mother, from her incarceration in the Prison Barrier. Yuuma had cooperated with Natsuki's investigations into LCO for this purpose, for the Attack Mage Section had promised Aya would be released once LCO was destroyed.

If it was just to spring Aya, though, she didn't need the Attack Mage Section's help.

If she defeated Natsuki, the warden of the Prison Barrier, the prisoners therein would be automatically freed. Accordingly, the devil possessing Yuuma did not see combat with Natsuki as a violation of the pact. Yuuma was using this to cooperate with Kojou and try to protect Itogami Island from destruction.

"You think your power is enough to defeat me, Yuuma Tokoyogi?"

Space around Natsuki distorted, from which countless silver chains shot out like bullets. Yuuma manipulated space as well, desperately evading the arcs of Natsuki's attacks. Unable to avoid all of them, she was forced to teleport to escape. Overwhelmed by Natsuki's control over space, she'd wound up on the defensive.

"That's difficult in terms of raw might. If I could beat you, you wouldn't have captured Mom to begin with."

Yuuma was breathing a little hard as she formed a strained smile.

Yuuma's blue knight construct Guardian was her inheritance from her mother, Aya Tokoyogi. However, Aya's ability as the Witch of Notaria was to reproduce grimoires from memory, making her Guardian fundamentally unsuited for combat. Of course she'd be overwhelmed by Natsuki in a head-on clash.

"That's if you can use your abilities to their full potential, though."

The blue knight construct's rusted sword carved a symbol at its own feet. The next instant, Yuuma vanished from Natsuki's sight.

"Self-acceleration…! The Witch of the Fall's time control ritual?!"

Natsuki engaged in repeated teleports as she unleashed a horde of teddy bears. The bears approached Yuuma with unexpectedly agile movements to self-destruct once they came within a set range.

Yuuma, however, evaded every last one of them at speeds beyond human limitations. Then she fired off a pressurized, bladelike shockwave in Natsuki's direction.

"Demonslayer, Witch of the Void! You can't use your Guardian's power to destroy the keystone! That's because the pact you made with your devil…the wish at the very bottom of your heart, is for *humans and demons to coexist!*"

"…!"

Unnerved, Natsuki's doll-like face betrayed human expression for the first time. Grazed by Yuuma's shockwave, the frills of her extravagant dress tore off and danced in the air.

"When you were young, you had a prayer, a wish so very pure—you paid a heavy price for that off-the-wall pact, and that's how you got that vast amount of magical energy!"

"Aya Tokoyogi, was it? So she told you about that…"

Landing on top of a wire cable, Natsuki gazed down at Yuuma with emotionless eyes.

Destroying the last of the bears, Yuuma wiped the sweat off her brow as she nodded.

Few knew of the wish of the Witch of the Void, feared by her other alias of Demonslayer. Aya Tokoyogi, Natsuki's friend from long ago, was among these few.

"That's why you can't destroy Itogami Island. This is a Demon Sanctuary where humanity and demonkind live side by side—this place is the realization of your wish."

"You have me there."

Natsuki quietly murmured.

Bound by her pact with her devil, Natsuki could not destroy Itogami Island. This was the reason why the Gigafloat Management Corporation could trust her to act freely despite her being a witch.

"That doesn't mean I have no means of sinking the island. The duty of destroying the keystone fell to the Sword Shaman of the Lion King Agency to begin with."

Natsuki declared this with a frosty air. Floating around her were strange-looking magic circles made out of magical symbols. This was a ritual unknown to Yuuma.

"Figures… You're not soft enough to go down easy…"

Yuuma's cheek twitched nervously.

Natsuki summoned three black-haired dolls, finely crafted marionettes looking exactly like Natsuki. Aside from the colors of the ribbons on the dresses, there was no way to tell them and Natsuki herself apart—or rather, the Natsuki in the real world was herself a marionette. In other words, the three dolls she'd just summoned had the same abilities wielded by Natsuki herself.

"Of course not, little girl. As an educator, I have to give uppity brats like you a proper spanking."

The four Natsukis spread out to surround Yuuma.

"…Er, I think corporal punishment is frowned on nowadays, Teach…!"

Yuuma smiled impetuously, hiding her inner unease. She'd known from the start her power wasn't enough to beat Natsuki. Yuuma's job was to keep Natsuki busy—to buy Kojou and others enough time to neutralize Yukina. She wasn't going to last long against Natsuki like this, though.

Please, Kojou— Making that tiny plea under her breath, Yuuma glanced at Kojou in her peripheral vision.

"—Er, yikes!!"

Letting out an earnest yelp without any shame, Kojou leaped and rolled sideways to evade the arrows of light pouring down. He had no time for relief, though—fresh arrows flew to drive Kojou into a corner.

"Ms. Kitty's spirit archery thingy, huh…! Not knowing where they'll fly in from makes this rough."

Kojou breathed raggedly, spitting out the words as he fled to the blind spot of the pillar.

Back when he'd fought Yukari once before, Kojou had been neutralized in a single instant by her Spirit Archery. This was a little better compared to then because he had some grasp of the opponent's hand. Besides, Yukari's ability had to be greatly constrained when using it via a cat's body. In spite of this, Yukari's voice still felt very confident.

"The offensive power of The Blood's black Beast Vassals is too great. They are unsuited to defense. Surely you understand this yourself, Fourth Primogenitor lad."

Yukari calmly warned Kojou while looking down at him from atop one of the cables stretching through the chamber.

"Well, in that body, you don't have enough power to smash the keystone, do you?!"

Ghh, grunted Kojou, drawing in a breath as he pretty much snapped at her. He felt like the black cat was grinning with scorn.

"Hmm, I wonder?"

"…?!"

A moment later, Kojou was assaulted by a sense of unease that defied words. A sound like silence torn apart echoed in his ears—a sound that should not have existed.

Someone had jammed nonexistent time within the temporal flow.

Time with which to unleash an attack—

"Let there be light!"

"Wha…!"

Kojou drew in his breath, dazed when he noticed the girl in front of him, recurve bow raised. At some point, the supposedly wheelchair-bound Koyomi Shizuka had appeared before Kojou with a drawn recurve bow.

Paper Noise, the right of absolute initiative attack—by the time Kojou noticed her presence, Koyomi Shizuka had already loosed a cursed arrow toward Kojou.

The roar of the whistling arrow generated the same effect as a long-form ritual incantation, forming a ritual spell artillery attack with destructiveness on par with a vampiric Beast Vassal. Slow to react, Kojou had no way to evade it.

Yet the anticipated impact did not strike Kojou.

A giant, rose-colored Beast Vassal arm intervened, blocking the ritual spell artillery attack right before Kojou's eyes.

"Astarte!"

"There is no problem. My Beast Vassal has neutralized the—"

Enveloped in her humanoid Beast Vassal, the homunculus girl spoke with a flat, emotionless voice, but Kojou was uneasy for an entirely different reason.

"Not that! Above!"

A moment after the artillery attack was finished, Koyomi Shizuka leaped above Kojou's and Astarte's heads. Her left hand gripped a silver long sword, Rosen Chevalier Plus—the pseudo-spatial severing its slices generated were not something even Astarte's Beast Vassal could block.

Driven by vampiric survival instincts, Kojou's body moved faster than his mind. Drawing on a portion of a Beast Vassal's abilities, he rent space and intercepted Koyomi Shizuka's sword.

The collision of twin spatial severings made a high-pitched sound like grating metal echo around them. Koyomi Shizuka, blown back by the recoil from the collision, landed atop a cable with a dance-like flutter.

Her movements resembled Yukina's, but the degree of polish was off the charts. Even without her Paper Noise ability, Kojou could tell she truly was a supreme Attack Mage.

"So you deflected a pseudo-spatial severing slice with a slice by Primus Iris? That's quite something."

Koyomi Shizuka smiled as if praising Kojou. Kojou's lips twisted slightly.

"What...you faked being hurt that bad? You had me totally fooled..."

"No, I am quite gravely injured. However, I healed myself with will-power. One of the Three Saints of the Lion King Agency cannot remain off duty indefinitely."

"Is that so...?!"

Sweat oozed from Kojou's back. Whether Koyomi Shizuka's words were truth or lies, the girl who supposedly couldn't stand on her own power was fighting him just the same. To be blunt, having one of the Three Saints join the battle was a very unhappy surprise.

"It is over, ruler lad. Give up."

Circling around Kojou's back, the black cat stated this as countless arrows of light hovered around him. *Aw shucks*, Kojou seemed to say with a touch of his hand to the back of his head.

"You got me... I'd be in a real bind if I didn't bring extra help along."

"Extra help...?"

The black cat's whiskers twitched in surprise. The next moment, the cover of the lowest stratum's maintenance hatch blew open, and a crimson robot tank leaped in from it.

"*—It would seemeth I have arrived in time! I am sorry to have keptest thou waiting, Sir Boyfriend!*"

Lydianne Didier announced her arrival in a loud voice as she launched smoke rounds. A scent similar to pesticide pricked Kojou's nose, spreading around him and the others.

Yukari Endou instantly loosed her arrows of light—yet her aim was slightly off, each and every one falling short of Kojou and Lydianne.

"No, this smell, this is...catnip...!"

The black cat wobbled and tottered, rolling onto its back as if it was flat-out drunk. Even a superb Attack Mage like Yukari Endou couldn't put up a proper fight when her familiar's body was intoxicated. Lydianne had loaded her tank's smoke discharger with catnip rounds as a counter to Yukari's black cat.

"Yukari!"

Gracefully dropping from the wire cable, Koyomi Shizuka sliced down at Lydianne's tank.

Faced with Rosen Chevalier Plus's slashes in space, the robot tank's fiber-reinforced plastic armor didn't stand a chance, but Koyomi's slash never reached Lydianne's tank, for a figure leaped out from within the smoke barrage to parry Koyomi's sword.

"Wha... Sayaka Kirasaka...?!"

"—Lustrous Scale!"

Shaken by the unexpected interference, Koyomi was physically forced back by Sayaka. Sayaka's and Koyomi's weapons had identical characteristics. The two swords' abilities canceled each other out, causing the naked blades to cast off sparks.

"I was right to bring along Miss Sayaka."

"Truly, one's own kin often proveth the greatest of foes!"

Yume, riding the tank's back, and Lydianne, in the driver's seat, respectively let out satisfied impressions.

"—The Witch of the Night's mind control, is it?"

Brushing aside the blatantly hostile Sayaka's slices, Koyomi Shizuka quietly murmured with irritation.

Once before, Yume had controlled Sayaka, making her attack Kojou and company. Yume was simply repeating history—but this time, as Kojou's ally.

"We asked Kirasaka to protect Itogami Island. I hear from Yume that even a succubus's power can't make someone obey an order they don't really wanna, though?"

Kojou was holding down the now-immobile black cat as he explained.

"In fact, given an order reflecting the person's desires, all doubts vanish, causing her to exhibit greater than normal strength… What a troublesome thing you've done." Koyomi Shizuka calmly replied.

Both she and Sayaka had weapons of equal potency. In combat skill, Koyomi had the edge, but she was in a great deal of pain, so Sayaka had a chance if the fight became prolonged.

Knowing this, Koyomi activated Paper Noise. A momentary silence was followed by a roar. With preparations to attack complete, Koyomi appeared from Sayaka's blind side, smashing her sword hilt in without hesitation, but—

"Wha…?!"

It was an unavoidable blunt strike, yet Sayaka stopped it just short of hitting. Shock hovered in Koyomi's eyes as Sayaka drew from her latent potential to its utmost limit, raising her reflexes to a superhuman level above Koyomi's attack speed.

"Leave this to me, Kojou Akatsuki!"

Sayaka spoke these words strongly as her swordsmanship dominated the shaken Koyomi.

"R…right…"

Kojou nodded, somewhat overwhelmed by Sayaka's oddly high level of fervor, probably owing to Yume's mind control. He then turned around.

That very moment, Yukina and Shizuri were locked in genuine mortal combat in front of the keystone to Itogami Island.

"Sayaka...why...?"

Yukina was heavily thrown off when she noticed Sayaka fighting with Koyomi Shizuka.

Sayaka was a Shamanic War Dancer, an elite in the Lion King Agency assigned even to the protection of figures of national importance. It was utterly unthinkable that Sayaka would turn against Koyomi, one of the Three Saints.

"So your vision strays even against an opponent like me, Yukina Himeragi!"

Not letting Yukina's opening slip past her, Shizuri unleashed a savage slashing attack.

Shizuri's crimson long sword was a demonic blade that increased in power using the demonic energy absorbed from the opponents it cut. It could also release demonic energy accumulated in its blade as a kind of shockwave. It wasn't a weapon any human in the flesh could stand up to, but Yukina was the sole exception.

"Snowdrift Wolf—!"

Yukina's spear caused the demonic energy covering the crimson long sword to dissipate.

Snowdrift Wolf, able to nullify demonic energy, was the mortal enemy of Shiziru's Hauras. Losing the demonic energy stored within, Hauras was nothing more than a long sword with an unorthodox shape. In a fight of sword versus spear, having the weapon with the longer reach surely gave Yukina an advantage.

In spite of this, Shizuri swung down her long sword with a ferocious smile.

"It is futile! Hauras!"

"Wha...?!"

Yukina barely blocked the demonic energy blade Shizuri's long sword unleashed a second time.

Hauras's dissipated demonic energy had returned. Yukina knew the true nature of that black, malevolent demonic energy. After all, Yukina and the others had fought Beast Vassals with the same auras the night before.

"That demonic energy, it couldn't be, the black Beast Vassals'…!"

"…It is the blessing of a paladin."

When Yukina inquired, Shizuri averted her eyes and replied in a flat tone. Yukina's voice ran ragged despite herself.

"Liar! You're drawing that demonic energy straight from Akatsuki-senpai, aren't you…?!"

"Th-this is my right as Kojou Akatsuki's Blood Servant!"

Shizuri defiantly shouted back as she pointed the tip of her sword at Yukina.

Shizuri was an ogre, a rare species of demon. Provisional or not, her pact as Kojou's Blood Servant provided her a far greater boon than Yukina's prior case. She was able to use her supply of demonic energy from Kojou to unleash demonic energy from Hauras effectively without limit.

"Lay down your arms, Yukina Himeragi. Having betrayed Kojou, you cannot draw upon sufficient spiritual energy. You have no chance of victory!"

"…Eh?"

Yukina's mouth stopped moving as she murmured. Shizuri's casually spoken words drove a fact into Yukina that she'd desperately tried to ignore.

"Betrayed…I, betrayed…senpai…"

"Ah…no, wait…wait, please!"

Seeing how Yukina hung her head, shoulders trembling, left Shizuka unnerved. She thought Yukina might burst into tears. Keeping her crimson long sword raised, Shizuri looked around awkwardly.

"I admit that I went a little too far just now…! In other words, what I wished to say is, this battle is fruitless, so I wish for you to listen to reason…"

"…Even I understand that this battle is meaningless!"

Yukina screamed, interrupting Shizuka's words.

Yes, this battle was meaningless. Shizuri and Kojou weren't even Yukina's enemies.

The ones Yukina should have been fighting were the Devas seeking to rule humanity through the fear known as Beast Vassal Warheads—Shahryar Ren and his coconspirators.

In spite of this, on top of Yukina's own powerlessness, here she was trying to sacrifice Itogami Island's innocent populace.

Kojou and Shizuri were blameless for trying to stop Yukina. Yukina understood this, yet there was nothing she could do about it.

Shizuri was suddenly assaulted by silence as Yukina vanished from her sight.

"Y-Yukina Himeragi?!"

Subconsciously sensing that something was wrong, Shizuri instantly backed away and went on guard, but by then, Yukina's attack preparations were already complete using Paper Noise, the right of absolute initiative attack—

"But what's right… What I should do… I don't know any of that!"

"Nyaaa?!"

Yukina's mighty thrust caught Shizuri's unguarded right shoulder. She'd thrust with the butt of her spear but hadn't held back at all. It was enough power to shatter the collarbone of even a resilient ogre.

She should have expected Shizuri would instantly twist her body and avoid taking a square hit. Even so, she surely had not escaped unscathed. Shizuri was thrown heavily off-balance, leaving her chest wide open.

"So this is the only thing I can do!"

Letting go of her spear, Yukina activated Paper Noise once more. Using blank time that did not properly exist, she moved right in front of Shizuri, placing both hands upon her heart to pound a decisive palm strike into her at point-blank range.

"Distort!"

"I thought that was coming!"

When Yukina appeared right in front of her, Shizuri, who should have been completely off-balance, slammed her own forehead into Yukina's. The incredible blow sustained right between the eyes sent Yukina flying with ease.

"Gaaah…?!"

"…If it's against humans, I can trade hits with the best of them!"

Covering her own chest as she coughed, Shizuri triumphantly curled up the corners of her lips. Yukina finally realized Shizuri had lured her in.

Shizuri hadn't been off-balance at all. Knowing she couldn't block Yukina's attack, she'd immediately aimed for a mutual strike. She'd deliberately baited Yukina to attack from a direction she could counter with ease.

The damage was still heavy on both sides, and Shizuri had already played the ace in her hand. Shizuri would never be able to evade the next Paper Noise.

Instantly calculating as much, Yukina leaped in the direction of her relinquished Snowdrift Wolf. With the damage to her right shoulder, Shizuri could no longer use Hauras to emit demonic energy. She couldn't attack at that range—she shouldn't have been able to, at least.

"Radia—!"

From behind her uniform, Shizuri's left hand drew out a second weapon. After the crimson Hauras, this was the second demonic blade belonging to the royal family of the ogres—the blue curved blade once wielded by Izea Nios, ogre acolyte of the Order of the End.

"Gaah...!"

Taking the hit from the demonic energy shockwave, Yukina cried out as she was blown into the air. She enveloped her entire body with ritual energy to defend herself, but the impact was still enough to roll over a small car. Her vision constricted, and her mind grew distant. Her body was numb, leaving her unable to stand.

For Shizuri's part, she fell to one knee and cringed after launching the attack.

Yukina's blunt strikes were still having an impact. In the first place, that afternoon Shizuri had seemed too gravely wounded to even walk on her own power.

In spite of this, she was firmly carrying out her role of stopping Yukina, her role of protecting Itogami Island as Kojou Akatsuki's Blood Servant—

"If I...if I don't destroy the keystone...a great many people...will be sacrificed..."

Yukina's mind was hazy as she grabbed her fallen spear and stood up.

Natsuki was engaged in combat with Yuuma. It was grueling for Yuuma, but she was tying down Natsuki and buying plenty of time.

Yukari's black cat familiar was limp and immobile, captured by the machinations of Lydianne's tank. It seemed the cat had fallen into a drunken sleep.

Unbelievably, Koyomi was being pushed back by Sayaka. Even if she was one of the Three Saints, she was in a state of great pain, and Astarte's support had to make it very difficult for her to neutralize Sayaka. Meaning Yukina was the only one able to destroy the keystone at the moment.

"I must…do this…"

Dragging herself with the silver spear as her crutch, Yukina moved close to the anchor for the keystone.

Yukina no longer knew why she had to do this. Perhaps she believed it was her duty for the Lion King Agency. Perhaps she truly believed this was for the sake of the many.

The one thing she knew was that if she destroyed the barrier before her, everything would be over. She would sacrifice her precious friends on Itogami Island to save people around the world whose faces she did not know. Even though Yukina knew this, there was no going back.

The silvery spear she was accustomed to wielding felt so very heavy. The spear was enveloped in a pale glow as Yukina raised it, an emotionless, machinelike expression on her face.

The next moment, Yukina gasped, for a boy with a languid air about him stood before the tip of her raised spear.

"Looks like you're having a hard time, Himeragi… It almost looks like you're crying?"

Kojou Akatsuki looked back at Yukina with pity in his eyes.

"Sen…pai…I am sorry…"

Yukina exhaled in a daze. Seeing Yukina shaking like that, Kojou made a strained, exasperated smile.

"You're righteous heroes smashing Itogami Island on the government of Japan's orders, right? Then you should be up front about it. I'm the big villain defying the decision of the great Holy Grounds Treaty Organization, y'know?"

"I am…sorry…senpai…I'm sorry…I'm sorry… I'msorryI'msorryI'msorry I'msorryI'msorryI'msorry!"

Unable to stop the emotions pouring from the bottom of her heart, Yukina gave off a high-pitched scream.

"When this mission is over, I can never be by senpai's side again…so!"

Ritual energy beyond her limits surged out from Yukina's entire body. There was no longer any demonic energy supplied from Kojou to offset the spiritual energy. Pure white wings with a radiant glow spread from Yukina's back. She was angelicizing, resolved to vanishing, never returning to the ranks of humans again.

"Aaaaaaaaaaaaaaaaaaaaaaaaaaa—!!"

With a cry of sorrow, Yukina sprinted. Charging at speeds beyond human limitations, she meant to destroy Kojou's body and the keystone barrier behind it both. She was driven by the thought that Itogami, Kojou, and Yukina herself should all vanish together.

Kojou made no attempt to evade Yukina's attack.

Kojou stood defenseless as Yukina mercilessly thrust her silver-colored spear toward Kojou's heart.

The purging spear nullified demonic energy and rent any barrier. Even Kojou's Beast Vassals could not stop it. Even an unaging, undying vampire would turn to dust and vanish, yet—

"Wha—?!"

The strange feedback conveyed through her spear made Yukina's expression freeze over. The right palm Kojou thrust forward emitted a crimson glow. The membrane of light generated by that glow stopped Snowdrift Wolf's attack cold.

"That light?! Senpai, how could you use The Cleansing…?!"

Yukina desperately poured strength into the hands gripping her spear, but the spear would not move. The glow of The Cleansing, the forbidden spell able to rewrite the physical laws of the world, was completely holding Snowdrift Wolf's Divine Oscillation Effect at bay.

Yet this was impossible. It took vast demonic energy to activate The Cleansing and extremely complex magical calculations—and deep knowledge of The Cleansing itself.

Even if Kojou could pull it off on the demonic energy side, the knowledge and magical calculations weren't things he could do on his own. Yes, were it Kojou by himself, that is—

"Sorry, Himeragi. But..."

Aiba Asagi, poking her head up from the shadow of the destroyed maintenance hatch, held her favorite smartphone in one hand as she spoke in a somber tone of voice. A glow was coming from the plain silver-colored ring on her left ring finger.

The instant she saw this, Yukina understood. Kojou had consumed Asagi's blood memories of The Cleansing by taking her as his servant.

"I'm not giving you Kojou. Not when you're like this."

Asagi crisply spoke those words to Yukina. Yukina stopped moving as if she'd been slapped in the face.

Kojou slowly raised his left hand. The pitch-black bloody mist gushing from his arm transformed into an enormous beast: a mass of demonic energy so dense as to possess sentience, a summoned beast from another world—

"C'mon over, Primus Crystallus!"

"...!"

Appearing in the isolated lowest stratum of Keystone Gate was a beautiful, obsidian-like gleaming aquatic dragon.

Kojou had inherited this pitch-black Beast Vassal from The Blood. Its giant, gemstone-like eyes entered Yukina and Koyomi's vision.

That instant, strength drained from Yukina's whole body. Her mind was growing distant, seemingly enveloped by white mist. Yukina's silver-colored spear left her hand, tumbling onto the floor. Yukina herself fell to her knees then and there.

"...Senpai...I am sorry..."

Murmuring without conscious thought, Yukina closed her eyes, completely depleted of strength.

A single tear slowly rolled down her cheek.

4

The next morning—

Crowds of people flooded the streets at the center of Itogami Island's urban zones.

The sight, reminiscent of a large-scale protest march, had no chaos within its ranks.

They were gazing at footage displayed on a huge screen on the side of a building showing an interview with a Gigafloat Management Corporation executive. He was conducting the first public policy announcements following the conclusion of the Electoral War and concerning the Necropolis and the gate to Nod that had appeared in the sky above the island.

"Looks like your dad an' them finished their presentation."

Motoki Yaze addressed Asagi as he listened to the earthquake-like sounds of cheers erupting around Keystone Gate in the urban areas on the other side of the canal.

"Looks like it."

Asagi, lying on an office sofa, toyed with her smartphone as she gave that curt reply.

Asagi's father, Sensai Aiba, was the former mayor of Itogami City and a current councillor on the Itogami City Council. Even after retiring from the position of mayor at the end of his term, he had exhibited shrewdness in negotiating with the government of Japan after the War of the Primogenitors, garnering the absolute trust of the citizens in the process.

That morning, Sensai Aiba was scheduled to address the citizens in the form of a press conference. He was to say negotiations with MAR for the purchase of Itogami Island should be wholly entrusted to the Gigafloat Management Corporation, a pretty arrogant thing to say in one sense.

The citizens' response to this would be assessed in an instant online poll. In other words, the address put Itogami Island's very fate on the line. It wasn't that they lacked the odds for victory, but even Yaze and company had no way to know the results of the vote. That was why Yaze was being fidgety.

Sheesh, thought Asagi, making no effort to hide the blatant exasperation on her face as she slowly sat up. It was then that she heard steady footsteps approaching the door to the office.

The first one to enter the room was a blue-haired female secretary, bringing Kazama Yaze with her. As senior director of the Gigafloat Management Corporation, he was in charge of the presentation and the online vote.

"How's it looking, Bro?"

Yaze impatiently asked Kazama that.

"The citizens' reaction isn't bad, thanks to Councillor Aiba, that is."

The corners of Kazama's lips faintly relaxed as he looked behind him. It was that very moment Sensai Aiba himself entered the office room. He was a middle-aged man with a stern face. He wasn't all that hugely built, but the sense of presence he emitted was remarkable. He gave off the impression of a politician's politician.

"It's the effect of the Gigafloat Management Corporation's manipulation of public opinion. From the citizens' point of view, Itogami City-State being the only one to negotiate independently with MAR, who are able to drive even the HGTO military back, can't feel that bad at all."

Sensai spoke in a low, calm voice. Glancing at his daughter sitting on the sofa, he smiled, seeming a little amused.

"The existence of that boy Kojou Akatsuki looms larger, though. MAR doesn't even fear the three primogenitors, but he has Itogami Island negotiating with them on equal terms. The people believe in the works of the new ruler who survived and won the Electoral War. Rumors are even spreading that it's young Akatsuki who's the World's Mightiest Vampire—the Fourth Primogenitor."

"Isn't that the result of your public opinion manipulation?"

Asagi spoke bluntly. She didn't come off as all that pleased with his praise for Kojou, but Asagi was at a difficult age where she couldn't be honest with her own father about that.

Yaze had a pained smile as he shrugged his shoulders.

"It ain't really that at all. He's been standing out, acting up all over the place... Of course, there were witnesses, so there's been more than a little talk about him until now."

"You've done a good job of controlling information via the Internet, but word of mouth isn't something even we can deal with."

Kazama rationally pointed this out.

Hmph, snorted Asagi as she showed them the screen of her smartphone.

"—Wait, most of the eyewitness info going around is about Himeragi, not Kojou...!"

"Well, that girl stands out on a visual front..."

Yaze seemed conflicted as he lightly scratched his temple.

Asagi's cheeks puffed up, clearly not finding this an amusing twist at all.

"…We have received acceptance that the meeting with Ladli Ren is due to begin at sunset today. We can't help you any further than that."

Sensai looked straight at Asagi, speaking with a serious look on his face.

Many of the citizens of Itogami City had agreed with the Gigafloat Management Corporation conducting negotiations with MAR, but that didn't mean they accepted selling the island to them, never mind making it part of the Devas war machine.

Itogami Island would have to reject MAR's demands while avoiding being enveloped in the fires of war. On top of that, they had to nullify the Beast Vassal Warheads in the Devas' possession and stop the plans of Shahryar Ren in Nod—these negotiations, difficult beyond anything realistically achievable, were the needle Itogami Island had to thread.

Also, the only one designated to negotiate with Ladli Ren was their ruler, Kojou Akatsuki. Neither Sensai nor Kazama could intervene in these negotiations.

"You're really going to do this on your own?"

Sensai frankly aired the worries everyone must have felt.

Asagi looked up at her father's worried face with a little smile. It was a powerful smile of absolute confidence.

Then she gave her brief reply.

"Of course."

5

Bathed in light shining through the window, Yukina slowly awoke.

"Uuu…"

The first thing she saw wasn't her own room—and yet the ceiling felt familiar to her. She was enveloped by an oddly comfortable scent. She was confused, wondering if she was still dreaming, for Yukina had awoken in the apartment that was the Akatsuki residence. She was in a cluttered study used by a male schoolboy. In other words, Yukina was lying in Kojou's bed.

"Ahhh, Yukina, are you awake? Good morning! You all right? Do your wounds hurt any?"

Perhaps sensing Yukina had awoken, Nagisa opened the door without knocking and entered the room. She must have been making breakfast. It didn't seem as if she was wearing an apron over her uniform for show.

"Nagisa…why am I…?"

Yukina put a hand to her forehead as she asked. Yukina remembered fighting Kojou and the others at Keystone Gate's lowest stratum and taking a mental attack from the black Beast Vassal, but she couldn't remember anything else.

She'd plotted to sink Itogami Island and had even tried to kill Kojou— she couldn't comprehend any reason why someone like her had been sleeping in Kojou's bed.

Nagisa, though, looked back at the bewildered Yukina with mild amusement.

"Since you asked why, Yuu brought you, Kojou, and the rest back here in the middle of the night. Your upperclassman or superior or whoever was with you, the triple-braided older girl."

"Eh…?"

"I mean, wow…I was so surprised. They told me you fainted in the middle of a fight with Shizuri. Your clothes were all a wreck and you had such a bump on your head… I wanted to have Mimori take a look at it but she was, like, that's barely an injury, she'll be just fine and stuff. Ah, Mimori took your upperclassman to the hospital, though. Mimori was really ticked off about her forcing herself to move when she was hurt that bad to begin with."

"I-is that so…"

Sitting on the bed, Yukina nodded vaguely, overwhelmed by Nagisa's verbal barrage.

The upperclassman who was brought to the hospital must have been Koyomi Shizuka. Participating in combat despite her injuries really must have put a great deal of strain on her body.

She was glad that a doctor as capable as Mimori Akatsuki had been the one to examine Koyomi—or maybe she should have thanked Kojou for bringing them home so that Mimori could do so.

"Ah, these are your clothes, Yukina. I washed and ironed them for you."

Nagisa dropped the clothes she clutched against her chest at the foot of Yukina's bed. It was then that Yukina realized she was wearing Nagisa's pajamas. When she looked closer, she saw that her entire body was covered in brand-new compresses and adhesive bandages. Mimori had probably done that, too.

"So why were you and Shizuri fighting anyway? It's because of Kojou, right?"

"Er...that's, ahhh..."

The question posed in such an innocent tone made Yukina go *uhhh*, hesitating to reply. The situation made it really hard to tell Nagisa she had been stopped while trying to sink Itogami Island.

Showing consideration for Yukina being caught red-handed, Nagisa giggled and smiled with amusement.

"Well, fine. If you can't say it with me around, just talk to him and settle it between yourselves quick. I'm going to Keystone Gate so see you."

"Keystone Gate?"

"Yeah, Asagi called me over."

Later, waved Nagisa, leaving the room. Finally, Yukina heard the patter of steps as Nagisa headed out the front door. Yukina was still sitting at the edge of the bed, listening to that sound in a complete daze.

She was overcome for another two to three minutes before she finally regained her senses.

Snowdrift Wolf hadn't been left inside the room. To Kojou and the others, Yukina was clearly an enemy—someone who'd tried to destroy Itogami Island on the government of Japan's orders. Of course they'd disarmed her.

The issue was, why had Kojou brought Yukina into his own home, then? Furthermore, she wasn't restrained or even under guard. She knew that Koyomi had been brought to the hospital, but she didn't know how Yukari or Natsuki was being treated. She had no grasp of the situation whatsoever.

"..."

Yukina sighed a little and put a hand on the buttons of her pajamas.

She wasn't going to solve anything staying in the room by her lonesome. She figured it'd be best to leave the room and gather information.

Stripping off the pajamas borrowed from Nagisa, she put her hands on her freshly washed uniform. She was a little thrown off that even her underwear had been washed. Right after Yukina picked up her bra—

Fwaaa, yawned a relaxed voice with a creak of the sofa.

Yukina, half-naked, lifted her head, only then realizing that the door to her room was still open.

She could see the Akatsuki residence living room straight ahead. On the sofa at the center of it rested Kojou, stretching his back. Looking like he'd just woken up himself, he noticed Yukina standing still, blinking his eyes with a mystified look. For a while, Yukina and Kojou looked at each other like that.

"Eh…?"

"Ah?"

After a brief silence, Yukina and Kojou let out their voices at virtually the same moment.

Apparently, because he had lent the wounded Yukina his own bed, Kojou had slept on the living room sofa, upon which he was just now waking up. Remembering that Nagisa had said just earlier to settle it between themselves, she apparently meant Kojou was right there in the apartment.

"H-Himeragi?"

"Y-yes…er! How long are you going to look at me like that?!"

Yukina covered her breasts with the underwear she'd just grabbed and objected in a shrieking voice.

Kojou swiftly averted his eyes.

"Er, wait, Himeragi. I was just waking up; you were the one suddenly standing there naked, right?!"

"I was in the middle of changing! I never imagined senpai would be here, and besides—"

"I get it already! Sorry! I'll turn this way so change clothes quick…er, shit, tissues! I need tissues…!"

Pressing both hands over his nose, Kojou let out a muffled yelp. Apparently his nose started bleeding from arousal. It was something you'd never expect from the mightiest of vampirekind.

The sight of Kojou's languid figure felt oddly nostalgic, leaving Yukina feeling bewildered. His attitude toward her was so very normal, so usual.

"...It finally stopped... Damnit, why do I have to go through this in the middle of the day..."

Pinching his nostrils, Kojou let out a weary sigh.

Glaring straight at him, Yukina wrung out a tiny voice as she inquired.

"Why...are you?"

"Er, why, I was just surprised...seeing Himeragi's...breasts all of a sudden..."

Kojou blushed as he awkwardly replied. Yukina's face flushed red as she hid her body behind the door.

"That is not what I meant...! I betrayed Akatsuki-senpai and tried to sink Itogami Island! Why aren't you saying anything about that?! It's only natural for senpai to hate me...!"

"Betrayed...whaddaya mean?"

Kojou looked at Yukina with a questioning look. His reaction left Yukina utterly confused.

"Eh?"

"Himeragi's an agent of the Japanese government to be the watcher of the Fourth Primogenitor, right? You're the one who said at the start you came to eliminate me, so what's this betrayal business?"

"Th-that may...be so..."

Like a rusty gear, Yukina made a creaky nod. Certainly, just as he'd said, Yukina's main mission was to watch Kojou, to determine the true nature of the boy named Kojou Akatsuki, and if she judged his existence was a threat, she was granted permission to eliminate him. That was the righteous purpose for which she had been granted the divine armament dubbed Snowdrift Wolf.

"An Attack Mage ordered by the government to come and kill me got ordered by the same government to sink Itogami Island. That all makes sense, right? It's not like I think you betrayed me, Himeragi, so I don't have any reason to be ticked at you..."

"B-but...but...I...!"

Without thinking, Yukina raced out of the bedroom, closing the distance with Kojou.

She understood why Kojou's attitude was unchanged, but she couldn't simply be happy about it. In the end, just how much did he think of her as a watcher, and nothing more?

That said, she had no business blaming Kojou for that. Yukina herself was the one who'd put her Lion King Agency mission ahead of her bonds with him and who'd tried to destroy Itogami Island.

"So, Himeragi, if that doesn't sit well with you, that's your problem."

Kojou calmly spoke those words. He was neither blaming nor admonishing her. He said it in a soft tone of voice as if he were speaking to his own sister.

"My…problem?"

Yukina murmured weakly. *Yeah*, nodded Kojou, with a serious expression she'd rarely seen on him.

"You girls failed in your mission. Ms. Kitty and the Three Saints lady both got captured, so new orders from the Lion King Agency ain't reaching you any more, Himeragi. You've gotta think it over and decide for yourself what you're gonna do from here out. You gonna go to wreck the island, or lend me a hand and help save it?"

"Save…this island?"

Yukina looked at Kojou in surprise. With the Holy Grounds Treaty Organization signatory nations falling silent owing to the Beast Vassal Warheads, the three primogenitors included, there was only one way to save Itogami Island—to sell the island to MAR and live under the Devas' so-called protection.

"Senpai, do you truly intend to sell Itogami Island to MAR?"

"…Maybe I do."

Kojou curtly replied to Yukina's earnest question.

Yukina instantly dismissed his words.

"Liar."

"Eh?"

"That is a…lie. You absolutely will do no such thing… Someone arbitrarily determining the fates of others, is that not what senpai hates most of all…?!"

Yukina declared it without the slightest hesitation. Yukina had watched him all that time. She knew. When Kojou had possessed the power of the World's Mightiest Vampire, he had never even tried to use it for his own sake.

He'd sought power to protect the weak—like his little sister, Nagisa, and the twelfth Avrora—from those who would toy with their destinies and trample upon their dignity through violence. Those were Kojou's enemies.

That was why he would absolutely never accept Deva rule. Kojou could never accept Shahryar Ren's way of thinking, seeking to rule humanity through fear via the Beast Vassal Warheads.

"However, senpai, should you reject Miss Ladli's proposal, MAR will probably use the Beast Vassal Warheads, and millions of people will pay the price... If that happens, you'll be shouldering the responsibility for those who die all by yourself... That's why...!"

Yukina's teary eyes wavered. Her voice was incoherent; her words caught in her throat.

Kojou seemed perplexed as he looked back at Yukina.

"Himeragi, could that be the reason you tried to sink Itogami Island? Because you didn't want me to feel responsible for mass genocide...?"

"I didn't know what else to do...!"

Yukina raggedly shook her head like a little girl.

Kojou wanted all peoples to be safe—Yukina's feelings couldn't compare to that. She thought she could at least bear the sin of destroying Itogami Island in Kojou's place.

"...It's all right, Himeragi. We'll deal with the Beast Vassal Warheads somehow."

Since Yukina wore a desperate expression, Kojou stood up and gave her head a gentle pat.

Yukina wiped her tears with the back of her hand.

"You will...senpai?"

"No. *We'll* deal with it. We're not gonna let Shahryar Ren do whatever the hell he wants."

Kojou said this in an oddly firm tone. Then, seemingly just remembering, he handed Yukina a musical instrument case standing behind the sofa. It was a case for a bass guitar.

"So, Himeragi, I'm returning this to you. Do whatever you want with it."

"Snowdrift Wolf…"

Yukina widened her eyes in surprise as she accepted the gig case. With Snowdrift Wolf, Yukina could go and try to destroy the keystone all over again. Kojou surely understood as much, but it was as if he was saying, *I don't mind. I trust your decision, Himeragi.*

"…Er, it's this time already? Yikes, I overslept. I'd better get ready and go."

Realizing it was past three in the afternoon, Kojou hastily began dressing himself.

"Get ready?"

Yukina inquired, still hugging the case. *Yeah*, nodded Kojou casually.

"I'm meeting Ladli Ren tonight at seven PM right after sunset. What are you gonna do, Himeragi? Coming with me?"

"…I'm not…qualified to participate in a meeting with MAR, not anymore…"

Yukina weakly shook her head. Yukina had tried to sink Itogami Island to obstruct negotiations between Kojou and MAR. *How can I show my face at the meeting now?* thought Yukina.

"Qualified? I don't think Asagi or Cas are qualified for that, or me, for that matter."

Kojou looked at Yukina with a mystified expression. Then he shrugged his shoulders, thinking, *Well fine.*

"…Guess you can't give an answer at the drop of a hat, huh. If you wanna come, come. Decide whatever you want, Himeragi. Later."

Plucking several pieces of candy off the table and popping them in his mouth in place of lunch, Kojou hurriedly went out the door. Not even locking the door seemed like careless behavior, but Yukina thought it was just like him.

It was the same as giving back Yukina her spear. *He trusts me* sounded a lot nicer, but the point was, he was far too open and trusting with people. Did he really plan on working as Itogami Island's ruler armed with great vampire powers and that half-baked personality? She couldn't help but worry. She couldn't take her eyes off him.

That was why she had to watch him, diligently, properly.

"Goodness…what a troublesome vampire you are…"

Furiously wiping the tears from her eyes, Yukina sharply lifted her chin.

There was a powerful glint in her eyes—the glint of someone who'd put something behind her.

6

In the northern tunnel entrance to Keystone Gate, a young girl's sobbing voice echoed throughout a detention cell at Island Guard Headquarters. It was a crying voice full of melancholy and gloom.

"Uuu…let me die already… Even if I was under mind control, slicing my belly is the only way I can make up for turning my blade on Lady Koyomi of the Three Saints… Yukina, I'm so sorry… Forgive me for being the first to pass from this life…!"

The speaker was a tall, slender girl with her knees pulled up to her chest. For all her exaggerated words, both hands were bound behind her back, making it hard for her to use the toilet by herself, let alone slice her belly. Originally, they hadn't even planned on detaining her, but her crying and ranting got annoying, so they tossed her into the Island Guard detention cell to dispose of the nuisance.

"Shut up. You're too noisy, Lion King Agency ponytail girl. If you're going to slit your belly, do it somewhere else! Er, hey, you stray cat! My dress isn't a scratching post! Hey, don't bite it!"

Natsuki Minamiya, confined inside the same cell, spoke with clear displeasure.

Having failed in their raid on the keystone, Natsuki and the others were being treated as sorcerous criminals by Itogami Island. Setting aside the wounded Yukina Himeragi and Koyomi Shizuka, it was only natural for the unscathed Natsuki to be detained like this.

The problem was that she was sharing a cell with the deeply depressed Sayaka and Endou's black cat familiar.

Now that the magical link with Yukari had been cut off, Yukari's familiar had turned into an ordinary, poorly behaved cat. On top of that, the cell interior was covered by a Cleansing barrier, so she couldn't use even a single spell. Even Natsuki couldn't break out, which served to build up a considerable amount of stress.

That was when a teasing voice spoke to Natsuki from the other side of the bars.

"Heya, Teach. Wow, look at you, you're just like a captive princess. Well, you're not quite sexy enough for the role, though."

The man's face had a chummy smile on it. Natsuki glared up without a word.

It was a middle-aged, well-tanned man with an impetuous look. His hair was unkempt, seemingly cut with a knife, and the stubble on his chin stood out. He wore a leather trench coat that was color coordinated with his other clothing. He looked like a member of the Mafia from days gone by, or maybe a down-on-his-luck private detective—he was Gajou Akatsuki, archeologist.

"What do you want, grave robber? I'm not lending you any money."

Natsuki spoke with an air of heartfelt scorn. Gajou grimaced as if faintly taken aback.

"Hey, I didn't come here to ask you for a loan. My idiot son asked me to pay you a visit."

"Kojou Akatsuki…asked *you* for a favor?"

Natsuki's eyes bulged in surprise. Her expression was that of a girl watching pigs flying through the sky.

"Hey now, you don't have to be that surprised. I'm his father. His actual biological father!"

Gajou stressed his words, seemingly offended. *Hmph*, huffed Natsuki, dismissing Gajou's objection.

"Wait, Death Returner…! Just what did you tell him?"

"Hah…ain't you a good guesser. That's Teach for you, huh."

The corners of Gajou's lips rose in a leer.

Natsuki audibly clenched her teeth. Gajou Akatsuki—aka Death Returner—was one of the scant few who'd invaded a Deva ruin and had come back alive. At a time like this, the only thing Kojou would be asking his father about was information concerning the Necropolises.

"Well, if anything, I'm more a man of action than a windbag, but the brat really insisted, so I talked to him a bit about old times."

Deftly evading Natsuki's follow-up, Gajou kept rambling with no small measure of pride. Apparently he was quite pleased his son had depended on him for something.

"…Your son intends to begin something with MAR?"

Natsuki inquired, making a point of cutting Gajou's long explanation short.

"Why don't you find out with your own two eyes?"

Gajou made a pleasant sound in his throat as he touched the door on the detention cell's lock. *Cliiiiick*, echoed a creepy little metallic sound as the resilient lock opened at once.

Gajou Akatsuki had come back from the Necropolis, but even at present, his body still straddled the border between the real world and another. Putting his hand right inside the metallic object and forcing the mechanical cylinder lock open was about as difficult for him as tearing a stretched-out plastic bag from the nearest supermarket.

"Well, as his guardian, it would feel better to have Teach taking good care of him. And you, as a bridal candidate for my son, you need to show off your good side, right?"

Guiding Natsuki and company out of the cell, Gajou made a conceited wink. Sayaka's cheeks reddened at the mention of being his son's bride. *Oh no, I couldn't*, she thought, blushing as Natsuki sighed with deep annoyance.

"Obsessed parent."

Smacked straight in the face by Natsuki's insult, Gajou raised his eyebrows with amusement.

"Ain't denying it."

As he spoke, Gajou picked up the black cat playing around with Natsuki's dress in one fell swoop.

7

As the sun set, Saikai Academy grew unusually silent.

The nearby residents taking shelter inside the school had gone home with the conclusion of the Electoral War. Since classes hadn't resumed, there were no students around, either. The rays of the setting sun dyed the desolate campus building red, with complex shadows cast only by the desks and chairs in the classrooms.

A few students had snuck onto the rooftop of that campus building—

Yaze and Asagi, Shizuri Kasugaya Castiella, and wearing a black cloak he wasn't used to, Kojou.

Thanks to the effects of Sensai Aiba's speech, the surroundings of Keystone Gate were in an uproar, a situation making any careless approach unwise. There were ongoing clashes in the streets between supporters and opponents of the Gigafloat Management Corporation's policy of splitting with the Japanese government and negotiating with MAR on its own.

It wasn't much of a situation for negotiating with terrorists, but even as this went on, the time for the meeting with Ladli Ren approached.

That was when Kojou and the others suddenly decided to change the venue for negotiations.

They wanted a site with a decent amount of size to it, no sign of life in the area, and its own private network connection to Keystone Gate. Hence, Kojou and the others picked a place they knew well—in other words, Saikai Academy.

"Sorry, Kanase, pushing the most dangerous role onto you like this."

Leaning against the rooftop fence, Kojou spoke into a borrowed smartphone.

Its screen showed Kanon Kanase.

It was a real-time video call, but the poor transmission situation made the image dark with a lot of static. Even so, it was more than enough for Kanon's soft, beautiful face to shine through.

At the moment, Kanon was wearing a perfectly skintight wetsuit. This emphasized her delicate yet surprisingly feminine figure, somehow leaving Kojou unsure where his eyes should rest.

Whether she knew of Kojou's indecent thoughts or no, Kanon raised both arms above her head as if to emphasize those body lines on purpose.

"It is all right. It is very cute."

"C…cute…is it?"

The smartphone's little screen cut it out, but the memory of what was outside of the video frame brought a conflicted expression over Kojou.

"There is no need for concern. I am with Miss Kanon, after all."

Cutting into his conversation with Kanon, Yume Eguchi poked her head up into the bottom of the screen. She was wearing the uniform of a famed girls' academy, same as usual.

"Yeah. You take care, too, Yume."

Kojou spoke earnestly. For various reasons, Yume and Kanon were taking independent action far removed from Kojou and company. They were Kojou's trump cards in the negotiations with MAR.

Of course, there was no guarantee everything would go well. If the plan was a bust, the girls would be exposed to great danger. Yume and Kanon understood this full well yet had accepted their duties regardless. They'd requested a fair bit of compensation, though—

"Yes. In exchange, please do not forget your promise. It's a date, just the two of us."

Yume pulled her face close to the camera as she asserted this. Kojou gave her a strained smile and nodded.

"Yeah...all right, I won't forget. How 'bout a sandbox in the park?"

"Do I look like a kindergarten student to you?! Please, I want a more adult-feeling date!"

"Er...you say adult-feeling but, um..."

Yume's genuinely indignant objection put Kojou in quite a bind. Even if she was pretty mature for her age, Yume was still a primary schooler. Kojou felt as if he'd get treated like a criminal if he took her to the wrong place.

"Um...I would like that as well."

Listening to the exchange between Yume and Kojou, Kanon bashfully, reservedly raised her hand.

"You too, Kanon?"

"Yes. An adult date."

Kanon strongly standing up for herself for once made Kojou feel driven even farther into a corner.

Setting aside the age issues, going on an adult date with a close friend of his little sister's felt bad in its own right, all the more so because Kanon was already Kojou's Blood Servant.

"It is a promise. Do not forget."

"Do not forget."

After the pair's voices spoke those words to drive in the point, the video call cut out. They were genuinely beyond signal range.

Kojou sighed with relief, feeling like he'd been bailed out. Abruptly, a voice addressed him from behind.

"Heh…an adult date, is it…? Is that so…?"

The flat, glacial tone made Kojou look back awkwardly. Standing there was a Saikai Academy schoolgirl with a very familiar black gig case on her back.

Her sudden appearance didn't bring about any change in Yaze's and Asagi's expressions. The only one surprised was Kojou.

"…Himeragi?"

"To think, in the brief time you escape my sight, you have promised an adult date not only to Kano, but even to little Yume… I truly cannot let my guard down around a vampire like you for a single moment."

Yukina's expression was clearly annoyed as she sighed very deeply.

Quite so, concurred Shizuri. For some reason, neither Asagi nor Yaze tried to refute them.

"Er…wait a sec; you have to understand what you heard just now, right? It's payback for their cooperation; it's not like I asked them to go out to have fun; they're the ones who—"

"Well, it is fine, really. I shall observe you very closely until the very end to ensure you do not act indecently toward Yume and Kano, senpai."

Yukina sharply lifted her face and shot Kojou a powerful gaze. Her demeanor left Kojou bewildered. He didn't know what had changed her mental state, but Yukina seemed like a completely different person than she had that morning.

"Observe… Wait, Himeragi, your mission's over already, right?"

"I am a Sword Shaman of the Lion King Agency. In accordance with the Attack Mage Act, Section Sixty-Five, I have the duty and authority as an Attack Mage to act to prevent large-scale sorcerous terrorism, even when off duty."

"…Huh?"

Yume's official-sounding words made Kojou blink hard. He found what she'd said utterly incomprehensible.

In place of Kojou, left completely adrift, Yaze laughed with a *kuh, kuh*. Sitting in classic delinquent style on the corner of the roof, he stood up, looking at Yukina with admiration for reasons unknown.

"…I see, an Attack Mage's duty is to stop crime. It's a bit pushy, but checks all the right boxes."

"Yes."

Yukina nodded firmly. Kojou still couldn't understand what they meant.

"Whaddaya mean, Yaze?"

"As long as they don't have a good reason not to, anyone with an Attack Mage license who has knowledge of large-scale sorcerous terrorism is duty-bound to stop it, even if off duty or outside their jurisdiction. In other words, Himeragi can act as watcher of a heinous sorcerous criminal totally independent of the Lion King Agency."

"Heinous sorcerous criminal… Wait, you're not talking about me, are you?"

This ain't right, bespoke the way Kojou twisted his lips, but Yaze spoke with a rational air.

"Until now, the government of Japan never publicly acknowledged that the Fourth Primogenitor exists. That's why Lil' Himeragi ended up tailing you on the Lion King Agency's orders. Now, though, you're the unknown vampire who inherited the Beast Vassals of The Blood. That's reason enough to make you an observation target."

"Considering the damage you've inflicted on Itogami Island to date, you're a pretty heinous criminal as it is."

Asagi grinned heavily as she spoke.

That's all unavoidable stuff, muttered Kojou to himself in clear dissatisfaction. In the first place, Asagi was wrapped up in a lot of the incidents happening on the island, so she counted as a coconspirator for at least half his misdeeds.

"Yukina Himeragi, this is the answer you have reached?"

Shizuri, silent to that point, glared at Yukina, inquiring with a sharp expression on her face.

Koko had a bad feeling as he looked between the pair's faces.

Shizuri and Yukina had been at each other's throats pretty seriously in the lowest stratum of Keystone Gate only the night before. The fight had ended in a draw rather than with any clear winner. Knowing how both hated losing, he was a little worried they'd throw down the gauntlet and pick up where they'd left off.

"Yes…I am Akatsuki-senpai's watcher, just as I have been and always will be."

Yukina stared right back at Shizuri as she spoke. The two continued glaring at each other for one more second. *Hmph*, huffed Shizuri, smiling as she lowered her shoulders.

"Not because the Lion King Agency commands it, but because you decided it? That makes us equal from now on, then…"

"So it does."

Yukina smiled as well.

Shizuri, the Last Paladin of Gisella, had chosen to lend Kojou her strength of her own free will. Now Yukina was the same, acting independent of orders from the Lion King Agency. Perhaps thanks to that, the powder keg atmosphere between Yukina and Shizuri vanished as if it had never existed. Realizing this, Kojou breathed out in relief like a deflating balloon.

Shizuri sighed with exasperation, staring hard at Kojou as he acted like that.

"I really must say, Kojou…is that mantle not somewhat…pretentious?"

"You're the last person I wanna hear that from…but yeah, it is kind of hard to move in this thing."

Looking back at Shizuri, still wearing her blue wimple, Kojou rotated a shoulder.

Kojou was wearing a pitch-black cloak coat. Asagi had forced it onto him, saying it raised his intimidation factor. He also had a gel-hardened hairstyle, which gave off a very different impression than normal. He had no idea if it looked good on him, but the fact remained he just couldn't calm down in the unfamiliar getup.

"This is your fault for not wanting to wear a suit, so put up with it. You can't show up to negotiations in a Saikai Academy uniform."

Asagi chided the sour-faced Kojou. He was forced to concede that she had a point, but still.

"These negotiations with Ladli ain't public, so why can't I wear whatever?"

"Because you look more dignified like this."

Asagi gave him a tongue-lashing as if she were scolding a recalcitrant child.

Yukina interrupted Kojou and Asagi's pointless war of words with a very serious expression.

"More importantly, senpai…how do you intend to negotiate with Miss Ladli? Do not tell me you intend to join forces with MAR and become enemies of the whole world?"

"Well, I thought that wouldn't be so bad, either."

Looking back at the worried Yukina, Kojou gave her a very suggestive smile. Asagi narrowed her eyes with visible amusement.

"If we do that we'll as go down as some of the biggest criminals in history."

"Do you truly mean that…?"

The look in Yukina's eyes sharpened. The fate of the world rested upon these negotiations, yet Kojou and the others were not behaving tensely at all. This seemed to be annoying the girl, but Kojou looked at the irate Yukina with an amused-looking smile.

"If I do that, you'll stop me, though, right, Himeragi?"

"Ah…"

Yukina stopped moving, seemingly shaken. Then, for whatever reason, she acted her usual, overly serious self, nodding with powerful resolve.

"Yes. I am your watcher for just this purpose."

Soon after that, Itogami Island was enveloped by an intense magical aura.

Complex magic circles supported by vast magical energy floated in the sky, still tinted by vestiges of red light. It was the enormous gate leading to Nod.

Its final traces extinguished, the sun completely sank over the water's horizon.

"Sunset, huh?"

Unconsciously, a rugged smile crossed Kojou's face as he spoke. This announced the end of daytime on the artificial isle of everlasting summer, signaling that night had come to the Demon Sanctuary.

A roar like thunder echoed, and an ashen sphere appeared above Kojou and the others' heads.

The enormous fortress floated in the sky like a second moon, the lordly castle hailing from another world.

"That is…a Necropolis…!"

A quiet murmur trickled from Yukina as she gazed up at the sky.

The Demon Sanctuary was encountering this Necropolis for the second time.

It was the beginning of the negotiations with the fate of the world at stake.

CHAPTER FOUR
FORTIFIED NECROPOLIS

1

"My shadow is mist and mist not, blade and blade not—"

Kiriha Kisaki raised her spear as she danced. All sight of her vanished, melting into thin air.

Using physical enchantment to heighten her body's capabilities paired with illusion targeting observers, this tactic enabled her to attack at speeds beyond human recognition.

"Slice as a phantasm, reverberate as the echo of catastrophe!"

Appearing right in the middle of the heavily armed troops, she swung her spear as it reverberated with the beautiful echo of a tuning fork. Fresh blood splattered as one soldier cried out after the next.

They were at the tiny cape floating in the sea of clouds. An MAR special forces unit of eight men had disembarked from a transport craft only for Kiriha to utterly crush them single-handedly.

"So that is...a Priestess of the Six Blades of the Bureau of Astrology..."

A grave look came over Yuiri as she spoke, hiding behind a rise in the ground.

Aside from directly targeting vitals, Kiriha hadn't really held back at all. The sight of her smiling gently while showered in blood spatter made it all the more ghoulish and terrifying. The hardened special forces soldiers' faces were twitching in fear as they began to retreat.

"How did Kirasaka win against that...I'd heard she beat up a girl until she cried and apologized, but..."

Lowering the bow with which she had meant to back up Kiriha, Shio wearily exhaled.

"I heard you, Lion King Agency. Of course no such thing happened."

Seeing that the enemy had been sent packing, Kiriha was wiping the blood from her cheeks as she glared at Shio. Then she looked behind Shio and Yuiri—directing her gaze at the badly sewn teddy bear Avrora was hugging.

"Well, fine. Mogwai, you said? Might we continue our earlier conversation?"

"...*Hmm, what conversation was that?*"

Mogwai, still in Avrora's embrace, blatantly averted his eyes. Kiriha pointed the bloody tip of her forked spear right at him.

"Don't play games with me. I'll kill you in a heartbeat. Don't tell me you brought us all the way to Nod to help with small fry like that?"

"*Hey, don't call 'em small fry. They're MAR elites with Deva blood in 'em.*"

Keh-keh, Mogwai laughed sarcastically as he watched the fleeing transport craft go. Kiriha furrowed her brows in silence.

"Devas...they are with Shahryar Ren?"

"Shouldn't ancient superhumans be tougher than that?"

Yuiri and Shio prompted back, mildly bewildered.

Until Shahryar Ren had revealed his own ancestry, the race known as Devas was thought to be a legendary existence that had died off long ago. They were said to be ancient superhumans possessing a high degree of sorcerous technology served by beast people, giants, and many other demon races. It was said that they wielded a supernatural force known as divine power, and that the spiritual energy Yuiri and company possessed was obtained through cross-breeding between Devas and human ancestors.

To be blunt, if the soldiers from earlier represented the superhuman might of the Devas, they seemed to have expected too much. Mogwai, though, made a shrug-like gesture with his little head.

"*Seems like just having had Deva ancestors a bunch of generations ago doesn't give 'em combat abilities that much different from humans.*"

"So they really were small fry."

Kirha coldly spat out the words. *Keh-keh*, laughed Mogwai in his throat.

"Well, there's another reason why those guys felt weak to you."

"I am not interested. More importantly, foul creature, speak about these Beast Vassal Warheads. What do you mean, this facility is for sealing the warheads?"

"Pretty much what it sounds like. The artificial isle Senra you can see from here was built as a Beast Vassal Warhead stockpile to begin with, a safe place where there's zero chance of 'em going off."

Mogwai, making a pained smile at the *foul creature* remark, lifted his face up toward the surface of the sea above them.

"What do you mean, a place where they cannot go off?"

Kiriha's expression remained unchanged as she inquired further. Mogwai grinned with amusement.

"Didn't ya hear from my Fourth Primogenitor Bro? Ya can't use demonic energy in Nod."

"Can't use demonic energy?"

Shio widened her eyes in surprise. Yuiri gasped, looking back as she just remembered something.

"So that's why the special forces team from just now felt so fragile?"

"Most of 'em should have equipment that runs on demonic energy. Without magic energy, their gear and their magic users ain't all that powerful."

Mogwai added an exaggerated wave of his hand as he explained.

"It's worse for actual demons. Demons who need demonic energy just to live can't survive in Nod to start with. Even if it ain't that severe, most demons are gonna be weakened. You can't bestialize, and vampires can't use Beast Vassals. Well, with one exception."

Speaking those words, Mogwai glanced up at Avrora, the one hugging him against her chest. Avrora's gaze drifted as if nothing going on seemed real.

Shio and the others knew that the Fourth Primogenitor was a special vampire.

To destroy Cain the Sinful God, who could not be felled by any other means, the Devas produced a god-killing weapon expressly for that purpose. The girls didn't know the methodology involved, but if only those particular Beast Vassals could be summoned in Nod, a place where demonic energy supposedly did not exist, they could understand what made the Fourth Primogenitor so special.

"—MAR brought seven Beast Vassal Warheads to the surface. The rest of 'em are still in the storage facility. I'm using Blondie here's power to keep the facility sealed, y'see."

"I see. So that's why MAR's after this place."

Makes sense, thought Shio, nodding in response to Mogwai's words.

Avrora, the Fourth Primogenitor, had enough demonic energy to open the gate connecting Nod and Itogami Island all by herself. Mogwai was employing her demonic energy to stop the Beast Vassal Warheads in the storage facility from being hauled away.

"That's why you brought us here? To protect you?"

Kiriha glared at Glenda, standing beside Yuiri and Shio and looking a little bored.

Dah, thought Glenda, nodding immediately. Shio and Yuiri spontaneously shielded Glenda behind them.

"More like she brought us and you just got caught up in it, Kiriha Kisaki."

"S-Shio, you can't just say something like that!"

"…This doesn't sit well with me."

Kiriha spun on her heels and turned to face Avrora and Mogwai.

"Avrora Florestina inherited the Beast Vassals of the Fourth Primogenitor from Kojou Akatsuki, right? Shouldn't she be able to easily send mongrels like that packing without needing our help?"

"Keh-keh…you'd have a point—if Blondie here really could control the Fourth Primogenitor's Beast Vassals, that is."

Mogwai replied in place of the wordless Avrora. *I get it*, Shio murmured aloud.

"The Beast Vassals don't recognize Avrora as their master yet, do they?"

"'T-tis my failing."

Avrora continued to clutch Mogwai as her delicate shoulders narrowed even further.

According to the reports from Yukina Himeragi that had reached Shio and Yuiri's ears, the Beast Vassals of the Fourth Primogenitor had particularly dangerous dispositions. Kojou Akatsuki himself hadn't been able to summon the Beast Vassals freely until just prior to the conclusion of the War of the Primogenitors. That was after the passage of nine months since inheriting the Fourth Primogenitor's power.

It was likely that, just like him, Avrora did not yet have a handle on her own Beast Vassals. Compared to the human Kojou Akatsuki, she should have had considerably greater compatibility with the Beast Vassals, but trying to simply force them to obey ran a high risk of making them go berserk.

"So, Bureau of Astrology miss. I forgot to mention one other important thing."

Mogwai spoke in an atypically serious tone of voice. One of Kiriha's eyebrows twitched higher.

"I wonder what?"

"Even if she could use the Fourth Primogenitor's Beast Vassals, it ain't easy to protect this place. This is Nod, after all."

"You've been beating around the bush since the beginning. What are you trying to say?"

Kiriha stared intently at him in annoyance. Shio gasped with a serious expression on her face.

"Oh…right, he's here in Nod, too…"

"Got it in one, short-haired miss."

Mogwai curled up only one side of his mouth. Kiriha dubiously prompted back.

"Him?"

"Right, you haven't actually met him yet have you? Him—the other pinnacle of demonkind right up there with vampire primogenitors."

Mogwai spoke in a provocative tone of voice. Kiriha drew in a breath slightly. She realized what Mogwai had been hinting at.

"Yuiri, Shio."

Glenda abruptly addressed the pair. It was in a clear voice, not her usual lisping tone.

Yuiri and Shio were perplexed when they casually turned their eyes toward her. Standing there was not the silver-haired girl the pair knew.

Along with the young Glenda, another Glenda stood there, pale and transparent like a ghost.

They resembled each other like sisters, but the two were clearly different from one another. The physical Glenda looked ten years old, give or take. The other one, the illusion, looked as old as Yuiri and Shio at minimum. Also, just like Avrora, she was wearing a school uniform greatly resembling that of Saikai Academy.

"Glenda…?"

"Are you…Glenda, too?"

"Yes, I am. More accurately, I suppose I am who Glenda used to be."

Gazing gently upon the bewildered pair, the Glenda illusion spoke in a teasing fashion.

That instant, Yuiri and Shio instinctively understood. The physical form of this Glenda illusion no longer existed. It had probably vanished thousands of years ago.

The Glenda that Yuiri and Shio knew had traces of artificial genetic manipulation. The dragon had probably been created as a successor to the being known as Glenda long ago.

"I ask that you, my friends beyond the bounds of time, lend me a small portion of your strength, so that the wish of my master, Cain the Sinful God, might be fulfilled—"

The Glenda illusion glanced at Mogwai as she spoke. Mogwai blatantly averted his eyes.

"Cain's…wish?"

Seeing Shio ask that guarded question, the illusionary girl nodded warmly. This left Shio and Yuiri unable to ask any more, for her eyes contained the same undiluted trust that shone in young Glenda's eyes.

"…Sheesh. Speak of the devil…"

Mogwai abruptly looked overhead, commenting as if it were someone else's problem. Avrora, holding him against her chest, twitched her shoulders in visible fear.

Once more, MAR transport craft were approaching from Senra, the steel-colored artificial city floating on the sea's surface.

The tilt-rotor transport craft was the same model as those they'd sent packing earlier, but these were weaponized types equipped with air-to-ground rockets and machine guns.

Furthermore, they could see a copper demon beast behind them, spreading its giant wings.

The enormous, hostile creature was larger than the transport craft. It had a long tail and four stout limbs. Vast heat generated by its cells made its entire body seem to shimmer like a mirage. It was a legendary monster that lorded over all demonkind.

"Dragon incoming."

Mogwai acted pretty casually about it as he spoke.

Flying above their heads, Kreyd the Flame Dragon savagely roared as soon as it spotted Mogwai and the others.

2

Back on the rooftop of Saikai Academy's school building, a girl in a gaudy outfit appeared, surrounded by the mirage-like shimmer that went hand in hand with teleportation magic.

"Good evening, Mr. Ruler. We meet again."

Twirling her cane like a stage magician, Ladli Ren surveyed the members of Kojou Akatsuki's group gathered on the rooftop one by one: Kojou and Yaze, Asagi, and then Shizuri, at which point she tilted her head with a questioning look.

"Mr. Motoki Yaze, representing the Gigafloat Management Corporation, Miss Asagi Aiba, Priestess of Cain and Mr. Ruler's Blood Servant… now then, who might you be? You would appear to be ogre royalty?"

"I am Shizuri Kasugaya Castiella."

Shizuri spoke boldly and plainly, her demeanor utterly unchanged even in the face of one of MAR's top executives. *Er*, thought Ladli, looking like she was taken aback. *Pfft*, laughed Kojou.

"She's my Blood Servant, too. You don't mind if I have a bodyguard here with me, do you?"

"Blood Servant—wife, in other words? But of course. Many wives lead to prosperous lives, quite a prize…"

Ladli glanced between Asagi and Shizuri, beaming and quite proud of herself. Apparently she thought *wives*, *lives*, and *prize* made for quite a rhyme.

"…May I cut this woman down?"

"Calm down, Cas."

When Shizuri mercilessly put her hand on the hilt of her long sword, Kojou stopped her with an annoyed look. *Who is this Cas?* said the way Shizuri bared her teeth as she glared at Kojou.

Yukina sighed a little as she gazed at the complex expressions on the pair. Yaze looked very amused for some reason as he rudely indicated Yukina with a thumb.

"And one prisoner in the custody of the Gigafloat Management Corporation."

"...?!"

Yukina nearly blurted something out. For whatever reason, she was being treated in that place not as Kojou's watcher but as a prisoner associated with the Japanese government.

Ladli glanced at the bewildered Yukina with a dubious air.

"...Prisoner?"

"Yeah, actually, last night, a bunch of people tried to destroy the keystone of Itogami Island on the government of Japan's orders."

Asagi replied to Ladli's question. Yukina silently bit her lip.

"Oh my...I guess they struck out at the plate? The keystone they tried to destroy became their tombstone."

Ladli commented with amusement, glancing at Yukina's reaction out of the corner of her eye. Shizuri gripped the hilt of her sword and subdued her anger, but Asagi indulged in a giggle.

"Pretty much, yeah."

"I see, so that is the reason why you decided to engage in negotiations with us?"

I see, I see, Ladli nodded in understanding.

It was very much true the government of Japan had used Yukina and company to attack the keystone. It might have been for the laudable cause of destroying the gate to Nod, but she'd betrayed Itogami Island all the same.

In one sense, Itogami Island joining hands with MAR in defiance was a natural decision to make. On both military and economic fronts, the only chance of defying the Holy Grounds Treaty Organization military rested with MAR and its vast number of Beast Vassal Warheads.

"Very well. May I ask, then? Do you agree with MAR's purchase of Itogami Island, or do you not?"

Ladli posed that blunt question to Kojou.

Yukina stopped breathing as she looked over at Kojou. A smile had formed on his lips. Thanks to the unfamiliar cloak coat, Kojou seemed like a completely different person from the one Yukina knew.

"Before we do that, won't you show us your power, Ladli Ren?"

Kojou shot Ladli an intense gaze.

"Our power...you say?"

Ladli puffed out one cheek in a slight pout. Kojou smiled and nodded.

"I mean, that's just obvious, right? A while back we sent an HGTO fleet packing all by ourselves. Coming and bragging about doing the same thing just makes a guy wonder."

"You would test us, Kojou Akatsuki? As a Deva, I am somewhat chagrined, but you make a reasonable point."

Ladli strove to maintain a composed tone as she spoke. Back during the War of the Primogenitors, Itogami Island had engaged in combat with an HGTO military multinational armada, sending it running with its tail between its legs. She must have been recalling that.

Itogami Island had The Cleansing, and Kojou had his black Beast Vassals. Kojou was asking MAR if it truly had commensurate power.

To Ladli, this was most likely an unexpected proposal, but she agreed to it with ease.

"Very well. Please state whatever you desire that would satisfy your side."

This time, it was Ladli's side testing Kojou with a question.

Kojou nodded with satisfaction and spoke casually.

"We wanna see the might of the Beast Vassal Warheads one more time. A fleet's too puny a target. I'm interested in what happens if you fire one at, say, a big city for instance."

"Senpai?!"

Yukina's eyes flew wide open as she looked at Kojou, but a cold blade was pressed to her throat before Yukina could continue with further objections. Shizuri had drawn her crimson long sword, turning it toward Yukina.

"Calm thyself, Yukina Himeragi. This is a negotiation."

Shizuri spoke in an emotionless voice. Yukina was incredulous as she listened. She didn't think Shizuri, self-proclaimed Paladin of Gisella, would so easily sacrifice millions of innocent people.

The same went for Kojou, but it was the government of Japan that had attempted to sacrifice the uninvolved people of Itogami City. If the Japanese government's attempt to sink Itogami Island truly made Kojou and the others furious, the condition they'd issued was certainly not incomprehensible.

"It seems this is no mere bluff from you, Kojou Akatsuki...but are you truly fine with this? Once a Beast Vassal Warhead is fired, there is no going back."

Ladli pressed the point with Kojou. To her, Kojou and company's terms had to be more than a little outside her expectations, but Kojou nodded with a cold smile.

"The government of Japan laid a hand on my turf first. Even if we blow Tokyo off the map, they can't really complain, can they?"

"Sen...pai..."

Yukina murmured in a broken voice. Not knowing Kojou's true intent left her in chaos. Just as Ladli had said, once fired, a Beast Vassal Warhead could not be stopped. Even if the objective was to reduce the Beast Vassal Warheads remaining, blowing up Tokyo for that purpose was far too great a sacrifice. She didn't think goading MAR into firing a warhead held any meaning.

Asagi and Yaze made no move to stop Kojou even so. Shizuri's blade remained immobile against Yukina's throat.

"Very well, Mr. Ruler. Just as you wish, we Devas shall demonstrate our power."

Ladli shrugged her shoulders in a show of exasperation as she spoke. Then she looked over Kojou's assembled group, pointing to the spherical fortress floating overhead.

"Now then, allow me to invite all of you to our Necropolis, Castle Kalenaren—it's showtime! Just kidding."

3

The sky of Nod shuddered with a screech-like roar.

This roar wove huge magic circles in the sky and became spells chanted at an ultrahigh density impossible for human vocal cords.

The magic circles created and amplified a shockwave accompanied by a destructive ray of light. It was Freikugel Plus's ritual spell artillery attack.

The beam of light mowed down the MAR soldiers and the moss-covered soil of the cape with them. A tilt-rotor transport craft caught in the attack lost its balance, falling into the sea of clouds below.

Even so, as she kept her silver-colored recurve bow raised, Shio's expression was hard and tense with fear.

The ritual spell artillery attack beam vanished, leaving the gouged soil exposed to sight. Wriggling upon it was a horde of bizarre monsters—a horde of soldiers covered with white exoskeletons.

"What are these things?! They shrugged off my artillery attack…?!"

Shio's voice trembled with nervousness. Freikugel Plus's ritual spell artillery attack could exhibit might close to that of a Fourth Primogenitor's Beast Vassal for a brief instant. These skeletal soldiers had taken a direct hit from her attack, yet remained active, virtually unscathed.

"Ahh, those must be Spartoi."

Still in Avrora's arms, Mogwai whistled, visibly surprised. Shio narrowed her eyes, perplexed.

"Spartoi? What are those…?"

"Apparently, artificial demons made from culturing dragon cells. They're not sentient, but they have magic resistance equal to a dragon. They're tough. That bastard Shahryar Ren must've figured out normal troops weren't gonna cut it so he sent these things in."

"Like it's not your problem, too?!"

Shio bit her lip as she notched a fresh arrow, but the Spartoi moved faster. They closed the distance, moving like bugs as they assaulted Shio before she could take aim.

"Rosen Chevalier Plus, Boot Up—!"

Yuiri leaped in, swinging her silvery long sword downward. Charging undaunted into the horde of Spartoi, she sliced into them along with their thick exoskeleton armor. Granted an effect equal to slicing through space itself, Rosen Chevalier Plus's slicing attacks were effective even against Spartoi, with flesh as hard as that of a dragon.

"Yuiri!"

"Shio, get back! Take care of Avrora and Glenda!"

Cutting down six Spartoi in the blink of an eye, she'd apparently gained a feel for fighting them. Yuiri smiled strongly toward Shio and the others.

Yet as she watched, the expression rising over Shio was one of surprise, foreboding, and despair.

"No, Yuiri! Not yet! They're still moving!"

"Eh…?!"

The Spartoi she thought she'd defeated were rising behind Yuiri once more. They weren't so much regenerating as forcing their sliced bodies to reconnect, which was more than sufficient for the *hollow* Spartoi, which lacked internal organs.

The cutting edge of Rosen Chevalier Plus was so fine, it kept them mostly intact.

"Why, youuu…!!"

Shio shot a cursed arrow toward the regenerating Spartoi. A small-scale whirlwind arose to envelop Yuiri's surroundings, blowing the Spartoi remains in every direction. It wasn't a real solution, but even the Spartoi couldn't bounce back right away if they were missing body parts. Denying them their combat abilities was good enough for the moment.

"Ohhh…not bad, missies."

Mogwai spoke with obvious praise. Avrora's blue eyes were wide open as she clapped excitedly.

"This is nothing."

Shio replied with a strong tone as her shoulders rose and fell. The fight with the Spartoi made her truly understand the peculiarities of Nod and its lack of demonic energy.

Magic spells and ritual spells greatly resembled each other, but there was a fundamental difference in how they worked. Magic used real-world elements like ley lines and celestial bodies to create supernatural phenomena. In contrast, ritual spells drew on the living energy from the caster's own flesh and blood and the natural world.

Shio and the others were able to use ritual spells in Nod, where magic energy did not exist, through the caster sacrificing her life force, using it as fuel to generate ritual energy. The Spartoi were probably able to function in Nod because they were constructed from a dragon's flesh.

The issue being, Shio and the others could only use as much ritual energy as their bodies could withstand.

If anything, thanks to being unable to borrow strength from ley lines or the natural world, their ritual energy depletion was more severe than on the surface. On top of that, Freikugel Plus wasn't exactly a ritual energy–efficient weapon. The same applied to Yuiri's Rosen Chevalier Plus. Prolonged combat was dangerous. They had to concentrate their forces as much as possible and settle this as soon as possible.

"Where is Kiriha Kisaki…?"

Shio posed this question to Avrora, standing right next to her. Avrora gasped and lifted her face.

"She is…right behind thee."

Avrora's unexpected reply made Shio unwittingly spin around. Shio's back was struck by the impact of someone suddenly kicking her hard.

"Out of my way, Shio Hikawa!"

Shio heard Kiriha's jeering voice as she rolled on the ground, with Avrora caught up in the process. A severe, hot wind blew at her back. An incandescent beam unleashed by the dragon raced past Shio and the others from overhead.

"What's the big idea?! That's dangerous, Kiriha Kisaki!"

Enduring the pain at her back, Shio looked behind and lodged her complaints.

Hah?! Kiriha's scornful glance seemed to say, before immediately returning her gaze to the copper Flame Dragon whirling in the skies above.

"I wonder, are the Lion King Agency's monkeys incapable of speaking a single word of thanks for saving them? I have my hands full against a dragon. I have no time to worry about deadweight."

"No time? I thought you Priestesses of the Six Blades were experts in antidemon beast combat?"

"Would you like to trade places with me, then? Right now perhaps? You should be thanking me for holding an ancient dragon at bay without proper manpower or equipm—!!"

Before Kiriha finished her words, the Flame Dragon belched fire once more. Shio and Kiriha picked up the still-on-the-ground Avrora on both sides, hastily fleeing outside of the flames' effective range.

"Hold back an ancient dragon? Don't you mean being chased around by it?"

"Shut up. I'll kill you...!"

Shio's unwittingly caustic remark caused Kiriha to shoot her a hostility-filled glare. Being forced to run around in circles had apparently piled up quite a bit of stress upon her.

"That girl you called Glenda, can't she fight?"

Kiriha surveyed the area as she posed that question. The dragon girl with steel-colored hair should have been inside the tower at the tip of the cape at present. She didn't seem to be hiding, but rather, doing something that she felt she had to do.

"Hey... Don't tell me you want to make Glenda fight that thing head-on?!"

Shio objected to Kiriha's line of questioning as she gazed up at the huge Flame Dragon overhead. Even if she was a fellow dragon, the ancient dragon Kreyd was at least twice as large as the barely hatched Glenda. Shio didn't think it would be much of a contest.

For her part, Kiriha sullenly tapered her lips.

"What? She's a dragon, too, right?"

"Keh-keh...sorry to disappoint you, but that ain't happening. She's in no condition to do that right now."

Mogwai, clinging to Shio's hip, interrupted in a grandiose tone. Tossed when Avrora rolled to the ground, he'd apparently hastily clamped on to Shio's skirt.

"What do you mean? Is that related to why you were holed up in this facility?"

Shio picked Mogwai up roughly. From the comfortable touch, weight, and feel of the material, he really did seem to be just a teddy bear.

"Sorry, but no time to explain that. He's comin'."

"What?"

Mogwai dodged the subject as Shio looked up at the dragon overhead.

Kreyd the Flame Dragon wasn't breathing fire, perhaps out of fear Avrora would be caught in it. In turn, he landed at the center of a force of Spartoi, digging up the ground as he touched down. Enveloped by an incandescent glow, his huge body suddenly shrank, turning into a large-statured dragon-man with scales covering his entire body.

"What does that ancient dragon intend to do...?"

"He released his dragon form so he can take Avrora with him...!"

Kiriha and Shio stepped forward to shield Avrora.

Yuiri put distance between herself and the group of Spartoi, getting into a low, guarded stance.

Shio and Yuiri, unaccustomed to fighting demon beasts, found this kind of fight easier than taking on a huge dragon, but Kreyd the Flame Dragon didn't feel any less intimidating in his dragon-man form. Working in concert with the Spartoi arguably made him even more dangerous.

"Avrora...Florestinaaaaaa...!"

White steam leaked out of the edges of Kreyd's lips as he roared.

Avrora, hiding behind Shio and company's backs, drew in a sharp breath in fear.

Seemingly controlled by the dragon's thoughts, the Spartoi began advancing all at once. They accelerated at an incredible rate that contrasted with how weighty their exoskeletons looked.

"*Tch!* Back me up, Lion King Agency!"

Arbitrarily dropping those words in Shio's lap, Kiriha raced out toward Kreyd. Ignoring the destroyed but soon to regenerate Spartoi, she must have wanted to neutralize Kreyd first.

She hated taking orders from Kiriha, but her assessment was on the money. Shio notched a fresh ritual arrow and aimed at Kreyd. She tried to draw Kreyd's attention to her to support Kiriha.

Kreyd's attack proved swifter. Before Shio could even fire her cursed arrow, his enormous jaw opened wide, and the dragon-man released a scorching beam.

"Wait...! He can breathe fire in humanoid form, too?!"

The unexpected counterattack startled Shio, making her break off her ritual spell artillery attack. Grabbing Avrora, she leaped to the side to evade the flames. Using physical enchantment past her limits made her entire body groan, but she had no time to care.

"Black Thunder—!"

Kiriha accelerated to superhuman speeds, slamming her forked spear into Kreyd's thin flesh. She'd imbued her spear with the ritual of pseudo-spatial severing identical to that of Rosen Chevalier Plus. No matter how resilient a dragon's flesh, it absolutely could not withstand such an attack…if Kiriha's attack actually hit.

"Wha…?!"

Kiriha's expression twisted in shock. In dragon-man form, Kreyd's reaction speed far exceeded Kiriha's acceleration, even with her ritual energy at its utmost limit. Kiriha's attack futilely sliced through the air as she was struck by an impact in turn.

The swing of Kreyd's dragon-man fist made a dull sound of bones breaking echo forth. Ricercare flew out of Kiriha's hands. Her left arm bent at an unnatural angle, Kiriha smashed to the ground, unable to even cry out as she rolled around.

"Kiriha Kisaki!"

"Miss Kisaki!"

Shio and Yuiri both shouted. Seeing Kreyd with an eye on the fallen Kiriha, the pair instantly leaped forward, each launching simultaneously timed attacks.

"—Reverberate!"

"Rosen Chevalier Plus!"

Shio used all the spell tablets she had on hand to summon bird-of-prey-style *shikigamis*. Using these as a distraction, Yuiri unloaded a lethal slicing attack. Their paired attack was timed so perfectly, it was as if they'd worked it out beforehand. Surely even a dragon's reaction speed couldn't defend against this.

Shio's and Yuiri's thoughts were easily shattered by the dazzling beam. Kreyd's breath of incandescent flames burned away Shio's *shikigamis* in an instant and blocked Yuiri's approach.

Blast winds slammed Shio all over her body. As she lost her sense of equilibrium, her consciousness grew distant. She'd somehow evaded a direct hit from the flames, but she couldn't fend off the shockwave as well.

Also, in the corner of Shio's hazy vision, she saw Yuiri slowly fall to the ground. Yuiri had been bathed in Kreyd's flames head-on from point-blank range. Her upper half cruelly burned by flames, she collapsed onto the molten soil, her silver-colored long sword clanging as it rolled across the ground.

4

Nagisa Akatsuki stood still in the corner of a dimly lit room resembling the bottom of a very deep well.

She was inside an isolated block hidden under Keystone Gate.

Above her, walls spiraled upward. Carved upon the walls were strange symbols in lines like some sort of spell. The unfamiliar characters carved into the stone's surface covered the entirety of the walls.

These were characters that had never existed in all of human history.

These were the records—the memories—left behind by someone inhuman.

Looking up at these, Nagisa's eyes showed no hint of fear. What she felt was the kind of reserved curiosity of a girl peeking into someone's private diary.

"Hello, Nagisa Akatsuki. Welcome to Cain's Coffin."

A mechanical, synthesized voice echoed through the center of the room. It was a little girl's voice.

"Hello. Um, so you're the AI Asagi told me about?"

Looking up at the strange 3D image hovering in midair, Nagisa tilted her head a little, seemingly unsure.

If she had to put it into words, the 3D image was like a dog with a beak growing on it, a very strange look for a plush toy. She wouldn't exactly call the design creepy, but at the very least, it wasn't cute. She thought there were a few…minor issues with Asagi's sense of aesthetics.

The AI avatar ignored Nagisa's impressions and smiled.

"Yes. I am Version VII of the Spriggan Series—please call me Kikimora."

"Got it. Nice to meet you, Kikimora. So what should I do? Er, also, why did I have to change into a swimsuit?"

Looking down at herself, Nagisa voiced that question while blushing a little at the competition swimsuit she was wearing. The outfit had electrodes and sensors all over it, but even if no one was watching, she felt a little embarrassed by how the skintight outfit accentuated her body lines.

Kikimora calmly evaded Nagisa's question.

"Master has instructed that it is faster to explain to you through experience than through words."

"Er…meaning what…?"

Nagisa brought her eyebrows together and glared at Kikimora. That moment, Nagisa felt a cool sensation on the soles of her feet through her high socks. Unbeknownst to her, at some point a large quantity of water had begun coursing into the sealed chamber Nagisa was in.

"Wa…Wait a… Water? Why is…? Er, it's cold?! Wait, hold on, what's the big idea?! I'm not exactly good at swimming actually…!"

Nagisa was very nervous as she closed the distance with Kikimora. She'd been told the room known as Cain's Coffin was actually part of a huge submarine. Any way she thought about it, having the inside fill with water was a fairly bad situation to be in.

"*Connection to the Gate, complete. Throughput stability confirmed. Entering synchro mode with 'Glenda.' Beginning memory projection—*"

In contrast to the consternated Nagisa, Kikimora spoke with an emotionless, mechanical air, seemingly checking off items on an unseen list.

During that time, the volume of water inside the room increased further, reaching as high as tiny Nagisa's chest. The flow of the water undermined her footing, making Nagisa tumble. She sank to the bottom.

Her long, bundled-up hair came undone, spreading and hovering within the water.

Freed from the forces of gravity, she lost her sense of what was up and down.

Strangely, even though she was floating inside water, she didn't have any difficulty breathing. She didn't feel the cold of the water. It wasn't dark. The walls faintly glowed, projecting an unknown landscape from afar. Nagisa knew this feeling. The vague memories of her prior experience came into the back of her mind.

"This is…like back at Kannawa Lake…"

Someone's memories flowed into Nagisa's mind.

They were unclear, haphazardly connected memories, like some sort of jury-rigged contraption, but this was all the girls had to offer. These were girls kept asleep in a fresh, newborn state.

At least until someone granted them genuine joy, genuine sadness—

"*—Do you love this island, Nagisa Akatsuki?*"

"This island? You mean Itogami Island?"

The AI's abrupt question threw off Nagisa a little.

She hadn't wanted to move to the island. Heavily injured by a demon attack, she was told she needed the technology of a Demon Sanctuary to heal her. She'd spent a lot of time in bed. It had only been lately that she'd been able to walk freely. Even in the present, she felt pangs of fear every time she passed a demon on a city street.

The sunrays were too strong, and the artificially constructed skyline lacked elegance. The sea breeze made her hair stick, and she had to admit, it rained too much. Even so, asked whether she loved it, Nagisa did not hesitate to answer.

"Yeah. I love it… Even though I've been through a lot, I still…love this place. I mean, I got to meet everyone, Asagi, Yaze-cchi, Yukina, Kano, everyone else in class…and…yeah… December and Avrora, too—"

Nagisa's vision was filled by a soft light. The strands of her hair floating in the water became pure white spiritual essence, stretching who knew how far. The warm feeling filling her chest spread out like a wave. She felt like her own thoughts were being conveyed to girls whose faces she did not know in a world unfamiliar to her.

"He has been waiting for you all this time—for a priestess whose heart has reached the Kaleid Bloods. Cain the Sinful God has awaited someone who can bestow false memories, and hope for the future, to the pitiable Numbers—"

Kikimora's robotic voice overlapped with hundreds, thousands of girls' voices. They were the voices of those who had passed down Cain's will over a span of time great enough to boggle the mind—the voices of the Priestesses of Cain throughout all of history.

"Cain's…hope…I see…now I understand…what I can do…"

Amid that light, her hazy vision became more vivid.

An unfamiliar landscape floated up. Beneath her eyes, all was buried by a white sea of clouds. Above her head spread the surface of a limitless sea. Upon its twinkling waves floated an artificial isle greatly resembling Itogami Island.

"I just need to send this to the girls, huh?"

Murmuring, Nagisa slowly stepped forward, steel-colored hair swaying behind her.

5

"Yuiri…!!"

Shio's cry, nearly a scream, echoed through Nod's sky.

The heavily wounded Yuiri was on the ground, limp and unmoving. Kiriha tried to stand up, but managed only to violently cough up fresh blood. She'd taken a lot of damage herself.

Kreyd gazed down at Shio and the others with emotionless eyes. The scales covering his entire dragon-man body were emitting a great deal of heat. He was preparing to breathe fire once more.

Realizing this, Avrora stepped forward with an uncertain gait. She was trying to shield Shio and the others. Even as her entire body quavered in fear, she glared at the combat-ready Kreyd.

"…B-begone…Flame Dragon…!"

Avrora stretched her right arm toward the dragon-man. The gesture was as if to summon a Beast Vassal. She was trying to threaten him with all her might.

"Avrora…quit it…!"

"R…un!"

The wounded Shio and Yuiri weakly shouted. Dragons were considered among the strongest of demonkind, right up there with vampire primogenitors. Avrora couldn't use her Beast Vassals properly. They didn't think she stood a chance.

"It is…futile, Avrora Florestina… Come…with me…"

Suspending his attack, Kreyd spoke in a grating, difficult-to-hear voice.

Avrora made tiny shakes of her head. A distinct aura of rejection hovered in her radiant blue eyes. Kreyd made a low growl in his throat.

"…If you will not…obey…I shall…make you."

Kreyd slowly spread out both arms. Avrora paled when she saw this.

Still in dragon-man form, Kreyd's fingertips exposed huge talons resembling razor-sharp knives. Imbued with great heat, the talons caused shimmers in the air around them.

"You are an unaging, undying vampire… Therefore…if I rip off your limbs and burn your head, you will not perish…!"

The dragon-man kicked the ground, accelerating as if hurled by a catapult. He was sprinting straight at Avrora.

"C...come forth, Minelauva Iris!"

Avrora shouted, seemingly spurred on by her fears. A huge, rainbow-colored Valkyrie materialized behind her back in a single instant, swinging her gleaming, demonic energy blade.

Minelauva Iris, Beast Vassal Number Six of the Fourth Primogenitor, was originally sealed by Hekatos—in other words, the Beast Vassal had been in Avrora's current body. In her current state, this was the only Beast Vassal that Avrora was capable of summoning.

Kreyd took Avrora's attack head-on. The dragon essence surging from his entire body collided with Avrora's demonic energy, splitting the air with a violent creak.

The clash between the two powers lasted for a brief instant. The Beast Vassal blade unleashed by Avrora shattered, vanishing in the blink in an eye, leaving a largely unscathed Kreyd remaining.

"Is this...all...Fourth Primogenitor...?"

Looking down at the light laceration carved into his own right arm, Kreyd exhaled, somehow seeming disappointed.

"Hiii...uuu...!"

Avrora's sensitive eyes wavered.

Shio and the others bit their lips in despair. Avrora hadn't summoned her Beast Vassal in its complete form. She really hadn't tamed the Beast Vassals of the Fourth Primogenitor yet.

Maybe Avrora wasn't cut out to rule the Beast Vassals to begin with. She hadn't been created to be the Fourth Primogenitor, but as one artificial vampire of many to seal away the Beast Vassals. She was too kind and gentle to make the ferocious, destructive Beast Vassals submit to her.

"Uuu...uuu..."

Avrora stretched her hand out to try and summon a Beast Vassal once more, but no Beast Vassal responded to her call. Her slender vampiric arm flailed futilely in the air, nothing more.

Scorning Avrora's powerlessness, Kreyd slowly drew closer to her.

The dragon-man stopped moving, seemingly perplexed. A tiny figure had walked right past Shio and the others, gently approached Avrora, and nestled against her.

"Glenda...?!"

Shio blinked in a daze. The dragon-girl, supposedly inside the tower, was supporting the frightened Avrora with her shoulder.

Kreyd wore a bewildered expression as Glenda's outward appearance slowly transformed before his eyes. She was no longer the dragon-girl, but someone else entirely.

"Thou art…!"

Avrora's voice trembled.

The girl who had been Glenda several moments prior shot Avrora a gentle smile.

Her long, steel-colored hair had turned into a glossy black. The tiny Glenda's back had grown ever so slightly, making her height equal to Avrora's. Thanks to this, the two looked practically like sisters for a fleeting moment. The lips of the girl who had been Glenda formed a friendly smile.

"Nagisa…Akatsuki…"

Shio murmured the girl's name. She was confused but, at the same time, oddly accepting.

Once, Glenda had adopted the form of Yukina Himeragi before Kojou Akatsuki. The same thing was happening now. As opposed to back then, the current Glenda was clearly moving according to Nagisa Akatsuki's will, not her own. Nagisa had to still be on the surface. She'd possessed Glenda by projecting her own mind.

"Looks like they made it in time…"

A voice came from Shio's feet. A syrupy smile crept onto the face of Mogwai, splayed out on the ground, when he saw how Glenda had transformed.

Shio looked at Mogwai in surprise.

The powerful spirit medium Nagisa Akatsuki had used her abilities to possess Glenda. It was likely this badly sewn teddy bear and his partner, Asagi Aiba, were responsible for piecing together this situation.

In other words, this was the will of the Priestess of Cain, no—the will of Cain the Sinful God himself.

But what for? wondered the perplexed Shio when Kreyd went into motion.

Kreyd had been briefly perplexed by the appearance of his kin Glenda, but he'd no doubt judged that the girl possessing her, Nagisa Akatsuki, posed no threat whatsoever.

His talons gave off a dull gleam as they assaulted Avrora once more.

Nagisa/Glenda calmly glared right back at the dragon-man without displaying any hint of fear. Then she strongly called out to Avrora.

"It's all right. We can do this, if we join together as one—"

Nagisa's left hand wrapped around and embraced Avrora's right. With a *gasp*, Avrora opened her eyes, firmly pursing her lips.

The pair then turned straight toward Kreyd, hand in hand. The demonic energy surging from both of their bodies was so vast as to fill the entirety of Shio and company's vision, pure white and incredibly cold.

"Come forth, Alrescha Glacies—!"

The girls' voices rang out simultaneously. The demonic energy gushing from Avrora's body transformed into a giant Beast Vassal, a beautiful icy raptor, Beast Vassal Number Twelve of the Fourth Primogenitor—

"Wh...at?!"

The onrushing, extreme cold fiercely unnerved Kreyd. He spewed out an incandescent beam in an attempt to resist the Beast Vassal's demonic energy, but the cold unleashed by the Fourth Primogenitor's Beast Vassal exceeded the Flame Dragon's breath. The incandescent flames vanished in white mist, and the dragon-man's entire body became enveloped in a block of ice.

The Beast Vassal's attack included the Spartoi behind Kreyd, too. Their exoskeletons, strong enough to rival dragon hide, fragilely broke apart like sand once exposed to ultralow temperature. There was no sign that the fragments piled upon the ground were regenerating. The intense cold emitted by the Beast Vassal completely destroyed the ritual to create the Spartoi that had employed dragon physical composition as a catalyst.

"Oooooooooooooo...!!"

The huge, copper dragon shattered the block of ice as it emerged. Returning to dragon form, Kreyd used the flames emitted in the process to thaw his own frozen flesh, soaring up into the sky in turn. However, his right arm was missing, with only a tiny bit near the shoulder remaining. Avrora's Beast Vassal's attack had frozen and shattered it.

"GUROOOOOOOOOHHH!"

Kreyd the Flame Dragon made an earsplitting roar. His voice was no longer something humans could decipher, but the curses and hate in his voice were clear to all. He directed a splitting rage toward Avrora, the one who'd wounded his flesh.

The Spartoi he'd brought were already wiped out, however. He'd surely judged that taking on Avrora in her current state on his own was too risky, even for him. The Flame Dragon flew off, glaring hatefully at Avrora all the while. He was retreating to the artificial isle floating on the surface of the sea overhead.

Avrora had no capacity left with which to pursue him. She fell to her knees, her strength depleted from forcibly summoning her Beast Vassal.

"…Thank you, Avrora. Thanks to you, we made it in time… Now it's my turn."

Nagisa/Glenda smiled as she gently touched Avrora's back.

As Shio raced to the injured Yuiri, an expression of surprise came over her, staring straight at the incredible rays of light emitted by Nagisa/Glenda's body.

"Nagisa Akatsuki…you're…!"

Shio murmured in a daze. The rays Nagisa/Glenda was releasing were actually dazzling, radiant strings of spiritual essence. She was freely controlling thousands of these strings like a veteran puppeteer.

Shio knew the true nature of this skill. It was Teokratia—the mind control ritual employed by Shirona Kuraki, one of the Three Saints of the Lion King Agency.

The ability to control thousands, even tens of thousands, of targets was the secret art of the Kuraki clan. Nagisa Akatsuki had personally experienced this ritual once previously. She'd probably reproduced Shirona's technique based on her memories of the event.

The spiritual threads woven by Nagisa/Glenda went through the steel-colored tower before spreading into the sky of Nod.

Shio was following the glows when she realized something was changing around her.

The cloud-covered sky of Nod was clearing. The cold from the Beast Vassal of the Fourth Primogenitor had frozen water in the atmosphere, rendering it unable to maintain its vapor form.

"I see...this is a..."

With the clouds clearing, Shio looked around the now-vivid sky, breathing out like she was beside herself.

Why were sky and ground inverted? Why did no demonic energy exist in this land? She felt like she finally understood the secret of the world known as Nod.

"So this is Nod's true form..."

Assailed by fierce dizziness, Shio fell to her knees on the spot. A sea spread forth above Shio's and the others' heads. What spread far beneath their eyes was also the surface of the sea.

The place they'd thought a cape floating in a sea of clouds was part of a shaft cutting horizontally through open space.

They were on the inside of a metal, cylindrical world dozens of kilometers in diameter.

The world known as Nod was itself a giant, artificial structure.

6

Their teleport finished, Kojou and the others stepped into a vast chamber enveloped by darkness.

Countless cylindrical pillars of varying heights and diameters soared indiscriminately up, down, left, and right, filling Kojou and company's vision. Stairs and corridors stretching out like arteries had been grafted to these pillars.

Each and every one of those cylindrical pillars was built like a castle tower, probably also serving as the supporting framework for the giant exterior wall. This was the interior of Castle Kalenaren—one of the Deva Necropolises.

Kojou and the others were standing on the top of a cylindrical pillar about ten meters in diameter.

The place, illuminated by burning braziers, looked like a spherical stage.

Some distance away, upon one of the cylindrical pillars standing taller than the others, was a single, extravagant throne. Kojou and the others had to look up a bit to gaze at that vacant seat.

"—Welcome to Castle Kalenaren. What do you think? A beautiful sight, is it not?"

Ladli Ren turned around, standing on the same stage as Kojou and the rest. Based on the proud way she gave her nose a little scratch, she didn't seem to be speaking ironically.

"So this is a Deva castle, hovering between the real world and another, huh?"

"Seems an awful lot like a haunted house…"

Yaze and Asagi genuinely grimaced as they spoke. To human beings with any sane sense of aesthetics, the irregular geometry of the chamber made it very hard to feel at ease.

"It is not to your liking? What a pity."

Ladli tapered her lips peevishly at Asagi and Yaze's less than enthused reaction.

A moment later, a man's voice echoed through that dark, creepy chamber.

"Welcome, Ruler of Itogami Island."

The supposedly vacant seat straight ahead had a man of indeterminate age sitting on it, a light skinned, blue-eyed Asian man with a wry, gentle smile reaching all the way to his eyes.

"Shahryar Ren…"

Kojou spoke the man's name. Shahryar Ren, supposedly in Nod, was sitting in the extravagant throne-like seat, looking down at Kojou and the others.

He was dressed in an ornate robe reminiscent of ancient royalty. The attire no doubt indicated that he was king of the Devas.

"I truly did not think I would be speaking with you ever again, Kojou Akatsuki."

Ren spoke in a frigid tone. Kojou and the rest had already realized it wasn't his real body talking. The Shahryar Ren here was just an illusion. This wasn't even magic, just a hologram.

Ladli turned to her holographic brother, reverently going down on one knee. It was a dated gesture like that of a knight serving her liege. Ren nodded, apparently satisfied with the propriety of her demeanor.

"Allow me to say you have made a wise choice, particularly since you desire to meet Dodekatos…no, Avrora Florestina, once more."

"Save the small talk. More importantly, you know why we've come here, right?"

Kojou cut off Ren's words with his own.

Kojou's unexpectedly rude behavior made Ren's eyebrows twitch several times. Even so, he kept his emotions in check, shifting his eyes to his little sister below.

"...Ladli."

"Yes, yes. Let's tune in to events in progress. Your Excellent Excellency Kul Zu of Castle Zu?"

Ladli said, returning to her usual clownish tone.

She was looking at a small cylindrical pillar jutting sideways out of the darkness to Kojou and the others' right side. A small, elderly man was standing on that cylinder's uppermost portion.

"...Lady Ladli, I ask that you be restrained in your jests."

The old man she'd called Kul Zu stood near Ladli and looked up to speak.

If he was the owner of Castle Zu, that made him the owner of a different Necropolis. He was actually the one who'd fired the Beast Vassal Warhead, instigating the sinking of the HGTO military's battle fleet.

"Forgive my rudeness. The situation has been conveyed to you, Your Excellency?"

Ladli double-checked without the faintest sliver of guilt. Apparently Kojou's request—fire off a Beast Vassal Warhead into Tokyo—had already reached Castle Zu.

Kul Zu, however, shifted a reproachful gaze toward Ladli.

"You have provided no resupply, yet you tell us to use our final Beast Vassal Warhead?"

"I'm asking you to overlook that. We've already arranged replacement warheads."

Ladli grinned and pressed both hands together.

For whatever reason, the girl smiled teasingly as she shifted her gaze toward her older brother above. Her expression was basically saying the dried-up supply of Beast Vassal Warheads was Shahryar Ren's fault rather than hers.

"Wait until roughly half past four. We will move our Necropolis. Its destination will be the airspace above Tokyo Bay."

Kul Zu spoke brusquely.

"I thank you, Your Excellency."

Ladli bowed courteously. The braziers illuminating that cylindrical pillar vanished, and the old man sank into the darkness. The connection with Castle Zu had been cut.

"Arriving in Tokyo Bay in thirty minutes... You'd planned to attack Tokyo from the start whether we asked you to or not, didn't you?"

Asagi shifted a critical gaze toward Shahryar Ren. They didn't understand the process by which the Necropolises moved, but she didn't think an object over a whole kilometer in diameter could turn on a dime at high speeds. If it was going to arrive at Tokyo Bay in thirty minutes, Castle Zu must have already been heading toward Tokyo for the last several hours. They must have intended to attack Tokyo to begin with.

"Negotiations are all about discerning what cards are in the other side's hand, Priestess of Cain."

Ren triumphantly gazed down at Asagi as he spoke. It was tantamount to saying he'd anticipated Kojou and the others' reaction to the government of Japan trying to sink Itogami Island every step of the way.

"Thanks. I'll keep that in mind."

Asagi shrugged her shoulders as she spoke. She squinted at him with a sarcastic air.

"To pay you back, I'll tell you something nice from my end. It's a bit of an old story—it's about the old memories carved into Cain's Coffin, the deepest part of Itogami Island."

"...The memories of Cain's Coffin, you say?"

Ren's brows twitched faintly. Apparently, even he couldn't remain indifferent to the mention of the memories of Cain, mortal enemy of his fellow Devas.

Amused by Ren's reaction, Asagi opened her mouth with a theatrical air.

"In the first place, Beast Vassals are beasts summoned from another world using a ritual spell. They're masses of demonic energy powerful enough to possess sentience. No one can control them—that's why the Devas used them as weapons of mass destruction, hence the Beast Vassal Warheads, yes?"

"That's right."

Ren quirked his brow. *You only understand that now*, said his expression mockingly.

Asagi paid no heed and continued.

"Summoning a Beast Vassal takes a sacrifice to serve as its icon, but human and normal demon bodies can't take the strain of having a Beast Vassal dwelling in them. That doesn't mean you can sacrifice the precious few Devas instead. So you Devas built the vessels for Beast Vassals we call vampires, girls without memories or even names, just numbers—"

Kojou's cheeks twitched and tensed. Even the Kaleid Bloods in which the Beast Vassals of the Fourth Primogenitors dwelled were referred to by simple numbers. Small wonder the fire-and-forget Beast Vassal Warheads hadn't even been given names.

These girls were factory-produced, had a Beast Vassal stuffed into them, and were then encased inside a gemstone. They'd remained in dreamless sleep for millennia as nothing more but terrifying, abominable weapons of mass destruction.

"Also, the Devas were afraid, because the Beast Vassal Warheads were simply too powerful. It was clear that unrestricted release of them would destroy even the Devas themselves."

Asagi let her words trail off. Ren crossed his legs in apparent boredom.

"Yes, therefore, the Devas brought all the Beast Vassal Warheads in Nod under the administration of the royal family. In other words, all the Beast Vassal Warheads in Nod belong to the Devas. All that remained was for us, the proper and natural successors, to regain the Legacy of the Devas."

"I figured that's how you'd put it."

Giggle, chuckled Asagi, smiling with amusement.

"That's not what Cain thought, though. During The Great Cleansing—when humankind and demonkind challenged the Devas to battle—Cain closed the gate to Nod and refused to bring out the Beast Vassal Warheads. He was a Deva, yet he was a betrayer doing harm to the Devas... That's why he was slandered as the Sinful God."

"...What are you trying to say?"

A hideous scowl formed on Ren's face. Perhaps he was remembering anew the anger and hatred against Cain nurtured for thousands of years.

Asagi calmly took the brunt of Ren's hostile gaze head-on. She did not reply to Ren's question.

The braziers behind Kojou and company swayed, and a fresh figure appeared from them.

"Lady Ladli."

A man entirely covered in cloth bent one knee atop his cylindrical pillar as he addressed Ladli. Ren grimaced, displeased with the interruption. Ladli turned around and looked at her subordinate.

"What is the matter? We are receiving guests."

"Emergency message from Arnica Quad."

Ladli's subordinate reported in a hard voice brimming with apprehension.

Ladli extended her right hand in a beckoning motion, taking the sheet of paper offered by her subordinate. Her eyes bulged with surprise when she perused the contents of the message written upon it.

"It seems the HGTO military is attacking our MAR headquarters once more."

Ladli spoke with a perplexed air. The Holy Grounds Treaty Organization had to comprehend the might of the Beast Vassal Warheads by that point, so their trying to invade MAR's HQ a second time came as some surprise.

Then she shot Kojou a measured look.

"The main force is the airship battle fleet of the Kingdom of Aldegia's Knights of the Second Coming—the flagship is La Folia Rihavein's *Böðvildr*, it seems? Aldegia is a nation allied to Itogami City-State, is it not?"

"…Princess La Folia has?"

Yukina spoke in a voice too tiny for anyone else to hear her.

Certainly, the Kingdom of Aldegia was part of the HGTO, so it was little mystery why it was launching an attack on MAR, the HGTO's foe, but such an act was reckless to the extreme. An HGTO military battle fleet trying to attack MAR Inc. proper had already been struck and virtually destroyed by a Beast Vassal Warhead. There was no guarantee the

Aldegian airship battle fleet La Folia was flying aboard would not share the same fate.

"…Your point?"

For his part, Kojou replied in an unemotional voice.

Oh my, said Ladli, warily narrowing her eyes. She maintained a grinning expression even so.

"This places us in something of a bind. We are forced to counterattack against the HGTO military in order to defend ourselves, but at this rate, poor Princess La Folia will be caught in the middle."

"That so? Well, it can't be helped."

Kojou calmly brushed off Ladli's warning and the threat implied within.

"Senpai…!"

Yukina raised her voice, unable to endure Kojou's stony indifference. The situation was not like when she'd faced Kojou's black Beast Vassals on Itogami Island. Even La Folia had no chance against a Beast Vassal Warhead releasing demonic energy without any restraint. Kojou's statement was tantamount to saying he'd stand back and watch her die.

"You're sure about this? Truly? The princess is one of your companion candidates, is she not?"

Ladli checked to make sure, seemingly at a loss. Kojou's demeanor was unchanged even so.

"As ruler of Itogami Island, my negotiations with you come first. That's only natural, right?"

"…I thought you would give up the ghost before your princess became a ghost."

Ladli sighed casually. Then she shifted her gaze to the subordinate beneath her.

"Send word to Lord Alda Ba. I request that he annihilates the HGTO military."

Understood, said the silent nod of Ladli's subordinate as he vanished from sight. The braziers shining upon him vanished as well, leaving only the faint sounds of receding footsteps.

"Annihilate, huh? You guys can actually pull it off?"

Kojou mused aloud in a casual fashion. Ladli took no special offense as she gazed at Kojou with deep interest.

The next moment, the interior of the Necropolis bustled with activity.

Numerous people, enough that Kojou had to wonder where they'd been hiding, appeared around Kojou and the others one after the next. These were operators serving under Ladli.

Various screens hovered before them in midair, projecting vivid holographic images.

The screens displayed a metropolis's nighttime cityscape. It was a real-time image of different parts of Tokyo taken from high above Tokyo Bay.

"Castle Zu has reached Tokyo Bay airspace. Materializing now."

"Beast Vassal Warhead safety released. Beginning firing sequence."

The operators reported the situation one after the other.

Shahryar Ren leaned forward in his seat, listening to the reports with unmistakable delight.

Kojou's expression was completely unchanged. The same went for Asagi, Yaze, and Shizuri, too.

"Senpai, are you really fine with this?! Senpai!"

Yukina was being held back by Shizuri's arm as she desperately pleaded with Kojou. The only one able to stop the firing of the Beast Vassal Warhead then and there was Kojou. Kojou could sell Itogami Island's territorial rights to Shahryar Ren. There was no other way to save the ordinary people in Tokyo.

"Castle Ba launching Beast Vassal Warhead! Also, Castle Zu entering countdown! Three, two, one…fire."

As if to mock Yukina's apprehension, the operator reported with a neutral expression.

Kojou didn't budge until the very end.

"Japan's storied capital, vanishing in a single instant? Well, shoot. Just kidding."

Ladli let out a disinterested cough. Somehow, her voice sounded a bit wistful.

7

"Incoming fire confirmed! Beast Vassal Warhead! Entering our airspace in twenty-five seconds!"

The sensor operator's voice reverberated across the bridge of the armored airship *Böðvildr*.

The ship was sailing above the Celebes Sea in the Western Pacific Ocean. The *Böðvildr* served as the flagship for an armored airship fleet of fourteen ships approaching the MAR headquarters known as Arnica Quad. Their objective was to take over Arnica Quad with a lightning raid, whittling away at MAR's military strength.

Their operation had been obstructed by the appearance of a Deva Necropolis from another world. It had launched a Beast Vassal Warhead without warning. Such an act of violence violated not just the Holy Grounds Treaty limiting the use of sorcerous weaponry, but the international laws of war.

The crew of the *Böðvildr* was not nervous, however. They'd expected from the beginning that the Devas would respond with drastic measures. The Devas were so short on manpower that the Beast Vassal Warheads were all they could rely on.

"*Böðvildr*, all ahead at forty-two knots!"

The weathered captain, looking much like a pirate, sent commands flying in a coarse, throaty voice. The beautiful, pale blue hull glowed with magical energy as it accelerated.

The other accompanying airships spread out some distance away. The *Böðvildr*, their flagship, ended up charging into the Beast Vassal Warhead's effective range alone.

"Now then, what will we do? Taking on a primogenitor-class Beast Vassal is a bit difficult in the ship's current condition."

The captain murmured with a strained expression, furiously stroking his beard.

"We really forced it against Kojou's Beast Vassal, after all."

The princess sitting beside the captain—La Folia Rihavein—smiled with elegance.

Her words, irresponsibly spoken as if she had nothing to do with it, made the captain lift his eyes to the sky in exasperation. The *Böðvildr*'s hull remained deeply damaged, the cost of holding a primogenitor-class Beast Vassal at bay all by itself.

Not even three days had passed before they were facing a Beast Vassal Warhead. The princess's recklessness seemed to know no bounds. That all obeyed her without a single complaint despite this was no doubt the work of the tremendous charisma she possessed.

"We have a lock on the Beast Vassal Warhead. On-screen!"

The bridge's main screen switched to imagery of the Beast Vassal Warhead flying at high speed.

It was a beautiful crystal reminiscent of a gemstone. The faint silhouette within was that of a girl holding her knees as she slept.

"Five seconds to contact! Outer shell collapsing!"

The area around the warhead was enveloped in a faint light. The gemstone-like outer shell shattered, the fragments thereof reflecting the light. As the crystal fell away in tiny pieces, the girl inside it was much more vivid to the eye, the girl within which a ferocious Beast Vassal dwelled—

"Outer shell dissipated! No Beast Vassal on sensors!"

The operator's voice included a faint whiff of surprise.

The Beast Vassal Warhead's crystal completely shattered, casting the girl serving as the icon into midair.

Her long, golden hair spread into the night sky. A strong wind blew, causing the girl's naked body to dance in the air. The Beast Vassal did not emerge. The girl remained asleep as she gently fell toward the sea.

"Princess, this is…?"

The captain looked at La Folia in surprise. La Folia's blue eyes narrowed as she smiled.

"Just as Kojou and the others planned. As expected of you, Priestess of Cain…no, Asagi Aiba."

The still-accelerating *Böðvildr* crossed paths with the girl serving as a host, yet the Beast Vassal still did not emerge. The Beast Vassal Warhead fired by the Necropolis had misfired. Their attack had failed.

"Captain, recover the girl."

La Folia gently issued the command. The captain gasped and came to his senses.

"Understood. Drop the Aerial Knights!"

"Aerial Knights, first lance, second lance, dropping!"

Knights equipped with flight units flew from the *Böðvildr* one after another. La Folia had them on standby in the hangar beforehand.

In other words, La Folia knew from the beginning that the Beast Vassal summons would fail. The Beast Vassal Warhead had not misfired by chance. It had been set up to misfire from the beginning.

"Those Devas must be in quite a state right about now."

The captain glared at the Necropolis floating straight ahead with a hard look.

"We must bring down the Necropolis before it retreats into the ether."

La Folia spoke with a composed tone. The Deva Necropolis had the ability to submerge itself into another world. If they allowed it to escape, it would not be possible to predict where the Necropolis would emerge next.

"—Daughters of the Gods that dwell in my body, ye who select the dead to bring victory in the Age of the Sword!"

La Folia was enveloped by the glow of spiritual essence as she chanted. She was using her own flesh and blood as an icon in which to summon a spirit from higher-dimensional space. This vast spiritual energy coursed into the spiritual reactor of the *Böðvildr*, enabling it to exhibit exceptional output far beyond the norm.

"Deploy bow ram! Flank speed! Activate the Völundr System!"

The captain issued one command after another. The Necropolis was a floating fortress reaching an entire kilometer in diameter. On top of that, it possessed a powerful defensive wall employing spatial control magic. Most artillery attacks wouldn't even scratch it.

The *Böðvildr* had a trump card to break through that wall.

"Target is Necropolis center, Beast Vassal Warhead launch site! All hands, brace for impact! Ram her—!"

The captain let out a ferocious roar. They were using the Völundr System for a ramming attack, using the hull itself as a giant holy sword.

Protected by spiritual essence, the hull crashed into the center of the Necropolis. They impaled it through the gunnery hatch left wide open from just launching the Beast Vassal Warhead, smashing through the exterior wall.

The *Böðvildr* was struck by ferocious recoil, but the impact was less than they'd expected. The output of the Völundr System rivaled that of the Necropolis's own defense.

"Hull, damage report! Reactor, maintain output! Status of the Necropolis?!"

"Envelopes Number Four and Number Six damaged. Buoyancy down to eighty-four percent. No hindrance to sailing."

"Radar dome electrical system damage. Switching to spare circuit! Sixty seconds to reboot!"

"Necropolis outer wall magical energy reaction confirmed vanished. Mass suddenly increasing!"

Crew members replied one after another to the captain's questions. They couldn't allow themselves optimism, but the situation wasn't all that bad. The Necropolis's mass suddenly increasing was particularly good news. An increase in mass on the real-world side meant it had lost its ability to submerge into another.

"The Death Returner's report has proved true, I see. The Necropolis completely surfaces into the real world at the instant it fires a Beast Vassal Warhead...also, it is possible to penetrate the Necropolis's otherworldly defensive wall with an attack from a higher dimension."

Releasing her spirit summons, La Folia smiled as she gazed at the Necropolis's wrecked outer wall.

The lone archeologist dubbed Death Returner had conveyed the Necropolis's abilities and weakness to the Kingdom of Aldegia. As a result, La Folia had been able to achieve maximum results with minimum loss, inflicting mortal damage on the Deva Necropolis.

"Incoming message from the HGTO battle fleet, sender: Chaos Zone, Third Primogenitor—'We thank the Kingdom of the Valkyries for its valiant fighting.'"

The communication officer looked back at La Folia and reported. The multinational armada dispatched by the HGTO emerged from the sea to the *Böðvildr*'s rear, primarily composed of the Chaos Zone's submersible aircraft carriers. Judging from magical camouflage deployed on a vast enough scale to cover an entire fleet, the Third Primogenitor, Giada Kukulkan, was likely there in person.

Aldegia's airship fleet wasn't carrying enough ground fighting power to take over the Necropolis and Arnica Quad to begin with. It was best to leave all the annoying mopping up to her forces.

"It seems we've sorted out this end. That leaves Tokyo Bay..."

An expression of relief came over the bearded captain as he spoke.

The *Böðvildr* had already received word that the Necropolis appearing above Tokyo Bay had employed a Beast Vassal Warhead. The current government of Japan couldn't have had the firepower to stop it.

"There is surely no need for concern."

La Folia spoke those words without hesitation. The princess gazed at her left ring finger as a small smile rich in implication came over her.

"I am not the only servant born of the Royal Family of Aldegia—"

In a creepy chamber enveloped by darkness, a white-haired elder dressed in priestly robes screamed. It was the throne room of the Necropolis called Castle Zu.

"Why?! Why isn't the Beast Vassal Warhead activating?! What is going on?!"

The screen above the elder was displaying the nighttime scenery of Tokyo.

It showed the windows of electric trains moving to and fro unceasingly. It showed the headlights of cars traveling along highways. It showed commercial facilities all lit up. It showed the lit windows of skyscrapers. Everything was perfectly normal for a peaceful city.

There was no sign of the Beast Vassal appearing to lay all this to waste. The Beast Vassal Warhead fired from Castle Zu was a dud falling toward Tokyo Bay.

"Detecting ultrahigh-density divine essence! Range…four hundred! Castle barrier dissipating!"

A new screen floated up to show a girl spreading wings of spiritual essence. It was a beautiful girl with a cherubic face. There was a golden shield in her left hand. In her right, she gripped a dazzling sword of light.

"A Faux-Angel from the Kingdom of Aldegia?! Where in the world did it come from?!"

Kul Zu's eyes were bloodshot as he shouted.

The existence of the ritual known as Faux-Angel was known even among the Devas. The secret spell of the Royal Family of Aldegia was said to artificially increase one's spiritual cores, causing unlimited amplification of spiritual energy, making one a higher-dimensional being while remaining in human flesh.

What made the Devas view Faux-Angels as dangerous was not because they represented a spiritual evolution of mankind. They feared

Faux-Angels' capabilities as simple weapons. The vast divine essence at their disposal was able to inflict lethal damage to a Deva Necropolis's functions.

"Enormous demonic energy detected at sea level! I-it's Leviathan! Bio-energy laser, incoming!"

Castle Zu's enormous frame shook violently before the subordinate had even finished the report. An enormous monster rivaling the size of the Necropolis itself was surfacing in Tokyo Bay. It was Leviathan, "Weapon of the Gods," the World's Mightiest Demon Beast.

Kul Zu stood in a daze as he gazed upon the legendary monster. Leviathan was a divine-level biological weapon that had existed in the surface world since before the Devas emerged. He could hardly believe anyone had tamed such a creature, but the monster was right there, baring its fangs at Castle Zu.

A tiny figure stood on Leviathan's thousand-meter-plus back.

It was a young girl spreading pitch-black wings. He could scarcely believe it, but this girl had controlled Leviathan to make it attack Castle Zu.

"Submerge! Emergency otherworld submerge! Hurry!"

Kul Zu angrily shouted at his subordinates.

Even the nigh-absolute defensive power boasted by a Necropolis could not withstand attacks from a Faux-Angel and Leviathan at the same time. The Faux-Angel's divine essence would nullify the Necropolis's otherworld defensive wall, whereupon Leviathan's extreme firepower would pour down upon them. It was the worst situation his mind could fathom.

"S-submerge not possible! The castle wall has been cut through…!"

A subordinate reported in a voice threatening to vanish. This time, Kul Zu simply gaped.

The silver-haired, blue-eyed Faux-Angel had created an enormous sword of light, slicing right through Castle Zu's outer wall. It was no longer possible to redeploy the otherworld defensive wall. Castle Zu was practically naked.

"The Völundr System…that's ridiculous…was the Aldegian battle fleet not headed to the Celebes Sea?"

Kul Zu listlessly shook his head. The Kingdom of Aldegia's Völundr System was one of the very few rituals capable of penetrating a Necropolis's otherworld defensive wall, but he'd heard that only the princess-priestesses of the Aldegian Royal family could activate this ritual. Yet the girl before his eyes was employing the Völundr System, employing the overwhelming spiritual power of a Faux-Angel—

"B-Beast Vassals! Vampire Beast Vassals directly above! Numbers in the hundreds…no, four hundred…over a thousand…!"

The subordinate looked at Kul Zu with a face twisted in despair. Kul Zu could no longer even speak.

The Beast Vassals filling night sky were a flock of enormous-winged dinosaurs supposedly gone extinct in a bygone era.

The enormous flock was really a single Beast Vassal. In that entire wide world, the vampires able to control such an exceptional Beast Vassal numbered precisely one.

"The Second Primogenitor's 'In Memorial Garden'…! Ha…haha… hahahahahaha…! So you use even the three primogenitors as your pawns, Empire of the Dawn!"

"Y-Your Excellency?"

When Kul Zu suddenly burst into laughter, his subordinates looked up at him with confusion.

"It is just as the other clans spoke… They told us, do not raise your hand against the Fourth Primogenitor… It is nothing like the primogenitors we know… I feel like a fool watching a nightmare."

Shoulders still lowered in dejection, Kul Zu continued his listless laugh. Of the seventeen Deva clans, only two entwined themselves with Shahryar Ren's ambitions. Kul Zu finally understood the reason why. For the sake of a puny artificial island floating in the Pacific Ocean, another nation's princess wagered her own life, the controller of a legendary divine beast had come forward, and even other primogenitors had lent their strength. So far as Kul Zu knew, such things had been impossibilities since The Great Cleansing, not occurring even once since that time.

At least not until the Fourth Primogenitor had emerged on Itogami Island—

"…We will surrender."

Regaining his dignity, Kul Zu spoke with a quiet air.

Expressions of relief spread among the subordinates inside the Necropolis.

The spherical fortress appearing above Tokyo Bay opened its castle gate, from which signal lights blinked on and off. It was an optical signal conveying surrender.

"Oh my? It is already o…ver? Unfortunate…but, that, is…fine…"

The elegant person riding on the huge Simurgh's back brushed up his purple hair and released his summons of the thousand-plus Beast Vassals. Aswadguhl Aziz was slightly deflated as he sighed.

Word had already come that the Necropolis Castle Ba, under full-scale attack by Third Primogenitor Giada Kukulkan's forces at the Celebes Sea in the Western Pacific, was falling to pieces. Compared to that, this ending seemed rather plain somehow.

That said, the lord of Castle Zu was no doubt worthy of praise for averting fruitless conflict.

Had the battle been prolonged, Japan's Self-Defense Forces would surely have deployed as well. Aswad, guilty of violating another country's airspace, was probably better off withdrawing before they showed up.

"You have also done…well, pretend angel girl."

Aswad switched moods and looked back. Two girls were riding on the Simurgh beside Aswad—Kanon Kanase, wearing a wetsuit, and the little artificial vampire she held in her arms.

"I am glad this girl was not harmed in any way."

Kanon looked down at the completely nude vampire girl and smiled.

It was the artificial vampire sealed inside the Beast Vassal Warhead. The girl with short, rainbow-colored hair was limp with her eyes closed. She was as pale as the dead, but her nearly flat chest was rhythmically rising and falling. She remained asleep, with the nameless Beast Vassal still dwelling inside her.

"To think Simurgh would permit any other to ride atop its back…my, my. Also, the Lilith who controls Leviathan…"

Aswad's red eyes narrowed as he looked down at Yume Eguchi, standing on the back of the giant demon beast leisurely floating on the sea's surface. The beautiful Second Primogenitor smiled, covertly baring his white fangs.

"*Giggle*…truly, you do not fail to…amuse. Someday, we must take our time playing… again."

8

In the core of a Necropolis—

Yukina, standing in the chamber atop a cylindrical pillar, was beside herself as she gazed up at the sight shown on-screen.

At Celebes Sea and above Tokyo Bay, black smoke rose from the Necropolis's broken castle walls. The Völundr System of the Royal Family of Aldegia had sliced through the Necropolis's outer walls protected by otherworldly bulwarks, inflicting critical damage to each.

On the other hand, the Beast Vassal Warheads fired by the Necropolises had not produced the expected results. The girls had been recovered as girls, their Beast Vassals unsummoned. The two Beast Vassal Warheads had failed to detonate.

Shizuri, gripping Yukina's arm, sighed with relief and patted her chest. Noticing Yukina's glaring gaze, she averted her eyes with a decidedly guilty look.

Looking closer, she spotted similar expressions hovering over Kojou and Yaze. Yukina stopped breathing for a while, followed by her shoulders quaking as ferocious anger rippled up through her.

She didn't think the twin Beast Vassal Warhead misfires had been the product of chance. Kojou and the others knew from the start that they would fail. That was why they'd taunted Ladli into using them.

Drawing out the Necropolises in the process—

"This is your doing, Priestess of Cain…?"

Ladli asked Asagi this in a low voice. Asagi shrugged her shoulders in a somewhat casual manner.

"Unfortunately, no. This was set up by Cain himself from the moment he took the Fourth Primogenitor, the 'god-killing weapon' made to destroy him, under his wing—"

"Huh? Wait a second, what are you saying—?!"

"You're breaking character, Ladli Ren."

Asagi smiled sardonically at Ladli, whose voice was ragged from getting so worked up. *Ghh…*, growled Ladli in vexation.

Ignoring Ladli, Asagi provocatively shifted her gaze to Shahryar Ren.

"Cain the Sinful God expected someone would eventually reopen the gate to Nod and bring the Beast Vassal Warheads sealed within to the surface. Shahryar Ren—he expected someone just like you."

"………"

Ren looked down at Asagi without a word, but his calm disposition was undermined by him biting his lip so hard, it turned pale. Asagi sighed with visible tedium.

"To stop that, he had no choice but to completely neutralize the Beast Vassal Warheads. That's why he came up with a plan to scrap the warheads entirely."

"…Neutralize the Beast Vassal Warheads? That is…not something achievable."

Ren spoke as if wringing his voice out of his throat. Asagi instantly shot down his words.

"No. Neutralizing Beast Vassal Warheads can be done. You already know of the precedent."

"…The vampire…primogenitors…?"

Clench, echoed the back of Ren's teeth.

"Vampire primogenitors are the first vampires to have Beast Vassals summoned via the warheads dwelling in their own bodies. They neutralize the Beast Vassal Warheads by taming the Beast Vassals within their own blood. The price they pay for that is accepting an eternal curse of immortality, though."

Asagi touched her right hand to her chest to indicate her respect for the primogenitors.

Fallgazer, Chaos Bride, and the Lost Warlord—

They were the ones who'd consumed countless Beast Vassal Warheads used in The Great Cleansing of Old to become the vampire primogenitors. The vampire primogenitors were the ones shouldering the sacrifice of the calamity known as Beast Vassal Warheads for humanity's sake.

"Neutralizing the Beast Vassal Warheads simply involves repeating the same process, making the artificial vampire girls the Beast Vassals are stuffed in their rightful hosts. That way, the Beast Vassals won't go on a rampage even if you break the girls' seals."

Asagi continued explaining with delight. She stomped the floor as if unable to contain herself.

"I said already, that is not possible! Those dolls lack the 'blood memories' to make those Beast Vassals obey them…!"

"What if they did have memories, then? Even false, artificially created memories?"

"Wh…at…?!"

Asagi's calm rebuttal struck Ren out of nowhere, silencing him.

Beast Vassals were information-based life-forms existing without physical form. To them, information was the feed necessary so that they could continue to exist. Accordingly, Beast Vassals instinctively acknowledged the one who fed them information as their host and obeyed that person. Joy, sadness, anger, sadness—the host's powerful emotions, and the memories binding them together, were the finest of delicacies to Beast Vassals, and any host not sating this hunger would cease to be, his or her life force consumed to the last wisp. That was why the Primogenitors hated boredom. They needed pleasures to farm out to their own Beast Vassals.

All the same, there was no rule that said the information fed to the Beast Vassals couldn't be fabricated.

"If you take the five hundred and sixty thousand people living on Itogami—no, if the networks are up, you have past memories from people around the entire world. We did samplings of these, created new personalities to farm out…enough for six thousand four hundred and fifty-two people…and built an illusionary school in virtual space for the girls to experience further."

Asagi said this calmly as if it were nothing major at all. Yukina abruptly remembered something while gazing at the side of Asagi's face.

Asagi hadn't used her partner AI Mogwai at all in the past several days. She'd heard that Itogami Island's main computer had been short on resources, too.

This was because Asagi was working behind the scenes to disarm the Beast Vassal Warheads. She'd given new memories and personalities to six thousand four hundred and fifty-two girls. She'd created an illusionary school for this purpose so that they could experience school life for themselves, all so that the girls gained the power of will with which to rule and tame the Beast Vassals—

"Do you mean to…save the Beast Vassal Warheads with these false memories?"

Ren spoke with a tone of bitter hatred.

"At first, fake memories are fine. If they live on, they'll get plenty of memories on their own. I mean, these girls have an unlimited future in front of them."

The corners of Asagi's lips rose in a powerful smile. Besides, the girls' experiences weren't complete fabrications anyway. After all, the artificial vampires' virtual personalities had been based on Nagisa Akatsuki's own experiences.

Nagisa had used the ritual called Teokratia to implant her own memories of daily life on Itogami Island into the girls serving as the Beast Vassal Warhead icons. To these girls, the memories of Nagisa fused with Avrora's soul had to feel nostalgic and easy to absorb. As they gained understanding of Nagisa's feelings, the icon girls would seize their own future, a future where they lived together with the Beast Vassals they had themselves tamed—

"This was Cain's plan? He expected Deva descendants would build an artificial island to open the gate to Nod, a plan to use this island to neutralize the Beast Vassal Warheads? A vague plan like that couldn't possibly go this well?"

Ladli shook her head with incredulity.

Even if it was possible in theory, Cain's plan had far too many uncertain elements. It didn't seem even remotely realistic that he could anticipate the construction of Itogami Island thousands of years down the line and use it to realize the disarming of the Beast Vassal Warheads.

Asagi, though, proudly pushed out her chest.

"That's what we're here for, all the Priestesses of Cain throughout history."

"…You're saying, even MAR was dancing on the palms of your hands all along…?"

Ladli made a limp, pained smile. Her voice had a ring of exasperation to it.

Even Asagi's plan to make all this a reality hadn't been anywhere near as sure a thing as Asagi implied. She was constantly walking along a cliff's edge, in many cases getting by only by the skin of her teeth.

Even so, the Beast Vassal Warheads really had been neutralized, two Necropolises had fallen, and the Priestesses of Cain had fulfilled their objective.

"Well...guess this means the negotiations are shot. You guys can't use Beast Vassal Warheads anymore, so the HGTO and the Japanese government don't have any reason to do as you tell 'em."

An invigorated expression came over Kojou from nowhere in particular as he stripped off the stuffy mantle. In the blink of an eye, he was back to wearing his parka, rotating his shoulders as the load on them eased.

"You entered negotiations with us with this objective? You made us fire the Beast Vassal Warheads on purpose to broadcast to the entire world that they'd been neutralized...?!"

Ladli warily put distance between her and Kojou's group and went on guard. Appearing within her hands were little sticks with spheres looking like lollipop candies on the end. These were sorcerous devices for summoning Spartoi.

"We figured you'd stick one Necropolis with protecting MAR HQ. Knowing the other would appear over Tokyo made it easy to ambush. If the three primogenitors know where the Necropolises will appear, they don't need to be stuck protecting their own turf, now do they?"

A profound smile came over Kojou as he spoke.

Ladli gasped, her expression freezing over. The Third Primogenitor in the Celebes Sea and the Second Primogenitor at Tokyo Bay had subdued a Necropolis each. That left only Castle Kalenaren in the airspace above Itogami Island.

"—Castle Kalenaren, emergency submerge!"

Wary of a surprise assault by the First Primogenitor, Ladli forcefully lobbed a command to her subordinates in an angry voice. Kojou and the others were struck by an unpleasant, dizzying sway as the Necropolis tried to submerge into space separate from that of the real world.

"You think you can run?"

Kojou glared at Ladli and asked this. Ladli smiled back at Kojou, not the slightest bit perturbed.

"It is futile, Kojou Akatsuki. No one can summon a Beast Vassal inside a Necropolis hovering between the real world and another, even for you and your black Beast Vassals. If not, I would never have invited you."

"You sure sealing only my Beast Vassals is enough?"

"Eh…?"

Ladli blinked hard. She was unable to immediately comprehend just what Kojou was saying. Ladli's expression abruptly hardened.

Suddenly, ridiculously powerful demonic energy surged behind Kojou. The source of this demonic energy was Shizuri Kasugaya Castiella—or rather, the crimson long sword she held in her hands.

"Counting on you, Cas!"

"Leave it to me! Hauras—!"

Shizuri swung down her long sword with all her might. The flame-like undulating blade was imbued with dazzling, pitch-black demonic energy, which she unleashed as an explosive shockwave. Pouring demonic energy supplied by Kojou into it without any restraint, she unleashed an attack of pure, unadulterated destruction.

"Wha…?"

Ladli stood still, forgetting all about trying to stop Shizuri. The cylindrical pillars filling the Necropolis's core shattered one after the other, crumbling down with a thunderous roar.

Kojou probably couldn't summon his Beast Vassals inside the Necropolis. It was with this expectation that Ladli had so easily invited Kojou and the others into the Necropolis.

This was why Kojou had brought Shizuri to the negotiating table. As Kojou's Blood Servant, she could release Kojou's demonic energy through Hauras effectively without limit.

"Cas, you missed a few. A little to the right, one o'clock, range is four hundred meters, diagonal slash up, please."

"Who is this 'Cas' person—?!"

Following Yaze's directions, Shizuri swung her sword once more. The now pitch-black blade's shockwave tore through the darkness, sending intense tremors throughout the entire Necropolis. Shizuri's slices had inflicted fatal damage to the Necropolis's power plant.

"Engines, full stop! Spiritual reactor, emergency shutdown!"

"Otherworld submerge impossible! Castle Kalenaren is surfacing!"

"Our propulsion is…at this rate…the castle will…!"

Ladli's subordinates cried out one after the other. Castle Kalenaren's otherworld submerging had failed, meaning it would be completely defenseless in the real world. For that matter, it had lost its buoyancy and had begun to fall to the surface.

"Motoki Yaze…are you determining Castle Kalenaren's layout with, echolocation…?"

Ladli barely listened to the cries of her subordinates as she glared at Yaze.

"Underestimated the 'Deva knockoff,' did we?"

Yaze feigned innocence as he smiled.

A Necropolis's layout was complex, its interior spaces twisting without regard for the laws of gravity. On top of that, the critical sections were protected with multiple labyrinth-like defensive walls. Even divination magic couldn't identify the Necropolis's weak points, yet Yaze had exposed them with ease. He was relying on mere sound echoes—no, it was precisely because he relied solely on sound echoes that he'd slipped beneath Ladli's radar.

"Kojou! We've returned to the real world!"

Asagi clung to the fiercely swaying cylindrical pillar's floor as she shouted.

Got it, said Kojou's silent nod as he thrust his right arm forward.

"C'mon over, Primus Mercury!"

An explosive torrent of demonic energy came forth as a pitch-black Beast Vassal appeared. It was an enormous, twin-headed dragon with both necks intertwined. It took an enormous bite out of the very center of the Necropolis, the Shahryar Ren hologram included, and kept going until it burst straight out the Necropolis's outer wall.

Moonlight illuminated the interior of the Necropolis as a powerful sea breeze blew in. They could see the nighttime skyline of Itogami Island and the surface of the sea through the rift in the wrecked outer wall.

"…It would seem this castle is done for. All hands, I entreat you to retreat!"

Ladli ordered her subordinates in a casual tone, but the interior of the Necropolis had already fallen into great chaos, Kojou questioned whether her words had really reached anyone. In the first place, there was no guarantee that the Necropolis was even equipped with escape devices.

"You will pay dearly for this, Kojou Akatsuki—"

Ladli glared resentfully at Kojou as she took out a small sorcerous device from a breast pocket. The device rested in her palm like some kind of remote control. The instant she activated the sorcerous device, the sight of her was swallowed up by a ripple-like sway. She was escaping via teleport.

"—Senpai! If the Necropolis crashes like this, it will be a disaster for Itogami Island…!"

Yukina seemed to be at the very end of her wits, withstanding the violent tremors as she closed the distance between herself and Kojou.

Having lost its buoyancy owing to Kojou and company's attacks, the Necropolis was accelerating, pulled by the force of gravity as it fell toward Itogami Island's urban areas. If the Necropolis crashed into the surface with that kind of momentum, Itogami Island wouldn't stand a chance. It was the worst-case scenario Natsuki Minamiya had feared.

"Suppose you're right. Guess it comes to this in the end."

"'In the end'…?!"

Yukina raised her eyebrows at Kojou's irresponsible statement, but Kojou smiled awkwardly back at Yukina.

"Sorry, Himeragi. That's how it is, so will you stick with me to the bitter end?"

"Senpai…? What are you saying…?"

"Talk and you'll bite your tongue, Himeragi!"

"…Huh?!"

Yukina replied in bewilderment. Before her, Kojou quietly closed his eyes.

The next instant, his entire body unleashed a surge of massive demonic energy like never before. Touching his palms to the floor at his own feet, Kojou began summoning a Beast Vassal. Even Yukina, watcher of the Fourth Primogenitor and witness to a great many powerful Beast Vassals, was sensing demonic energy of such an incredible level for the very first time.

"C'mon over, Primus Ater!"

Kojou summoned his new Beast Vassal.

The interior of the Necropolis roared like a painful cry as it tore apart. A ridiculously huge sword with a blade surpassing a hundred meters pierced the Necropolis straight down from directly above.

Assaulted by an impact like never before, explosions began erupting all over the place in the Necropolis's interior. The few intact remaining cylindrical pillars snapped, and the outer shell creaked.

On the other hand, a change came over the Necropolis's movements. Its acceleration caused by the force of gravity diminished, and Yukina and others were assailed by a strange, floating feeling. Their falling speed had clearly slowed.

Finally, the Necropolis fell completely silent and began floating once more. It slowly gained altitude as if completely freed from the force of gravity.

"Beast Vassal…gravity control…!"

Yukina's eyes blinked wide open as she spoke. The pitch-black great sword was the black Beast Vassal able to control gravity. Using its abilities, Kojou was dragging the Necropolis higher into the sky. Its destination was the giant magic symbols drawn in the night sky—the gate that continued on to Nod.

"—*Lady Empress! Thou art safe?!*"

As the Necropolis continued to creak, a loud, speaker-amplified voice echoed within.

A crimson robot tank with a flight unit attached roared its way in through the giant hole Kojou's Beast Vassal had punctured. Kojou could make out Yuuma Tokoyogi on the tank's back, too. They'd been on standby in the upper atmosphere to secure an escape route for Asagi and company.

"Looks like our ride's here to pick us up. This is where our job ends."

Asagi sighed with her smartphone in one hand.

The Necropolis's interior was already in tatters. Few of the surrounding cylindrical pillars looked like cylinders or pillars anymore. The area around Kojou and company was only safe because Asagi had deployed a bulwark using The Cleansing.

Asagi could not use her ability in Nod, however. The Cleansing could not be activated without the support of the sorcerous device called

Itogami Island. That was why a conflicted expression hovered over Asagi. She must have felt like she was powerless to help Kojou when he needed it most.

"Well, it cannot be helped. Our abilities cannot be employed on that side after all."

Shizuri shot Yukina what seemed to be an envious expression. As an ogre, Shizuri would also lose her abilities in Nod, where demonic energy was nonexistent. The only people able to use their abilities even in Nod were Kojou, who'd obtained power on par with the Fourth Primogenitor, and Yukina, who wielded spiritual energy.

"—*I apologize for the wait, one and all! Now, now, let us swiftly depart!*"

Lydianne's tank batted aside falling fragments as it landed.

"Might be best to hurry up. Looks like MAR's reserves standing by in New Itogami Island are on the move. I think they're planning to conquer the main island as a last resort."

Yuuma, hopping off the tank's back, spoke with an atypically serious tenor.

Kojou gasped, his expression hardening. MAR had a large force garrisoned at its staging base on New Itogami Island. Just because the Necropolis was dead in the water didn't mean the threat they posed had vanished into thin air.

"Go get 'em, Kojou. I know you can bring Lil' Avrora back, too."

Kojou hesitated for a moment whether to abandon charging into Nod and move to Itogami Island's defense when Yaze encouraged him. Kojou looked back at Yaze in surprise. Then the two bumped fists without another word.

This was probably his last chance to bring back Avrora, a chance that the combined strengths of Asagi, Yaze, and many others had provided him. Kojou couldn't let it go to waste, no way, no how.

Besides, Yaze's encouragement held the subtext of *Leave this to us.* All Kojou could do was trust them to see things through to the end.

A jet engine noise whined and echoed once more as the robot tank lifted off. Yuuma activated a teleport. The crimson robot tank was enveloped in a ripple-like sway.

"I'm leaving Kojou in your hands—"

From the back of the tank, Asagi looked down at Yukina and spoke those words. She along with Yaze and Shizuri were clinging on to the tank any way they could. A two-seater tank was carrying five people, a situation that was really pushing it.

"Yes."

Asagi and the others completely vanished before Yukina's voice ever reached them.

Soon after, Yukina and Kojou were struck by an intense swaying of their own. The Necropolis had made contact with the gate to Nod.

Unable to endure the warping of space, the Necropolis's innards began to crumble. Their fields of vision darkened, and rubble poured down on them.

When Kojou seemed ready to bowl over, Yukina instantly squatted and grasped him in support. The two clung to one another as they breached the gate to Nod.

CHAPTER FIVE
DAWN TRIUMPHANT

1

They were assailed by an enormous impact unlike a normal teleport. The abrupt change in air pressure was dizzying. The Necropolis—Castle Kalenaren—had passed beyond the gate to Nod.

Kojou had a sense of glass shattering as the pitch-black great sword he had summoned vanished, its power exhausted. Taking this as its cue, the half-demolished castle walls began to completely fall to pieces.

Nonetheless, the great mass of rubble sent flying in the process did not pour down on Kojou's and Yukina's heads. Time seemed to come to a standstill as the remnants of the Necropolis floated into midair, and then...stopped.

"There is...no gravity...? What is this...?"

Yukina was still clamped on to Kojou's left arm as she looked around the area. Freed from the power of gravity, her hair gently spread out as if she were underwater.

"Looks like we made it to Nod safe and sound..."

Kojou seemed drained as he exhaled. Though this was the first time he'd physically visited Nod, there was an obvious environmental difference. At the very least, there was no room to doubt they weren't on the surface anymore.

"Nod? This is...Nod, you say?"

Yukina inquired, her tone still laden with surprise.

"Yeah, probably. Well, setting that aside...Himeragi, you're, ah, exposed."

Kojou awkwardly averted his eyes from the bewildered Yukina. Yukina's skirt was also freed from the force of gravity, fluttering up with her underwear in full view.

"Eh? Wa...waaaah!!"

Shrieking, Yukina let go of Kojou's arm and hastily pressed down her skirt. This time, the reaction sent Yukina's body twirling about, thrusting her butt right into Kojou's face.

"Wh-why is this happening to... aaa, wait a...d-don't look! Please do not look!"

Yukina tried flailing her legs about, but this did not alter her positioning in any way. Apparently, thanks to using both hands to push her skirt down, she was unable to control her posture anywhere near as much as she'd like.

Though stunned by the sight of her white thighs—which he had swiftly burned into his memory—Kojou nonetheless managed to grab Yukina by her arms and put a stop to her unorthodox spinning. Though this rectified her posture, embarrassment and confusion over the weightlessness had put tears into Yukina's eyes.

"Ahhh...you all right, Himeragi?"

Kojou timidly posed that question, seeing that Yukina was hanging her head without a word.

Yukina's shoulders quivered with anger as she resentfully glared at Kojou. Her big eyes were a mess, tears spilling from them as if something had been torn inside her.

"Sen...pai...!"

"Hey, wait. There's nothing to cry over, is there?! I just tried letting you know in a friendly way... I mean, I glanced over and saw for just a moment; it's not like I was staring nonstop or anything!"

Nervously, Kojou desperately tried to excuse himself. What happened just then was a pure and simple accident owing to being in an unfamiliar, weightless environment. Kojou was offended by being made responsible for it. That said, it remained a fact he'd seen Yukina's underwear, so Kojou did feel a decent amount of guilt nonetheless, but...

"I am not angry about you seeing my panties!"

For once, Yukina outright exploded in anger in Kojou's face. She swung a clenched fist down against Kojou's chest like a child having a tantrum.

"What in the world was that?! If you knew they couldn't use the Beast Vassal Warheads, why didn't you tell me that from the beginning…! Senpai, I thought you seriously meant to have Tokyo destroyed… Do you have any idea…how worried I was…!"

Yukina's words trailed off, vanishing into incoherent sobs midway. She was the only one at the negotiations with Ladli Ren who hadn't heard of Kojou and company's plan beforehand. She'd genuinely believed Kojou had goaded them into firing a Beast Vassal Warhead into Tokyo, something that had apparently caused her deep distress.

Naturally, Kojou felt very uncomfortable, wiping sweat off his own cheeks.

"Er, there wasn't any time to explain by that point, and thanks to you getting nervous like that, the Devas bought it hook, line, and sinker… and if you wanna get right down to it, you tried to sink Itogami Island without one word to any of us so…"

"Uu…uuu…uuuuuu…!"

"Owww! …Sorry, my bad! I won't do anything like that ever again!"

With Yukina so worked up, Kojou stroked her head and voiced words of repentance. Yukina's flowing tears turned into water droplets that floated around them, gleaming like glittery gemstones.

Somehow, crying made Yukina look so young that Kojou was stricken with the urge to hug her, but unfortunately, neither of them had the luxury for such a moment.

A vibration and a rumble at Kojou's and Yukina's feet sounded like something slamming together along with a repulsive roar. It was the earsplitting death cries of a kind of beast.

Wiping her tears with the backs of her hands, Yukina drew her silver-colored spear from the case on her back. Perhaps she'd become accustomed to weightlessness after a brief time, but there was no hesitation in her movements whatsoever.

Yukina was glaring at an ashen-colored demon beast that looked like a splice between bear and wolf. Its height was between four and five meters thereabouts. The inside of its gaping maw was lined with sharp fangs. It was likely some vile demon beast created and controlled with magic for military purposes.

It was the demon warbeast, but it was acting with the desperation of prey trying to escape a predator's grasp.

An enormous tree resembling a mangrove had the demon beast in its grasp. The tree branches over a meter in diameter writhed like snakes as they constricted the demon beast's torso. The tree trunk was split open like a shark's mouth, drooling with saliva that looked like powerful acid.

"Yateveo…?! What is such a thing doing here?!"

Yukina's voice quivered in fright.

The Yateveo was a plant-type demon beast, its range chiefly in the Chaos Zone in Central and South Americas. Its branches, moving via turgor, exerted hydrostatic pressure in excess of the brute force of the great majority of demon beasts, and secreted a cocktail of paralytic and nerve poisons to securely slay any prey that approached. On top of that, they had powerful magical resistance. Even someone as ill versed on demon beast ecology as Kojou knew about these famous carnivores.

"Probably Ladli Ren's pets. Seems like these Devas love raising and releasing demon beasts into their Necropolis mazes as a hobby of theirs."

Kojou spoke with an annoyed tone. He'd thought Schtola D's story about this was an exaggeration, but apparently the information Asagi and Yaze had gleaned from him was on the money after all.

As Kojou and Yukina grimaced, the Yateveo started eating the captured demon beast right in front of them. The demon warbeast wailed death cries as its bones were bitten into while it was still alive. They wanted to avert their eyes from the gruesome spectacle.

"The demon beasts are…eating one another…!"

"Hey, Pun Girl, at least feed the damned things!"

Yukina drew in her breath a bit as Kojou spat insults at the absent Ladli Ren, but that was as far as their leisurely observations could reach, for as soon as the Yateveo had finished feeding on the demon warbeast, its branches began stretching toward Kojou and Yukina.

"Guess this is no time to file complaints! Hang on tight, Himeragi!"

Kojou picked up Yukina's slender body. The downpour of castle wall pieces was in the way, so they had to get out of the Necropolis one way or another. It was faster to blow the rubble away than to search for another traversable route.

"…Complaints?"

Yukina looked up with a sober expression, seemingly reproaching Kojou for his casual comment, but Kojou ignored her gaze and summoned a Beast Vassal. Pitch-black, bloody mist scattered all about, transforming into a giant beast.

"C'mon over, Primus Cinereus—!"

The shelled beast Kojou called forth spewed mist the color of darkness. The Necropolis remnants touched by this mist became insubstantial, melting into the vapor.

Kojou's fourth black Beast Vassal inherited from The Blood emblemized a vampire's ability to transform into mist. However, there was no guarantee anything it turned to mist would ever regain its original form.

The Necropolis remnants turned into black mist scattered with the wind, retaining nothing of their original shape as they vanished. The Yateveo with high magic resistance struggled against vaporization to the bitter end, but once the ground vanished from under its roots, there was nothing more it could do. The rubble and the demon beasts and everything else were swept away, leaving only the Necropolis's lower half like a watermelon neatly split in two. Kojou's black Beast Vassal had swept away half the mass of the Necropolis nearly a kilometer in diameter in a single instant.

As the mist thinned, the first thing entering his eyes was sea. A vast sea as far as their eyes could reach spread above Kojou's and Yukina's heads. At their feet, they saw a starless night sky covered by clouds. The remnant of the half-destroyed Necropolis was hovering uncertainly between sky and sea.

"Why is…the sea above us…?"

Yukina spoke in a daze. The undulating surface of the sea didn't feel like it was going to come falling out of the sky it stretched through. It seemed that gravity pulled things upward the closer one got to the surface to the sea.

Yukina shifted her gaze farther, her big eyes opening wide, for she noticed the presence of the enormous wall completely covering the space behind the Necropolis.

A steel-colored sheer, vertical cliff spread from the surface of the sea above to the bottom of the sky below.

The surface of the wall was carved with odd, interlocking marks, clearly indicating it was an artificial construct. It was like a bulwark built to isolate the world.

The remains of the Necropolis the pair were in clung to that wall, halfway caved in like a crushed ping-pong ball.

"What is this wall…?!"

Yukina weakly shook her head. The series of abnormal, mind-boggling spectacles were apparently causing even her to lose her cool.

"Ahhh, this is the end of Nod. We can head outside from here."

Kojou calmly explained in sharp contrast to Yukina's surprise. He was acting like a tourist visiting a place with mildly rare scenery.

"Outside?! What do you mean by that? Outside of Nod…?"

"Right, Himeragi didn't know."

Seeing Yukina approach, Kojou grappled with internal conflict.

"Himeragi, Nod's apparently a world inside some super-huge artificial island floating in space."

"Huh…?"

The sudden term *space* made Yukina freeze, her expression vanishing.

"…An artificial island floating in space… Are you saying this is a space colony?"

"Yeah, that… I feel like I've heard that somewhere."

Kojou readily nodded as he gazed upon the steel-colored "world wall."

For a time, Yukina stopped entirely as if frozen solid, after which her tiny voice quavered.

"Then this weightlessness, the sky and sea being inverted…and not being able to use demonic energy in Nod…it's all because this is inside a space colony?"

"It's not so much the sky and sea are upside down as the inside of the colony walls are all one big sea. Apparently this keeps the bad effects of cosmic rays on living creatures to a minimum. All that said, the gravity here is artificially made with centrifugal force so it figures gravity's weak near the center like we are right now."

Kojou flicked a piece of rubble floating in midair with a fingertip as he continued.

They were floating in a void far removed from the earth inside a gargantuan space colony over two hundred kilometers in length—this was the true nature of the otherworldly land known as Nod.

As a result, Nod's sun always floated right around the water's horizon. Eternal twilight without any noonday sun and long, starless nights—such were the days in Nod.

"And the gate to Nod only opening at night is…"

Yukina aired that question with an expression that was still incredulous. Kojou narrowed his eyes as he recalled some kind of vague memory.

"That's related to the Earth's own rotation. This time of the year, Nod's on the opposite side of the sun from Earth's point of view, so the gate only opens when the sun sets. It can be the other way around dependin' on the season."

"Ghhh…just how far from the earth are we in tangible terms?"

"Asagi guesstimated it was somewhere between the orbits of Mars and Jupiter, but she doesn't know that for sure. There's not even any proof it's inside the solar system."

Kojou sighed casually. Maybe an expert in spatial control magic like Natsuki could accurately determine its coordinates, but Kojou was an amateur. What he did know with crystal clarity was that this place was far, far removed from the earth. The very fact that Fourth Primogenitor–class demonic energy was required to maintain a teleportation gate was proof of that.

"Just who did this…and for what purpose…?"

Yukina shook her head with visible confusion.

"This is a way station. It seems to be some kind of corridor for headin' to planets outside this solar system. Did you know? They call themselves Devas 'cause they're visitors from the heavens to start with."

Kojou made a pained smile as he continued.

There was no proof the Devas really were visitors from another planet, but the fact remained that at the peak of their glory, they had built and employed the space colony known as Nod. They intended to use Nod as a way station en route to other solar systems.

"Seems like the decline of the Devas starting even before The Great Cleansing means they don't have the technology or the passion to actually continue space development, though."

Kojou mused aloud in a tone that somehow felt forlorn. In the end, Nod never had a chance to shine as that way station and was used as a simple storage facility for Beast Vassal Warheads. The only thing left in the Great Sea of Nod was the steel-colored artificial island, deserted and abandoned.

"...You know quite a bit about this, senpai."

Yukina kept her voice calm as she glared at Kojou with a deeply wounded look. Her reproachful gaze shook him up a bit.

"Eh?"

"Senpai, why do you know all of this? I thought you were bad with history classes?"

"Ah...er, that's..."

"This is Aiba's knowledge, isn't it? You drank Aiba's blood and gained her Priestess of Cain memories in the process, didn't you?"

Yukina pressed the issue with Kojou with half-lidded eyes. Kojou gently averted his eyes in silence. It was exactly right that Kojou had drunk Asagi's blood and made her a servant during Yukina's absence.

Scrutinizing Kojou's deep, awkward silence, Yukina sighed deeply.

"Senpai, you really do rush to do indecent things with other girls when I take my eyes off you for even a second..."

"It wasn't exactly indecent."

"...Yet you would not drink my blood."

Yukina ignored Kojou's half-hearted rebuttal and pursed her lips, visibly peeved. She was apparently still nursing a grudge over the incident at the hotel the prior morning. She was surprisingly stubborn about such things.

Kojou shook his head in exasperation, abandoning all resistance.

"Well, it's fine. More importantly, we've gotta go look for Avrora, huh..."

"I suppose we should...but how would we look for her...?"

Yukina slapped her own cheeks and got serious. At great pains, they had arrived in Nod, only to find it far vaster than she had imagined. She didn't feel like they could find Avrora in any kind of random search, but...

"...*Kojou.*"

Kojou and Yukina were at a loss when someone abruptly called out to them. It was a very familiar voice.

Turning around, the pair saw a girl with long black hair who'd appeared out of the blue.

"Nagisa?!"

"Nagisa, how…?!"

Kojou and Yukina called out her name in surprise. Floating there while enveloped by a glow was Nagisa Akatsuki. She was wearing a monochrome sailor suit greatly resembling her Saikai Academy uniform.

"Nagisa…the hell are you doing in Nod…?"

"Wait, senpai. You are mistaken. This is not the real Nagisa…"

When Kojou tried to rush over, Yukina swiftly stopped him.

The girl in front of them changed shape. Her long black hair adopted a metallic glint, and her sociable face changed into one that seemed a tiny bit mature.

Kojou knew a girl who could change her shape like this. She was the one who'd appeared before Kojou when once caught up in encroachment from Nod, saving his life.

"You're…Glenda…?"

"…*Giggle, so we finally meet, Kojou Akatsuki…*"

A Glenda grown to sixteen or seventeen years of age looked at Kojou with a smile. Seeing this expression, Kojou instinctively knew that this was not the Glenda whom Kojou knew, but someone else—no, a different Glenda.

"*Over here…the last daughter of Mizen is waiting.*"

Beckoning the bewildered pair with her hand, the girl with steel-colored hair started walking.

Kojou and Yukina nodded to one another and chased after the second Glenda.

2

Thin air swayed like a ripple. A woman in a gaudy outfit appeared from it. The place to which Ladli Ren had teleported using a sorcerous device was inside the bridge of a hospital ship moored at New Itogami Island.

"Lady Ladli, are you all right?"

The head of MAR's security division—a man known as the Colonel—addressed her with an expression of relief.

Ladli glared back at him.

"I am hardly all right. The Necropolis was savaged and heavily damaged."

"R-right."

"Negotiations have failed, so we are forced to subdue them with might. Send orders to all units garrisoned on New Itogami Island—we are shifting to Plan C. Also, release the Gaminodons, please."

"The...Gaminogigants? But that's—"

A rare look of hesitation came over the Colonel. The expression was a product of mistrust and disgust for the Gaminogigants. Internally, he strongly resisted using weapons that would indiscriminately slaughter civilians.

For her part, Ladli smiled, seeming downright delighted.

"Oh, I don't mind. As long as we get control of Keystone Gate, everything works out. Even if Itogami Island is ruined as a city, we'll cross that bridge when we get there."

The Colonel nodded without a word and issued a curt command to his communications officer.

Fifteen minutes later, MAR's remaining forces launched an all-out attack on Itogami Island.

The crimson robot tank equipped with a flight unit descended from the night sky with a roar.

The tank's expected landing point was the roof of Keystone Gate. Yuuma and Asagi sat on the back of the tank while Shizuri and Yaze clung to its left and right legs respectively. The tank was clearly over its carrying capacity, but Lydianne somehow succeeded in landing it. Yaze and the others got off, standing on the roof with weary faces.

New figures appeared on the roof as if awaiting their return. They were a little witch wearing an ornate dress, a blue-haired homunculus wearing a maid outfit, and a tall, slender, chestnut-haired Attack Mage.

"—You kids have really done it this time."

Natsuki spoke, glaring at Asagi as the latter dismounted the tank.

Asagi looked back at her diminutive homeroom teacher with a bit of surprise on her face.

"Natsuki? How'd you get out of the detention area? It had a force fi...*taaah*?!"

"Don't address your teacher by her given name."

Asagi reeled back from the shockwave smacking her on the forehead as Natsuki spat the words out with pronounced disdain.

"Er...that's the part you're complaining about...?"

Yaze sighed with exasperation. Asagi, clutching her forehead with both hands, was crouched over with tears in her eyes.

During the time Natsuki had been shut in the detention center, her pupils had engaged in negotiations with MAR, caused them to fire Beast Vassal Warheads, and brought down the Necropolis in Itogami Island airspace. He wasn't exactly surprised she was cross with them.

By rights, Natsuki wanted to say a lot more than that, but the lack of time made her hold her tongue. A legion of emotions thus filled the shockwave with which she'd delivered that smack to the forehead.

"Where's Yukina?! Weren't Yukina and Kojou Akatsuki with you?!"

Sayaka looked at everyone getting off the tank as she spoke in an earnest tone.

Shizuri calmly pointed to the magic symbols hovering in the night sky.

"Those two went to Nod aboard the Necropolis."

"Hah?! Nod?! Wh-what's the meaning of this?! Why did only he and Yukina...?!"

"Wait a...h-hard...to...breathe!"

Shizuri yelped fervently as Sayaka wrung her by the collar with incredible force. Yaze and Astarte swiftly intervened to make Sayaka stop.

Yuuma watched this with a strained smile but soon turned to face Natsuki with a sober look.

"—So, Teach. What's the situation?"

"The MAR attack units garrisoned on New Itogami Island have begun invading Itogami Island proper."

Natsuki shifted her eyes toward Itogami Island's northern reaches. New Itogami Island, which floated all around Itogami Island itself, had been pockmarked by MAR bases during the back-and-forth of the

Electoral War. The closest part of New Itogami Island was only ten kilometers away. Keeping them from landing forces was an exceptionally difficult job.

"With all other options exhausted, they have no way to turn things around except by conquering the island through force. They're probably attacking with a do-or-die mentality."

Natsuki's calm explanation created a grim atmosphere on the rooftop.

Itogami Island was fundamentally a city of scientific study. It had not been constructed with urban warfare in mind. The Island Guard was armed only with the objective of maintaining public order in a Demon Sanctuary. This left it with a devastating lack of combat strength with which to resist an all-out military invasion. By rights, since Itogami Island had no dedicated military forces, its defense fell under the government of Japan's jurisdiction.

Yet this very same government of Japan had attempted to sink the island, so relations between the two had significantly deteriorated. On top of that, the greatest combat strength Itogami Island had—in other words, the Fourth Primogenitor—was absent. This was the worst scenario any of them could think of.

"So in reality, is this winnable?"

Shizuri's question got right to the point.

"MAR's main force went into Nod, so the remaining forces should be logistics units primarily. Even the Island Guard's combat strength should give them a pretty hard time."

Natsuki voiced her cold analysis of the facts. *That's right*, said Sayaka, totally agreeing, having visited one such MAR base just a few days earlier.

It was generally held that, in war, it was easier to defend than to attack. If the forces on both sides were equally balanced, the Island Guard should have had an overwhelming home field advantage.

On top of that, being a Demon Sanctuary, Itogami Island had over twenty thousand registered demons, plus numerous Attack Mages, Natsuki and Sayaka included. Even without Kojou present, one could fairly say the balance of power was in their favor.

"But," continued Natsuki, "MAR has to understand all of this."

"Certainly…barring simple desperation, invading despite all that must mean they have some sort of trump card in their hand."

Shizuri's brow creased as she sank into thought.

Yaze, lazily leaning against the tank with eyes closed, seemed immersed in sound as he shook his head.

"Looks like that trump card's bein' played already."

"What?"

Natsuki and all others turned their eyes in the direction Yaze pointed.

It was the sea coast of Island North. Rising like the tide from the sea side of the breakwater, a flurry of giant figures emerged from inside the sea. The figures exceeded ten meters in length with room to spare. They were humanoid monsters with enormous heads, as if sperm whales were able to walk upright.

The monsters' whole bodies were covered in hardened, armor-like hides with countless tentacles protruding from their backs. The heads had sets of gleaming, crimson eyes. Shizuri and the others recognized them.

"Those are…Unknowns! Unknowns walking on two legs…!"

"*Such a…monstrous visage…!*"

Shizuri and Lydianne shouted simultaneously. These six-eyed giants were likely the final version of Nine-Four—the Unknowns that had appeared on Itogami Island once before.

MAR had apparently developed Gaminodons into these humanoid demon beasts, keeping them in reserve as their trump card for invading Itogami Island.

"Guess they had one more nutty rabbit to pull out of the hat…"

A pained expression came over Yaze as his gaze roamed the seacoast.

MAR hadn't sent a mere handful of demon beasts into combat. Demon beasts were rushing Island North and East's coastlines one after another. The demon beasts that had landed already exceeded a dozen. Island Guard positions on the coast were trampled and uprooted, defeated in the blink of an eye. At that rate, the conquest of Itogami Island was only a matter of time.

"Asagi Aiba, how many of those can you crush with your Cleansing?"

Natsuki inquired in a tiny voice. Asagi grimaced and reluctantly shook her head. The Cleansing was no simple attack spell—it was a forbidden, high-level spell that rewrote the physical laws of the world. Certain destruction of the humanoid demon beasts was within its capabilities no matter how powerful their magic resistance—but only if she could activate The Cleansing in the first place.

The Cleansing was so overpowered that activating it meant magical calculations so vast, they chewed up Itogami Island's entire information network. They didn't have the luxury of such an operation. Most of the main computer's computational capacity was being used to neutralize the Beast Vassal Warheads.

"If Mogwai's corporeal form wasn't eating resources, I could take out several, but under these circumstances, maybe two? It's not like I can make leading citizens to safety a lower priority, either..."

"If that is how it is, it is my turn, yes? May I take it that all I need do is cut those oversized things down?"

While Asagi murmured with regret, Shizuri replied, brimming in confidence for some reason. She was ready to leap into combat that very moment when Yaze pulled her back in a hurry.

"No, you need to stay put, Cas. You flung around all that crazy demonic energy in the Necropolis, but your body's in tatters, right?"

"W-who is this Cas?! And this damage handicap only makes it fair for them!"

"—Yuuma Tokoyogi. Take this preening paladin and the Lion King Agency ponytail girl and support the Island Guard in East. Astarte and I will handle North."

Natsuki calmly issued orders with a resigned expression.

"Roger that, Teach."

"P...preening paladin...?!"

Yuuma nodded with a strained smile as Shizuri's shoulders shook from anger.

Only high-level Attack Mages could go up against Unknown-class living weapons. Since they couldn't depend on Asagi's Cleansing, the only option was to duke it out with everything they had.

"And I shall defendeth Lady Empress and Keystone Gate?"

Lydianne spoke with a delighted tone. Natsuki brusquely nodded.

"That's how it is. Also, Yaze, you understand what your job is, don't you?"

"My job…er, ahhh…so that's it…"

Yaze seemed to feel a heavy weight upon him as he looked toward the sky. In terms of pure combat capabilities, Natsuki and the others had Yaze beaten, but he had alternate ways of fighting. That's what Natsuki was conveying to him.

"Hurry. We won't last long with just the people on hand."

Natsuki left those words behind before vanishing from sight. She'd teleported to the field of battle. Next, Lydianne's tank lifted off, and Yuuma and the others vanished, too. Yaze was the only one left on the roof.

"Guess I gotta… Time for me to do my job."

Shaking his head as if resigning himself, Yaze took his smartphone out of his pants pocket. He called a hotline reserved for the exclusive use of president of the Yaze Consortium.

3

The isolation wall Kojou had called the end of Nod was not one flat surface, but countless facilities merged together as a series of intersecting structural blocks. It was a little like a miniature spaceship similar to what you'd see in old superhero shows.

Many of the facilities were tiny structures like containers, but in the middle was a large-scale structure reaching numerous kilometers in total length.

The place Glenda Number Two was taking Kojou and Yukina to was a ridiculously huge transmission tower inside this section. The tower jutted vertically toward the night sky. The tower was five or six kilometers tall. Kojou estimated its diameter to be a couple of hundred meters or so.

This structure, enveloped by clouds of thick steam, looked more like a cape or a floating bridge than a tower when you looked straight up at it. The way it floated in a sea of clouds gave it a surreal, ethereal feel.

Because it was a little removed from the colony center, there was a weak amount of gravity on the bridge's surface. Thanks to this, Kojou and Yukina, unaccustomed to weightlessness, were able to walk along it with ease.

Their guide, Glenda Number Two, had vanished from sight at some point.

Kojou and Yukina subconsciously held hands as they walked together along the bridge into the clouds—and then a small figure leaped out at them from a pure white cloud.

"Daah! Kojouuu!"

The girl with long, steel-colored hair hugged Kojou with the vigor of a puppy. Owing to the low gravity, Kojou staggered, unable to withstand her momentum.

"Glenda! So this is where you've been!"

Seeing that it was the real Glenda this time, Kojou fluffed up and stroked her hair.

A heartwarming smile came over Glenda as she rubbed her cheek against him. Watching this, Yukina exhaled in relief.

Glenda had been in front of a small building standing at the tip of the bridge. Kojou could make out familiar girls nearby and, also, a creature looking like a badly sewn teddy bear.

"—Er, Kiriha Kisaki?! What are you doing here…?!"

Noticing the raven-haired beauty with a foul look in her eyes, Kojou blinked, visibly perplexed.

Hmph, huffed Kiriha, snorting with contempt as she gripped her tuning-fork-style spear.

"Miss Hikawa…Miss Yuiri, too…"

Noticing that Yuiri and Shio were sitting on the ground, Yukina broke into a small run and approached them.

Yuiri and Shio were wearing High God Grove uniforms, but Shio wasn't wearing her jacket. Yuiri was wearing Shio's jacket in her place. The right hand poking out of the jacket's sleeve was red and inflamed, hanging limply. Yukina's expression grew grave when she realized this.

Beside her, Yukina felt Kojou gasp.

"Avrora…"

Kojou was staring at the willowy, golden-haired girl standing stiff, still clutching the badly sewn teddy bear in her arms. Her radiant blue eyes drifted left and right from worry. Her cheeks were red.

"Avrora…I'm so glad you're safe."

"I-indeed."

When Kojou tensely called out to her, the vampire girl gave him a little nod.

The girl was maintaining an odd degree of distance as Kojou awkwardly scratched his head.

"Ahh…sorry I'm late. I'm here to pick you up."

"Th-thou hast done well. Thine efforts are praiseworthy."

"R-right."

Neither of the two met each other's eyes, and after exchanging words like complete strangers, Kojou and Avrora fell silent. This was the first time they'd properly met face-to-face in ages, so neither had any idea what to say.

For a time, Yukina and the others watched the tension-filled exchange between the pair with bated breath.

"—What are you, a couple of cousins who haven't seen each other in forever?!"

Finally, unable to endure the silence, Yuiri gave them a tongue-lashing from behind.

Shio indulged in a deep, weary sigh.

"There's more to say than that, isn't there?! Like, hug and stuff, cry tears of joy over being reunited, something?! After you went through all that trouble just to see each other again…!"

"That's true, but it's just straight-up embarrassing with everyone else watching…!"

Kojou retorted, his own face red. *Yes, yes*, said Avrora's little nods.

"He's acting quite a bit differently than he does with us, isn't he?"

"Dah…"

Yukina and Glenda shot Kojou cold stares. *Oh, give me a break*, said Kojou's heavy grimace.

"Right, Avrora. You hungry? Wanna eat some, um, candy?"

Reaching into his parka's pocket, Kojou took out a handful of colorful candy pieces.

"Kojou, when did you get ahold of…"

"Probably when I decided to bring Avrora back. Figured I'd lure her with food."

Yuiri and Shio whispered to each other with tiny voices. Yukina sighed as she watched on. Avrora, however, peered into Kojou's hand with glimmering eyes, as if to say, *'Tis as expected of thee.*

Then she noticed a tiny, silver-colored ring mixed in with the candies.

"A ring of pacts..."

"Eh? Ah, this...well, this isn't food."

"Aaa..."

When Kojou tried to put the ring back in his pocket, Avrora reflexively grabbed his hand to stop him. Kojou found Avrora's reaction a little surprising.

"Wait, you want a ring, too?"

"Uuu...ah...i-if thou desirest it..."

Avrora spoke those words, glancing at Kojou's expression as she implored him. After a brief contemplation, *Well fine*, thought Kojou, handing her the ring. Either way, it wasn't something Kojou had any use for himself.

Shio and the others were beside themselves as they watched.

"H-hey, Kojou Akatsuki...! Are you all right with this?! If you hand that to Avrora, you'll become the Fourth Primogenitor's Blood Serva... Ah, wait, you're both vampires, which one becomes whose servant...?!"

"K-Kojou...wait a...owww!"

Yuiri tried to stand up in a hurry but moaned frailly as she pressed on her right arm. Yukina instantly moved to support the tottering girl's back.

"Miss Yuiri...um...your right arm..."

"Ahh, this...I was...kind of a klutz and tripped..."

Hehe, said Yuiri, bashfully sticking out her tongue. She was maintaining her calm, but her arm was hurt even worse than it looked. Even if it was given time to heal, Yukina didn't think it would ever regain full motion.

"Shahryar Ren's flame dragon companion got her. This never would have happened if I'd properly supported Yuiri at the time..."

Shio went down on one knee, her face twisting with deep regret. Yuiri shook her head, a bit in a bind.

"It's not your fault, Shio. Besides, Nagisa healed it so it'll be all right in a little while. That girl's healing spells are incredible. Ah...it'll be hard to use this arm for real combat, I suppose."

I'm sorry, Yuiri, Yukina expressed with a bow of her head. Yukina bit her lips, unable to reply aloud.

"What do you mean, Nagisa's healing spells? She really did come to Nod, too?"

Kojou cut into the conversation. He remembered that Glenda Number Two had been adopting Nagisa's form when she'd appeared before them only a little earlier.

"Ah, no, it's not that… I mean it's not that Nagisa came in person…"

"In one sense, I guess she did come, but it was really Glenda doing the talking, you see…"

Yuiri and Shio seemed at pains to explain as they glanced at one another. Apparently even they didn't have a firm grasp on exactly what had happened.

"Well, that'd be a long story so maybe wait until things calm down a little more before gettin' into it?"

The badly sewn teddy bear interrupted to arbitrarily drag the conversation back on track. Glancing at the teddy bear still in Avrora's arms, Kojou let out a languid sigh.

"You're…Cain?"

"Eh?"

Yukina widened her eyes in bewilderment when Kojou suddenly brought up that name.

The girls were right to be skeptical. The name of the Sinful God was straight out of mythology, whereas this was a badly sewn teddy bear fit for a kindergarten. There seemed to be nothing in common between the two whatsoever, but…?

"Well, that's pretty close to the mark, I'd say."

Baring its triangular teeth, Mogwai smiled, downright proud of itself for some reason.

"More accurately, I'm an emulated personality from data taken while Cain was alive. My personality was engraved in stone inside of the 'Coffin' on Itogami Island. It learned to reconstitute itself as an AI. This is a mock body made with The Cleansing. Pretty cool, huh?"

"Freeing the icons of the Beast Vassal Warheads, that's your objective, right?"

Kojou inquired without any hint of surprise. Drinking Asagi's blood and sharing her memories meant that Kojou already knew Mogwai's true nature.

"Well, that was kind of my one and only regret in life, y'see."

Gazing at the artificial isle floating overhead, Mogwai narrowed his eyes with a nostalgic look.

"You have my thanks, Kojou My Bro. Thanks to you protectin' Lil' Dodekatos, I learned all about the icons. To free them, I needed a sample—I needed one of Mizen's daughters in my hands more than anything."

"…Were not you and the Fourth Primogenitor supposed enemies…?"

Yukina seemed perplexed as she posed this question.

In the history known to Kojou and the others, the Fourth Primogenitor was a god-killing weapon created for the purpose of slaying Cain the Sinful God, yet Mogwai spoke the name of the original Fourth Primogenitor as if they were old friends.

On top of that, the emulated personality calling itself Mogwai was in the embrace of the current Fourth Primogenitor. These incongruous facts were leaving Yukina and others confused.

"At the very least, it's a fact that the Devas left behind on the surface made the Fourth Primogenitor to kill me. I gotta say, when I found out about the existence of Star Beast Vassals made out of pure hatred, guided by the stars so that you could summon 'em even in Nod, far removed from the surface world…man, even I had to shudder."

Mogwai gazed on the bewildered girls with visible delight as he spoke.

"So you and the Fourth Primogenitor took advantage of that?"

Kojou glared at Mogwai reproachfully.

The human boy named Mizen was tamed by Cain the Sinful God. The Devas used his flesh and blood to give birth to the Fourth Primogenitor to extract payback from Cain, whom they considered a traitor.

Yet even this became but one component of Cain's plan.

"You made sure they saw you, the administrator, getting killed, and closed the gate to Nod, making sure the Beast Vassal Warheads you left behind couldn't be used by anyone."

Kojou turned a glance toward Avrora, standing still and baffled.

"It takes the power of the Star Beast Vassals to open the sealed gate again. That's why you and the Fourth Primogenitor made him rip his own body apart to hide the Beast Vassals. You forced twelve Beast Vassals onto twelve girls who didn't know a thing."

"For the record, that's somethin' Mizen did all on his own. I didn't order him to do it."

Mogwai justified himself with a slightly sulky tone. Apparently even Cain hadn't expected his friend the Fourth Primogenitor to choose to end his own existence.

"Mizen's the one who made that Order of the End thing, then?"

Yeah, nodded Mogwai, in response to Kojou's question.

"That bastard The Blood got things kinda wrong, but the point of instilling fear about the Fourth Primogenitor into people to stop the Fourth Primogenitor from bein' revived was the Order of the End's original role. It would have sucked for the gate to Nod to open before preparations were ready."

"…Preparations?"

"I mean preparations to neutralize the Beast Vassal Warheads and free the icon girls. It took two indispensable things to carry that out. One, humankind had to have enough technology to at least revive me. The other is the arrival of peace. From the bottom of my heart, I want the icon girls freed from the Beast Vassal Warheads to live well, and they need happy, everyday lives for that."

"So by chance, Itogami Island fulfilled those two conditions."

"By chance, huh… I suppose you're right. If the day you met Lil' Dodekatos was by chance, then I guess you're right, Bro.

"Keh-keh," said Mogwai with a sardonic smile.

Cain, revived inside Itogami Island's main computer as an emulated personality, had been working under the radar, preparing to neutralize the Beast Vassal Warheads. Asagi Aiba, Priestess of Cain, and Avrora, excavated from an island in the Mediterranean Sea, had been assembled in a Demon Sanctuary, a boxed garden in which humankind and demonkind could peacefully coexist. He probably had something to do with that, plus choosing Itogami Island as the site of the Blazing Banquet so that the Fourth primogenitor might be revived.

"Gotta say, Bro, havin' a supposed mere human like you getting' the power of the Fourth Primogenitor had even me clutching my head. Well, it worked out pretty well in the end so I ain't complaining."

"I have a whole mountain of things I'd like to say to you, though... Hey, you can't pull the 'I'm just a teddy bear' card out now!"

Kojou shouted in anger when Mogwai stopped moving completely on purpose. Mogwai circled around Avrora's back in an effort to escape from Kojou's follow-ups.

Yukina and the others gazed at the earnest exchanges between Kojou and stuffed animal with incredulous looks on their faces. Their minds didn't seem to have caught up with what Mogwai had said just yet.

"—None of that crap matters, so could you put it off until later?"

Kojou was locked in difficult combat to peel Mogwai off Avrora's back when Kiriha interrupted with a furious voice. Her glacial tone threw Kojou for a loop as he looked back.

"Er, it kinda does matter but... Wait, aren't you hurt real bad yourself...?!"

"Be quiet or I'll kill you. If you don't like it, drink my blood. As in, right this second!"

Kiriha stripped off the scarf of her sailor suit and showed him her slender, exposed neck. Setting her personality to one side, in terms of looks alone, she was quite a beauty.

Kojou put every shred of his rationality to work as he tore his eyes away from Kiriha's pale skin.

"Drink your blood... Wait, what do you want that for?!"

"If I become your Blood Servant, I will regain regenerative ability on par with a vampire, yes? I will be able to properly heal these wounds so that I can fight again. Then I can go murder that piece-of-shit dragon!"

Kiriha unloaded a barrage of words. Cowed by her fury, Avrora stiffened like a little animal in the throes of despair. Kojou was a little taken aback by Kiriha's forcefulness himself.

"Er, ah, I get the logic, but that's weird, right? You shouldn't be fighting a dragon; you should get your butt back to the surface and go to a hospital."

"That dragon hurt me! I'm supposed to let it go? Don't toy with me; I'll kill you! Stop complaining and Drink! My! Blood! We're bath-mates who've immersed in the same hot water, are we not?!"

"Hey, that's got nothing to do with this?! It's not like I went into the bath with you; you're the one who showed up uninvited to the guys' bath after the fact, right?!"

When Kiriha stubbornly grabbed him, Kojou tried to fling her away in annoyance.

At the corner of Kojou's gaze, Shio began loosening her own necktie. Without a word, she undid her buttons one after another, greatly opening her collar.

"—Er, why is even Miss Hikawa beginning to strip?!"

Noticing Shio's actions, Yukina swiftly tried to stop her, but Shio had a completely serious look on her face as she walked in front of Kojou.

"I hate to admit it, but Kiriha Kisaki is right. Please, Kojou Akatsuki. Do whatever you want with me. If you tell me to take my clothes off, I'll strip. I don't mind if you put me through humiliating things just like Himeragi. Please, heal Yuiri's wounds…!"

"Um…has he done any such things to me…?"

Yukina froze, seemingly shocked by Shio's words. In her place, Yuiri rushed over to Shio.

"W-wait, Shio…you don't need to do anything embarrassing for my sake…! If Kojou tells me to strip, I'll strip for him…!"

"Er, why is this premised on me telling one of you to strip exactly…?!"

Yuiri and Shio were working each other up when Kojou objected with a weary voice.

Glancing between Kojou and the girls, Glenda blinked hard and tilted her head.

"Dah…should Glenda strip, too?"

"No, you should not!"

"Keh-keh, you sure are popular, My Bro."

Mogwai poked his head out from behind Avrora's back and sarcastically pointed that out.

"How does this situation look like popularity to you?!"

"So whose blood are you gonna go for, Bro?"

"Whose blood… Sheesh, when you put it like that…"

Kojou's words died in his throat as he felt powerful gazes from Shio and company on his cheeks.

A vampire's Blood Servant meant a semi-eternal existence living alongside one's master. Even if this was provisional, he keenly understood the reasoning that servants were not something to create lightly.

On the other hand, the fact remained that this would be an effective means of healing Yuiri and the others' wounds. *If I can save the girls with my actions, shouldn't I drink their blood without hesitating?* anguished Kojou.

Kojou's clouded thoughts were swept away by the explosion that occurred without the slightest warning.

"—Wha?!"

Enveloped by crimson flames, the little tower standing on the floating bridge crumbled. It was an incandescent beam not reliant on demonic energy—dragon breath.

"The control tower…!"

"The Flame Dragon?!"

Blown down by the blast winds, Yuiri and Shio shouted at the same time. Kiriha and Yukina were sent flying but regained their balance right after, raising their respective spears.

Kojou, Avrora, and Glenda rolled on the ground as one tangled pile. Kojou tried to shield the two, but he'd been sent rolling, unable to withstand the impact.

Something strange happened to Mogwai's body inside the fallen Avrora's arms. Faint static ran throughout his body as he rapidly faded.

"The connection to Itogami Island's been cut, huh…"

Gazing at his own hands as they crumbled further, Mogwai mumbled like it was no big deal.

"Cain…!"

Kojou called out to Mogwai. The badly sewn teddy bear looked back at the unnerved Kojou, making what felt like a smile of satisfaction as he raised his voice.

"Later, Bro. We'll meet again…soon enough."

"Uuu… aaa…!"

Avrora tried to hold Mogwai tight, but her arms managed only to futilely pass through him. Watching Mogwai vanish without a sound, Kojou stopped moving, his thoughts completely blank.

The next moment—

"Senpai!!"

Silver-colored sparks ferociously scattered in the corner of Kojou's vision. Yukina had used Snowdrift Wolf to shoot down a silvery bolt flying amid the flames.

"Wha…?!"

Kojou looked down in shock at the remnants of the bolt impaling the ground.

It was a fully metallic bow gun bolt. It was short and thick, resembling a stake more than a bolt.

It was a silver-colored stake imbued with spiritual energy. It was just like the purging stake for destroying vampires that Kojou had once used to slay Avrora.

If that stake had been made by the Devas, it wasn't strange if Shahryar Ren had one of his own, but the sudden return of memories of an abominable past left Kojou frozen stiff for a second. This was a fatal opening.

"Eh…?"

Warm droplets fell onto Kojou's cheeks. They were glossy, crimson droplets, seductive in their beauty.

Yukina's body wobbled. Bereft of strength, she dropped to one knee.

Yukina's shoulder was dyed a deep red from the fresh blood gushing from it. Kojou didn't know what had happened. All he could do was stare in a daze as the fresh color spread through Yukina's uniform.

"Hime…ragi…?"

Behind the wobbling Yukina, he spotted Shahryar Ren clad in a combat suit.

He'd unleashed an invisible slicing attack—but Yukina took the unseen blade about to slice Kojou and Avrora apart in their stead. Yukina had no time to reposition Snowdrift Wolf right after batting down the purging stake. That was why she had no choice but to use her own body to shield them.

"I am sorry, senpai…I…"

Yukina smiled weakly. Fresh blood spilled from those lips. The slicing attack unleashed by Shahryar Ren had sliced through her shoulder blade all the way to her lungs. It was so grave a wound, she could have died instantaneously.

The instant he realized this, Kojou's simmering anger was blotted out with white-hot rage.

"Uwaaaaaaaaaaaaaaaaaaaaaaaaaa—!"

With that scream, the bloody mist gushing out of him turned the sky of Nod pitch-black.

4

"Shahryar Ren...! Why, youuuuu!"

Holding Yukina's bloody body, Kojou howled as demonic energy flooded out of him.

Shahryar Ren was visible at a spot only thirty meters away. Behind him, armed MAR infantry appeared one after another.

Ren and the others had apparently teleported to near the center of the colony, taking advantage of the low gravity to come up behind Kojou and the others without a sound. Thanks to that, even Yukina and the others hadn't noticed the surprise attack beforehand.

"Your anger is a delight to behold, Kojou Akatsuki."

Bathed in demonic energy waves sufficient to shake the entirety of Nod, Ren said this without moving an inch.

The MAR infantrymen turned their guns toward Kojou as one. There was no sign of any warning. They intended to slaughter Kojou and the others, no questions asked.

"But my anger at your stealing the Beast Vassal Warheads from me is nothing so petty!"

"C'mon over, Primus Adamas!"

There was a roar of gunfire before Ren's words had even finished, but Kojou had already finished summoning his Beast Vassal. The pitch-black bloody mist transformed into an enormous bighorn sheep that became a wall of black diamond crystals reflecting the bullets back at them.

The gunfire bouncing off the black diamond crystals mowed down one MAR infantryman after the other. The pitch-black divine sheep had the trait of returning an opponent's attacks back upon him with equal force.

With many of their men felled by their own gunfire, Ren's unit suddenly became incapable of action, but Kojou's Beast Vassal vanished as well. It wasn't that Kojou had released his summons. The divine sheep had shattered into tiny particles and vanished, its strength seemingly exhausted.

"…Senpai…that's…?"

Yukina inquired in an anguished voice, but Kojou said nothing in reply. It wasn't because he didn't know the cause of the Beast Vassal dissipating. It was precisely because he knew that silence was his only response.

"So it is true. I didn't think the Beast Vassals of that failed prototype The Blood could possibly hold out for long."

Shahryar Ren laughed profoundly, not even sparing a glance at his injured and fallen men.

Properly speaking, the black Beast Vassals of The Blood that Kojou had obtained should have vanished with The Blood back at Keystone Gate. Zana Lashka had pretty much forced them into a seal so that she could hand them over to Kojou, but this was little more than a temporary respite.

The black Beast Vassals had begun slowly vanishing since immediately after Kojou had obtained them. Their collapse had only hastened since Kojou's arrival in Nod.

Nod was a place where only the Fourth Primogenitor's Beast Vassals could be properly summoned. The black Beast Vassals could be summoned only a single time. Once their one final summons was complete, each would completely vanish.

"How many Beast Vassals do you have left, Kojou Akatsuki?"

Ren laughed delightedly, taunting Kojou to back him farther into a corner.

"I only need one to blow you away, Shahryar Ren!"

Kojou glared at Ren head-on. His MAR infantrymen were already routed. Kreyd the Flame Dragon was circling overhead, observing the battle between Kojou and Ren.

He just had to defeat Ren. That fact made Kojou hesitate just a tiny bit.

Deva or not, if Kojou used a black Beast Vassal on an opponent in the flesh at that range, he was highly likely to kill Ren. That fact was making Kojou hold back.

Scorning Kojou's indecision, Ren let a tiny laugh slip.

"What do you think is the reason an exceedingly proud dragon like Kreyd obeys me?"

"What?"

"It is nothing dramatic. Put simply, I am stronger than he is."

"…!!"

The impact to the side of his head made Kojou's vision wobble. He fell to the ground, holding Yukina's body in his arms. Shahryar Ren's invisible blow had shaken Kojou's brain.

Even if vampires had nigh-immortal levels of regenerative ability, putting the body off-kilter made that virtually useless. Kojou realized that Deva divine power held far more danger than pure destructiveness.

"Besides, aren't you getting something quite wrong? I am not the one you should be fighting."

Looking down at the staggering Kojou, Ren took out a sorcerous device shaped like a dagger. It was the sorcerous device for controlling the artificial vampires known as Kaleid Bloods—in other words, Avrora.

"Aaaaaaaaaaaaa!!"

Behind Kojou, Avrora let out a high-pitched scream.

Turning back, Kojou set eyes upon Avrora's whole body, releasing a torrent of thick demonic energy swirling around her. Under the sorcerous device's control, Avrora was trying to summon the Beast Vassals of the Fourth Primogenitor.

"Avaaa!"

"Stop, Avrora Florestina…!"

Glenda and Kiriha tried to stop Avrora, but the pair, impeded by the demonic energy Avrora was giving off, couldn't even get close to her.

Avrora summoned only a single Beast Vassal.

This, however, was no Beast Vassal known to Kojou. The mirage-like creature floating above Avrora's head was an enormous, ghoulish chimera fusing all twelve of the Fourth Primogenitor's Beast Vassals together.

It had the body of a minotaur, a twin-headed dragon for a tail, the wings of a monstrous bird and the arms of an undine, the horns of a bicorn and the claws of a lion—it was a mixture of all, a partway fusion of each, taking the form of an enormous monster. This was the result of Avrora's inability to properly control the Beast Vassals, instead taking only part of each, so that they materialized as one incomplete monstrosity.

"Oh...shit...!"

Kojou summoned all of his remaining black Beast Vassals.

The Beast Vassals summoned by Avrora didn't even have the intellect of beasts remaining. They were simply an enormous mass of demonic energy that would destroy everything in sight in accordance with its fighting instincts.

If Kojou didn't neutralize the Beast Vassals somehow, it wouldn't end with the slaughter of Kojou and company alone. In the end, it would destroy Nod itself. Of course, it was highly probable the host, Avrora, would break completely before it came to that.

Even if this was an incompletely summoned monstrosity, it was composed of Beast Vassals of the Fourth Primogenitor nonetheless. *Mizen's* demonic energy was overwhelming. In contrast, Kojou's black Beast Vassals didn't have enough power left to oppose it.

"This is bad... The Beast Vassals, they're...!"

Sounds like breaking glass echoed as the black Beast Vassals dissipated one after the other. In contrast, Avrora's Beast Vassal was unscathed. If anything, they'd increased in demonic energy, all the better to squash Kojou and the others flat.

The final black Beast Vassal vanished before Kojou's eyes. Avrora's Beast Vassal howled, moving to slice Kojou asunder with a lightning-imbued claw.

The swing of one slender blade stopped this claw cold. Gripping her silver-colored spear, Yukina blocked the Beast Vassal's blow head-on.

"Himeragi...?! Quit it! If you move in that body, the bleeding'll—!"

Kojou screamed with a plaintive voice. As Yukina gripped her spear, her body was unceasingly bleeding fresh blood. Even so, a fleeting smile came over Yukina as she called out to Kojou.

"Senpai...please...get to Miss Avrora while you still can...!"

"U...aaaaaaaaaaaaaaaaa...........!!"

Kojou let out an incoherent yell as he broke into a sprint.

Now that Avrora was in a berserk state, there was only one way left to stop her: to drink Avrora's blood and overwrite her Beast Vassal control rights.

Kojou had lost his black Beast Vassals, but his vampire factors still remained. The possibility of taking control of her was better than zero.

"Avrora!"

"Ko…jou…!"

As Kojou desperately raced over, Avrora feebly stretched out her arms. She, too, wished for Kojou to drink her blood—to be overwritten by him.

Fortunately, the scent of Yukina's fresh blood splattered on him had already kicked Kojou's vampiric urges into high gear.

Kojou roughly grabbed Avrora's outstretched fingers. Picking up her slender body, he sank his fangs into her defenseless neck.

The instant he sipped droplets of fresh blood, Kojou heard a sound behind him.

It was a ridiculously soft sound, like that of a razor-sharp blade thrusting into soft bread.

It was the sound of a fresh purging stake unleashed by Shahryar Ren's bow gun impaling him.

"That's what I thought you'd do, Kojou Akatsuki."

Ren spat the words out in an indifferent tone. He'd sought the moment Kojou tried to stop Avrora's rampage from the very beginning.

"Senpai…!"

Seeing Kojou's heart impaled from behind, Yukina let out a soft scream.

"Hi…uuu…aaaaaaaaaaa……Kojou! Kojou!"

Avrora's face twisted in despair. Fine cracks ran over Kojou's entire body, beginning to crumble away like sand. Avrora desperately tried to hold on to Kojou but could not stop him from falling apart.

"Begone, sham Fourth Primogenitor. Not even a single piece of ash will remain of you."

Shahryar Ren spoke coldly, tossing away his bow gun now that its job was done. His voice never reached Kojou. Kojou's flesh had already lost its human form, changing to a pile of ash. Finally, even the ash of him left behind melted away, fading into the darkness of Nod.

"Sen…pai…no…"

Yukina sat down on the spot, depleted of strength.

There were no longer even tears in her lifeless eyes.

5

"—This Fang is the Light that rends our Darkness. Its Breath is the Flame that repels Evil! Thy Name is the Fire-Eating Serpent. Born of the Soul of a Saint, thou art the Immutable Blade!"

Using the incantation to heighten her demonic energy to its utmost, Shizuri fired it out along the blade of her crimson long sword. She split the humanoid demon beast over ten meters tall from shoulder to hip, driving it to one knee.

Despite this, the humanoid demon beast remained active. It approached Shizuri, crawling using its left arm alone. Shizuri yelped fervently at the scene straight out of a horror film.

"Er, even that attack did not defeat it?!"

The tentacles on the humanoid demon beast's back lunged straight at Shizuri. She instantly raised her long sword, but her movement lacked speed. Thanks to a series of large-scale demonic energy releases, her fatigue was at its peak.

The moment she tried to counterattack against the initial tentacles, unpleasant sounds came from all over Shizuri's joints. Then—the beam unleashed from behind Shizuri blew away the head of the humanoid demon beast. This time, the monster fell completely silent.

"This makes the third, Lady Paladin!"

Lydianne, poking up her head from the back of the robot tank, shouted in a buoyant tone. Her tank's large-caliber laser was what had rescued Shizuri from peril.

"…I feel like I should harbor pangs of regret, but that is fine."

Shizuri felt conflicted as she wobbled to her feet.

Nearly three hours had passed since MAR's remaining forces began their invasion of Itogami Island. They'd just managed to keep those forces from invading city limits, but the Island Guard's defense line kept on being forced back. The humanoid demon beasts MAR had sent into combat were the cause, of course.

Compared to the Unknown Nine-Fours that had previously appeared, their propagation and regenerative abilities were greatly diminished. Regardless, the shocking endurance and attack strength they possessed remained unchanged. These were more intelligent, working together with the advance of infantry units, which if anything made them even more dangerous weapons.

The total number of humanoid demon beasts exceeded fourteen. Sixteen of them had landed on the coast of Island East alone. Shizuri and company taking down three or even four felt like a drop in the bucket.

That they'd been able to hold the line even so was due to Sayaka's valiant efforts.

"Most Brilliant Flaming Horse, Illustrious Kirin, He Who Governs Heavenly Thunder, pierce these evil spirits with thy wrath…!"

Raising her silver recurve bow, Sayaka launched a ritual spell artillery attack.

Bathed in a direct strike from a vast curse, four humanoid demon beasts crumbled away. Additionally, the thick miasma unleashed dulled the movements of the remaining demon beasts. She was fully living up to the reputation of Shamanic War Dancers, experts in curses and assassination.

Yet Sayaka was clearly approaching the limits of her endurance, too. She breathed raggedly as she leaned against the wall of the building behind her. Her sweaty forelocks clung to her forehead, and the right hand with which she drew her bow oozed with vivid blood.

"You all right, Kirasaka?"

Yuuma posed this worried question to Sayaka. For her part, Yuuma's face looked pale. She'd been teleporting beyond her limits to provide aid to Island Guard casualties.

"I'm just out of cursed arrows, but I can still do close combat."

Sayaka transformed Lustrous Scale into a sword as she spoke those words. It was clear to anyone's eyes that her fingertips no longer had the strength with which to grip her sword, however.

"You should get some rest, Sayaka Kirasaka. I shall take over from here."

"Nah, I felt like I heard a sound I shouldn't be hearing from your right arm during that last attack."

Shizuri put on a strong front, but Yuuma looked at her and calmly pointed this out. Shizuri, however, huffed, smiling as she puffed out her chest.

"As a Blood Servant of Kojou Akatsuki, this is nothing but a trifle to me!"

After saying this, clearly for her own benefit more than theirs, Shizuri gasped and stiffened, coming back to her senses. Her cheeks reddened before the other girls' eyes.

Shizuri vigorously shook her head, looking desperate to deny the real feelings she'd subconsciously let slip.

"—T-that was in error! I take that back! I meant to say, as a pomp…as a Paladin of Gisella…!"

"Well, either way's fine, really."

Yuuma gave her a strained smile and lowered her shoulders.

The very next moment, the entirety of Itogami Island shuddered from demonic energy so powerful as to burn one's skin.

It was a malicious aura on par with that of a Beast Vassal of the Fourth Primogenitor, a malevolent surge so great that Shizuri and Sayaka went on guard out of raw fear.

"What in the world is that ridiculous demonic energy…?!"

"Did Ms. Minamiya call out Rheingold…? Guess she's having a pretty hard time on her end, too."

Yuuma's musings sobered Sayaka's and Shizuri's faces.

Natsuki Minamiya was one of the rare witches who did not employ her Guardian, for her own Guardian was so ridiculously powerful that its mere appearance warped space and time around it, something with ill effects for Itogami Island.

Put another way, she was being pushed back into a position so dangerous that using Rheingold was her only option.

"—Everyone still alive?"

Whirrr, whined the spherical tires of a robot tank other than Lydianne's as it appeared. This was the older Hizamaru model left with the Gigafloat Management Corporation. From the hatch on its back, Asagi poked her face out with a smartphone in hand. It was an ominous greeting, but Shizuri and company were beat-up pretty badly, making the greeting oddly apt.

"Lady Empress…what is the situation on thine end?"

Lydianne inquired, her tone sounding a bit worked up with nostalgia at seeing her beloved machine.

"The civilian evacuation's complete. The front line's pulling back to right in front of Canal Number Four. During that time, you girls on foot had best recover a bit of physical energy while Tanker charges up and reloads—"

"Unfortunately, I can allow you to do no such thing."

Upon abruptly hearing that amused voice, Asagi and the others gasped and turned about.

In the middle of the intersection they'd secured as their line of retreat stood a woman wearing a gaudy outfit and holding a short stick. The countless lollipop sticks she'd scattered along the roadside were changing into sorcerous infantry covered in white exoskeletons.

"Ladli Ren…!"

"Since combat will become quite prolonged at this rate, it's time for a surprise attack to the back. My dear Spartoi, kill them, would you? It's time for some payback—!"

Ladli clapped her hands as she sent the Spartoi after them.

Filled with impatience at the humanoid demon beasts' slow progress, Ladli had come to eliminate Shizuri and the other obstacles personally. For her, the commander, to take the field of battle personally was less a display of recklessness and more a display of confidence in her own abilities.

"Khhh…at a time like this…!"

"Quite the stubborn bunch!"

Sayaka and Shizuri raised their swords and engaged the Spartoi in combat.

If you set aside their off-the-charts defensive strength and high magic resistance, the Spartoi didn't have all that much in the way of combat capabilities, but Shizuri and company had already used up most of their physical energy, and there were simply too many of them. Sayaka and Shizuri each found themselves surrounded and forced into a one-sided defensive battle.

Lydianne and Asagi fired antipersonnel machine gun barrages, but they weren't much good against Spartoi with their resilient exoskeletons. Yuuma tried directly attacking Ladli herself, but she was baffled by her opponent's lack of openings, which got her pinned down instead. Ladli, who'd lived far longer than her appearance would suggest, had fighting experience in another league compared to Yuuma and the rest.

"Oh my, you are better than I thought, but aren't you forgetting something rather important?"

Ladli slowly licked her lips, openly teasing Sayaka and the others as they desperately continued to resist. There, opposite her, was an enormous humanoid demon beast that had closed the distance at some point during the fight.

Countless tentacles imbued with untold strength swung down toward Sayaka and the others as one.

"Tanker!"

"Understood! Releasing full salvo!"

Asagi and Lydianne fired every weapon they had, using missiles, lasers, machine guns large and small, and even antipersonnel rubber bullets to offset the humanoid demon beast's attacks.

The demon beast didn't stop attacking, though. Its whiplike tentacles split the ground, and the vibration waves flung about turned into explosive impacts that assailed Asagi and company.

Unable to withstand such blows in the flesh, Sayaka and other girls cried out as they were sent flying. Asagi and Lydianne's tanks were smashed into buildings. Both robot tanks had been rendered inoperable. Even Shizuri of the resilient ogre race had been knocked completely unconscious with no sign of revival.

"Hmm...it would seem the Priestess of Cain's blessing goes no further."

Ladli muttered this while gazing at the blood flowing from Asagi's forehead.

Even the life of the Priestess of Cain, protected by the will of Cain the Sinful God, was now no more than a candle in the wind. Gaining a sadistic sense of satisfaction from this fact, Ladli swung her right hand upward.

She didn't need to command her Spartoi for this. She would unleash an invisible blade and end Asagi Aiba's life with ease. Yet a moment before swinging down her hand, Ladli noticed that something was slightly... off.

"...This is?"

Faint, yet malevolent demonic energy was springing forth from near the fallen girls. It pulsated like a beating heart. To her, it looked like something was being drawn from them.

The sources of the anomaly were the girls' left hands, or specifically, the small rings worn on their ring fingers.

These were giving off a crimson glow that spread over the bare skin of the girls wearing the rings. They were greedily, mercilessly devouring the girls' living blood.

6

"Kojou…Kou…jo…u…"

Avrora was in a detached state as she kept deliriously repeating the same word.

Since she was unable to maintain the incomplete summons of her Beast Vassal any longer, it returned to mist and dissipated immediately.

The golden-haired girl's body had countless cracks running all over it. Her skin had lost all color as if she were turning to stone, and droplets of fresh blood dripped from the deep cracks. Unable to withstand the backlash from summoning the Beast Vassal, she had begun falling apart.

"Hmm…a disposable artificial vampire in the end…so this is its limit…"

Shahryar Ren murmured in an indifferent voice.

He'd already lost all interest in the battlefield. Kojou Akatsuki had dissipated, and Avrora was beginning to crumble away. The Attack Mage girls and the dragon girl remained, but they were little threat to him. Ren didn't even need to take them out himself.

"What of the…gate, to my homeland…?"

Upon landing, Kreyd the Flame Dragon inquired, remaining in his dragon form.

The demonic energy of the Fourth Primogenitor was necessary to open the gate to Else, homeland of the dragons. Kreyd seemed concerned that the dissipation of Avrora's body would lose any means of doing so.

"There is no need for concern, Kreyd. Nod has over six thousand artificial vampires. We need only use one of them as a vessel for the Star Beast

Vassals in Dodekatos's place. Indeed, managing them should prove a far easier task."

Smiling as he spoke those words, Ren then called over his surviving subordinates. There had been casualties from the combat with Kojou, but such sacrifices were well within expectations. He had higher priorities than healing and recovering the wounded.

"—Prepare a replacement doll at once. After that, put those Attack Mage girls in chains. I do not care if you break their limbs, but ensure you do not damage their heads. It has been quite some time since I've obtained such lively prey. I must take pains to enjoy them."

Ren looked down at the Attack Mage girls as he issued those tyrannical commands to his subordinates.

To the Devas, who required acts of vampirism just to remain alive, humans were nothing but food to them. Among these, Attack Mages with strong spiritual energy were the highest class of prey and rare captures. Ren planned to savor every bit of the girls' suffering, fear, and lamentations as he wrung every last drop of blood from them—even he could not fail to feel a stirring in his chest.

Yet those very Attack Mage girls were glaring at Ren and his people, yet to sheathe their weapons.

"You still intend to resist? Kojou Akatsuki, the one you relied upon, has dissipated without so much as a single cell remaining. Do you really think you have any chance of victory...?"

A scornful smile arose over Ren as he addressed the girls. A faint doubt of misgiving hovered in his eyes because he noticed the crumbling Avrora picking up a tiny, metallic object.

Amid the ashes of the dissipated Kojou Akatsuki, this had remained until the end.

It was a silver-colored ring.

The still-collapsing Avrora tightly squeezed that precious ring.

The tears of blood flowing from her dripped down onto the ring in her palm.

"Kojou..."

Avrora pressed the red-colored ring against her own chest.

Thump, thudded the large heartbeat they felt.

✝

On the back of Leviathan, floating in Tokyo Bay, a silver-haired girl let out an agonized breath.

"Nnn…aaa…"

Kanon Kanase curled up and writhed as she pressed on her left hand.

Her cheeks were red from the blood rushing to them. Her blue eyes were moist as if they were running hot. With the faint moonlight shining on her, the sight somehow felt…obscene.

"*Haaa…haaa…* Miss Kanon…this feeling…"

Yume Eguchi, sitting alongside Kanon, breathed raggedly over and over. The young succubus girl had bewilderment, fear, and unconcealable euphoria on her face.

"It is all right…let go… It only hurts at the beginning."

"But I…I've never, felt like this bef…aaa…noooo!…"

Yume's entire body shuddered within Kanon's gentle embrace.

The rings on their left hands gave a sense of drawing something out of them as their bewitching glows increased.

"Ahhh…!"

On the bridge of the armored airship *Böðvildr*, La Folia Rihavein's back twitched and shuddered. Her white skin had turned the slightest shade of pink. Her blue eyes were watery.

"Princess? Is there something physically amiss…?"

Interceptor Knight Justina Kataya, attending at La Folia's side, inquired with concern. La Folia squirmed, rubbing her thighs together, shaking her head with a strained smile.

"There is no need for concern. It would seem that my partner is doing something indecent again."

"Partner…do you mean Sir Kojou Akatsuki? I shall urgently check upon Itogami Island."

The dead-serious Justina spoke with a particularly earnest tone. La Folia, however, gently pressed the ring on her left hand to her chest and shook her head, an oddly sensual expression coming over her as she smiled.

"No. Such consideration is unneeded. This is a secret between just the two us—"

"Having this happen…is a bit…embarrassing, even for m…mnn!"

Half-buried by rubble, Yuuma Tokoyogi's body twitched and squirmed. Her normal voice had a deep, boyish air to it, but at that moment, Yuuma sounded as lovely and sensual as a voice actress.

At a place a small distance removed, Sayaka and Shizuri writhed in similar manners.

"Nooo…more…no…I can't take this…save me…Yukina…Yukina…!"

"Uuu…what is this…why is this happening to…n-no…aaaaa!"

Sayaka let out a sweet voice that made the usual impression she gave seem like a mirage. For her part, Shizuri was simply bewildered at experiencing such sensations for the first time.

Also, inside her own wrecked robot tank, Asagi was biting her thumb as she desperately endured the waves of pleasure crashing into her.

"…That idiot…what are you doing, at a time like this… It's too mu… aaa…!"

Asagi was still halfway hurled out of the tank's driver's seat when her entire body suddenly stiffened. Then she limply collapsed facedown on the ground, letting out a frail, trembling breath.

"Lady Empress…what is doth happening…?"

Lydianne, the only one keeping her cool, asked over the radio. When that voice finally dragged Asagi back to lucidity, she shook her head with a guilty look.

The glow had already vanished from Asagi's ring. The strange pulsing and the agony and pleasure of having her blood sucked into it were gone, too. In its place, she felt a deeper connection. She felt like *he* now existed deep inside her body. That sensation was giving Asagi strength, literally the strength to—

Asagi crawled out from under the robot tank, shoving the frame back with brute force. She didn't feel any of the wounds she should have from the humanoid demon beast's attack. There wasn't even a scar.

"Keh-keh…you look like you're having a pretty good time, Lil' Miss."

She heard a voice from the smartphone in her pocket. The oddly human-sounding synthesized voice felt downright nostalgic. The phone didn't even wait for Asagi's input before a badly sewn teddy bear avatar came on-screen on its own.

"Mogwai? You've finished your business?"

Asagi rudely greeted the partner AI she hadn't seen in some time. Maybe it was a simulated personality reproduced from the memories of Cain the Sinful God, but to Asagi, it was just her mouthy partner.

Mogwai replied in a perfectly normal tone of voice, too.

"Yeah, I got a huge load off my shoulders, thanks to you."

"Oh really. Then you'd better move your ass to make up for all the slacking. I don't come cheap."

"Please be gentle, Lil' Miss."

Mogwai laughed with a sardonic *keh-keh* as his real body—the main computer of Itogami Island—began a vast amount of magical calculations. Asagi called forth a crimson light from the magic symbols floating on-screen.

This was the light of the fearsome forbidden spell that could overwrite the physical laws of the world.

When the crimson bullet shot through the humanoid demon beast, it changed into pure white salt crystals and fell apart.

The Unknown's magic resistance and regenerative abilities were meaningless in the face of that radiance. The humanoid demon beasts MAR had sent into combat were being erased as if they had never existed to begin with.

"O…oh my?"

Ladli Ren raised a bewildered voice when she saw which girl had destroyed the humanoid demon beast—a high school girl with a flamboyant hairstyle and a stylishly mis-worn uniform.

Surrounding her were countless floating bullets of light shaped like perfect squares. The humanoid demon beasts into which these bullets were shot turned into salt, dissipating one after the next.

"Asagi Aiba's Cleansing?! Why did its strength spike all of a sudden?!"

Thrown for a loop, Ladli ordered her Spartoi to attack Asagi. Yet two girls with swords in hand stood before the horde of Spartoi once again.

"Lustrous Scale!"

"Hauras!"

Sayaka Kirasaka's silver-colored long sword rent the resilient Spartoi exoskeletons like tissue paper. Also, Shizuri Kasugaya's crimson long sword was pulverizing the Spartoi with brute force.

"Th…this can't be happening…!"

Ladli took out her teleportation device from a side pocket, but the sorcerous device failed to activate. Yuuma Tokoyogi's Guardian—her faceless blue knight construct—had prevented its activation using even more powerful spatial control magic.

"What is the meaning of this? You'd used up your strength mere moments ago, yes?"

Ladli looked over Asagi and the others out of sheer confusion.

Yuuma and Shizuri should have been depleted of strength, yet their demonic energy was as if they were well rested. Asagi and Sayaka's heavy wounds had been completely healed. They'd been on death's door from humanoid demon beast attacks, yet something had happened to the girls in less than a minute.

The girls had obtained a source of inexhaustible demonic energy and nigh-immortal regenerative ability. That simply wasn't possi—

"The tables have turned, Ladli Ren."

Asagi spoke while toying with the smartphone in her hand. Ladli's face twitched with anger.

"…Do you truly think so, Priestess of Cain? You may have become a little perkier, but the tides are still against you."

Ladli spoke with a theatrical tone as she turned her steel-colored stick toward the sky. Taking this as its cue, a giant sphere appeared over the sea near Itogami Island.

It was an enormous floating fortress, like a castle from the Middle Ages forced into a round shape.

"A Deva Necropolis…! You still had one of those blasted things?!"

Shizuri shouted as she looked up at the sky. She couldn't hide her surprise at seeing another one emerge after they'd worked so hard to destroy the other Necropolises.

"This is my Castle Laren. Don't you think this one is much cooler looking than my brother's Castle Kalenaren, the one you destroyed? It's a sphere...but it's edgy."

Satisfied with Shizuri's pronounced reaction, Ladli delivered those words with her typical composure. Judging from her negotiating with Itogami Island not as one of the Devas, but as an employee of MAR to the bitter end, she really hadn't wanted to send her own Necropolis into combat.

In other words, that was just how far into a corner they had driven her. From this point on, Ladli would probably attack without regard for the cost.

Though Asagi understood that full well, she smiled tightly out of pity for her opponent.

"I'm not sure about edgy, but you're the one with the tides against you, Ladli Ren."

"Eh?"

What do you mean? said Ladli's narrowed eyes. The next moment, the Necropolis above the sea was engulfed in explosive flames.

The Necropolis was being attacked by a squadron of fighter jets diving from directly above. The models were fifth-generation stealth jets from the NAU. However, the flags painted on their gray fuselages were those of Japan. It was a fighter squadron from the Japan Air Self-Defense Force.

"Fighters...why are Japan's Self-Defense Forces..."

Ladli murmured, eyes wide open in a daze.

Certainly, properly speaking, Itogami Island's defense was under the government of Japan's jurisdiction. Self-Defense Force craft attacking the Necropolis and MAR's invasion forces made sense.

Yet the government of Japan had decided to destroy Itogami Island a scant twenty-four hours earlier. She didn't understand why the situation had flipped on its head just then.

"Looks like we made it in time."

Surrounded by wind like a tornado, Motoki Yaze leaped off a building and landed beside Asagi. Seemingly following suit behind him and his weary-looking face, large armored cars appeared one after the other. They were APCs of the Special Attack Mage Regiment of the Japan Ground Self-Defense Forces.

"Pretty good job you did there. Thank you for your hard work, President Yaze."

Asagi waved casually as she spoke in a teasing tone of voice.

Taking his headphones off his ears, Yaze squinted at her with distinct annoyance.

Yaze wasn't just the director of the Gigafloat Management Corporation—he was also the president of Japan's Yaze Consortium. Though internal divisions had weakened its power in recent times, the Yaze family's pull with the Japanese government remained powerful.

Using those financial connections to the fullest, Yaze had made them rescind their order to destroy Itogami Island.

To the Japanese government, this proposal was a godsend. With the Beast Vassal Warheads already neutralized, the government of Japan had no reason to view Itogami Island as a threat anymore.

Also, Itogami Island was only three hundred and thirty kilometers from Tokyo as the crow flies. Military transports could cross that in a half hour. Supersonic fighters could cross that distance and land in less than fifteen minutes.

The Island Guard hadn't fought a retreating battle for no reason. They'd been buying time for the Self-Defense Forces to arrive.

"To think you would negotiate with the government of Japan... You've certainly pulled out quite a card..."

Ladli's face turned bitter as she gazed sidelong at the Self-Defense Force members beginning to engage the humanoid demon beasts in combat. Fighters were engaging the Necropolis over the sea. She had Spartoi left, but she was still running short on firepower.

"The government of Japan's not the only one I negotiated with, though."

Yaze casually shook his head. That instant, Ladli's expression grew graver still. She'd noticed a fresh source of demonic energy emerging above her head.

"—Dance, Gula!"

A thousand pitch-black daggers poured down like a storm, stabbing and piercing the remaining Spartoi. Even the high regenerative ability that Spartoi possessed couldn't stop the countless blades from pinning them to the ground. After that, they could be picked apart without any reservation.

Losing her backup in the blink of an eye, Ladli stood alone.

"Velesh Aradahl...!"

Ladli was shaken when she realized the identity of the dagger Beast Vassal's master. Ladli used an invisible slice to fend off Beast Vassal attacks as she turned her steel-colored stick toward Aradahl.

"Sorry, but I'm sealing that nasty petrification device—"

A fist covered in silver-colored metal pulverized Ladli's sorcerous device from the side. She'd dropped her bulwark to activate the device. It had left her open for a single instant.

"Zana Lashka...!"

With Ladli having lost her sorcerous device, a gorgeous, red-haired beauty pummeled her at point-blank range.

Zana slipped through Ladli's invisible slicing attacks with overwhelming speed. Sliced hair and blood droplets danced in the air. Ladli displayed unexpectedly high-caliber combat techniques, but Zana still had the edge in hand-to-hand combat. Taking kicks from Zana reminiscent of dance moves, Ladli was finally blown into the air.

"...How did you revive yourself, Zana Lashka? My sorcerous device should have sealed you in a barrier of equal strength to a Beast Vassal Warhead."

Glaring resentfully at Zana, Ladli wiped the blood trickling from her lips.

"If a barrier's made with the same technology as Beast Vassal Warheads, can't you remove it with identical technology in turn? For instance, yes...if one used the Beast Vassal Warhead maintenance equipment stored in Nod."

Zana spoke with a tone of feigned innocence. *Impossible*, spoke Ladli's shake of her head.

Surely Kojou Akatsuki and his allies hadn't had the luxury of time to haul Zana and Aradahl into Nod. Ren and his MAR troops certainly had no reason to help the pair.

Yet the fact remained that the two had been revived. There was one other person besides Kojou and company who could have visited

Nod and brought back the mechanism with which to save Zana and Aradahl—an ambusher Ladli had never expected.

"You couldn't mean, the one who revived you was—"

"Oh, right, a message for you from my husband."

Zana interrupted Ladli's quivering voice and forced a change of subject. "Message…?"

Ladli tensely went on guard. Zana was a Blood Servant of the First Primogenitor—in other words, her husband was none other than the Lost Warlord himself.

"He said, 'Since the Fourth Primogenitor brat destroyed a whole Necropolis, he'll show me up if I don't put in some elbow grease, too.'"

Zana giggled with a teasing smile. High overhead was the Necropolis floating above the sea.

The SDF fighters furiously engaged in combat with it suddenly fled from the combat area for some reason. The Necropolis was floating by its lonesome when a hazy, black shadow floated up behind it.

This shadow took the form of a beast—that of a wolf so enormous, it could swallow even the Necropolis in one gulp.

This was the starving wolf that ate all dead, the wolf that would never be satisfied, the one that had consumed the sun and the moon to taint the heavens with blood. This was Beast Vassal Number One of Ki Juranbarada, the First Primogenitor—Parhelion.

"It can't be…! Aaa…?! Wait, stop! I surrender! I surrender, I say! Let's all be happy. At least let me surre…no, stopppp!!"

Ladli Ren raised both hands up, lamenting with a desperate look.

Crunch—

The next moment, an enormous sound of something being chomped echoed through the night sky.

7

At the tip of the steel-colored bridge floating in the sea of clouds, the girls let out voices of agony.

"I'll…remember this, Kojou Akatsuki… You will pay dearly for my pure blood…khhh…!"

Biting her lip, the mortified Kiriha Kisaki pressed on her left hand.

The white nape of her neck poking through the gap left by her disheveled white hair was pink, and the hot breath she let out was mixed with a most lovely voice.

"No…noooo…I'm, Yuiri is…aaa!!"

"Uuu…uuu…I'm sorry, Yukii…I can't take any more…!"

Shio and Yuiri strongly embraced each other, desperately holding out against the surging ecstasy.

The powerful pulses from the crimson-dyed rings biting into their fingers continued.

From a place slightly removed, Shahryar Ren gazed at the girls' state with a grave expression.

"What is this…? A bacteriological weapon…no, some kind of curse…?!"

The President of MAR's eyes were filled with bewilderment.

Eliminating the immobile Attack Mages was simplicity itself, but if that meant he'd be infected by whatever bacterium or curse was afflicting the girls, that carried the possibility of an unfortunate occurrence he could never take back. Nod was a closed environment. The spread of bacterial contamination or any kind of curse was a threat deserving maximum caution.

For once, Ren was indecisive, unsure whether to attack or relent.

This was why he was slow to notice the final abnormality occurring at the exact same time.

"I, Avrora Florestina, inheritor of the Kaleid Blood, release thee from thy bonds…!"

Avrora, her body continuing to collapse, continued murmuring as if in prayer.

She was gripping in her hands the silver-colored ring Kojou had left behind. The ring was giving off a deep red glow as it absorbed the blood flowing from Avrora.

"Fourth Primogenitor, Kojou Akatsuki! I permit thee! Inherit all Beast Vassals dwelling within mine flesh—!"

Wringing out the final wisps of power remaining in her, the golden-haired vampire girl screamed.

The ring her fingers were grasping shattered. A golden mist flooded up from within.

In the blink of an eye, this mist increased in mass, changing into the form of a boy—a vampire boy wearing an expression that somehow seemed lethargic.

"Ooooooooooooooooooo…!!"

Revived in the exact same shape as when he had dissipated, he embraced Avrora, on the verge of crumbling away completely.

The silver-colored ring that should have been shattered was restored within Kojou's hand.

Kojou placed this ring on Avrora's finger. Avrora herself probably hadn't realized it: Sealed within the pact rings for the purpose of creating Blood Servants were fragments of Kojou's blood and rib bones—in other words, Kojou's cellular makeup.

Absorbing Avrora's blood, Kojou had been revived from a mere handful of cells.

"Absurd…Kojou Akatsuki has returned to life…!"

A dazed Shahryar Ren drew in his breath.

A vampire had been resurrected from being completely turned to ash. Even Ren couldn't maintain his calm at such an unexpected circumstance.

The commander's loss of nerve caught fire among his subordinates. The MAR forces with a supposedly overwhelming military advantage were riddled with pangs of fear.

"*Daaaaah—!*"

Glenda, overjoyed to see Kojou's resurrection, changed into her enormous dragon form. The air around her swayed, and from this swaying emerged a great mass of flying demon beasts. These swarmed around the steel-colored dragon as if to protect her, attacking the MAR troops as one.

"Houda?! Why are the environmental maintenance demon beasts attacking us…?!"

Ren's face contorted in shock.

The houda were artificial demon beasts created via genetic manipulation and programmed to maintain the space colony. These traits, similar to the hive-making instincts in bees, caused them to keep up and maintain Nod, the place where they were born.

Yet Glenda, the artificial dragon, had been granted the ability to summon these houda at will.

Houda had only moderate combat capability individually, but there were simply too many of them. The soldiers on the receiving end of an assault by hundreds of houda were driven into a vortex of pure chaos.

"Kill it! Kill the silver dragon!"

Baring his fangs at the dragon acting as the catalyst, Ren summoned his Spartoi.

Houda attacks were ineffective against the Spartoi and their resilient exoskeletons. They raised their bladelike arms, charging toward Glenda, the summoner of the houda—

A flash of a lead-colored blade pulverized the Spartoi.

"Not bad at all. I will graciously overlook your drinking my blood without permission this once, Kojou Akatsuki!"

The black-haired girl wearing an old-fashioned sailor suit uniform smiled ferociously as she gripped her forked spear. Swinging it with the right arm that had definitely been broken in the fight with the Flame Dragon, she activated the resonant destruction ritual. The Spartoi's exoskeletons shattered, unable to withstand the vibration.

"Glendaaaaaa!"

The dragon Kreyd breathed fire at the steel-colored dragon.

He burned away the horde of houda with one incandescent beam, but before it could score a direct hit on Glenda, it was impeded, as if striking some sort of invisible wall. A pseudo-spatial severing ritual had created a spatial rift bulwark.

Her silvery long sword poised, Yuiri stood before Kreyd to protect Glenda. Her right arm, the one cruelly burned black, was completely healed without so much as a single scar. It was her miraculous regenerative ability on par with a vampire primogenitor.

"Yuiri...your arm...!"

Shio asked this, sounding completely beside herself. Yuiri looked back with a vibrant smile on her face.

"Yeah. It's all right now. Thank you, Shio. I'll have to thank Kojou, too, huh."

"...Then this would be our chance to get some payback."

Speaking those words with a tearful voice, Shio shot a powerful gaze.

The copper Flame Dragon was circling overhead. Yuiri and Shio mounted Glenda's back, taking to the skies of Nod to pursue him.

Amid the furious conflict between the MAR troops and the horde of houda, a place of pure white silence emerged upon the floating bridge within the sea of clouds.

Within the open area in front of the destroyed control tower, a blood-ridden Yukina Himeragi was lying down. Rent by an invisible slicing attack from Shahryar Ren, she was gravely wounded. It was unbelievable that she was still breathing.

Yukina lay there as Kojou quietly approached.

In his arms, Kojou carried Avrora, who still slept after losing consciousness.

"...Senpai...how is Miss Avrora?"

Yukina posed this question to Kojou in a frail voice. *She's on the brink of death, and there she is worrying about someone else*, thought Kojou with a strained smile. It was very much like her.

"Don't worry. She's technically one of my Blood Servants now, y'see."

Kojou spoke as he laid the sleeping Avrora on the ground.

With her hands crossed over her chest, the silver-colored ring on Avrora's left hand was glowing. It was a pact ring for creating a Blood Servant—with that as a catalyst, Kojou was providing her with his own demonic energy.

Avrora, unable to endure summoning the Beast Vassals and on the verge of being completely broken, had become Kojou's Blood Servant, reviving her from the brink of vanishing altogether. Also, thanks to Kojou's overwrite, he'd obtained the twelve Beast Vassals dwelling within Avrora, the Beast Vassals of the Fourth Primogenitor—

"There you go, drinking another girl's blood at the drop of a hat... You truly are an..."

Yukina spoke with a joking tone.

Kojou smiled without a hint of guilt as he peered into Yukina's face.

"If you don't mind, there's one more girl whose blood I really wanna drink right now."

With Kojou staring straight at her, Yukina bashfully averted her eyes. Kojou picked her up without waiting for a reply. Yukina let out a little cough mixed with blood.

"Please do not look at me so intently... My face is terrible at the moment..."

Yukina pleaded with him in a voice sounding like she was about to burst into tears. Her entire body was wounded. Her cheeks were filthy with dried blood and mud. Her skin was ominously pale with barely a hint of blood. There was not even a trace of her normal loveliness.

Kojou, though, shook his head.

"No way."

"Why...?"

"I mean, Himeragi, you're cute, you know?"

"Why are you...saying that at a time like this..."

Yukina glared resentfully at Kojou. He looked straight down at her face.

"I can only say it out loud when it is a time like this."

Speaking quickly as if hiding a blush, he put strength into his embrace of Yukina. She smelled of fresh blood, but to him, the scent was utterly intoxicating.

"Senpai...you are a liar..."

Yukina squirmed, weakly resisting to what little extent she could.

"I am not. I've always thought it. You're super-serious but don't know much about the world, you're not honest and always bluffing, but you're always kind and helping others, and you've stuck with me all this time."

Kojou brought his lips close, whispering into Yukina's ear.

Strength drained from Yukina all over. She leaned her cold body into Kojou.

"Will you take responsibility?"

"...Responsibility?"

Kojou stopped moving, bewildered. Yukina sighed in exasperation.

"Stay with me forever. Never go to a place beyond my sight again... Never go away and leave me ever again...!"

Touching her hands to Kojou's cheeks, Yukina stared straight into his eyes. Even though she was critically injured, having lost the strength to

even stand, the powerful glint deep in her eyes was the same as the Yukina of old.

"Forever…er, Himeragi, you're all right with that? Never leaving my side?"

"Yes. I am your watcher, after all…so please…"

Yukina gently pulled up her hair. Then she offered her slender neck to Kojou like a sacrificial offering.

"Please, drink my blood—"

Kojou sank his fangs deeply into her defenseless neck. A fleeting sigh trickled out of Yukina's mouth as Kojou strongly embraced her.

The starless night sky of Nod gazed down at the sight of the pair seemingly melting into one.

8

"What are those two doing at a time like this…eh?! Aaa! Is it all right to do that?! Whoa! That's…eh?! Ehhh?!"

Riding on Glenda's back, Shio was beside herself when she noticed Yukina and Kojou embracing. As she gazed straight down on them from above, the pair looked like lovers in the throes of indecent actions.

"Ah-ha-ha…well, for this one moment, it's fine, right?"

Yuiri's cheeks reddened as she gave her friend a strained smile.

In the next moment, Yuiri batted down the incandescent beam flying toward them with one swing of her long sword.

The copper Flame Dragon was targeting Glenda as it circled Nod's night sky. A flock of MAR attack helicopters flew in concert behind him.

The mobility of the two dragons—Glenda and Kreyd—was roughly equal. Kreyd had the upper hand in lift and acceleration, but Glenda was able to make tight, swift circles. All the same, the overwhelming firepower advantage rested with Kreyd.

The houda summoned by Glenda were virtually powerless before Kreyd's breath. Even with Yuiri and Shio's support, it was all she could manage to keep things at a standoff.

For her part, Kiriha Kisaki remained in combat with MAR soldiers atop the bridge floating in the sea of clouds.

With the support of a horde of houda, the MAR unit's coordination was in tatters, but MAR had the Spartoi on its side. The numbers of houda were steadily diminishing in the face of the high attack power and regenerative ability the Spartoi possessed. On top of that, Shahryar Ren had sent in all the Spartoi at his disposal, so Kiriha was at a decisive disadvantage.

"This has become most unamusing…"

Tch, clicked Kiriha's tongue as she glared at the mangled edge of her forked spear.

Even if Kiriha's own abilities had increased, her equipment had not been strengthened in turn. Ricercare was unable to keep up with Kiriha's dramatically increased ritual energy and endurance from becoming a Blood Servant.

If her spear broke entirely, she'd lose her means of attacking the Spartoi. If it came to that, Kiriha's defeat was inevitable. Kiriha's beautiful face twisted as she foresaw this unpleasant future.

"—Sadalmelik Albus!"

Someone shouted from behind Kiriha. An immense Beast Vassal appeared from within the sea of clouds enveloping the floating bridge. This was a water maid—a pale undine with a body of transparent, flowing water.

As it swept across the ground with the sharp talons on its slender hands, the Spartoi turned into what seemed like fragments of fossilized bone. The Fourth Primogenitor's Beast Vassal Number Eleven had forcibly reverted the artificial demons to the raw materials they had been before being born.

"C'mon over, Al-Nasl Minium!"

Next, the air trembled, and a scarlet, twin-horned beast appeared in Nod's upper sky. With a roar, it spat out a cannonball of shockwaves that shot down the copper Flame Dragon and the MAR attack helicopters with it.

"Tch…Kreyd! What are you doing, you incompetent pieces of garbage…!"

Shahryar Ren, losing most of his side's combat strength in an instant, tore off his earpiece, slamming it to the ground in an act of pure rage.

Before Ren, wearing a bloody parka, a boy quietly walked forward.

It was Kojou Akatsuki.

*　　*　　*

"Sorry to keep you waiting, Shahryar Ren."

Kojou spoke with an utterly unconcerned tone. His demeanor was as warm as if he were passing a friend in the city by pure chance.

Outwardly, Kojou looked just like he had the moment before dissipating when Shahryar Ren shot him, yet the air enveloping him seemed gentler. The malevolent aura remained, but there was no leakage of uncontrollable demonic energy. Kojou himself seemed a little thrown off by the sensation.

"Kojou Akatsuki…is it…?"

Shahryar Ren glared at Kojou, crushing the wireless headphone underfoot.

His Spartoi were completely destroyed. The troops under him had begun to rout. He was facing Kojou all alone.

"Why does a mere human interfere with me? You resurrect after I slay you, you tame Dodekatos, seizing the Beast Vassals of the Kaleid Bloods for yourself… Do you think you are permitted to do this? Who in the world do you think you are?!"

Ren's questions serving as condemnations brought a genuinely pained smile over Kojou.

Vampire. Observation target of the Lion King Agency. Ruler of Itogami Island. High school student—there were many titles he could think of.

Yet that moment, there was only one thing Kojou could call himself.

"I'm the Fourth Primogenitor."

Kojou spoke in a joking tone. Ren's face twisted with lethality.

"There are only three primogenitors. The fourth is merely an urban legend spread by that fool The Blood…a mere rumor without any basis in fact."

"Nahhh. You're wrong about that."

Kojou quietly shook his head.

Certainly, it might have been a baseless urban legend at first, yet over the long, long months, that legend had turned into hard fact. Through the machinations of various forces, several layers of coincidence, and the desires of many people, they had made that legendary monster real.

"The Fourth Primogenitor is the name of the World's Mightiest Vampire, undying and immutable, with no blood kin, no desire to rule, served by twelve Beast Vassals that are disaster incarnate, a vampire who lives only to kill and destroy, standing beyond all the doctrines of the world—that's the enemy you've made."

"What nonsense…!"

The air around Ren shifted. It was an invisible blade spawned from Deva divine energy.

Kojou bared his fangs as he smiled.

"So let's get started, Shahryar Ren. This ain't got nothing to do with the Devas and Cain anymore. I'll make you pay dearly for the crime of using Avrora and Itogami Island for your stupid goal of ruling mankind! From here on, this is my fight!"

Kojou howled ferociously as Ren unleashed his divine energy blade toward him, but Ren's invisible slash shattered in a shower of beautiful sparks. A diminutive figure wielding a silver-colored spear leaped in front of Kojou.

"No, senpai. This is *our* fight!"

A small, beautiful smile came over Yukina as she launched an attack on Shahryar Ren. Her uniform was still drenched with blood. A huge gash in her clothing, from her shoulder down her chest and back, was still evident. Despite this, the flesh visible through that gash was as white as freshly fallen snow. Not even the slightest scratch remained. Having gained the status of a Blood Servant, Yukina had also obtained healing ability on par with a primogenitor.

"Filthy humans…! It's no use!"

"Eh?!"

Ren stopped Yukina's silvery spear with his bare right arm. There was a sound of two metallic objects clashing as Yukina's attack bounced right off him.

"Wha?!"

Yukina's body flipped in midair, and she landed like a cat. Her expression was stiff with raw shock.

Visible past his torn sleeve, Ren's arm was covered in a dark, silvery metal. The glossy surface changed to match his every movement.

He wasn't wearing armor or some kind of augmentation suit. It was his very body. Ren had replaced part of his own flesh and blood with a sorcerous device.

"That body...you stuffed it with sorcerous devices those Cleanser guys used...?!"

Kojou exclaimed in astonishment.

Shahryar Ren's divine energy was unnaturally powerful compared to fellow Devas like Schtola D and his little sister Ladli. This grotesque body was the secret behind it. Now Kojou understood why Ren had boasted he was stronger than Kreyd the Flame Dragon. He'd abandoned his own flesh to heighten his combat capabilities.

"The Cleansers? Ahh...you mean the fools who worship Cain like a god, fully ignorant of the truth."

Ren spat out his words as he spoke. A thin, pitch-black aura enveloped his entire body. The true nature of that pitch-black aura was encroachment from Nod that could sever even the demonic energy of the Fourth Primogenitor.

"I would prefer if you did not associate me with such refuse. This form is the crystallization of all Deva knowledge, built to wipe away the humiliation of The Great Cleansing! It is the ultimate physical form with which to strike down the primogenitors!"

Ren unleashed a divine energy blade, an invisible slash that could not be blocked with demonic energy. Kojou rolled to his side to evade the attack.

"The Beast Vassal Warhead nullification, felling several Necropolises— all you lot have done is futile. So long as I survive, one day the Devas will prosper as rulers once more! I...am...MAR! I...am King of the Devas!"

"Tch—!"

Kojou concentrated his demonic energy and released it like a cannonball. It was the one ritual spell–like trick he'd picked up from training with Shizuri at Onrai Island.

The attack was blocked by the pitch-black defensive membrane enveloping Ren.

"Also, I am far from bereft of cards to play, Kojou Akatsuki! After all, you have brought that all this way with you!"

Ren shouted loudly as he pointed to the wall behind him.

It was the space colony's isolating wall that Kojou had called the end of Nod. In the weightless zone at its center rested an enormous, smashed sphere resembling a crushed ping-pong ball.

It was the remnant of Castle Kalenaren—Shahryar Ren's personal Deva Necropolis.

"What...?!"

Enormous things emerged from the half-destroyed Necropolis, seemingly chewing through its outer wall.

Spreading their wings like birds of prey, they calmly flew toward Kojou and Yukina.

They had ferocious-looking heads reminiscent of a lizard's, snakelike tails, and four bestial limbs—they greatly resembled Kreyd and Glenda in dragon form.

These, however, were not dragons. For that matter, they weren't even alive.

Their flesh was rotting, fluids from decomposition scattering as they moved.

Their eyeballs had melted away to leave hollow sockets. They had unhealed scars and exposed bone.

They were corpses—dragon corpses controlled by magic.

"Dragon Zombies...!"

Yukina's voice quavered. Of course, profaning the dead to create zombies was a forbidden art. Making a zombie out of a proud dragon was an absolutely unforgivable act.

"What is left of the abominable Guardians of the Corridor."

Shahryar Ren spoke with scorn. Kojou knit his brows at the unfamiliar term.

"Guardian of the Corridor...?"

"That's right. Dragons are observers dispatched from another planet to watch over the Devas' activities, though once The Great Cleansing left no one able to use Nod, their duty came to an end and they left for parts unknown, save for the precious few individuals left behind on the surface."

"You took their corpses and made them into zombies? Why do such a thing...?"

Yukina inquired, looking up at the Dragon Zombies as they approached.

A foolish question, said Ren's shake of his head.

"To use them as weapons, of course. Even if they are corpses, a dragon's flesh is robust, and they do not lose their supernatural strength. More importantly, their corpses are quite obedient."

Ren made a low-toned laugh.

Seven Dragon Zombies crawled out from the Necropolis.

If they really did possess power on par with Kreyd the Flame Dragon, they most definitely posed a threat to Kojou and the others even as they had become. Small wonder Ren was triumphant.

"It's more trouble cleaning up after them than with Beast Vassal Warheads so I hadn't wanted to use them, but the responsibility lies with you and your continued useless resistance. Now choke on your regrets… ha…haha…!!"

Deploying his pitch-black aura, Ren walked toward Kojou and the others. The next moment, Ren was halted by an unexpected voice. It hailed from Kreyd, back to dragon-man form after being shot down by Kojou's Beast Vassal.

"Shahryar Ren…damn…you…!"

Kreyd glared at Ren with eyes brimming with anger.

Ren looked back at the wounded dragon-man and laughed with frigid scorn.

"What's wrong, Kreyd? Surely, you are not irate at my turning the corpses of your comrades into zombies? If so, how sentimental of you… for a filthy demon beast…"

"You…!"

Practically dragging his tattered body along, Kreyd launched an attack toward Ren. The dragon-man was struck by Ren's invisible slashes. Countless gashes were carved all over the dragon-man's body. Blood the color of magma frothed from them.

Ren seemed blood-drunk as a cruel smile came over him. That instant—

"…Nanda…Bannanda!"

"What?!"

Ren's smiling face froze over when, without warning, the skies were filled by flames.

One of the Dragon Zombies exploded. Yet another was split all over its body, turning it into fragments of scorched flesh. The flames dyed the night sky red, as silvery, glimmering lights streaked through it like comets.

"What...what is this...?!"

Shaken, Ren cried out.

Swimming in the sea of clouds was a gargantuan Beast Vassal over thirty meters in length. It was a serpent, its entire body covered in flames and swords—no, this was a vampire beast vassal in the form of an oriental dragon.

"A Beast Vassal...?! That's absurd! Why is a vampiric Beast Vassal besides the Fourth Primogenitor's in Nod?!"

Ren was quite naturally beside himself.

Beast Vassals couldn't be used inside Nod since it floated in outer space. The singular exception was the Star Beast Vassals of the Fourth Primogenitor designed from their inception to be used in space—that is what Ren had believed for millennia.

Kojou, however, was not all that surprised. If anything, he'd had a feeling this was coming.

Of course, a man who loved combat with powerful opponents more than anything would show interest in monsters as rare as Dragon Zombies.

"Heya, Kojou. As usual, you've become involved in a most amusing-looking battle, haven't you—?"

Enveloped by golden mist, a tall vampire appeared atop the wrecked control tower.

He appeared along with Jagan and Kira—his two young vampire aristocrat allies.

Even if they noticed the sleeping Avrora, neither batted an eye. In other words, they'd been watching the battle from the very beginning, including the moment Kojou had lost his power and dissipated, and the instant he had been resurrected as the Fourth Primogenitor.

"Dimitrie Vattler...?! Why are you alive...?! Why can you use your Beast Vassals in Nod...?!"

Shahryar Ren shook his head in what seemed like anguish, but Vattler did not reply to his question. He utterly ignored Ren as he summoned a new Beast Vassal, as if to say, *You are not worthy to face me.*

A serpentine Beast Vassal enveloped by a crimson radiance assaulted the Dragon Zombies one after another. Kojou knew the true nature of the radiance Vattler had unleashed.

"The Cleansing, huh…well, he was all pumped up about going to Nod to begin with…"

A wilted expression came over Kojou as he recalled their fight during the War of the Primogenitors.

Obtaining the power of The Cleansing with Asagi's help, Vattler had picked a fight with the Holy Grounds Treaty Organization like it was a good thing, causing Kojou and company no small amount of trouble in the process.

"Yes. He of all people must have modified his own body and Beast Vassals beforehand so they can operate in Nod just fine."

Yukina murmured with a weary expression mirroring Kojou's. When he thought about it, Dimitrie Vattler always had a poignant obsession with the existence known as the Fourth Primogenitor. He was probably trying to research the Fourth Primogenitor's Beast Vassals to find a way to wield power in Nod.

"Absurd…this is absurd, absurd, such an absurdity cannot…!"

Shahryar Ren's entire body shuddered, as if utterly unable to accept the fact that the Dragon Zombies, his trump cards, were being downed in a one-sided slaughter.

Ren turned his back on Vattler's combat with the Dragon Zombies and began to flee.

However, his legs came to a halt after no more than a few paces, for Kojou had circled around him to impede his path…

"Where do you think you're going, Shahryar Ren? I'm your opponent, y'know?"

Kojou said calmly.

His anger toward Ren had already vanished. The only emotion remaining was pity.

He pitied the man, treading water for thousands of years, clinging to his empty pride at having been born a Deva, flung to and fro by the meaningless ambition known as "ruling mankind."

"Kojou Akatsuki…! Do you not yet understand the likes of you cannot face me…?!"

Kojou fired a demonic energy cannonball, only for Ren to block it with his pitch-black aura. Then he unleashed countless invisible slashes toward Kojou.

Yet Ren's divine energy blades all dissipated without so much as touching Kojou.

Kiriha Kisaki's Ricercare had protected Kojou with a pseudo-spatial severing bulwark.

"You're the one who doesn't understand. Himeragi isn't his only Blood Servant."

Following the girl in the old-fashioned sailor suit's lead, Kojou ferociously curled up the corners of his lips.

The next instant, a beam of light rent the skies.

The beam became a spear of light, piercing through the pitch-black defensive membrane and Shahryar Ren's own body. The light spear bored a meter-wide hole, ripping off his right arm and right flank without so much as a sound.

"Wh…at…?"

Dazed, Ren shifted his eyes toward the source of the light spear.

He saw Shio and Yuiri poising a silver-colored crossbow. Freikugel Plus, Armbrust Mode—this was a ritual spell artillery attack that shaved away space itself. It was the pair's ultimate ritual, able to pierce anything that existed. Even Ren's "Encroachment" could not defend against that attack.

"I, Maiden of the Lion, Sword Shaman of the High God, beseech thee—"

When Ren stopped moving, Yukina took advantage of the momentary opening, leaping in to attack. With movements reminiscent of an elegant dance, she chanted as she thrust her silvery spear forward.

"O purifying light, O divine wolf of the snowdrift, by your steel divine will, strike down the devils before me!"

"This…cannot be…!"

Enveloped by the Divine Oscillation Effect, Yukina's spear thrust right through the tear Shio and Yuiri had made in the aurora, impaling Shahryar Ren through his shoulder.

Ren desperately tried to operate his sorcerous device to redeploy the aura, but the interference of the spear impaling him left him unable to completely close the aura again.

As Ren's face twisted in haste, he beheld Kojou raising his right arm aloft.

Fear hovered in Ren's eyes.

"C'mon over, Regulus Aurum—!"

The deep crimson bloody mist scattering from Kojou changed into an enormous beast—a ⸺ightning lion enveloped by a golden glow. Kojou imbued his fist with the Beast Vassal's demonic energy that was lightning incarnate, swinging it downward.

—Straight toward the metallic shaft of the spear impaling Ren's shoulder—

"It's over, old man! Try not to die on me, King of the Devas!"

A thunderous roar made the night sky of Nod shudder.

Remnants of a sorcerous device scattered everywhere as the man calling himself King of the Devas was sent flying.

9

The girl gazed at the golden radiance from the ruined city.

It was a girl of small stature with a face greatly resembling that of Yukina Himeragi.

The girl's clothes also strongly resembled the uniform of Saikai Academy, but the sailor suit had a slightly different design. The eyes with which she gazed up at the night sky of Nod glowed crimson like rubies.

"We came to watch over things just in case, but our turn didn't come up, huh?"

The girl looked down at the older half-sister sitting beside her as she spoke. Wearing a white coat, her older sister had an ultrathin tablet on her knees as she sat on the roof of a tall tower at the center of the artificial isle.

"I suppose not. Well, it'd be trouble for us if we had to intervene at a time like this, too."

The older sister replied bluntly, still with a straw in her mouth, its other end jammed into a tomato juice pack. The first girl pursed her lips slightly.

"Yeah, but it makes you worry, though. I mean, what'll happen down the road if it's this hard a fight against just a Deva?"

"...Yet in terms of results, he accomplished his objective, and in a way that could not be more perfect."

The older sister smiled a bit. From the screen of her tablet, a 3D image of a badly sewn teddy bear was smiling sarcastically up at her.

"Obtaining twelve Blood Servants, thus regaining his power as the Fourth Primogenitor, Kojou Akatsuki has come one step closer to being the ruler of the Empire of the Dawn."

Still looking up at the starless night sky, the girl voiced the words like a theatrical line.

Giggle, laughed her older sister, smiling with amusement.

"There's still a long way to go for that. At the very least, he's protected the possibilities linked to our future."

"Yep."

"So let's give them a little freebie for all their hard work, shall we?"

Speaking those words, the girl in the white coat executed a file she'd put together on the fly. Strange magical symbols were drawn on the surface of her tablet. The girl felt a network of demonic energy coursing out.

The girl smiled, staring at the side of her older sister's lovely face with a hint of surprise.

"You're more of a softie than I thought, Moegi."

"Well, I have to show filial piety once in a while."

Speaking in the candid manner she'd inherited from her mother, the girl's older sister—Moegi—shrugged her shoulders.

Yeah, said the girl's silent nod.

Over six thousand artificial vampires still slept within the artificial isle the girls were at, each innocent, guileless icons in which dwelled Beast Vassals on par with those of the primogenitors. It would be hard work giving all of them peaceful lives. Such was the dream for the future the man called the Sinful God had cursed them with.

The two girls believed Kojou Akatsuki would make this dream come true.

He'd come to Nod and retaken his power to do just that.

So, too, would he make his triumphant return to the island that would be called the Empire of the Dawn, his servants at his side.

"Welcome back, Kojou. See ya later."

Tee-hee, giggled the girl with a mischievous smile as the girls were surrounded by golden mist, and vanished.

All that remained in the ruined skyline was the quiet rush of the waves.

OUTRO

The girls sat on the edge of the steps of the seaside hill path on the commute to school.

One was a small girl with her long black hair tied up. Another was a vampire with mysterious golden hair that changed color like a rainbow depending on the angle you looked at it.

Their hair and eye color showed them to be different species, yet their gestures and the atmosphere around them seemed very similar. For some reason, when you saw them side by side, they looked like blood sisters.

Both were holding ice cream cups bought from a stall nearby.

The black-haired girl was eating chocolate. The golden-haired girl held a cup with triple ice cream: strawberry, caramel, and ganache.

The black-haired girl gently gazed at the golden-haired girl stuffing herself with ice cream as she inquired.

"Tasty, Avrora?"

The golden-haired girl seemed a little worked up, ice cream marring the edges of her mouth as she replied with a nod.

"Like the ambrosia of paradise…!"

"Is that so? I'm glad."

Wiping the face of her happily smiling friend with a handkerchief, the black-haired girl narrowed her eyes with equal amusement.

Then Nagisa Akatsuki's gaze abruptly fell to Avrora's left wrist.

Glimmering in the light of day was a black, metallic wristband—a brand-new demon registration bracelet. This recognized the golden-haired vampire as a registered demon of the Demon Sanctuary.

With this island, she'd finally gained a place to call home—

A homeland where she could live with all her friends.

A week had passed since Shahryar Ren's invasion of Nod.

Thanks to the exceptional healing ability of the supposedly unaging, undying Devas, Shahryar Ren had just barely clung to life. He'd been handed over to Holy Grounds Treaty Organization custody and would stand trial along with his younger sister, Ladli, and other terrorist coconspirators.

The sorcerous manufacturing conglomerate MAR had been dissolved, with each individual division announced as a brand-new, freestanding corporation. Anticipating great effects from wiping out a giant multinational concern, competing corporations had begun a bidding war, making competition over the technology and human resources freshly put into circulation, so the situation remained in flux.

On the other hand, the leaders among the Devas known as the Seventeen Clans issued a joint statement of regret the string of incidents their brother Shahryar Ren had caused, along with announcing vast reparations to be paid for the people sacrificed in these events and the undertaking of repairs to the damaged cities.

After this, the Devas restored the damaged Keystone Gate, the harbor area, and other Itogami Island critical infrastructure to their former states in a single night, displaying to the world that the Devas still wielded unfathomable power—but that is another story.

"So…in the end, the Demon Sanctuaries of the world have accepted the Beast Vassal Warhead icon girls?"

The western sun shone into the classroom after school. Kojou lazily leaned back in his chair as he posed the question.

"Yeah. Technically they're still with Itogami City-State; we're just calling it indefinite foreign studies. I mean it's not like even we can accept over six thousand vampires by ourselves."

Yaze, sitting opposite Kojou, smiled with a rather weary expression.

It had been seven days since the Nod Incident instigated by Shahryar Ren. Yaze, crushed by overwork from his duties as a corporate chairman, had only been able to pop into school that day.

"I believe that is very reasonable. Surely many nations would be uncomfortable with such a sudden increase in Itogami Island's demon population."

Yukina, having come all the way to Kojou's classroom to meet him, spoke in her usual overly serious tone.

The icon girls recovered from the Beast Vassal Warhead silos in Nod numbered six thousand four hundred and fifty.

Primogenitor-class Beast Vassals dwelled in the blood of each and every one of them. Shahryar Ren had proven that the girls were powerful strategic weapons in an unstable, freshly awakened state.

Even the Demon Sanctuary of Itogami Island would earn international ire if it monopolized all of those girls. In the first place, there weren't anywhere near enough foster parents and schools to accept all the girls.

All the same, the "lessons" in virtual reality employed by Itogami Island's main computer were indispensable for the girls' safe management. The girls' "foreign studies" were the logical compromise.

"Well, if they're treated like foreign exchange students, that means they won't be treated like guinea pigs at least."

Kojou murmured offhandedly, seemingly to assuage his own worries.

"To a certain extent, at least."

Sitting beside Kojou, Asagi spoke bluntly as she operated her smartphone with one hand.

"The three Primogenitors seem pretty concerned about that part, too. I don't think many people will try to lay a hand on the girls knowing the potential of the Beast Vassals inside them, though."

"Sure hope so…"

Yaze put his cheek against his palm and let out a concerned sigh.

After all, there had been no lack of groups willing to tangle with

Itogami Island despite knowing it had the Fourth Primogenitor, the World's Mightiest Vampire. If anything, troublesome people with the Fourth Primogenitor in their sights were countless, with Dimitrie Vattler at the top of the list.

With that in mind, Kojou felt like a future where he'd get involved in disputes over the six thousand four hundred and fifty icons scattered around the world would be inevitable, but he'd cross that bridge when he came to it.

"Come to think of it, Vattler was headed to that Else place, wasn't he?"

Trying to brush such ill omens aside, Yaze forced a change in subject.

"Yeah. That old dragon dude Kreyd hired him to guide the way."

Kojou spoke in a nonchalant tone. Vattler's reason for making his way to Nod was the corridor with Else at the other end—his objective being to investigate that planet lying outside the solar system.

With demonic energy on par with the Fourth Primogenitor, able to summon Beast Vassals in Nod, Vattler could open a gate even without the Fourth Primogenitor. Vattler wanted to reach Else, and the lonely dragon survivor wanted to return to his homeland—miraculously, their mutual interests coincided.

"Given who he is, that was his objective all along. It's an entire world where the other team has home field advantage."

Asagi let out a faintly weary sigh.

To Vattler, a widely acclaimed combat maniac, the forces of Else that had driven back even the Devas were the mightiest of foes he could hope to encounter.

That wasn't to say Vattler's eccentric activities were all fruitless so far as mankind was concerned.

If Kreyd and Dumblegraff's words were true, the forces of Else under dragon control had long plotted an invasion of Earth.

The fact that made Kojou's and the others' heads hurt more than any-thing was that Itogami Island becoming a window to Nod inevitably put them on the front line of any dragon invasion.

"…Hey, maybe in a little while, Mr. Vattler will take over Else and come back to this world at the head of its armies."

Heh, heh, laughed Asagi mischievously as she alluded to one possibility.

Kojou grimaced, looking repulsed from the bottom of his heart.

"Cut that out. That ain't funny. He'd really do it, too, you know."

"Then we'd better shore up our Dominion's military power to prepare for the upcoming battles, shouldn't we?"

A poignant smile cossed Yaze's face as he looked at Kojou.

"Whaddaya mean, increase our military power…?"

Kojou prompted back with a completely serious look. Yaze gazed at Yukina and Asagi with deep interest.

"Hey, if you wanna increase your Dominion's combat strength, the quickest way is to make second-generation vampires. Depending on the pair, the kids between a primogenitor and Blood Servants can have power equal to or better than a primogenitor's."

"Kids of a primogenitor and a Blood Servant…huh? Haaah?!"

Kojou's voice went shrill when he realized the significance of Yaze's words.

Asagi and Yukina glared scornfully at Yaze with blatant disgust brimming in their eyes.

"…Motoki, you creep."

"I suppose he is… Upperclassman Yaze, I believe such statements are socially impermissible."

"Hey, I'm just speaking the objective truth?!"

Yaze sullenly rebutted, thrown off by Asagi and Yukina's unexpectedly harsh reactions.

A chilly exhale trickled out from Asagi.

"This is why you got dumped by your what's-her-name."

"She didn't dump me! She just went back to the mainland to recuperate from her injuries!"

Yaze shot back with a beet red face. Sadly, the sheer desperation of his efforts made his words lose all credibility.

"Incidentally, Aiba. Do you know anything more about that information manipulation?"

Yukina posed that question to Asagi, ignoring Yaze's continued attempts at explanation.

The information manipulation Yukina had on her mind was a global-scale anomaly occurring right after Kojou's return from Nod. The rumored real name and anything else about the boy who had become the winner of the Electoral War, who then resolved Shahryar Ren's invasion of Nod, had completely vanished from people's memories and all physical records.

"Honestly, not one darn thing."

Asagi shook her head, seemingly unable to accept that fact.

The spread of information about Kojou Akatsuki had long exceeded the bounds of what could be managed with hacking and information management. Asagi and the others had steeled themselves for the Fourth Primogenitor's identity to have spread around the entire world.

Yet when they opened the lid and peered inside, they could not find a single ordinary person who remembered the Fourth Primogenitor's identity. It was the same for Shizuri and Yume's participation in the Electoral War. The remaining rumors about the mysterious vampire known as the Fourth Primogenitor were vague, and the only information on the boy named Kojou Akatsuki was his high school data.

The rampage against the Order of the End and the destruction of MAR's invasion forces had all been chalked up to the work of this Fourth Primogenitor of unknown provenance, and all records had been adjusted to conform with this belief. Someone had rewritten all the information on Kojou and company behind their backs.

"With Tanker's help, I conducted a thorough examination of the logs, but all traces were completely wiped clean as if time itself had been rewound. The only thing that's changed are the records about Kojou's identity."

"…The Lion King Agency's investigation obtained the same result. Only information relating to Akatsuki-senpai and the Fourth Primogenitor have vanished from the memories of people around the world save for spiritualists and magic users of very high skill. It is as if a large-scale Blazing Banquet took place."

"…The Blazing Banquet…huh."

Asagi puffed up her cheeks as Yukina invoked the abominable term.

It meant memory loss occurring when the Fourth Primogenitor's Beast Vassals were summoned in an unstable state. If someone could produce a similar effect artificially and combine it with Asagi-level hacking skills, it wouldn't be impossible to control people's memories around the world, but this was utterly impossible in reality.

"With our current technology, even using Mogwai at full capacity, information manipulation on this level just isn't possible. In ten...no, maybe twenty years of hardware advances, it might just barely be possible, though."

Asagi murmured with frustration. She turned off her smartphone's screen and rested the device on her desk.

"But why would someone use that level of tech just to hide my identity? I mean I'm really grateful not to be wrapped up in all kinds of trouble I don't need... Maybe someone real nice is out there."

Kojou let his honest impressions trickle out. It was only thanks to this mysterious information manipulation that Kojou was able to live as a normal high school student after getting the power of the Fourth Primogenitor.

"Technology...twenty years in the future..."

Yukina seemed to remember something as she quietly spoke those words to herself. Her eyes fell to the ring on her left hand, but she immediately shook her head, thinking better of it.

"Can't be all that optimistic when we don't know if it's from friend or foe."

For once, Kojou spoke seriously.

"I suppose not. Perhaps we truly must forge greater strength to prepare for all possibilities."

Yukina stared at Kojou with a smile. *I must become stronger as a watcher so that Kojou never vanishes again*, she vowed in her heart.

Upon hearing Yukina speak, however, Asagi's expression hardened.

"Greater strength...Himeragi, you're..."

"Eh?"

Yukina was thrown off, but in contrast, Yaze moved his shoulder close to Kojou with a smug smile on his face.

"My, my, Himeragi's such a forward thinker, isn't she? Ain't that great, Kojou? You have such a cutie-pie all fired up."

"Oh, shaddap! What are you so happy about?!"

Yaze was patting Kojou on the back when Kojou brushed his hand away like a nuisance. When Yukina overheard this, her cheeks blushed hard as she finally noticed her own verbal slip.

"Ah! Ah…no, you are mistaken! Just now, I did not mean in the sense of second-generation vampires… I simply meant I must train har… Y-you are mistaken…!"

"Well, fine. If that's how it is, then I don't need to hold back, either… It's not like Himeragi's my only foe after all…"

"No, that is not what I meant…!"

"Man…just like usual, this island's so…hot."

Listening to Asagi and Yukina's verbal scuffle, Yaze made a show of wiping the sweat off his forehead.

Kojou exhaled wearily as his gaze shifted to outside the window.

He gazed at the Demon Sanctuary landscape illuminated by the golden rays of the sun, languidly commenting to himself.

"…Gimme a break."

The city of never-ending summer—

The city's name was Itogami Island, a tiny island floating on the Pacific Ocean, an artificial island built with carbon fiber, resin, metal, and magic.

The golden-haired vampire girl sat in a nook off the coastal hill path, looking down at the city as the setting sun shone upon it.

It wasn't all that large a city. Monorails ran through the gaps in the densely packed buildings as if threading the eyes of needles. Humans and demons filled the same train cars as if it was the most natural thing in the world—

She heard the calls of gulls over the sea breeze.

Somewhere off in the distance, a melodious bell announced the end of school.

Gazing with regret at the cup of ice cream she'd just finished eating, she felt the black-haired girl sitting behind her suddenly rise to her feet and wave her hand.

She hastily followed her friend's gaze. A pretty girl with a black guitar case on her back was walking with an ordinary-looking boy.

"—Kojou!"

The golden-haired vampire girl's voice bounced as she spoke the boy's name.

Meeting her black-haired friend's eyes, the two set off in a run, hand in hand. Noticing the pair racing over, the boy gave them a strained, blushy smile. An ever so slightly pouty expression came over the girl with the guitar case as she grasped the sleeve of his parka.

This was an ordinary day in the Demon Sanctuary of the Orient—

The everyday life of the vampire called the Fourth Primogenitor.

Afterword

Series complete! And so the final volume of *Strike the Blood* has reached stores!

Truly, thank you very much to everyone for sticking with me this far. It became a longer series than initially planned, but being able to portray background material that was never going to be touched on was tough going but pretty fun. Of course, if I was to get greedy, there are plenty of characters I'd like to do things with and situations to portray, but there wasn't enough time or pages for all of it. I'm very sorry to Rui and Yuno, who had their appearances entirely cut. I didn't forget about you...

In the nine-and-a-half years after I began to write this series, there have been heavy shifts in the real world that surprise me even today. In particular, I believe there have been great changes in the environment around all the readers who have been following this work since the beginning.

Personally speaking, it's not so much that I've changed as weakened. Being gradually worn down might be the more apt description, but in contrast, what hasn't changed one tiny bit is that I was always happy when writing *Strike the Blood*. I was grateful from the bottom of my heart to have a place to write Kojou and company's adventures and that that many people were reading them. So if those who have read this series enjoy it even a tiny bit as much as I did, I can have no greater joy.

*　　*　　*

Now then, the book series itself may be complete, something I am extremely thankful for, but the new OVA under the title *Strike the Blood IV* will be on sale in a little while to come on Blu-ray and DVD. It's blessed with a fabulous staff and cast, and the contents will not betray your expectations in any way. There are also plans for a collection of original short stories. I'll be quite happy if you stick with me to the very end.

Also, e-book versions of the previously Internet-only "Strike the Blood—This Is Saikai Academy" four-panel comic spinoff by Ryuryu Akari-sensei are starting distribution with various e-book companies. I humbly request you check them out, too.

To Manyako, the illustrator, you've been a big help once again. As an author, I had the honor and good fortune to work with you until the very end of the series.

Also, I would like to say thank you from the bottom of my heart to everyone involved with the creation and distribution of this book.

Of course, my greatest thanks go to all of you who have read this book. I hope we meet again in my next work.

Gakuto Mikumo